Dean

M

Battle for Bi

Thank you so
much for picking
up the book!

Anupa.

The writing is very tongue... now very funny... sparkling ... much ... down...

What people are saying about *The Zoya Factor*

'Her writing is very young, very now, very funny. Sparkling with wit and cattiness, here's the much-awaited doosra of Indian writing!' – *The Times of India*

'Ms Chauhan had me laughing aloud so often that I'm sure my fellow passengers thought I'm a bit of a nut.' – *Headlines Today*

'Let's not beat around the bush. This book is gross and really funny. Chauhan has the craft, panache and talent for fiction writing.' – *The Week*

'It's a sweet, heart-hugging story that ends in a confetti of happy resolutions you will enjoy arriving at.' – *Hindustan Times*

'An entirely sophisticated first novel, *The Zoya Factor* brings the insouciance, humour and heart back into chick-lit.' – *TimeOut*

'Cute butts. Biteable chests. A saucy new read that has all that and more. It's a fascinating, unabashedly shallow world and I fell madly in love with it.' – *India Today*

Battle for Bittora

ANUJA CHAUHAN

HarperCollins *Publishers* India
a joint venture with

New Delhi

First published in India in 2010 by
HarperCollins *Publishers* India
a joint venture with
The India Today Group

Copyright © Anuja Chauhan 2010

ISBN: 978-93-5029-002-6

2 4 6 8 10 9 7 5 3 1

Anuja Chauhan asserts the moral right to be identified
as the author of this book.

HarperCollins *Publishers*
A-53, Sector 57, NOIDA, Uttar Pradesh – 201301, India
77-85 Fulham Palace Road, London W6 8JB, United Kingdom
Hazelton Lanes, 55 Avenue Road, Suite 2900, Toronto, Ontario M5R 3L2
and 1995 Markham Road, Scarborough, Ontario M1B 5M8, Canada
25 Ryde Road, Pymble, Sydney, NSW 2073, Australia
31 View Road, Glenfield, Auckland 10, New Zealand
10 East 53rd Street, New York NY 10022, USA

Typeset in 11/14 Adobe Garamond Pro
Jojy Philip New Delhi 110 015

Printed and bound at
Thomson Press (India) Ltd.

For my parents,
Pushpa and Revti Raman.
Thank you for the roots. Thank you for the wings.

'Jinni, I am *so* not imagining this!' said Gaiman Tagore Rumi earnestly, his sensitive face glowing with boyish zeal. 'The telltale signs are *everywhere,* you just have to read them! The flashy crotch-hugging costumes, hidden under conventional attire. The butts-encased-in-skintight-latex. The obsession with secrecy, the leading of a double life, the paranoia about being found out. Trust me ya, I *know* that every superhero is a homosexual struggling to break free from the shackles of society!'

I stared at him, intensely irritated. I love my superheroes. I mean, I fantasize about them. And I deeply resented the way Gaiman Tagore Rumi was trying to take them away from single girls like me, appropriating them for the LGBT club instead.

'You're just seeing what you want to see, Rumi!' I said fiercely. 'And anyway, Bruce Wayne is a total playboy. He does tons of chicks. He can't possibly be faking that.'

A secretive know-it-all expression crossed Rumi's mobile face.

'Ah, *Brute* Wayne,' he murmured musingly. 'I've always felt his chemistry with those silly girls was nothing compared to his chemistry with Robin.'

Gross. He'd just destroyed all of Gotham for me. Trying to shut out the horrid image of Batman and the Boy Wonder in a clinch in the interior of Batmobile, I said, with more assurance than I felt, 'That's just silly. And what about Spidey, huh? He's all man. *And* he's into a steady scene with MJ – he's loved her all his life!'

Rumi gave a throaty laugh. 'But that constant *fssssskkch fssssskkch* spurting of sticky grey stuff into the air is thoda sa phallic, don't you think?'

I gasped. 'Those are *webs*!'

He shrugged his thin shoulders. 'Then they're symbolic of his desire to entrap as many men as possible into the sticky web of his want.'

'Or women,' I replied doggedly. 'Spurting web goo doesn't mean you're *gay*. Just that you're, you know, full of the stuff and bursting your seams a little. Anyway, Superman's dead straight.'

Rumi threw me a quizzical look. 'Yeah, right,' he said. 'That's why Clark Kent always zips into a telephone booth to change. He dives in, wearing a boring pin-striped suit – and emerges resplendent in brightly coloured, skintight, nipple-enhancing lycra, complete with underwear on top! That's clear symbolism for coming out of the closet! Come on ya, it's as plain as the nose on your face.'

'My nose isn't plain,' I told him crossly.

He screwed up his face and looked at me critically. 'You're right,' he concurred finally, before hunching over his computer monitor again. Your nose is geometrically quite sound. It's your mouth that's a little, uh, *excessive*.'

He was right, of course. My mouth is definitely XXL. In profile, it actually sticks out a little more than my nose. But less than my boobs, thank god. My mouth is also really wide. In fact, it's so wide that I look like one of those stupid, smiling,

Disneyland dolphins. You know, the bright-eyed, over-friendly ones who are always leaping out of the water, frantic for fish. And it gets worse when I smile. When I was little, my mother used to have nightmares that I smiled so wide that the two ends of the smile *met* at the back of my head and made the top half of my head fall off. How scary is that?

Anyway, how did we get to the subject of my mouth? I spun Rumi's chair around till he faced me.

'Don't try to change the subject!' I charged him. 'You're just irritated because I said your stupid bathroom potty germs need some work. And it's true. They *do* need work. They're supposed to strike terror in every housewife's heart, make her jump out of her sofa, go to the kirana and buy a year's supply of Harpic. Right now, they look about as scary as Alok Nath in *Hum Aapke Hain Kaun*. Which is why I told you to make 'em look slimy and evil – and instead of taking feedback in a constructive, mature way, you're retaliating by launching this completely arbitrary attack on all my favourite superheroes.'

Rumi leaned back in his chair and surveyed me critically. This was not a good move because the so-called orthopeidically correct swivel chairs at Pixel Animation – where we both work in the 3-D animation division – are highly unpredictable and have a tendency to keel over if you lean back too far.

'Your problem, Jinni,' he told me in this very superior way, crossing his turquoise corduroy-encased legs, 'is that you have an entirely conventional mind. Your imagination isn't very... *original.*'

Hello, just because I don't while away the whole working day downloading gay *Avatar* porn off the net – thus giving a whole new spin to the phrase *blue* film – doesn't mean I'm not original!

'At least my name is original,' I shot back, stung. (This, because Rumi's actually made up his own name, mixing the names of the three creative artists he admires the most – Neil Gaiman, the dude who wrote the Sandman comics, Bengali literateur Rabindranath Tagore and the mystic Sufi poet Rumi. Which makes me positive that his real name is something totally mundane, like Ravi Bhalla.)

'Unfortunately, so's your haircut,' he murmured, rolling his eyes and twiddling his (tweezed?) eyebrows.

I touched my hair defensively, scowling. Everyone at work makes fun of my carefully-casual, unruly mop of hair. Just because I pay large sums of money to get it styled every month – by a dark dude with blonde streaks in a Bandra parlour called Percy's Cuts and Blow Jobs. Percy calls my hairstyle the Half-blown Rosebud Cut, claims that it's inspired by Japanese manga comics, and assures me glibly that its short, spontaneous bounciness shows off my long neck, brings out the point of my chin and the rosiness of my skin, and makes my luxuriantly lashed black eyes 'twinkal'. According to the Pixel gang, however, it looks like he randomly attacks me with a set of gardening shears every month.

'You concentrate on your kitaanus,' I advised Rumi coldly. 'I am ordering pizza. We should be all done by three in the morning, max.'

I ordered the pizza, tucked my feet under my butt and opened the Harpic Kitaanus file.

I soon figured out what was wrong. He'd made the eyes too big. That's why they were looking cutesy. The trick is to give them tiny eyes, low idiot foreheads, huge snout-like noses, slavering, downward-sloping mouths and weak chins. I know this because, in the two short years that I've been working at

Pixel Animation, the largest animation and special effects studio in Mumbai, I've animated dozens of germs and kitaanus. I have even earned the somewhat dubious distinction of being the best damn animator of germs, khich-khich, mosquitoes, cockroaches, larvae, viruses and bacteria in the city of Mumbai. In companies like Reckitt-Benckiser – the makers of Dettol and Harpic – I am practically a celebrity.

Jinni Pande, Kitaanu Queen.

I sighed and rumpled my hair a bit more.

In the beginning I had loved my job. I'd lapped up all the stuff the senior guys at Pixel had told me: Respect the kitaanus, Jinni. The battle of the kitaanu against the cleaning agent – be it medicated shampoo or nasal decongestant or toilet bowl cleaner – is the battle of Good against Evil. The Light triumphs, the Dark side is vanquished and crawls away to lick its wounds and plan revenge. It's like Spidey's fight for Good on the mean streets of New York. Or like Batman taking on all the Evil guys in Gotham City.

More like Gotham Shitty, I thought sourly as I added more warts to the kitaanus in the toilet bowl. The truth is less noble. Pixel just has to do a lot of kitaanu animation (instead of, you know, hardcore animation stuff like *Inception* or *300* or Tim Burton's *Alice* or whatever) because kitaanus – along with cheesy special effects for mythological TV serials like *Mahabharata* – are our bread and butter.

I'd been slaving away for ages, sucking on the foul Hajmola golis that were the only edible thing in the office, when we finally heard someone shuffling about in the deserted reception area.

'It's the pizza,' I told Rumi, as my stomach rumbled in anticipation. 'Go sign for it, quick.'

He came back three minutes later, a slightly stunned expression on his face. 'There's somebody outside,' he said faintly, 'asking for a Sarojini Pande. Uh, dude, is that your real name or something?'

I nodded, going a little red. Just my luck – somebody from my bank or my mobile phone billing company had wandered into office and ousted my old-fashioned name. It's *such* a lame name. It was given to me by my grandfather. He was totally into Sarojini Naidu, the famous freedom fighter and poet, the 'Nightingale of India', you know. Bauji loved all these really sappy, tinkling 'lyrical' poems she wrote. Like,

> Bangle sellers are we who bear
> Our shining loads to the temple fair.
> Who will buy these delicate, bright
> Rainbow tinted circles of light?
> Lustrous tokens of radiant lives,
> For happy daughters and happy wives.

I mean, was that all she could find to write about during the freedom struggle? Bangle sellers? Didn't she want to write rousing, gritty, Britain-bashing poems with plenty of blood and gore and beheadings in them? Really, if I had to be named after some old poetess, I would've preferred Subhadra Kumari Chauhan. Her 'Jhansi ki Rani' is my best poem ever.

'Yeah, that's my official name,' I told Gaiman Tagore Rumi as breezily as I could. 'Didn't you know?'

He shook his head, still looking stunned, and I started to feel a little annoyed. Okay, so I have a dumb name, but there was no need to look like he'd just seen a ghost.

'It means one-who-has-a-lotus,' I told him matter-of-factly. 'Not the car – the flower.'

Which was true enough – but not entirely. Because in Delhi, where I come from, Sarojini means one thing only. Sarojini Nagar Market.

Sarojini Nagar Market is this huge noisy market in South Delhi. It's named after the 'Nightingale' and is fully cheap and cheerful. You can buy the coolest Tommy Hilfiger vests for fifty rupees there. And the most happening embroidered jeans for two hundred bucks. Sweat-encrusted auntyjis throng there to buy massive, roomy panties, block-printed kaftans, mountains of sabzi and plastic Hello Kitty slippers. There are cows and garbage dumps. It's also peopled with aggressive beggars and snarling, taloned college girls looking for bargains. Whenever fundamentalists of any denomination want to create terror in Delhi, they plant a bomb and kill some people in Sarojini Nagar Market.

So being named Sarojini is not quite like being named Paris or Venice. More like being named Mumbai. And who wants that?

I certainly didn't. I had to spend years at the Loreto Convent, Delhi, surrounded by girls with trendy, short-n-snappy names like Rhea, Pia, Jia, Sia, Ananya, Mehek and Meher, while I had to answer to *Sarojini*. It had scarred me for life.

'How nice,' said Rumi in a decidedly weirded-out voice. 'Jinni... err... I mean, *Sarojini,* out there in the reception, it's not the pizza – it's...'

I frowned and looked beyond him, towards the door, and beheld a sight that turned my blood to ice.

A little old lady with her hair in a bun and a dainty gold naakphool in her nose stood framed in the doorway, draped in a light dhakai sari. Her soft white hair had a dramatic pink streak running through it. She had the delicate features of a

Mughal miniature painting and the pugnacious stance of a professional boxer.

'We are looking for Sarojini Pande,' she announced, peering around the room short-sightedly. 'See haj to come home with us, *immediately.*'

———

Busted.

That was the first thought that crossed my mind when I saw my maternal grandmother standing in the Pixel Animation lobby. The second was, okay, it's late, most everybody has gone home and Rumi won't recognize her anyway. The third thought, following fast on the heels of the second, was, yeah, *right*. Because Rumi, eyes alight with the gormless-groupie gleam that Delhi people get around movie stars and Mumbai folks get around politicians, was pouncing on Amma, going: 'Excuse me, ma'am, but aren't you Pushpa Pande? Of PP for Pragati Party, PP for Pavit Pradesh and PP for Pushpa Pande fame?'

And Amma was nodding graciously and replying in the affirmative.

'Duuuude!' squealed Rumi, like a housewife spotting kitaanus in her toilet bowl. 'Oh my *god*! Why didn't you *tell* us you know Pushpa Pande?'

This, from a boy who, barely an hour ago, was accusing *me* of a lack of imagination!

See, I'll admit that on the face of it, it's great to be politically 'connected'. You can get train reservations whenever you want and park anywhere simply by flashing the MP sticker on your car. You can also charge pretty much every kind of health screwup on your CGHS card. Even if you're one of those humble, in-denial, I'm-just-like-everybody-else type of political progeny, you still know you've got this big trump card in your underwear pocket which you can flash whenever life gets too hairy.

But think about it a little more, and you'll realize there's a whole social downside to it too. Because once you tell people you're from a political family (or *dynasty*, like the press types like to call it) they immediately start expecting you to embezzle the nation's entire GDP, buy them lavish dinners in five-star hotels every night with your ill-gotten gains and shoot the bartender dead in the head with your unlicensed revolver if he refuses you a drink.

And while there may be some classy, 'clean' lady politicians out there – the kind that wears FabIndia and Dastkar saris and big round bindis, speaks flawless English, hangs out in the Upper House and represents India at UN summits – my grandmother is *so* not one of them. Oh no. She's Pushpa *jiji*, a hard-core, three-time Lok Sabha MP, an MP3 so to say, hailing from the dusty badlands of Pavit Pradesh, one of north India's most populous states.

Which is why I've kept her a deep dark secret from all my recently-made Mumbai friends like Gaiman Tagore Rumi. I mean, Rumi's seen *Rang De Basanti* thrice. He even thinks the ending made sense. And he's still wearing those black armbands in remembrance of the victims of 26/11!

The last thing I want is for my Mumbai friends to know that my grandmother is *the* Pushpa. Even though she's now retired and concentrating solely on growing vegetables in her massive garden, they'll instantly start making snide *your-nani's-security-costs-the-state-exchequer-three-crores-a-year* and *why-don't-you-go-marry-Ritesh-Deshmukh* cracks. And worst of all, they'll start hitting on me to get them visas or school admissions or sort out pending lawsuits or any of the other million things that only pollies can get done in this country. Because despising me and my tainted bloodline wouldn't stop them from asking me for favours. Oh no.

'This is my grandmother,' I said gloomily, bowing to the inevitable, 'and Amma, this is my colleague, Gaiman Tagore Rumi.'

Amma was frowning. I could see she was trying to slot Rumi into a neat caste, creed and votebank pigeonhole and not finding it easy. Finally, 'Gay-man?' she hazarded, hovering closer to the truth than she realized. 'Isaaeeyee ho? Are you Christian?'

Rumi, hugely delighted to meet this alien from another planet, shook his head and proclaimed reprovingly, 'Ammaji, I am a devotee of Art.'

She grunted, looking singularly unimpressed.

'You pray to oil paints?' she asked him, as her face split into a grin of peculiar sweetness that revealed the thick-as-a-five-rupee-coin gap between her top two front teeth. 'Or...' she smirked, 'nude models?'

My heart sank at this typical Amma crack but Rumi, the fool, looked instantly charmed. It's so irritating; if old people say anything even remotely ribald, everyone ooohs and aaahs and gushes on about how cool, what good sports, what *rock stars* they are. When all they're doing is just being plain crude.

'Amma,' I said through gritted teeth. '*What* are you doing here?'

She sat down heavily on a chair and said, a little evasively, 'We have come to meet aawar granddaughter. What's there?'

Please. It could never be as simple as that. I regarded her suspiciously, warning bells ringing in my head. The general elections were coming up and, of course, all the parties were out there, their leaders grinning smarmily from every hoarding and television channel in Mumbai. We were constantly being bombarded with their so-called achievements, while hideously remixed versions of soulful Bollywod songs blared in the background. The visuals were all the same – nutritious mid-day meals and loan waivers and right-to-information and happy farmers counting money and smiling ladies administering polio drops to fat babies. There was the standard 'secular' shot of a Muslim guy with surma in his eyes and a white lace cap perched on his head, getting a rakhi tied on his wrist by a simpering Hindu girl with a Ganesha locket around her neck. Fully brother-sister vibes. Of course, no party had the guts to show a couple like that getting *married*. That would start riots nationwide.

But all this couldn't have anything to do with Amma. She was retired, right?

Right?

I opened my mouth to ask her this, but just then Rumi went, 'Oh, hey! The pizza's here! I'll sign, Jinni. Ammaji, you're in for a treat!'

He scurried off, reaching into his back pocket for a pen as he went. Amma watched his turquoise butt twinkle away and asked interestedly, 'Who ij this Article 377, Sarojini?'

'He's my *friend*,' I told her fiercely. 'And stop calling me Sarojini.'

'Toh kya *Jinni* kahen?' she said disdainfully, leaning back in her chair, her eyelids all wrinkled and tissue-papery over her closed eyes. 'Mohammedan sa name hai. You sound like a poor carpenterj fourth wife.'

And here we go again. For someone who's been in the public eye for most of her life, my grandmother is appallingly prejudiced. She turns up her nose at anybody who isn't a high-caste citizen of Pavit Pradesh. Bengali, Bihari and Gujarati women are man-eaters and husband-stealers. Their menfolk are impotent. Kashmiris are crooks and drug addicts and they don't bathe. Good Nepalis are nightwatchmen, bad ones slit the throats of their employers. Punjabis (of either gender) are permanently randy. Christians are scheduled caste and out to convert everyone they meet. And Musalmaans? They're all dirty, stupid, constantly breeding, Pakistani-cricket-team-cheering rapist-murderers.

I looked at her in exasperation. 'I see you've enjoyed a very happy Holi.'

She shrugged, touched her pink forelock and said resignedly without opening her eyes, 'Arrey bhai, it ij fast colour. We have tried to shampoo it away but it ij not coming off. Sahnaz herself could not make it go. Why did you not come home for Holi?'

It was my turn to shrug now. 'Too much work, Amma.'

She sniffed. 'Well, we had something very important to tell you. So we came here.'

'Really, Amma, you look exhausted,' I told her, feeling a little guilty. 'You should've just phoned me.'

She looked at me like I was really, really dumb.

'Buggers,' she said.

Huh?

'All aawar phones are bugged.'

I sighed.

'Well, this place isn't. So spill. What is this very important something?'

She sniffed again. 'If you were reading the papers, you would not ask such a stupid questsun,' she said loftily.

I looked at her, a Very Bad Feeling twisting my insides.

'What's in the papers now?' I asked suspiciously.

She said smugly, 'Pragati Party comj begging to Pushpa Pande…'

'And what do the Praggus have to say?' I asked, even more apprehensively. (I'm really wary of Amma's party machinery – because even though it purports to be a clean, meritocratic, non-partisan setup, it's actually about as democratic as the Mughal court of Aurangzeb.)

Amma lifted my chin with a bony finger, looked at me with suddenly starry eyes, and whispered, 'TB wants to give us the ticket from Bittora.'

TB is not tuberculosis. It is reverential Praggu shorthand for Top Brass, which is what they call their party president. He's this fair, cute, sixty-seven-year-old widower with very large nostrils, who belongs to the 'first family' of Indian politics. Basically, his mother and his grandfather have both been prime ministers of India before him. And now even his daughter – an attractive forty-plus woman whom everyone insists on calling a *girl* – has been launched into active politics. That should reveal to you how 'democratic' the whole setup is. The only reason why the Praggus manage to win again and again in India's free, fair, universal adult franchise elections is because the main opposition party, the Indian Janata Party or the IJP, is a weirdo hardliner Hindu outfit with some very scary screwball notions that equate rule-of-democracy with rule-of-religious-majority. I tell you, if the Praggus had even a halfway decent opposition against them, their ass would've been grass decades ago.

'But you've retired,' I pointed out.

Her eyes lit up and she began to speak but precisely at that point, Rumi returned with a huge Slice of Italy box and set it down before us. 'Pepperoni,' he announced. 'And chocolate mud pie. You're not veg or anything unhealthy like that na, Ammaji?'

She grinned and told him that of course she wasn't, while I

glowered at the two of them, annoyed that they were getting along so cozily. Rumi was such a fraud – he claimed to *hate* pollies, and here he was being so sycophantic, ripping open little packets of oregano and emptying them lavishly all over the pizza, then placing the largest slice on a *Lion King* DVD cover and handing it to Amma with a flourish.

She bit into the pizza with relish and watched me intently as she chewed, head cocked bird-like to one side, waiting for my reaction to the bombshell she'd just dropped.

Well, I was going to make her wait for it. Let her make PC with Rumi for a while.

Unfortunately, Rumi, instead of being difficult and saying Amma's appreciation of pepperoni was phallic or whatever, just took great draughts of Pepsi and said gushingly, 'Oh my *god*, this is such a privilege! I'm *such* a fan of your husband!'

'Thenks,' said Amma serenely, reaching for her Pepsi can and swilling the liquid around. Wow, her diet had changed big time since I saw her last, when all she would eat was a little tadka-less dal and brown rice. 'So are we.'

Hah, that was a load of bull! Amma had never been too impressed with Bauji.

His name was Pandit Madan Mohan Pande and he'd been a big freedom fighter in the old days when the Pragati Party was both democratic and idealistic and engaged in the fight for India's independence. He printed an underground newspaper, whose brilliant (and, according to the British, seditious) editorials influenced a whole generation of young Indians and earned him three years as a Grade C prisoner in the Yerawada jail. The wardens kept putting him in solitary confinement and assigned him arduous labour but I don't think it bothered him too much. At least, that's what he always told me. He said that he'd been young and strong and that he loved being alone – he could spend hours in meditation.

Anyway, post independence and after his arranged marriage to Amma (she had been fifteen to his thirty-three), Bauji contested the first Lok Sabha election on a Pragati Party ticket from his sleepy little hometown of Bittora in Pavit Pradesh, and won. Twice. He lost the third time he stood, and the party moved him to the Upper House, the Rajya Sabha, where he thrived in a low-key sort of way, sending long idealistic letters to the prime minister, writing editorials for the *Hindu* newspaper and generally acting like some sort of self-appointed, fiercely honest and therefore gently ignored national conscience. Amma, completely in awe of her terrifyingly well-educated, tall, fair and handsome superstar husband, stayed in the background, cooking his food and making sure he took his blood pressure pills.

But once he and all his 'batch', so to speak, swarg sidhaaroed for their heavenly abode, Amma moved in to take over his mantle with gusto. She'd been watching him carefully (and critically) from the sidelines for years and had quietly decided that he was too rigid in his ways. She reckoned she could learn from his mistakes and be a lot more 'adjusting' in her dealings with people.

So in giving the *Thenks, so are we* ones to Rumi, she was basically being a bit of a fraud.

'I loved *Shaadi, Khaadi aur Azaadi*,' gushed Rumi, revealing hitherto unsuspected depths of general knowledge and falling a few notches even lower in my estimation. God, what was *wrong* with the guy? Was he a closet Pragati Party groupie? Any minute now, he would whip off his shirt and reveal the Top Brass tattoo across his tits.

'Arrey!' burbled Amma happily, as she dug into a chocolate

mud pie. 'You have read aawar autobiography? You read political books? What are you doing in this computer office, making cartons?'

Rumi looked a little confounded at this.

'Cartoons, Rumi,' I clarified, taking pity on him. 'What are you doing in this computer office, making *cartoons*?'

'Oh!' His intellectual brow cleared. He said, earnestly, and I could tell he meant it, 'But Ammaji, your book is not a political book! It's unputdownable! It reads like fiction!'

It *is* fiction, I thought sourly. None of the stuff in the 1993 book, published the year Bauji died, actually happened. Amma and Bauji did not meet and fall passionately in love in the Yerawada jail. My mum wasn't born there either. And Amma contributed pretty much zilch to the freedom struggle. Bauji had married her two years after independence – in a bid to appease his parents, who were fully embarrassed to have an ex-jailbird on their hands. They'd hoped that her mix of beauty and pedigree would redeem him in Brahmin society somewhat. Anyway, in the book, she blithely claimed to be a good ten years older than she actually was, and basically used it as a tool to claw her way into the hearts of the frail, fast-fading freedom fighters club (who were all so senile they said they remembered her).

It worked like a charm. Amma was given the ticket to contest from Bauji's old seat in Bittora and won it by a landslide margin on the crest of a sympathy wave. To be fair, she did do some decent work for the people there – and got re-elected twice after that, dropping only one election in the middle.

But then things got messy.

Rumi asked, a little hesitantly, 'Um... wasn't somebody going to make a movie based on the book?'

'Yes,' I said shortly. 'Somebody was.'

The thing is that Amma had been under a pretty dark cloud, career-wise, for the last four years or so. And it all started when the film rights to her book, *Shaadi, Khaadi aur Azaadi*, were sold to an international film studio. News of the movie deal naturally reawakened interest in the book, and some shady photo studio in Noida gave an interview to a nosy news magazine about how Pushpa Pande had been their client for years and had got dozens of photographs of luminaries of the freedom struggle morphed to include her own image. A lot of these images had been included in the book. Amma had been sitting around smugly, speculating on who would play her in the film – Deepika (nah, too dark), Katrina (nah, too sturdy), Aishwarya (umm, maybe, only she played old Kokilaben Ambani, how can she play *me*?) – when the story broke and kicked her in the butt.

The party, totally red-faced and embarrassed, promptly slimed her out of the ticket from Bittora and Amma found herself, in the space of just a few weeks, reduced to being that most ignominious thing in India's political capital – an ex-MP. At once, a host of newly appointed cabinet ministers and Supreme Court judges started circling hungrily around her house on Tughlaq Road, it being a prime piece of real estate bang in the heart of Lutyens' Delhi.

Luckily, Anthony Suleiman, an old friend of hers on the Housing Committee, made sure she didn't lose her house by declaring that the nation owed the widow of the famous freedom fighter, Pandit Madan Mohan Pande, a home during her lifetime. So Amma stayed.

But I wasn't sure that was a good thing. At least, if she'd given up the house and moved to Bittora, she would've eventually gotten over the trauma of being politically irrelevant. Now she lived on a road chockfull of VIPs, a stone's throw from Parliament House, and kept picking savagely at her political sores. I tell you, during those first few months, it had been scary just watching her, sitting in the verandah and staring at the jamun trees, her hair all wild and scraggy.

Rumi, his sensitive side finally coming to the fore, changed the subject. 'Is your family very large, Ammaji?'

Amma shook her head, busily spooning chocolate mud pie into her face. 'There ij us, aawar daughter Jyoti and aawar granddaughter Sarojini. That ij all.'

My mother lives in Toronto. She migrated there when I was sixteen, partly because my late father's family is settled there, but mostly because Amma and she just didn't see eye-to-eye on the whole lying-about-your-age and pretending-you-had-been-to-prison and accepting-expensive-presents-from-shady-industrialists thing. That, and the fact that Amma had always thought Ma married beneath her. My father had been a college professor and Bauji had heartily approved of him but Amma had been keenly disappointed. She'd hoped Ma would make a brilliant political alliance and strengthen our 'dynasty'. In fact, practically the moment my dad died, when I was just three, Amma had been all, *Oh good, Jyoti, now you are free to entice Top Brass! We think he likes you...* Of course, Ma never forgave her.

She's really pretty, Ma, and smart too. She's dean at the Cohen University, and lives alone on campus, in a lovely house surrounded by apple trees, reading girlie magazines and books about monks who've sold their Ferraris.

I said, rather pointedly, 'Rumi, you want to go finish those kitaanus? I'd like to approve them before I leave.'

He pulled a bit of a sad face but got up to go. 'It's been a real honour meeting you, Ammaji!' he told Amma earnestly. Then he turned to me and drawled meaningfully, 'And *Sarojini*, you and I will have a long talk tomorrow.'

I gave him a shove in the general direction of his desk. Amma, more polite, dismissed him with her practiced, gracious smile and, swallowing the last of her chocolate mud pie, wiped her hands fastidiously with about sixteen paper tissues.

'That mud pie was loaded with triglycerides and unhealthy preservatives, by the way,' I informed her.

She shrugged magnificently. 'So what?' she said. 'Life is sort.'

Okayy.

Then she collected all the leftover chilli and oregano flakes sachets and calmly dropped them into her capacious handbag. Next, she produced a toothpick and proceeded to pick at her (all real, no fakes) teeth. Finally, she gazed piercingly at me and said firmly, 'You have to come and help us with the campaigning.'

I sighed.

'Are you sure you've *got* the ticket, Amma?' I asked. 'I mean, how d'you know they won't backstab you again? Has it been announced yet?'

She nodded. 'Hundred per cent,' she said. 'TB haj assured us *personally.* Dwivedi's patta has been cut. Pukka.'

So it hadn't been announced yet. Which meant that nothing was pukka. The last time too, they'd assured her she was getting it – that they had faith in her, despite the morphed photo scandal – and then they'd gone and announced her bête noir Pandit Dinanath Dwivedi's name, instead. And at the last minute too, when it was too late for her to get her act together and stand as a rebel independent candidate. Even then, all kinds of shady little regional parties had swarmed around her, offering her a ticket, but the Praggus cunningly promised her a Rajya Sabha berth if she sat out the election quietly, which got her really excited, as she thought the Upper House was the epitome of snooty, intellectual, political cool. Needless to say, it didn't materialize.

I sighed again.

'Amma, whyn't you go back to Delhi, and if,' I looked at her expression and hastily corrected myself, '*when* you get the ticket, you call me and I'll take the next flight down.'

She was sure she'd cut Dwivedi's patta last time as well. She'd told the press that she considered him a hypocrite, a bribe-eater and a skinflint. As proof of his hypocrisy, bribe-eating and skinflintishness, she had offered the fact that he and his family ate their vegetables *unpeeled*. A Brahmin so stingy that he grudged the cows in his courtyard his vegetable peels could not be good for Bittoragarh, she had declared.

The dirty tricks department within the Pragati had promptly used this bizarre reasoning to spread rumours that ageing veteran Pushpa Pande was suffering from Alzheimer's, pressurized her to resign from all her posts within the party, and forced her into retirement.

Amma shook her head vehemently.

'Arrey bhai, why don't you understand – everything we said about that incompetent, lauki-ka-chhilka eating Dwivedi turned out to be true! He haj exposed himself in hij true colors, and now they want us to leap into the burning pyre, fight the elecsun and save their ijjat. We are the cleanest person they could find.'

Which, if you thought about it, was a seriously scary thought.

'What'd he do?' I asked, intrigued in spite of myself.

Amma gave a low, girlish chuckle. 'You know how TB wants us to get clojer to the poor people?'

I nodded. This was one of the TB's new pet policies. For top-level politicos to go spend a night in the homes of the poorest of the poor in India's rural districts. Eat what they ate. Sleep where they slept. Endure what they endured. It was supposed to make the politicians understand the needs of the poor and thus go about fulfilling them. Of course, both the IJP and the media had scoffed at the initiative, calling it naïve, superficial, gimmicky and populist.

'So Dwivedi went. Only, he took with him, in a big matador van, his own Sleepwell spring mattress, his own sheets, his own AC, his own bottled mineral water, his own food and his own English-style, ceramic commode.'

'Are you serious?' I asked.

Amma nodded.

'He didn't drink the water the poor couple he stayed with gave him, because they were low-caste Dalits. He didn't eat their food. He didn't share *hij* food either! He slept in their main room and made them sleep on the roof, becauj of mosquitoes. And then, when he instructed his servants to turn on his portable window AC, the load was too much for the small electricity station in the village. It blew up and the entire village waj dark for three whole days.'

'Awesome,' I said, disgusted but not surprised.

'The press got a photo of him sitting like a king on hij unconnected English-style commode, making mosun in the middle of a field, reading hij newjpaper. It came out in all the PP dailies. TB was furious. He threw him out. And now he wants *us* to stand.'

I shook my head to clear it of the image of Dwivedi on his ceramic throne and tried to stick to the issue at hand.

'But you made a public statement that you've retired from

politics!' I pointed out. 'You can't go back on your word like that!'

She brushed aside this irrelevant remark.

'Arrey bhai, but naysun *needs* us,' she purred, her palms joining smoothly into a leader-like namaste. 'Janta ko hamari jaroorat hai!'

I groaned as she closed her eyes and the familiar, benevolent-politician smile slid across her face.

'Amma, no, please! What about the thirty-seven interviews in which you claimed that all you want to do now is grow vegetables and pray?'

Her eyes snapped open. 'That ij what you say when you are not having opsun! Now, we are having opsun! Why sud we become dark in the sun growing teenda-gobi, instead of fighting elections in Bittora if we have *opsun?* Hum mentally retarded hain kya?'

'Amma, *don't* say mentally retarded!' I groaned.

'Sorry…' she said grudgingly. 'Spesal.'

'D'you think you'll win?' I asked her, switching tactics. 'What's the buzz in Bittora?'

'Pragati ki hawa hai,' she replied breezily. 'The wind is changing and blowing for the Pragati. We will win, don't worry.'

Yeah, right. She always says that. She also said it that one time she lost. Rather badly too. By over seventy thousand votes.

'So the house must be overrun by a whole baraat from Bittora by now?' I asked. 'All of them dying to work for you and swearing that you will hundred per cent win?'

She nodded. 'Yes,' she said, just a little defensively. 'Don't turn up your nose, Sarojini. These people have worked for us many, many times. We think so they know what they are talking.'

They're a bunch of opportunists, I thought but didn't say. They'll work for anybody. They don't care if you win or lose, as long as they get to make some fast cash. Each time the elections roll around, they lift their noses, sniff the sour, currency-note scented air and close in like a horde of vultures.

'So you want me and Ma to come and campaign for you, is that it?' I asked her.

I knew how important this was. Constituents in the rural areas are never happy just to see *you*. They want to see you and your children and your children's children. They want to see the tiny black mole in the navel of your children's children. We are talking extremely nosy people here. Not that I mind. Meeting people is the good part actually. It's just the bit where they don't vote for you that sucks.

Amma pursed her lips. 'Your mother haj said see is not coming. So *you* have to come and campaign for us, Sarojini.'

Just like that. I was expected to drop everything and come running just because India is going to the polls for like, the *fifteenth* time and because my grandmother says so.

Feeling cornered, I pushed back my chair as far it would go and plunged my hands into my hair. Raking my fingers through my suddenly throbbing head, I said, my voice sounding unconvincing even to my own ears, 'Amma, I'm a big girl now. It was okay when I was little, the elections always happened in my summer vacations, but now I have work to do; anyway, I wasn't expecting this, you said you'd retired!'

There was a long silence.

Then an insistent, gnarled little hand closed over mine. It felt warm and pulsating and vibrantly alive.

'*Pleaj*,' she said. 'Last time. We will be dead before the next elecsun anyway.'

I sniffed. 'No such luck! You'll be rattling around campaigning when you're a hundred and ten!'

She grinned. 'Arrey bhai, so maybe you are right,' she relented. 'But come no, beta, this time we have *lot* of oxygen, bada maja aayega, it will be fun.'

I looked into her girlish, grey-flecked old eyes, and the magic word reverberated in my head over and over again.

Elecsun.

You know that word association game? You say a word to me and I say a word back to you instantly and it's supposed to reveal deep dark secrets about how I think? Like *hot* and *chocolate*, and *rock* and *star*, and *moron* and *Rahul Mahajan*? Well, if you said *election,* I would instantly reply *party time.*

When I was a child in Bittora, the excitement used to be so thick you could bite it with your teeth. Raised voices, singing and sloganeering, no proper bedtimes, people coming and going any time of the day and night. The smell of freshly printed posters and rose-chrysanthemum-tinsel garlands. An edge to Amma's voice I never heard at any other time. Eating sweets and being praised as *pretty-girl, clever-girl* in house after house. Folding my hands and prettily lisping *Vote for PP!* while everybody applauded. And the best part – driving down dusty roads, waving to the populace from the sky roof of a custom-made jeep, *band baja* blaring from specially-sanctioned-by-the-traffic-police loudspeakers.

Oh, I do realize, being grown-up now, that it is gruelling and chaotic and horribly stressful and heartbreaking and possibly heart-attack inducing. But I also know that the only thing worse than taking part in a Lok Sabha election is *not* taking part in a Lok Sabha election.

Nobody here needs to know, a little voice in my head whispered. You can just sneak out and be back in three weeks' time. You've got a month's leave that you haven't used, anyway. They won't have a clue where you've been. You could even do some work off your laptop. Besides, you haven't gone back to Bittora since you were sixteen.

I looked up at Amma and grinned. So wide I could almost feel the ends of the grin meeting at the back of my head. It was a wonder the top half of my head didn't fall off.

She grinned back.

Then she fished out a rather spiffy looking BlackBerry, peered at it short-sightedly and punched the speed dial with panache.

'Driver saab,' she said in a cat-that-got-the-cream voice, 'gaadi nikaaliye. We are leaving for the airport. *Now.*'

2

'What news?'

I stopped chewing on my hair, shook my head and sighed. 'Nothing,' I said.

For an entire week now, we'd been biting our nails and holding our breath, waiting for the list of Pragati candidates from Pavit Pradesh to be announced. And it wasn't just Amma and me. A large contingent of obsequiously smiling men with neatly oiled and parted hair, dressed in blinding white, were crowded into the front verandah of the house at Tughlaq Road, pressing up against numerous framed photographs of Amma and Bauji shaking hands with famous dead people.

And they weren't just confined to the porch. They were spilling into the three-acre garden, napping under the jamun trees, stinking up the loo in Amma's little office annexe, demanding endless rounds of chai, sweet biscuits and matthri, and every now and then sending up lusty chants of

> Give tikkit to Pushpa jiji,
> Winning elecsun will be eajy!

'We are losing *time,* didi,' fretted the MLA from Jummabagh, who'd been introduced to me by Amma rather vaguely as 'Aawar Pappu'. The moment we met, Pappu informed me, in a single, well-constructed sentence, that he was MLA-Jummabagh, a science graduate, a bachelor, an only son, a trained yoga instructor, from a business family, and totally at my service. Jummabagh is one of the eight assembly segments that make up Bittora constituency. 'All the other states' tickets have been announced! We will get very little time for campaigning. Others will get a head start.'

'Well, the IJP hasn't announced its list yet either, Pappu,' I told him comfortingly.

He didn't look convinced. 'Didi, you don't understand! Dwivediji had been preparing for almost a year! He was *so* sure he would get the seat. Now he will *not* get it – and god knows if the people he sweetened will still vote for Pragati Party!'

'I don't see why they shouldn't,' I said. 'After all, he'll have to come along and campaign for Amma, won't he?'

Our Pappu shook his head vehemently, the silver studs in his ears flashing. 'Not Dwivediji! He will stand *against* jiji on another ticket, just wait and see!'

I felt a little queasy. It was bad enough contemplating how shattered Amma would be if she didn't get the ticket! I didn't even want to start thinking about how shattered she would be if she *got* it, and *stood*, and lost. That too, to the peel-eater.

'Ummm, so d'you want some tea?' I asked in a bid to quell the rising panic in my belly.

He nodded eagerly. He loved tea. They all did. They could drink it any time.

'Just a small half cup, didi,' he said. 'And then we will do one more chakkar of the AIPC office – to check if there is any news.'

I nodded gloomily and went in to order the tea. I was beginning to dread the little chakkars to the All India Pragati

Committee office at Akbar Road – all kinds of weird rumours were emanating from there. In order of appearance they were:

- The big movie star Salmon Khan, nicknamed thus because he wore either salmon pink shirts or no shirt at all, was going to stand from Bittoragarh – he'd shot his superhit film *Jeevan Apnaa Saaraa, Sanam* there and the people loved him.
- The ticket was going to Pushpa jiji – it was all done.
- Top Brass wanted a young candidate and they were going over a list of all the Youth Pragati members from PP with a fine toothcomb.
- Top Brass's daughter was going to stand from Bittora – she had stayed at the Taj property there once and had become enamoured of the place.
- The Salmon Khan rumour was true!
- Dwivedi had visited TB's house in the dead of night, toting a suitcase stuffed with over a hundred crore in cash for the party fund, and clinched the ticket.
- Pushpa jiji's hopes were history.
- Top Brass had approved Pushpa jiji's name and left to kick off the campaigning in the south. Immediately, one of the AIPC general secretaries had dropped her name and replaced it with that of his brother-in-law.
- TB had returned, reviewed the list and rejected the name on grounds of nepotism.
- Pushpa jiji had visited TB's house in the dead of night toting a suitcase stuffed with over two hundred crores in cash for the party fund, and clinched the ticket.
- The search for a youthful, Muslim-friendly face was on. Pushpa jiji's chances were bleak.

I hurried to the kitchen in search of Amma's ancient cook-cum-housekeeper Joline Bai, who was even more grumpy than usual because of the strain the Bittorawallahs were putting on her kitchen. I found her in the vegetable garden, yanking out a massive, fish-belly white radish from the gooey grasp of the thick chyawanprash-like soil. It looked like the dismembered arms of some long-buried corpse. I hailed her with a cheery demand for tea, which she acknowledged grudgingly with a short grunt.

Joline Bai doesn't approve of me. She thinks I have too many newfangled notions about housekeeping, simply because I sometimes protest mildly about living in a house ridden with termites, overrun with large-as-small-dogs bandicoots and under siege by red killer ants.

She's Lutyens royalty, Joline Bai. Her family has lived in the quarters of the great white bungalows for years, since before independence in fact, flourishing in the criss-crossing service lanes behind the grand, tree-lined boulevards. They've been drivers, dhobis, cooks and sweepers to prime ministers, home ministers, the Pragati Party TB, even presidents! She's a big snob, of course, and had been extremely upset when Amma had her fall from grace four years ago. It was like Amma had let her down personally. Now, of course, she was on tenterhooks just like the rest of us, but too snooty to let it show.

As she stumped past me to make the tea, breathing heavily, I caught the smell of last night's mutter-mushroom emanating from her grubby checked apron.

'Where's Amma, Joline Bai?' I asked politely.

She plodded towards the kitchen, ignoring me, but deigned to point one dead-white radish in the direction of Amma's bedroom.

I trotted along to Amma's boudoir, which faced the garden and was done up in an overabundance of pink and peach floral prints. Amma was stationed behind her large wooden desk, reading newspapers from three different states.

Enormous gift boxes full of dry fruit, chocolate and seriously fancy, gold foil-wrapped gujia were stacked up like walls all around her, almost obscuring her from view. It was her Holi haul, and a good one – definitely a far cry from Diwali last year when the people's offerings had dwindled ignonimously to a single eighty-rupee Kurkure gift hamper.

As I peered at her through the rising walls of gilt and cardboard, I was reminded bizarrely of the scene from *Mughal-e-azam*, when Akbar gets Anarkali walled up with bricks to die.

She looked up when I entered, her light eyes all sharp and bird-like.

'What newj?' she asked.

'*I* don't know, Amma,' I said a little waspishly, though of course I knew what she meant. '*You're* the one reading sixteen newspapers!'

God, I was so sick of that question! Everywhere I went, people were going *What news?* at me. The Bittorawallahs outside, Amma inside, the sweeper, the gardener, the milkman, the security guards. Everybody wanted to know if Amma had got the ticket. We were all working ourselves up to a hysterical fever pitch of anticipation – all on the basis of some vague conversation Amma had had with TB over nine days ago. It was quite pathetic, really.

'What exactly did he *say*, Amma?' I'd pressed her over a million times. 'Did he promise you the ticket?'

'Arrey bhai,' she would answer vaguely each time. 'We think so he promised us.'

'You think so he promised you?' I would groan. 'What does that even *mean*?'

She would shrug evasively. 'He said, We need your presence and wisdom, Pushpa jiji. Are you willing?'

'But that could mean *anything*!' I would cry. 'It could mean he wants you to campaign for *Dwivedi*!'

'Oh no, we don't think so,' Amma would reply, serenely enough. But somehow, her eyes never looked too confident.

Now I waded through the strewn newspapers and gift boxes, plonked myself on her fluffy rose-print bed and helped myself to the plate of fried paranthas, mixed fruit jam and mango that was just sitting there, looking neglected.

'Amma,' I asked, my voice heavy with trepidation. 'You're okay, na?'

She threw me an irritated look, then picked up a large, hairy mango heart and started sucking on it, her expression inscrutable.

'We are *fine*, Sarojini,' she said as she ate. 'PP list hajn't been announced yet, that ij all.'

'I know, I know,' I said fretfully, 'but listen, everybody is saying it will be announced today, *definitely*. The IJP list will be announced tonight too. They can't possibly delay it any further. The date for withdrawal of nominations has already been fixed. At this rate, you may not have even three clear weeks for campaigning!'

'Oh, it might take longer than *that*,' said Amma vaguely, infuriating me. 'It ij a big state – Top Brass is approving every name personally, so list will take time. Stop eating aawar parantha.'

And with that, she picked up her plate and wandered into the garden while I gazed after her uneasily, listening to the chants of

Give tikkit to Pushpa jiji! from the garden, worried that she would be in for a huge disappointment tomorrow morning and hoping she would be strong enough to deal with it when it came.

'Jinni! What news?'

It was Gaiman Tagore Rumi.

He'd called, or at least he claimed he'd called, to tell me that the Harpic Kitaanus had been approved, even praised, by the client.

'No news,' I told him irritably, as I rummaged through my old clothes cupboard, searching in vain for frumpy salwar kameezes to go campaigning in.

'Didn't Ammaji get the ticket?' he asked, point blank.

Huh? I couldn't believe the big sticky *nose* on the guy!

'What makes you think,' I asked him a little scornfully, 'that Amma even *wants* a ticket? She retired five years ago.'

'C'mon, *Saro*jini,' he said knowingly. 'I've met your grandmother. There isn't a retired bone in her body!'

'Don't call me Sarojini.'

'See, I've been thinking,' he burbled on blithely. 'If Ammaji does get the ticket, and you go campaigning for her and stuff – I'm assuming that's why you've applied for a month's leave – I could tag along and shoot lots of pics. For an exhibition, you know. Titled Battle in Buttora. I googled Buttora, by the way – it looks *awesome*.'

'It's *Bitt*ora,' I snapped. God knows what the pevert had been googling. 'And if she *does* stand – which, of course, she may *not,* because she adores her retirement too much – it won't be some kind of rustic-exotic poverty tourism trip where you can strut around taking pictures! It will be serious business.'

'Hah, so she is standing,' he said smugly.

'Rumi, it isn't that easy!' I said, exasperated. 'Other people want the ticket too.'

'So kill them,' he replied blithely. 'Order their assassinations. Or, if you aren't too squeamish – which you're not – do it yourself.'

'This isn't *Rajneeti*,' I told him crossly. 'Now go away, I'm clearing out my wardrobe.'

'Be sure to throw out that tatty nylon bra then,' he shot back at me. 'The one with the frayed strap that keeps showing from under your shirts. And Jinni, one last thing. I did your tarot cards last night – watch out for *frenemies*.'

I frowned. 'Whatcha talking about *now*, Rumi?'

'Enemies who pretend to be your friends,' he said earnestly. 'You know, like Harry Osborn is Spidey's frenemy – there's a total sexual undercurrent going on there, of course…'

'Rumi!' I hissed. 'Do you mind? I'm *doing* something!'

'It's a political term, Jinni!' he insisted. 'India and Pakistan are frenemies. Steve Jobs and Bill Gates are frenemies. Observe all of Ammaji's friends carefully… one of them could be a *frenemy*. Isn't it a nice word? I like saying it, you've got to roll the Rs in a sinister fashion… frrrrrrrrenemy! Sounds like frrrenum – that's a tiny fold of skin just below the penis.'

'I know what a frenum is!' I groaned, totally grossed out. Then I cut the line and tossed the phone onto the tangled heap of clothes on the bed and sighed.

The tension was totally getting to me.

Outside, Our Pappu and his gang of merry Praggu men were busy chanting for the benefit of the news channel vans parked outside the gate.

> *Give tikkit to Pushpa jiji,*
> *Winning elecsun will be eajy!*

Meanwhile, Amma, displaying magnificent disinterest, was shut up with a home-delivered Shahnaz Hussain beautician, getting a thorough servicing.

I decided to tell Pappu and his gang to go do their sloganeering somewhere else. Or at least think of a new slogan.

'Dekhiye, Ammaji is very old,' I called out to them from the front verandah. 'She is trying to take rest. So why don't you—'

But before I could finish my little piece, an oldish gent sidled up to me and said in a hoarse whisper, 'Excuse me, beti, but my grandson's wife is not letting him consume.'

I blinked rather bemusedly and said, 'Consume what?'

He looked at me like I was a moron.

'Consume the marriage, of course! She is claiming that he is repulsive to her. She is claiming mental torture and dowry demands. It is not true! She is just after our two-crore property in Titotia. We want her to be told point blank that we Varmas are a decent family and that if she does not chup-chaap, very nicely, let him consume, then the marriage will be annulled because of non-consummation.'

I sighed. Part of the problem with staying with Amma at Tughlaq Road was that people were constantly dropping in with random problems. God knows how they expected Amma to fix them.

Still, I knew the drill.

I held out my hand. 'Gimme the file,' I said, all business-like.

'Thank you,' he said. He whipped out the inevitable file, handed it to me and scurried away, satisfied.

I folded my hands to the rest of the contingent and told them they were welcome to stay there, but *quietly*. Then I went into Amma's boudoir and chucked the file down next to an array of Shahnaz products.

She stopped getting her face massaged long enough to peer at it blankly.

'What newj?' she said.

'Mr Varma's granddaughter-in-law,' I informed her, 'is not letting her husband consume.'

'Good for her,' Amma said wearily, picking up the file and tossing it into a conveniently placed laundry basket. 'Sarojini, tonight we shall be attending a wedding.'

I looked up in surprise. I would've thought she would be too on-edge to attend a wedding. 'Okay,' I said. 'Whose?'

'Mixed marriage hai,' she said with a disapproving shudder. 'Civil ceremony ho gayee, and tonight is the walima – like a recepsun. See what we can give as a good gift.'

So Joline Bai and I went into Amma's immense, dusty store room and rummaged through the mountains of ugly stuff that people are always giving her. There were all these sandalwood elephants and camels of decreasing size walking in single file, grinning brass idols, a whole stack of Kerala urlis, ungainly silver tea sets, tons of melmoware crockery and a number of synthetic furry blankets in zip-locked bags. I started sneezing immediately.

Joline Bai suggested we pick out one of the silver tea sets but I shook my head. You can never tell which one of these is real silver and which is just white metal – we'd had an unfortunate accident in the past when we ended up gifting a very expensive set at the dhobi's wedding, and a cheapie-fake at a wedding in the home of a chubby lady chief minister from south India. She must've had a silversmith living in her house, because she spotted the fake instantly and presented Amma with a cheap cotton sari as a return gift.

Finally, I fished out a not-too-hideous brass lamp, the kind actresses light at the beginning of award functions, and sent it off to the Pavit Pradesh State Emporium on Baba Khadak Singh Marg to be gift-wrapped. That way, the bridal couple would think it had been bought *specially* for the occasion.

'Whose wedding is it, Amma?' I asked curiously, as we sat out in the front hall, drinking our evening tea.

'Oh, some industrialist family,' she said vaguely. 'Big Pragati Party supporters. The important thing is, Top Brass will be there. And everyone else too. It will be good to be seen there tonight.'

Awesome. I couldn't wait.

An hour later, as we rolled up to the wedding venue on Kushak Road, just off Rashtrapati Bhavan, I looked at all the VVIP cars in the drive and frowned.

'Amma,' I said.

'Hain…?' she answered distractedly, screwing in the back of her massive stud earrings grimly, wincing as she did so. Her ear lobes, if you look closely, are a truly grisly sight. She's had to have them stitched up surgically a couple of times because they split right down to the end under the weight of the thick, heavy gold earrings she's always wearing.

'The IJP list for Pavit Pradesh was announced today, wasn't it?'

She winced and continued to screw in her earring. 'Yes,' she said shortly. 'But not the name of the Bittora candidate.'

'How come?' I asked uneasily.

She shrugged. 'Who knowj? Maybe they are trying to broker a deal with that fool Dwivedi. You sud have pinned your hair up, Sarojini. So untidy it looks!'

'It's the Half-blown Rosebud Cut,' I explained glibly. 'Its spontaneous, bouncy unruliness shows off my long neck, brings out the pointiness of my chin and the rosiness of my skin and makes my eyes twinkal.'

Amma grunted. 'Looks like Half-Mad Full-Crack Cut to us,' she said. 'Must have paid one thousand rupeej for it, extravagant girl.'

As I had actually shelled out two thousand, I wisely said nothing to this. Anyway, she was a fine one to talk, with all her Shahnaz Hussain ShaSmooths and ShaYouths and ShaTooths. Instead, I said, 'And your usual IJP opponent, what's his name... Pant? Didn't he just die or something?'

'He did not *die,* he just had bypass,' she said. 'It could still be him – or they may bypass him, who knows?'

It figured. Really, it's sick how old some of these pollies are. Guys in their *fifties* are still in the Youth Pragati. Guys in their sixties are referred to as Young Turks. And every time there's a party meeting at the Akbar Road office, the driveway gets jammed because there are so many wheelchairs toiling up the hill. Some of them are so decrepit that you're scared they may actually *die* on you while you're talking to them at a function. You'd be sparkling and going all *so-how-are-you-uncle* at them and suddenly you'd realize the uncleji's so quiet because he's popped it.

The car stopped. As I adjusted my sari, Amma said fretfully, 'And ij this any way to wear a sari? One choochi in and one choochi out! Drape the pallu higher, Sarojini.'

'This is the *style,* Amma,' I said, rolling my eyes. 'If I drape it over both my breasts I'll look like the Dalai Lama. Besides, I'm wearing a blouse, aren't I?'

'*We* would not call that thing a blouj,' she grumbled. 'It doej not match your sari colour, and the neck is so deep, if you bend even a little bit, your partition will sow.'

'My *what* will sow?' I asked her, frankly baffled.

She reached forward and jabbed one bony finger right in the middle of my chest. '*That*,' she said austerely. 'Cleevaze.'

'Uff, I promise I won't bend, okay?'

'Okay,' she said in this really martyred voice as she heaved herself out of the car. 'Chalo, let us do some jasoosi. Find out who the IJP is fielding…'

The house was brilliantly decorated. There were a million twinkling lights strung across the trees and hedges. We walked in, me shivering slightly, out of sheer nervousness obviously, because the April evening was very pleasant and my red wine coloured velvet blouse and emerald green georgette sari were, if anything, a little too warm for the weather.

The bride and groom were standing on a massive, gerbera-and-orchid festooned stage at the other end of the lawn, but Amma was in no hurry to wish the couple. The extremely invasive frisking at the gate (*hold out your arms madum, spread your legs madum*) had alerted her to the fact that the big shots were already here. With a few whispered questions, she figured out where the 'VVVIP' seating was, and headed that way. I felt a little nervous for her, worried someone might snigger *ho-ji-morphed-photos-morphed-photos* when we approached, but everybody was super obsequious and she swept in regally, while I scurried along in her wake, right into the heart of the Ugly People Mafia.

'Coz they're all really ugly. Pollies, I mean. I've never been able to figure out exactly where the vicious circle starts – ugly people join politics and therefore make it look ugly, or regular-looking people join politics and *become* ugly because it's so ugly.

Whichever way you look at it, it can't be denied that, with about three and a half exceptions, Indian pollies are an unbeautiful lot. The exceptions include Amma's darling TB and one quite dishy-looking minister-of-state – but his good looks don't actually count 'coz the guy's an ass. Like, right after the 26/11 terrorist attacks, he actually went all Shahrukh-from-*DDLJ* and told an outraged media that *bade bade shehron mein aisi choti choti baatein hoti rehti hain*. And okay, I'll grant that one or two of the 'young' fifty-plus MPs aren't entirely hideous either.

As I stood there, a little behind Amma, gloomily eyeing the many wondrous specimens of manhood on display, a clammy hand landed unerringly on the bare patch of skin above the back of my blouse and a cheerful, husky voice declared, 'Hello, dear! How are you?'

It was Amma's old buddy, Anthony Suleiman. The one who'd done her the dubious favour of letting her stay on in the house on Tughlaq Road.

In the politically correct Noah's Ark that is the Pragati Party – stocked with representatives of every conceivable religion and caste in India – Anthony Suleiman has a *double* advantage, being half Muslim and half Dalit-Christian. Elevating him in any way appeases *two* minorities at once. He's milked the minority card for all it's worth – scrambling onto all sorts of committees and becoming AIPC General Secretary to boot – and is whispered to be seeking a girl who is half Brahmin and half Sikh for his son. So that they can get together and produce a female child (what with the women's reservation bill having been approved and all) who would be *so* comprehensively representative of all Indian vote banks that she could grow up to be the sole denizen aboard the Pragati Party Ark, rendering all other candidates redundant.

Looking at him now, I realized that Anthony Suleiman was also an exception (kind of) to the whole Ugly People Mafia theory.

He was resplendent in an electric blue bandhgalla, his eyes glinting yellow-green in the wedding lights. With his thick head of grey hair, extremely bushy white eyebrows and moustache, he looked for all the world like a good-humoured, debonair tomcat.

'Hi, uncle,' I said with a smile. 'Amma, look who it is!'

Amma, who had been heading for Top Brass like a guided missile, allowed herself to be deflected from course long enough to say carelessly, 'Arrey, Tawny. Kaise ho?'

And then she kept walking.

I winced. The dude's name is Tony. But Amma is incapable of pronouncing it any other way than how Nirupa Roy says Kumar Gaurav's name in *Teri Kasam*. Tawny.

Still, Tawny uncle looked pretty sanguine. He beamed at me affectionately.

'You are looking *lovely*!' he proclaimed, rocking back and forth on his heels a little. Then he leaned in, indicated the high-level Praggus around us and added, his eyes twinkling, 'Come to study some cartoons, hain? Or should I say *kitaanus*? Swimming about at the bottom of the Pragati Potty?'

I laughed. I like Tawny uncle. Four years ago, he talked Ma and Amma into letting me take up animation after college. He argued that a couple of very big Maharashtrian leaders were cartoonists too, that it was a time-honoured route to joining politics – and Amma had totally bought it.

'I'm just visiting, uncle,' I said, mindful of the fact that officially, Amma had retired and wasn't hankering wildly after the Bittora seat.

Then, because Amma was waggling her eyebrows and looking daggers at me, I went up to the Praggu Top Brass and folded my hands.

'Jyoti's daughter,' said Amma with a meaningful wink.

'Hello,' I said lamely.

I got a charming smile in return. Some light remark about how he'd heard so much about me, and then Amma filled the silence with some total *lie* about the suuuperb social work I had done all my life. Then they all started talking to each other again, Amma pausing only to ask me to bring her some galouti kebabs.

I raised my eyebrows. 'Amma, that's pan-fried red meat,' I said. 'Your doctor won't like it.'

She dug her thin sharp fingers into my ribs.

'Arrey bhai, life is *sort*,' she said. 'Go and get us some, Sarojini.'

And so, leaving Amma triumphantly ensconced at the TB's table, chatting animatedly about this and that while professing a complete disinterest in who would get the ticket from Bittora, I made my way into the thick of the gathering.

I walked past a massive pink sherbat fountain, huge stalls of fruit and salad, past laughing, happy groups of people who all seemed to know each other, until I reached the delicious smelling galouti kebabs. There was a long, rather noisy queue, full of ladies chattering gaily. I picked up a plate and stood in line.

The ladies in front of me finally departed, their plates piled high. I moved forward and the waiter-type behind the tawa came to a sudden stop. He just stood there, staring at me, twin skewers loaded with raw glistening chicken, gobi, simla mirch, tomato and button mushroom, held aloft like a sword in each hand.

I stared back at him.

'I know you,' he said, in a voice so intimate it made me jump a little.

'Uh… really?' I said, looking at him blankly. Wow, he was one hot waiter. Tall, with tousled dark hair and what my art teacher in school would've called a 'nobble' forehead. His black achkan was exquisitely severe, though a hint of deep rose satin showed at his breast pocket. His skin seemed to glow pale honey gold, but that could just have been the light from the coals.

I said the first thing that came into my head, which was, moronically, 'Did you go to Loreto too?'

He flashed a grin at me with slightly crooked, very white teeth as he shook his head and said, 'Err… no… that would've been biologically impossible…?'

His voice, which held a faint hint of 'abroad', trailed off with a teasing upward inflection, and still he just stood, holding aloft the loaded skewers, looking at me expectantly, waiting for me to say something.

I stared at him, looking for clues.

His features were strong. Slightly aquiline. He was clean-shaven but slightly stubbly. His sleeves were rolled up to just above the elbows, revealing lean but muscular forearms. A black thread was tied tightly around one sinewy wrist. A tiny scar lurked at the corner of his seriously sexy mouth.

'Come on, Kirti Nagar,' he said grinning. 'Jog that memory.'

I frowned. Only one person had ever called me Kirti Nagar. Or Lajpat Nagar. Or Malviya Nagar. It was supposed to be this big *joke* about how my name was the name of some random, overcrowded Delhi locality, only he could never remember which…

But surely this tall waiter couldn't be…

A couple of sparks leapt up from the tandoor, startling me, lighting up his quizzical eyes.

I knew those eyes.

———

It was the first day of the summer holidays in Bittora. He'd hauled me up our favourite mango tree and I, bursting through the leafy branches, landed backward into his arms. Instead of shoving me away like he usually did, he went very still and kept holding me. Then, leaning forward, he pressed a soft, hesitant kiss on the bare skin at the back of my neck.

A light, skipping sensation ran through my veins.

We were both thirteen.

Just then, the branch beneath us snapped, almost as if to warn us that such activities were forbidden in a place where children played.

We tumbled down, more or less unhurt, and set the ducks squawking. As they flapped away, protesting loudly, I began dusting the mud off my jeans, and he said, touching his face gingerly and showing me his fingers, 'It's bleeding, look.'

'Serves you right,' I answered confusedly, not looking at him. 'See what you've gone and done… the mali's going to kill us.'

'I'm not sorry,' he said defiantly, and I knew he wasn't talking about the branch we'd just broken.

I felt my cheeks flame as I retorted, 'Well, I am!'

He stared back at me, his dark eyes suddenly stormy. Then he spun around and walked away. I called out to him. But he didn't stop.

———

'Maruti Zain!' I exclaimed, beaming happily.

'Whoa!' He put a hand to his heart and staggered back two steps. 'I'd forgotten that smile... it's like someone suddenly turned on a stadium light. Hey, you should've been in that Happydent chewing gum ad! Grinning down dazzlingly from the chandelier as the Nawab eats his dinner.'

'And you should've been the Nawab,' I retorted instantly. 'Spoilt rotten. Exploiting the serfs on your estate for electricity.'

Zain Altaf Khan – for it was he – put down the skewers carefully and folded his arms across his chest. 'Still worrying about the *pure* people, I see,' he remarked.

I flushed. '*Poor* people,' I said. 'You don't need to keep correcting my pronunciation any more, you know.'

He took no notice of this remark.

'You still have two of my Zorro comics,' he said instead.

I gasped at this ungrateful attitude. 'You ate in my house every day! What about all the stuff I gave *you?*'

He wrinkled his forehead. All these deep lines popped up instantly, making him look not just hot, but extremely intelligent too.

'That would be... lots of attitude,' he said musingly. 'And lice. And chicken pox.' His dark eyes glowed warmly. 'And three incredible kisses.'

I felt my face go hot. I remembered, suddenly, the curiously caressing, rough velvet texture to his voice.

'And a scar that deformed me for life.'

'Oh, please!' I snapped unnecessarily to cover my confusion. 'You anyway looked deformed 'coz your ears were so big!' I looked up at him with a frown. 'Hey, what did you do...?' Then I snapped my fingers. 'Oh! You keep your hair longer so the ears don't stick out so much. Smart move.'

'Thanks,' he returned drily.

The first spontaneous spurt of conversation over, an awkward silence fell between us. I was remembering the weirdness of our last parting, and god alone knows what he was thinking about. He whistled tunelessly between his teeth as he turned the skewers, and I remembered how clever he used to be with his hands.

Finally, he said, 'So where did you net out in the end? Are you even five feet tall?'

'Five feet *two* inches,' I replied. 'That's taller than the average height for Indian women.'

He didn't look too impressed. 'You should've eaten the yolks of your boiled eggs,' he said. 'Instead of feeding them to the ducks. You turned them into cannibals, shame on you.'

'I only did that *once!*' I said, feeling a twinge of guilt. 'And anyway, they weren't duck's eggs, only hen's eggs. That's not cannibalism, strictly speaking. How tall are *you* now, anyway?'

'Tall enough,' he countered with a grin.

'Matlab?' I asked, puzzled.

His dark eyes danced as they looked around the crowded reception. 'Matlab, I'm over five ten which, if I remember correctly, used to be your cut-off height for anybody you would even *consider* getting involved with.'

I giggled. 'Really? God, I was pretty obnoxious.'

'Oh, I was obnoxious too,' he admitted. 'I had some high standards of my own, which you now...' he paused, his eyes flicked assessingly down to my chest, then rose back up to meet my gaze, '*just* about manage to fill.'

I resisted the urge to check if my pallu was in place and gave him what I hoped was a glacial look.

'I *think*.' He grinned, as he sneaked another assessing look.

I choked, but managed to say, with a little self-possessed laugh, 'This has got to be the most bizarre conversation happening at this party.'

'Oh, I don't know,' Zain replied. 'There are some pretty bizarre people here...'

'True,' I said ruefully.

Silence for a bit.

Then he said, 'You did well in your boards, I presume? Since Mr Pahuja didn't have to kill you?'

He was referring to our old tuition teacher back in Bittora. An ancient, soft-spoken, mild-eyed gent, Mr Pahuja was very proud of his 'record' which was that no child he had tutored ever got less than ninety per cent in their tenth class boards. Zain's theory was that Mr Pahuja had achieved this extremely impressive average by bumping off all students whom he suspected of being in danger of scoring lower than a ninety, a few weeks before the exam. Zain said he crept up behind them, eyes gleaming manically, and stabbed them to death with a geometry-box compass.

'So what would you like to have?'

Huh?

I looked at the empty plate in my hands.

'Why are you making kebabs, anyway?' I demanded. 'Did your family go bankrupt and have to sell the crumbly fort?'

'Yes,' he replied soberly.

I looked up quickly, concerned. He grinned.

'Ufff!' I said, rolling my eyes.

He picked up the skewers again

'I like doing it,' he said, shoving the skewers into the tandoor with the restless energy I remembered so well. I tried not to look at his sinewy forearms. They were affecting me strangely

– making my heart pump like that of an aging Praggu cabinet minister in desperate need of bypass surgery. 'And everybody else seems to like it too. So I always do something for family functions, you know?'

'Wow, I never thought you'd grow up to be so... metrosexual,' I managed to say. 'Cooking and all.'

His eyes glittered combatively. But all he said, the buddy-buddy camaraderie in his voice just a little off-key, was, 'So, where are your dopey plaits? Did someone die in your stupid Hindu family... or did you just get lice again and have to cut them off?'

'I hate you,' I said, regressing promptly to the nursery.

'I know,' he said lightly.

I looked up quickly. His lips were smiling, but his eyes weren't. They were oddly vulnerable.

'You look really nice in that sari,' he said abruptly.

I felt my cheeks go hot. 'Thanks,' I said, matter-of-factly. 'You look...'

Awesome. Superheroic. Biteable. Incredible.

'... nice too.'

'Hey, thanks!' He grinned. 'But don't come too close or you'll smell the mothballs.'

'I wasn't planning to,' I said defensively.

'How's Ma?' he asked, ignoring this weird reply.

He used to be really fond of my mother. And he couldn't stand Amma, but that's another story.

'How's your horrible dad?' I countered, then immediately wanted to kick myself.

The sparkle in his eyes died instantly. His face shuttered over. I looked away, wishing I'd kept my extra-wide mouth shut. The erstwhile royal family of Bittoragarh was, frankly, seriously weird. Zain's dad lived entirely in the past. Luckily for her, Zain's mom had died young. Not so lucky for Zain, though. We'd become friends because our bereavements had been so inversely symmetrical. Me with no dad, Zain with no mom. He used to love our house. And I didn't blame him because, really, those dudes in the crumbling palace had had absolutely no sense of interior décor. There were huge heads of animals mounted on walls all over the place. Lion. Tiger. Moose. Boar. Deer. Elephant. All glaring at you with glassy, accusing, you-killed-me-sicko-burn-in-hell eyes. I couldn't eat a thing with them watching me. God knows how Zain did. There were intricately carved ivory tusks all along the dining room wall, forming a sort of a tunnel that led to the table. There were tiger-skin carpets. All the dustbins and umbrella stands were elephant legs, chopped at the knee and hollowed out. They had toes and everything. And then there were these tall lamps scattered around the place, with heavy wooden bases, upon which stood erect elephant trunks with a wire threaded through them, topped off with lacy beaded lampshades.

'He died,' said Zain shortly. 'Four years ago. Didn't you know?'

Oh good! I thought.

'How awful,' I said.

He looked at me, his expression sardonic, and then suddenly said, in a louder, more formal voice, 'Hey, Mr S!'

I blinked, confused.

'Hello, young man! Barbequeing, hain?'

I looked around and realized with a start that Zain and I were not all alone on a desert island, after all. We were at a wedding, and Tawny uncle, with his son the Rapist in tow, had just joined us. The Rapist was blatantly ogling me.

(He isn't really a rapist. At least, we don't have any *proof* of it. Ma said, the last time she came to India, that he as good as raped you with his eyes every time he looked at you, and the name had stuck.)

'Titu dear, remember Jinni?' said Tawny to the Rapist.

'Of course!' said the Rapist, addressing my breasts with the welcoming air of someone greeting old friends. 'I remember...'

Both of you? I thought irately, as I yanked my pallu higher.

'And Zain toh you know...' Tawny uncle trailed off.

The Rapist held out his hand, but Zain, whose hands were messy from threading kebabs onto skewers, shrugged and smiled hello.

The Rapist laughed foolishly, picked up a kebab and chewed on it jauntily.

A little silence followed.

Finally, Tawny uncle broke it with an awkward, 'So! I will leave you youngsters to enjoy!' and rolled away. The music on the dance floor changed abruptly, from a fast song to a slow, romantic one. The Rapist, sensing an opportunity to grope, brightened instantly and turned to me. 'Would you like to dance?'

At which point, Zain, who had just been asked to whip up some kebabs by a very pretty girl in a spangled silver sharara, said smoothly, 'These galoutis will take some time to cook, Sherry. Whyn't you dance with my friend here till then?'

Sherry smiled in a friendly manner.

'I love this song!' she announced.

The Rapist smiled beatifically at her gorgeous décolletage.

'Titu, meet Shahana,' Zain told the Rapist. 'Great dancer.'

'Hi, Titu.' She smiled.

'Call me Tits!' the Rapist beseeched her instantly. 'Would you like to dance?'

Looking a little stunned, she nodded and the two of them floated away.

'I've always wondered,' Zain mused, as he flipped the galoutis expertly, 'what it must feel like to have *three* moustaches...'

'Like who?' I asked, a little irritated at the way he'd just assumed I wanted to stay with him and not, you know, burn the dance floor with the Rapist.

He looked up, his dark eyes dancing.

'Like your grandmother's buddy,' he said, waving the flat steel ladle about dramatically. 'Tawnyyy Suleimannnn!'

I gave an involuntary snort of laughter.

'One above his mouth and two above his eyes?'

'Exactly.' He grinned. Then he added, his eyes disturbingly warm, 'You always know what I mean, Jinni.'

'Yeah...' I muttered, looking away uncomfortably. 'Don't be mean about Tawny uncle, okay? I like him.'

'Okay, dear, okay,' he replied peacably.

I giggled again.

'You still do that weird snorting thing when you laugh,' he said, shaking his head. 'Like a koala with a cold. It's disgusting.'

Then he smiled and tilted his head in the direction of the beautifully lit sprawling white house behind us.

'Shall we go inside and talk?'

He led me through the cobbled courtyard into a carelessly expensive country kitchen, which opened into a cozy study, stocked with overstuffed armchairs and lined with old bookcases.

'Why don't you sit, I'll just wash up and come,' he said, heading for the massive silver and chrome sink.

'Okay,' I said somewhat dazedly as I sank into the cushy sofa, kicked off my absurdly high-heeled golden sandals and crossed my legs under me, my ears buzzing strangely. I was experiencing the weirdest sensation of sliding back in time.

Zain and I had been unwilling friends at first, thrown together during every summer vacation since we were five or six, because our grandfathers were thick buddies. I spent most of that early time together making fun of Zain's crumbling, termite-infested palace and his weird dad. He reciprocated by being snide about my goody-goodiness and oily plaits. But since all the local kids in Bittora thought the two of us out-of-towners were a pair of zoo exhibits, we had no choice but to quit squabbling and become friends.

The first thing we would do when we met was stand butt-to-butt to see who had gotten taller, then race out to the mango grove to climb our favourite tree and, inhaling the cool, intoxicating aam-ki-bor, tell tall tales about what we'd done all year. Zain had large dark eyes, spoke very fast, ran like the wind, and was wickedly inventive in the games he made up. His skin seemed golden in the Bittora sunshine, almost transparent, a thin blue vein lightly visible along one cheek. He made me laugh a lot, up in the branches, as we swung our legs and the bees buzzed around us, but he was also oddly intense and could be very moody at times.

As the sun climbed higher into the sky, we would slide down the tree trunks, trample through the gay, black-eyed sunflower beds and strut into the house to feast on slices of tiny, slightly sour King's Bakery bread, slathered with thick, fresh cream and sprinkled with crunchy sugar. We would pore over the stash of superhero comics in my room, play grimly competitive games of carom in the verandah, or swarm up the raat-ki-rani growing along the pillars and whack the lazy lizards dozing on the walls with rolled-up newspapers. The idea was to build a collection of their tails which dropped off if you whacked hard enough and wriggled about on the floor for hours.

Sometimes, fired by the tales of independence Bauji used to tell us, we would write out long, freedom-fighter type speeches and declaim them to each other in the garage, using the bonnet of Amma's old Ambassador as a podium. Bauji would patiently hear us out, pointing out flaws in our rebuttals, raising points we had missed, and awarding a crisp five-rupee note to the better speaker. Or we would recite poetry – Zain loved Ramdhari Singh Dinkar's *Singhasan khali karo ki janta aati hai,* because it was all about abdicating the throne for the people, and he was rather hung up on the grand gesture his dadajaan and all his 'royal' cronies had made back in the fifties. Of course, I was always quick to point out to him that they hardly had a choice in the matter. They were a bunch of indolent, decrepit dudes with no armies, disgruntled populaces and landlocked states. Zain retaliated by sniggering at my favourite poem, the gutsy *Khoob ladi mardaani woh toh Jhansi wali Rani thi,* pointing out smugly that it hailed Laxmi Bai as '*mardaani*', which meant as-good-as-a-man. So obviously, being a woman wasn't good enough, smirk smirk. We also created our own comic book series called *Enforcer 49*, with Zain providing the text and me doing the drawings. That's what got me hooked to superheroes in the first place.

Zain was sent off to some fancy public school in England when we were both twelve and returned in the holidays all snooty and proper. He winced whenever I spoke, and kept correcting me: 'Don't say *roits*, Jin, it's *riots*. And my shoes are not Naaik, they're Naai*kee*. And it's not *veemin*, you idiot, it's women.' I had to break a few badminton racquets over his head just to cut him down to size.

After that, I saw a little less of him, as our holiday terms no longer synchronized completely and also because he got totally obsessed with cricket and spent a lot of time playing with a gang of husky local boys. But he would still come over in the afternoon, when it was too hot to play outside, and lie around, eating entire trayfuls of ice cubes and crushing me at carom. That year, he wrote to me from England, sprawling untidy letters full of four-letter-word-peppered limericks.

The next summer, we didn't quite know what to say to each other, and started having the most idiotic fights. Also, my sharp-eyed grandmother cottoned onto the fact that my teenage 'haarmoans', as she called them, had started to play the harmonium every time Zain showed up. She pretty much forbade him to enter the house, even telling Ma I should spend my holidays in Delhi so I could concentrate on my studies far away from that 'always-coming' fellow. Thankfully, Ma, convinced the yearly visits to our hometown gave me 'roots', vetoed this.

Finally, one afternoon, just a few weeks before my tenth class board exams, when the music from the harmoniums had waxed into a full-scale *symphony*, Amma said a whole lot of typical uncalled-for things and Zain dropped out of my life forever.

Okay, so he's hot, I admitted to myself, as I sat on the overstuffed sofa in the cozy study. So what? Don't forget he walked out on you and never got in touch. He may not have valued the romance – but we were *friends*, right? Surely that counted for something? Unless... hey, unless he spent all these years working out and becoming Taller, Stronger and Sharper, striving to reach the epitome of suave, masculine hotness, so he could totally wow me when we met again... and now that he had hit his exquisite, incredible peak, he had contrived to casually bump into me at a wedding. It *could* be!

Even as I was thinking this, the new, taller, hotter Zain walked in, dropped down at the other end of the sofa, and in one fluid movement, swung his long legs over the arm of the sofa and deposited his dark head into my lap.

'Hey,' I protested, my heart banging hard inside my little velvet blouse. 'Back off, okay? I barely know you.'

'That's okay,' he said, his eyes dancing. 'I know you *really* well. I know you hate logarithms and love rock music and...' His voice grew huskier and one lean hand rose up to brush my cheek caressingly. 'I know you have a little, cream-coloured, South America-shaped birthmark way up on your... um... left... right, no, definitely *left* thigh – wanna hear more?'

'No, thanks,' I said hastily, and tried to haul his head off my lap.

But quick as a flash, he caught my hand and pressed a soft kiss on the inside of my wrist.

Fireworks.

And his lips had barely brushed my skin.

I gave a shaky laugh. 'Zain, if you're going to be like this, I'm going outside,' I warned him.

'Get me off your lap first,' he countered with a grin, clutching my fingers tightly.

I glared at him.

'Okay, o*kay*,' he said and swung himself up easily, his tousled dark hair falling into his eyes. He threw himself along the other end of the sofa, stretched his long legs out in front of him, tapped one foot impatiently, and said, 'You want to talk, right? So, talk!' He threw one arm up into the air. 'Taqlia!'

'That means "Leave us",' I told him sweetly. 'Should I?'

'Really? God, my Urdu sucks.'

'What-of-yours doesn't?' I said, trying for sarcasm but ending up giggling.

Encouraged, he caught the edge of my pallu and started weaving the pliant fabric in and out between his fingers.

I glared at him.

He gave the pallu a light tug.

I yanked it back from him and stood up. 'I'm going outside,' I said.

He raised one dark eyebrow lazily. It looked pretty cool, but I wasn't impressed. I'd seen him practise the gesture too many times when we were ten years old.

'Longing to dance with Tits?' he enquired.

'Dying to,' I returned.

In one smooth movement, he reached out, grabbed my wrist and pulled me so hard I fell back on the sofa and came up close against his side with a thud. 'That's better,' he said smugly.

Suddenly furious, I tried to break his grip but couldn't, and had to settle for twisting my face as far away from his as I could, which wasn't much.

'You can't,' I said tightly, 'just walk into my life after nine years and try and revive some juvenile little romance. I've forgotten all about you.'

He didn't say anything, just looked down at my averted face for a long time.

Then, very deliberately, he bent his head and pressed a contrite, lingering kiss on the soft skin at the back of my neck.

The same place where he'd once kissed me, my first kiss ever, eleven years ago.

I closed my eyes, gritted my teeth, and heroically managed to stifle the stupid little sigh that threatened to escape my lips.

He removed his hands, releasing me. Then he stepped back, shrugging his shoulders a little, and said formally, his public school accent suddenly prominent, 'You're right. My apologies. Please go outside if you wish.'

But of course I didn't wish. I reached up, found his extra-large ears, pulled down his head and kissed him.

Anything could have happened on that overstuffed sofa if somebody hadn't knocked on the door a few minutes later.

I think it was the catering crew, passing though with some big utensils, but whatever it was, it brought me to my senses. I sat up quickly, ignoring Zain's groan of protest and started gathering my unspooled sari.

Zain sat up, blinking, looking adorably confused, and demanded, 'Where are you going, idiot?'

'Outside, of course!' I said, frantically tucking my pleats in. 'There are *people* out there! You'd better come too – your Sherry must be back at your stall by now, desperately seeking galouti!'

He continued sitting there, his head tilted to one side. 'I like your hair like this,' he said.

'Oh, I like your *everything*!' I returned fervently, throwing his achkan at him. 'Now come on *out* – but five minutes after me, okay?'

'O...kay...' I heard him mutter resignedly, and then I was out on the verandah again, picking up a glass of cool red sherbat from a passing bearer. My head was spinning.

What was *wrong* with me? I'd never been much of a swinging party girl. I'd gone to university with some fairly cool guys, but I hadn't slept with a single one of them. Honest! I hadn't even *wanted* to. I'd hung on to the 'precious gift of my virginity' till I was twenty. Then I met a cute sensitive banker, just *one* measly banker, and got pretty serious with him. But it had ended badly, he claimed I didn't love him the way he wanted to be loved, and that was when I decided to get a job in Mumbai. There, I had a tepid two-month scene with a dark, sarcastic music engineer which had gone nowhere fast. That was the sum total of my sexual encounters. Some nice, callisthenic-type sex with the banker, *one* vastly unsatisfying session with the music engineer.

And here I was, behaving like some feisty, get-on-the-carousel-boys chick and unbuttoning achkans like I did it every day of my life. And within sight of the Top Brass and most of the Praggus. Not to mention my grandmother. Who, I now saw, was on the podium, wishing the couple, handing over our present and posing for pictures. I smiled vaguely in her direction, sipped my drink and then sniffed the glass suspiciously. Had they laced the sherbat with some kind of aphrodisiac?

'Jinni…?'

Zain had emerged, looking incredible. His mouth was a little bruised. My doing, I thought, feeling appalled.

'Can we just talk?' he asked.

'What about?' I snapped, trying desperately not to remember how he'd looked with the achkan off.

(Lean, taut, chiselled and honey gold.)

Zain made a vague gesture in the air.

'About… anything. Like, what you're doing here for instance. I thought you lived in Canada?'

'I did,' I told him. 'I went to cartoon college there.'

He looked a little startled.

(Lean, taut, chiselled and honey gold.)

'What I mean to say,' I continued, babbling moronically, 'is that I studied computer graphics and animation there. But then I got so India-sick I picked up a job at an animation studio in Mumbai.'

'Welcome back,' he said approvingly. He'd always been a patriotic, live-in-India type. 'And your job – is it fun?'

I laughed, a little sarcastically. 'Oh, it's a total blast. I animate kitaanus all day. And what do *you* do when you 're not barbequing at weddings?'

'I'm an engineer,' he said. 'At least, I have a degree in environmental engineering. What do you mean, you animate kitaanus?'

I sighed.

'Have you seen all those creepy, computer-animated germs inside toilet bowls in ads for Harpic and Domex?'

'You make those?'

'Yeah.' I nodded.

'No superheroes?' he asked, just the slightest trace of laughter in his voice.

'No,' I said, my cheeks very red. 'What do *you* make, anyway?'

Now he looked really amused.

'Oh, I make enough,' he said smugly. 'Didn't you ever google me?'

'No,' I replied. 'You dropped clean out of my life and out of my mind.'

He grinned. 'I bet you did.'

'I bet *you* did!' I returned.

He laughed so hard he spluttered sherbat all over the railing.

(Lean, taut, chiselled and honey gold.)

I ignored him, adjusted my pallu and looked around the garden in what I hoped was a queenly manner.

'When can we meet again?' he asked abruptly.

I shook my head, saying nothing. Things were going a little too fast here.

He leaned in and said in an urgent undertone, 'Would you relax? *Please?* And regarding... um...' he waved an arm vaguely in the direction of the study, *'that...* can I just say, I'm really sorry if I came on too strong.' He paused, his forehead lining up again, a lock of dark hair falling into his eyes. 'Wait, scratch that, actually. Why am I saying I'm sorry? I'm not sorry at all!'

He stood there frowning, like this was some momentous discovery.

Then the sudden grin flashed.

'Are *you* sorry?' he said.

I felt my cheeks go hot.

'Yes,' I said decidedly.

He winced. 'You're always too quick to say you're sorry, Jinni,' he complained. 'It's the most irritating thing about you.'

'I have a generous nature,' I retorted. 'Unlike *you,* who sulks for days... or months... or *years.*'

'Well, I'm not sulking anymore,' he said lightly. 'Say you'll meet me again, Kaka Nagar. C'mon.'

I shook my head and began to speak, but we were interrupted once again – this time by Amma, who barrelled in on our deserted island like an oil tanker, foghorns blowing.

She grabbed me by the arm and hissed peremptorily, 'Sarojini! Come with us. *Now.*'

But I swung her around to face Zain.

'Amma, guess who this is!' I said excitedly. 'Go on, guess! You'll *never* guess!'

A rather weird silence followed, while Zain looked at Amma and Amma looked at Zain. For at least three minutes.

'Adaab,' he said finally, formally, one hand going to his chest. He wasn't stand-offish exactly, but he didn't smile, and his fine nostrils flared a little. Well, the way things had ended back then, I couldn't have expected him to fall into her lap and start kissing the inside of her wrist or anything – but hey, he'd just claimed that he wasn't sulking any more.

'Haan haan, hello,' said Amma grudgingly. Her benevolent politician smile did an extremely brief, blink-and-you-miss-it flit across her face. 'Sarojini, come!'

And with that she dragged me away! I tell you, that's why I have such a pathetic love life. My family is like a social millstone around my neck.

I tried to protest, but she hissed 'Enough!' and marched me to the car, smiling and nodding and folding her hands in farewell to everybody we encountered on the way, her grip on my upper arm as unyielding as steel.

When we reached the car, she snapped at the driver to go take a walk, and then got in. I got in after her and she reached over and banged the door shut.

'Amma, what is *wrong* with you? That was Zain! How could you be so rude?'

She snorted loudly.

I pushed the hair off my face and continued. 'I know you're really tense nowadays, but that was so uncalled for! Especially when,' a new thought entered my head, 'hey, especially when he could've *campaigned* for you and everything!'

She snorted again. Louder. More ominously.

'You know, you could totally asphyxiate yourself if you keep doing that,' I told her. 'Stop it.'

Silence. I think she was gnashing her teeth in the dark.

I said, a little worried now, 'What is it, Amma? Is it the ticket? Oh god, have you not got it?'

'Yes,' she said flatly. 'We have not got it.'

'Oh *no*, Amma,' I said, sickened at the disappointment she must be feeling.

Reaching out, I put my arms around her stiff little body and started babbling out the soothing speech I'd been preparing for a week. 'Listen, it's probably a blessing in disguise anyway. The Pragati is going to lose that seat. It's way too much of an uphill task after the mess Dwivedi's made of everything. I've got a great idea. Let's just screw all this. We'll go to Canada for a holi—'

She pushed me away. Hard. Really hard.

Then she said, her voice throbbing with emotion, '*You* have got it.'

'Sorry, what?'

She said, just to make it clearer, so that there could be no mistake, '*You* are standing on the Pragati Party ticket!'

My heart plummeted, like a boulder in slow motion, right through my stomach.

I stared at her, my head spinning.

'And that ij not all,' she continued, her voice extremely bitter, 'you wanted to know na, who the IJP is fielding? Well, open your yearj and listen! It ij that puppy, that too-much eating, always-coming *pilla*, your great childhood friend, that over-smart, over-educated Zain Altaf *Khan*!'

3

We drove home in complete silence. I tried to get Amma to talk to me, but she just waggled her eyebrows violently, indicating the driver in the front seat, and shushed me into silence. So I sat back, watched the old neem trees of Lutyens' Delhi whiz past, and tried to make sense of what she had said.

It was insane – much too insane to be true – but it *had* to be true; Amma wouldn't make up such a story. I stepped gingerly around the proof of Zain's perfidy – *watch out for Frenemies,* Rumi had said, and reluctantly I saluted him – and zoomed into the issue that affected me the most at this current moment. My candidature.

'How come,' I asked Amma finally, choosing my words carefully, very aware of the driver in front, 'they picked... uh, you know... who they picked?'

She snorted. 'How do we know?' she said. 'We don't claim to know what goes on inside the minds of the mad men who run the IJP!'

I shook my head. 'No, I meant -- in *your* party, Amma.'

'Alwayj thinking about yourself,' she said, somewhat unfairly.

I didn't say anything.

The silence between us deepened, but finally, she sighed and said, massaging her ear lobe, 'The newj came when we were eating – that the IJP had announced the pilla's name from Bittora. It waj quite a sok for all of us – you look in front!' This to the poor driver, who hadn't even *glanced* our way.

The hapless man instantly hunched over the wheel in a desperate bid to appear invisible. Amma burned holes through his back for a while, then threw up her hands, shrugged and exclaimed fatalistically, 'Oh, what doej it matter? It ij all public knowledge now, anyway!'

Then she turned back to me and started to spill.

'Anyway, so TB immediately said that we must get a young candidate to stand also. Then somebody suggested Tawny's son's name.'

'The Rapist? No way!'

She ignored me. 'We pretended to agree with the suggestion. It ij only polite, and poor Tawny ij aawar friend, after all. But of course, we were already thinking of you. So when TB said, quite snappily, ki wajn't there any other candidate besides the son of the AIPC General Secretary, we said humbly that We are there. But immediately, TB said, just as we knew he would – No no, Pushpa jiji, you are too senior to take on this young whippersnapper, it would be insulting to you! So then we quickly said ki haan haan, we may be old, but there ij *young* Pande blood willing to serve you…'

'You said that?' I exclaimed, totally appalled. 'Amma, you *didn't*! That is so *feudal*! Why do you insist on acting like some kind of loyal knight talking to a king?'

'Arrey, what foodle foodle?' she said belligerently. 'Seat was slipping out of the familyj hands, we had to do *something*! Then everybody argued for a long time, and finally TB said – People, people, time is running out! We simply have to take a decision on this seat today! I'll be damned if I pick that disgusting Dwivedi fellow, and so I vote we give the ticket to Pande junior. It is a tough seat to win and we have pledged to give thirty per cent of tough seats to the youth. Good luck to her! And that,' she said, not a little bitterly, 'was that.'

I looked at her, at a loss for words, my brain racing.

Then I spotted a loophole.

'But I'm not even *registered* as a voter from Bittora!' I said triumphantly. 'I've been in Canada all this time. My name's not on the electoral rolls, and it's too late to add it now – so I can't possibly stand! You'll just have to go back and tell TB sorry.'

But she didn't even blink.

'Don't be silly, Sarojini,' she said. 'Of course you are registered. We got it done long ago. You think we don't know aawar duty?'

Oh god, what was this?

'Amma, I can't take *your* place,' I said beseechingly. 'Who am I, after all? Nobody!'

She grunted. 'That ij true enough. And let us tell you, with the pilla in place, winning Bittora ij almost impossible. Tawny Suleiman thinks so too. He came up to us afterwards and thanked us for not letting hij son get the Bittora ticket. He said it waj an impossible seat, that IJP will sweep. He warned us not to expect too much election funds either, because the party won't want to throw good money after a lost cause.'

'Fuck,' I whispered. 'Amma, this is a total disaster.'

She squared her shoulders.

'Oh, no,' she said rallyingly. 'We can still turn it around. Let us make one or two phone calls, we have some friends who will fund us…'

Her eyes got a dreamily speculative, faraway look, like she was flipping though a virtual filofax of owed favours. Then they zoomed into the neckline of my skimpy velvet choli, which the newly anointed IJP candidate had been unbuttoning passionately not half an hour ago. 'Better get some decent bloujej stitched, Sarojini,' she said. 'Sari hum de denge. Salwar kameez won't do, now that you are the candidate.'

I swallowed convulsively. This couldn't be happening, I thought numbly, as I flopped back against the cool white upholstery of the old Ambassador.

'Err… no chance I can duck this thing, is there?' I said hesitantly.

A small, incoherent, choking sound came from her side of the car.

'Amma?' I said uncertainly into the near dark.

She thrust her face into mine, her pointy chin almost hitting me in the eye. 'Of course *not*!' she declared. 'People spend their whole lives waiting for this apportunity! Who do you think you are… some *star*?'

'Okay, okay,' I said, trying to swallow the wave of panicky bile that was lurching towards my mouth. 'I'll do it. You'll have to help me a little, though.'

'Oh, no,' said Amma grimly, tightening the jooda pins in her bun, as we swung into the gates of the Tughlaq Road house and an army of Bittorawallahs rushed up to greet us. 'We will have to help you a *lot*!'

Ballot Boxing
Part 7 in our continuing series of reports from
Lok Sabha constituencies across India

People-Like-Us Bratpack
Battles it Out in Bittora

It's a sleepy little town in central Pavit Pradesh. It boasts of an engineering college, a state-of-the-art hospital and a palace converted into a seven-star heritage hotel. There are innumerable beauty parlours and a rather self-important looking, brand new Pizza Hut, but the feel of the town is largely rural, set as it is among large swathes of *channe ke khet*. And yet, few constituencies in the nation provide such a perfect microcosm of India's political paradoxes as does Bittora, capital of the erstwhile princely state of Bittoragarh and home turf of the redoubtable Pushpa Pande – she of *PP for Pushpa Pande, PP for Pavit Pradesh and PP for Pragati Party* fame.

Bittora constituency, comprising the town of Bittora and 600 surrounding villages, spread over 804 densely populated, tough to traverse by road or rail kilometres, is an electoral candidate's nightmare and a psephologist's delight. *Kos kos pe paani badle paanch kos pe bani* is a truism here. Bittora has a 27 per cent Muslim population, amongst the highest in India. Add to this numerous Dalit and OBC groups, Christian tribals in the Bitwa Reserved Forest, a tiny but extremely vocal and influential Brahmin bloc and a strong environmentalist lobby protesting against the modest dam that is being proposed on the Bitwa

river, and the mix can confound the wiliest of veteran campaigners. And now the ancient streets of Bittoragarh are plastered with smiling images of the two youngest candidates in this General Election.

Sarojini Pande, PP, 25 years old, Electoral Symbol: The Pointing Finger. Post-graduate degree in animation and film graphics from Tuck University, Toronto, schooling from Loreto Girls' Convent, Delhi. A last-minute nominee, pretty little Sarojini Pande is a political novice and seems to have nothing to recommend herself except a warm, wide smile, a scrubbed clean image and the Pande name tag. Her grandparents have always been sympathetic to the plight of the poorer sections in Bittora and the party is obviously hoping that she will provide a healing touch to the section of the electorate which was bitterly upset by Pandit Dinanath Dwivedi's recent insensitive antics during a homestay at a Dalit dwelling in Durguja.

These, coupled with the now infamous bribe-soliciting 'You did not vote for me for free, why should I do your work for free?' dialogue he was seen to mouth to a TV journalist posing as a Muslim teacher seeking CBSE recognition for an Islamic school during a sting operation a fortnight ago, have sealed Dwivedi's fate with the party Top

Brass. To make matters worse, Dwivedi referred to the school as a 'madrasa' and expressed the opinion that 'these people do not require education beyond class five'.

The footage caused major outrage in Pavit Pradesh. In the words of a prominent Muslim cleric, 'the synthetic green veneer has been ripped from the bosom of pseudo-secularists to expose the throbbing saffron heart beneath.'

Dwivedi, who was a shoo-in for the PP ticket from Bittora, and had been preparing for the election for almost a year, was shooed out summarily. With no other contender in sight, his ticket was handed over to Pande.

A visibly jubilant Pushpa Pande is now fielding her granddaughter with great aplomb. The campaign headquarters is likely to be Saket Bhavan, the old family home of Pandit Madan Mohan Pande, famous freedom fighter and Sarojini's grandfather. But young Sarojini Pande's 'healing touch' promises to the poor Muslims of the region may not cut any ice as her main adversary is the scion of the erstwhile royal family of Bittoragarh, Zain Altaf Khan.

Zain Altaf Khan, Indian Janata Party, 25 years old. Electoral Symbol: Marigold Flower. Engineering degree from MIT, schooling from Winchester School, England. Khan is both handsome and charismatic even though his credentials are mainly that, unlike most young men of his privileged background, he has never run anybody over with a speeding BMW under the influence of alcohol or drugs. His worst crime is probably a series of trophy girlfriends and a passion for rally driving. The ladies of Bittora seem especially vulnerable to his intensity and stormy good looks and view these shortcomings with a tolerant eye. Khan is universally credited with bringing progress and commerce into the area by converting the mouldering Bittora palace into a heritage hotel in partnership with the Taj group, post his father's death a few years ago. Khan's campaign base is to be the Zain Mahal, a luxury suite named after him at the property.

Unlike most erstwhile royal families from the north, the Altaf Khans are well loved, as one faction chose to stay on in India post Partition and has done a lot – especially in the first thirty years after independence – for the people in the area.

Khan's appeal to Muslim voters may, however, be diluted by the fact that he is standing on an IJP ticket. This Hindu hardliner party has occasionally followed a strategy of fielding ex-royals, with mixed results. But this is the first time that they have found themselves a Muslim ex-prince – that too from a royal house which is not entirely decrepit. Purged by several *chintan baithaks,* and with its new secular face on, the party seems proud of its handsome young protégé. But Muslim voters are naturally wary. 'IJP is trying to put a lamb's face on its vulture body,' they said. 'But we are not so easily convinced. Hum sochenge, we will not be so quick to decide where to cast our vote.'

But Khan seems sanguine. 'Everybody knows the old IJP is dead,' he stresses. 'This is a *new* party, one which has emerged after intense introspection and soul-searching.

The ideals of secular janta stalwarts of the seventies are very close to its heart. Minorities and backwards will be well-represented here. IJP aims to give the voters a genuine option to the hypocritical, populist, overfed leadership of the Pragati.'

Meanwhile, there's also a little band of spoilers out to queer the pitch. Forty-year-old college professor Vir Singh, a popular if controversial local figure, has secured the KDS ticket and could end up splitting the high-caste Brahmin vote three-ways.

Another last minute candidate could well be the disgraced Pandit Dwivedi himself, who, having been denied the Pragati ticket, is rumoured to be standing as an independent, simply to block Pushpa Pande and her granddaughter.

But Khan minor is clearly in the lead, with Pande junior hot at his heels.

It's a battle of foreign-returned local brats who are both probably much more at home in the air-conditioned environs of big cities than in the dusty hearths of Pavit Pradesh. But they are even now travelling down to Bittora to file their nomination papers. And they seem to be in earnest.

So is this the new, post-26/11 India? Genuinely concerned, young, educated people-like-us, coming to a head at the hustings? Or is it just a sordid continuation of dynastic politics? Whatever else it may be, it is certainly a piquant situation when a Brahmin girl from the Pragati fights a Muslim ex-royal from the IJP.

The media is watching closely. Unfortunately, voter involvement, at least at this initial point, three weeks before Bittora goes to the polls, seems to be rather low.

'Quite a nice article, isn't it?' Gudia aunty cooed in breathless cloying accents, her large watery eyes locked into mine. 'Such a big picture also! Madam, you must be so proud of your famous granddaughter!'

Amma grunted.

I plastered a polite smile across my face and merely said, 'Thanks, Gudia aunty.'

It was a swelteringly hot day, forty-one degrees according to Our Pappu, and we were sitting in the verandah of the Tughlaq Road house, getting ready to depart for Bittora by the evening train. It was to be a large contingent – lots of workers, the core team for the campaign, Joline Bai, who was joined at the hip with Amma, Amma and me. And also, it now appeared, Gudia aunty.

Gudia aunty gambolled into our lives when Amma entered politics after Bauji's death, and has been holding on grimly ever since. She looks rather like a middle-aged Sesame Street muppet, one of those over-eager, hyper ones, with bulging ping-pong ball eyes, a huge nose and a gulping, whiny little voice. She trails behind Amma, running her errands, being yelled at and pushed about, always smiling a nervous, appeasing smile. She has proclaimed herself Amma's 'second daughter' and says she'll do *anything* for her because Amma got her some sort of secretarial job at the All India Pragati Committee headquarters when she was down and out many years ago.

She fully creeps me out. She's kind of like that weirdo nanny in *The Hand that Rocks the Cradle*. You know, the one who insinuates herself into the heart of a family and then starts killing them off one by one.

'Are you coming with us, Gudia aunty?' I asked, fervently hoping she would say no.

Gudia aunty turned her huge watery eyes upon me, blinked and said gushingly, 'Of course! I'm going to be madam's election agent! Oops—' She raised one ungainly, red, knuckled hand to her mouth. 'I mean, ha ha, *your* election agent!' She swatted my arm in an awkward attempt at playfulness. 'This will take some getting used to!'

'Well, then get used to it, Gudia,' Amma said wearily. 'Now go and organize some tea.'

Gudia aunty flushed a little at Amma's dismissive tone, but got to her feet immediately. 'Of course! I am not a *guest* in this house, to sit in the hall and be served tea!' she said archly. 'I know madam's kitchen like the back of my hand! Jinni, can I offer you some tea? *You* are the visitor here, really! *I* am quite at home!'

You see how totally creepy she is? Talking to her is like biting into a slice of extra-sweet dussheri mango, and then discovering it's been cut with the onion knife.

'Why do you put up with that woman, Amma?' I asked crossly, when Gudia aunty had blundered away towards the kitchen. 'And why is she coming with us?'

Amma shook her head. 'Gudia haj had a very sad life, Sarojini,' she said reprovingly. 'She was orphaned at ten, had a hysterectomy at twenty, and then her hujbend left her – not even to go and live with another woman – just to be alone!'

'I would've left her too,' I muttered.

'See ij an excellent election agent,' Amma said stubbornly. 'We won't have anyone else.'

'What does an election agent do, anyway?' I wondered aloud. I was pretty hazy about all the nuts and bolts of campaigning stuff. My expertise was mostly limited to smiling winsomely and saying *Vote for Pushpa jiji! Vote for Pragati!*

Amma rolled her eyes. 'The election agent is the candidate's most trusted person. The core of the core team. See can sign documents on the candidate's behalf. Also, see visits the office of the district commisner every two days and submits full accounts of all the monies her candidate is spending. With bills and everything.'

'Why is that such a big deal?' I asked, not particularly impressed.

Amma rubbed her ear lobe tiredly. 'Do you have any idea,' she asked, 'how hard it ij to spend six-seven crores and make it look like you spent only twenty-five lakhs?'

'Six-seven *crores*?' I gasped. 'That's *insane*.'

Amma just looked at me.

'Don't be Nave, Sarojini,' she said sternly.

I flushed.

'I'm not being naïve,' I said doggedly. 'You *know* Bauji wouldn't have approved.'

Amma sniffed.

'Bauji wouldn't have approved of your *haircut!*' she shot back. 'Times *change,* Sarojini.'

I backed down. 'So you want her to diddle your accounts. Fine, I get it. Just – don't treat her like a dogsbody, okay? Or push her around, that's all I ask of you.'

'We won't,' said Amma indignantly. 'We never do,' she added as an afterthought.

Then she looked around furtively, lowered her voice and said, 'Only, you will need to watch her, little bit – see haj a small problem… *you* know.'

Oh god. I'd forgotten all about Gudia aunty's little problem.

I groaned. 'Amma, the woman is a full blown klepto!'

Amma shook her head. 'No, no, we have no *proof,*' she said vaguely, not looking me in the eye. 'Besides, see ij very honest about money… only rings and one-two perfume bottles and all disappear sometimes when see is there…'

You see? It's completely illogical. Only my grandmother would pick a kleptomaniac to be her election agent and trust her to handle large bundles of sweet-smelling cash.

'And that too, only after parties when see haj had one-two drinks…'

Make that an *alcoholic* kleptomaniac.

'You only like her,' I said resentfully, 'because she sucks up to you.'

'Well,' said Amma, poking me with her bony fingers, 'at

least *somebody* doej! Now come, it ij almost time to go to the stasun.'

I got up, glancing again at the news article as I did so. Gudia aunty hadn't been sucking up for once. The picture of me *was* nice, an arty black-and-white portrait that Rumi had shot on Marine Drive one rainy afternoon, but the picture of Zain was even nicer. He was wearing a retro Def Leppard T-shirt and laughing, looking a little rueful, surrounded by a crowd of doting girls on the campus of Bittora Women's College. Just looking at him made my belly flip over.

Meeting him last night had been so incredible.

And not just because he had turned out to be lean, taut, chiselled and honey gold. Or because his kisses had made my head spin. That helped, of course. But it had been incredible, mainly because meeting him again had been, in a way, like meeting myself again.

I picked up the newspaper for another look at his picture. Was one of the girls groping his butt? Well, *good* for her.

The caption below the picture said *Zain Altaf Khan, IJP candidate, at the BWC's inter-college western music festival.*

Was he a snake? An opportunist?

Or was he – my eyes widened – a closet *mujahideen* or something? Worming his way into the IJP and then trying to finish them off from within. Was that his big plan?

Or was he trying to finish *me* off from within? Was *that* his big plan?

I mean, the way he'd just shown up, out of the blue – and been so nice and everything. Surely, that couldn't be a coincidence? Oh my god, supposing he *hadn't* spent all those years working out and growing tall to be worthy of me? Supposing he'd spent all those years nursing a grudge and figuring out how to *destroy* me? And I'd let him lead me to the study with the big comfy sofa. I'd let him kiss me, *more* than kiss me. *Much more* than kiss me. My insides began to squirm in painful embarrassment. He had seemed so well-prepared... what if there were *cameras* in that study?

Supposing he'd known, somehow, that I would be standing? When Amma and I alighted the train in Bittoragarh, would we find the constituency plastered with pictures of me in a clinch with him? Talk about getting screwed by the opposition! I'd be doomed before I even began!

Sweaty and panicking, I decided it was time to do something I'd been putting off for almost ten days now. I sneaked into the garden – which was sizzlingly hot, but at least finally free of Bittorawallahs – and called my mother.

The phone rang about sixteen times before she picked it up.

'Hello!' she said, sounding out of breath. 'Please say you're calling about the broken boiler!'

'No, I'm not,' I said grumpily, perspiring in the heat. 'I'm your broken, boiling daughter.'

'Jinnniiiii!' she squealed. 'How are you, baby?'

'Good,' I said. 'What's wrong with your boiler?'

She sighed.

'That,' she said in her lecturing-professor voice, 'is a deep, far-reaching question, too long to be answered in the international phone call format.'

'Okay. Listen, Ma, I, uh, need to ask you a question,' I said awkwardly.

'Wow,' she said chirpily. 'Are you on *Who Wants to Be a Millionaire*, Jinni? Am I your Final Lifeline?'

'Very funny,' I said crossly. 'Listen, do you have any issues with my joining politics?'

'Hey, who am I to have issues?' she replied breezily. 'You're an adult. Do your own thing!'

Phew. Thank god. I relaxed.

'Having said that,' she added, her voice switching smoothly back to professor mode again, 'I would much prefer you stick to the intellectual, high-minded, spiritually rewarding and society-serving job of animating cartoons than sink to the squeaky, frivolous, make-believe world of politics.'

'I've been given the ticket from Bittora,' I blurted out, unable to stand the tension any more. 'And I'm standing.'

Silence. Almost a whole minute of it.

'Score one for Pushpa jiji,' said Ma finally.

'Umm… Ma?' I said, my voice pleading. 'Score one for *Bauji*, actually.'

'I hope so, Jinni,' she said. 'I just *hope* so.'

I didn't say anything.

See, that's the whole thing.

Amma's politics are different from Bauji's.

I remember a conversation I had with Amma, back when she was still an MP. She had taken Ma and me for a free holiday to a luxury beach resort, whose owner was fighting a court case involving infringement on the no-permanent-construction-within-five-hundred-metres-of-the-high-tide-line clause of the Environment Protection Act. I asked her if it was in good taste for her to holiday there and she explained it all to me, very reasonably. She was always good at explaining stuff.

'Dekho, Sarojini,' she said. 'We respected your Bauji but we learnt from his mistakes.'

'Matlab?' I asked.

She was quiet for a moment. Then she said, 'Just becauj some fellow gives you flowerj and one-two small prejents and takes you out to dinner, that doej not mean you will let him get into your bed, na?'

'That's not the same thing at all!' I exclaimed. 'And anyway, if I was *sure* I didn't fancy the guy, I wouldn't lead him on by accepting his presents!'

'Not even if they were very *nice* prejents?' she asked. 'Not even if they were very nice prejents he could *eajily* afford?'

'No!' I said, feeling absurdly prim and a little untruthful.

'Then you are a fool,' she said with finality. 'Arrey bhai, look at inflation! People from the constituency just get up and come to our house *anytime*! We need to maintain twenty-four-hour office and kitchen. We need to have some standing within the party! Also, we get invited to three weddingj a week, minimum. Where we have to give at least thousand rupee lifafa, to keep our nose from being cut off, yes-ki--no? How to manage on twelve thousand a month MP selery? Bhai, we are not proud. Pride ij a sin. If kind friends want to subsidize our lifestyle a little, we just accept humbly and gracefully.'

I pointed out to her that the twelve thousand bucks MP salary was a bit of a scam. If you added all the other perks they were entitled to, like office expenses, travelling concessions, DT-TA, house and electricity, plus the fact that they could fly business class forty times a year for *free* – the whole deal came close to three lakhs a month! But Amma just waved me away.

Four years later, she had a ready justification for the morphed photo scandal too. She told me, as persuasively as ever, that Bauji *knew* all the people in the pictures, he'd told her all about them, she'd even *met* some of them, all she'd done was fake some pictures of meetings that might have actually happened. It wasn't like she'd been involved in some multi-crore scam like most of her other colleagues. It wasn't like she'd embezzled money. Why were Ma and I being such self-righteous prigs? What was the big deal?

She didn't realize that, for Ma and me, it *was* a big deal.

A long gusty sigh from Ma brought me back to the present.

'Well,' she said lightly. 'When you were little, you were always drawing up these elaborate plans – India's Poor People Plans – you couldn't say poor, you used to pronounce it "pure", remember?'

I flushed. Trust her to remember. It's true. I used to be fully megalomaniacal. I would sit in Bauji's old armchair at Tughlaq Road and draw up complex, detailed plans about how to fix the nation's ills. Massive, state-of-the-art skyscrapers would spring up everywhere, replacing the slums. The 'pure' people could stay there for free, provided they all had a thorough bath, took their vaccinations, had regular health check-ups and sent their children to school. All the rich people, I confidently assumed, would gladly fund these programmes, because they were so rich they wouldn't miss the money. Besides, it would give them a chance to Get in Good with God. At that point in my life, cuddled up to Amma or listening to Bauji's stories every night, I used to think that the most important goal in everyone's life was to Get in Good with God.

'And don't tell me you've gotten over that phase,' Ma continued. 'All you did, the last time I came to India, was sit in front of the TV and gaze soppy-eyed at Kiran Bedi as she meted out swift but sure justice to the masses on *Aap ki Kachheri*. You have the soul of a benign dictator, Jinni.'

'I don't,' I said automatically, recalling with a pang that Zain too, had once dismissed my 'pure' people plans as borderline fascist. 'Ma, come campaign for me.'

'No way,' she replied promptly. 'So much proximity to

Pushpa jiji might derail my menopause. Have you *any* idea how long I've been waiting for it to hit?'

'Alwayj thinking about yourself,' I said snidely.

She laughed. 'Who else is in attendance?'

'Gudia aunty,' I said gloomily. 'And someone called Rocket Singh, though I haven't met him yet.'

'Ughh to both,' said Ma darkly. 'Gudia toh you know my opinion of... and that Rocket Singh... he's a Saakshaat Fart. A fart incarnate. If flatulence could ever assume human form, it would look exactly like Rocket Singh. Anyone else?'

'Some dude called Pappu,' I continued. 'And lots of nameless hordes.'

'Well, get to know them, Jinni,' Ma advised. 'Or you'll only have Gudia to talk to. And how's Pant-the-elephant?'

'Half dead, I think,' I said vaguely. 'He had a bypass. Why?'

'Arrey! Surely he'll be standing against you on the IJP ticket?'

'Err... it's not Pant this time,' I said, feeling my face go hot.

'Oh, okay. So who is it? Anyone I would know?'

I hesitated. I didn't really trust myself to say this out loud. Ma can read me like a book.

'It's... Zain, Ma. Zain Altaf Khan,' I said casually and braced myself.

Dead silence.

And then a tiny choked squeak.

'*Whatttt?*'

'You heard,' I said, rolling my eyes.

'Hamara Zain? *Maruti* Zain?'

I nodded, forgetting she couldn't see me.

'What's he doing in the IJP!'

I said patiently, 'It's a long story, mother.'

She had one of her random lapses of logic then.

'But you're in love with him!' she said.

I gasped in outrage.

'I am so *not* in love with him,' I spluttered.

A knowing silence.

God, sometimes I *hate* my mother.

'And these phones are *bugged*!'

More silence.

'Okay, so I fancied him a bit back then,' I admitted. 'But what did you expect? Between Loreto Girls' Convent and Bauji's house in Bittora, I didn't *meet* any other guys till I was seventeen!'

'But Jinni,' she said, in this gentle, understanding voice that totally got my goat, 'you've stuck all those brooding Jim Morrison posters in your bedroom in Mumbai.'

'So?' I demanded.

'So, he looks like Zain – like an emaciated Zain in the terminal stages of AIDS, actually. And you like that raspy singer, whatshisname – who sounds just like Zain. And you *cried* when you saw that Airtel ad, the one where Saif carries a photo of his childhood sweetheart around for years, and searches high and low for her and then, when he finally finds her, dumps her for Kareena Kapoor. C'mon baby, you don't need to keep secrets from me. I'm your *mother*.'

'I cried because it was such a *lame* ad!' I said, feeling really hassled now. 'And anyway, you're just remembering selectively! I wanted to be a cheerleader. I loved Britney Spears. I even had a blonde boyfriend! The banker, remember?'

'That was just peer pressure, baba,' she said pityingly. 'Oh dear, I'm really worried now. Maybe I *should* come to India… you're going to be *such* a wreck after you lose…'

I ground my teeth and banged the phone down on her.

—◆—

Our extremely large contingent boarded the train at nine o'clock that night. We were all in the same first AC bogie, but only a privileged few would actually end up inside Amma's compartment for a short conference. So of course, as soon as Amma, Gudia aunty and I were seated, and I had, in anticipation of playing Need for Speed, plugged in and flipped open my laptop, everybody started trying to shoulder their way in through the doorway.

Pushing and shoving and muttering under their breaths, even as they smiled fulsomely at Amma, every single one of the workers stuck in the door seemed grimly determined to hold their ground. One dude even thrust a steel tiffin-box at Amma, which he claimed was filled with home-made *atte-ke-laddoo* prepared by his wife.

Gudia aunty let out a small, smug giggle. 'So *desperate* these people are!' she said in a superior voice, from her perch on the berth next to Amma.

Amma sighed wearily. She picked up a bottle of mineral water, ripped off the plastic seal, took a sip and said, in a small, tired voice, 'Rocket Singh. Munni. Pappu. Jugatram.'

The selected four almost died of happiness. They strutted into the compartment, and with an imperious wave of her hand, Amma dismissed the rest of the gang. To the outer darkness, I thought fancifully, where there is wailing and gnashing of teeth...

'Sarojini?'

I started.

Amma said, not very enthusiastically, 'Hello bolo, Sarojini. This is your crack team.'

The way she enunciated 'crack' made it sound like they were all *nuts*, and not, you know, 'ace' or 'expert' or 'the best' or whatever.

'Hello,' I said, looking at the crack team gravely.

'Hello,' they chorused back, looking at me with a total respect I'd done absolutely nothing to earn. I wondered if they knew that the big noises at Akbar Road had declared my cause a lost one.

One of them, I realized suddenly, was a woman. She was sturdily built, with an aggressive ponytail and a thick pink khaddar dupatta wound very tight round her neck, and a surprisingly sweet, chubby face, with long-lashed, slightly protruding round eyes. Taking in her grey kurta, track pants and Lotto sneakers, I realized she was the one who'd been pushing and shoving the most in the corridor. She'd slapped a couple of people rather hard and definitely kneed at least one guy in the groin. Now she looked at me and smiled, a sweet, guileless, almost childlike smile.

'Hello, didi,' she said breathlessly. 'Myself Munni.'

'Oh, *hiii.*' I smiled at her. I knew Munni's story, everyone did. She'd blazed into the public eye a few years ago when her college professor, a high-caste Brahmin, had promised her, a Dalit student, good grades in return for sexual favours. She'd agreed meekly enough, gone for the rendezvous with a tiny camera taped to the neckline of her straining kurta, strung him along nice and proper and then sneaked out through the loo window at the penultimate moment. The clip had run on all major channels that same night, the professor was suspended and Munni soon became a Youth Pragati leader to reckon with.

Our Pappu, of course, was the silver-earringed, puffy-with-muscles little guy who'd been hanging around Tughlaq Road, sloganeering for over a week now. He was all bright eyes and chubby-cheeked and waggy-tailed. As he shook my hand, he informed me yet again, in one well-constructed sentence, that he was MLA-Jummabagh, a science graduate, a bachelor, an only son, a trained yoga instructor, from a business family, and totally at my service. Between noisy slurps of tea, he kept repeating, 'Sarojini didi, I will do *anything* for you! *Anything! Any* service! Whatever you want, I will give! How *many* times you want – I will give! *Anything* to satisfy you, *anything*!'

It sounded vaguely indecent. I wondered if he was propositioning me.

Next to him was the Saakshaat Fart. Rocket Singh was a brown man-mountain, with a sloping paunch, loose flapping arms and a complexion like sludge-coloured bubble wrap. He was an ex-wrestler who earned the sobriquet 'Rocket' when he was in his prime, because he moved as fast as a rocket in the wrestling pit. He won the gold medal at the '82, '86 and '92 Asiads but then somebody managed to slip a vicious one to his vitals, and he had to retire. He always looked like he was in pain, and he never smiled, only occasionally letting a constipated little grimace twist his lips. He ran a very popular amateur wrestling gymkhana in Bittora and right now he was wearing a shiny white tracksuit embroidered with his Gymkhana's logo – a tiny gold rocket.

Rocket folded his massive hands in a namaste and winced a stiff hello at me. I returned the gesture, before looking beyond him to the fourth member of the crack team.

Jugatram, Amma's some-time driver and man Friday was very handsome in a grizzled old Sean-Connery-from-*The Rock* sort of way. He was an ex-serviceman and a Vir Chakra winner and I remembered him very clearly, mainly because, when I was twelve years old, he had taught both Zain and me to drive.

He taught us on one of the Normal Public School buses,

which he drove, shouting encouragement and instructions over the screams of the children. When we were a bit older, he used to give Zain and me constant updates on the situation in 'Gargle', as his grandson, who was also in the army, was posted there during the war. He had bought us a huge watermelon to celebrate the Indian victory, I remembered, and his grandson had thankfully returned home unhurt.

Zain and I had totally idolized Jugatram when we were children, but now I looked at him with misgiving. What kind of man, I wondered, lets twelve year olds drive a school bus filled with little kiddies?

'Jugatram and Munni,' said Amma, as I goggled at Jugatram, 'are trusted Pragati Party workers. And Rocket Singh and Pappu are sitting Pragati Party MLAs.'

'Uh, how many MLAs do we have?' I asked hesitantly, hoping this wasn't a stupid question.

'Just us two, didi,' Our Pappu informed me. 'Other six are IJP. State gourmint is theirs, no.'

'I knew that,' I said defensively.

There was an awkward little silence.

Then Munni stood up and said with breathless sincerity, 'Didi, I want to take this apportunity to say how proud we are to have you as our candidate...'

Okay, this sounded like the beginning of a speech, which I would have to answer with a short speech of my own. Thankfully, I was ready for this. In fact, I'd sat up for a while last night, thought of a few points that I wanted to make to the core team and typed them out on my laptop. I reached for it, as unobtrusively as I could, and quickly double-clicked my Word file open.

Meanwhile, Munni was going on and on. 'Your international

qualifications... all that you have learnt at the feet of jiji... your illustrious grandfather... your love for Bittora...' and other remarks of the same variety. I calculated that I had a good ten minutes before I had to reply.

Looking down at my laptop screen, I realized that a new mail notification icon was popping up and down on my screen. Automatically, I clicked it open. It was from Facebook, which is weird because even though I have a Facebook account, I hardly ever use it. It's too full of these over-smart, acknowledge-how-clever-my-status-update-is types. Or the show-offy, check-out-the-photos-of-my-holiday-in-Peru variety. Or some forty-plus old fogeys looking for their school friends or whatever.

Still, there it was, and my eyes couldn't help skimming over it automatically.

Zain Altaf Khan wants to be friends with you on Facebook, the mail stated blandly. *To confirm (or quietly ignore) this friend request go to* – and a link followed.

I choked.

And looked around quickly.

'And so, didi,' Munni was saying reverentially, as she brought her speech to a surprisingly quick conclusion, 'we would like you to say a few precious words to us!'

Everybody in the compartment turned to look at me with eager expectancy.

I quickly flipped the laptop shut.

Pushing it away gingerly, I stood up, cleared my throat and said, 'Uh... thank you! I am honoured to have such a fantastic crack team! I am sure that with your support and guidance, we will taste victory! As I am young... and inexperienced, I would like help and suggestions from all of you. Pappu, what do *you* think we need to win this election?'

Having thus neatly tossed the ball back into the crack team's court, I sat down again, my brain gibbering dementedly. *He sent you a friend request. A friend request! A friend request! Maybe he's uploaded pictures of you smooching him in your velvet choli and unravelled sari on his Facebook account! Maybe he's even tagged them!*

Meanwhile, Our Pappu had grabbed the ball with enthu.

'What we need,' he declared importantly, springing up, his big black eyes flashing, 'is a Plaan.'

He pronounced it to rhyme with 'barn'. Then he dived into a shiny black Rexine rucksack and produced a bunch of impressive, spiral-bound, one-inch thick plastic files. He handed them around smoothly, and we all studied them, stunned by his efficiency.

'Jiji and didi,' said Our Pappu in hushed tones, 'these are the findings of famous survey expert, Mr Urvashi! He may have the name of a woman but he has the brain of a man! His team of dedicated interviewers melt into The Masses and ask them questions. Yesterday, we commissioned him to conduct a snap survey of entire Bittoragarh and tell us what our chances of winning are. Please read and absorb.'

The first page said, in big, fat, slightly erratically written typewriter font:

```
BITTORAGARH   CONSTITUENCY   SURVEY   AND
BREAKUP

Only for eyes of honourable, respected,
venerated, most gracious, motherly big
sister Smt. Pushpa Pande jiji and small-
big sister Sarojini didi.
   Eight  assembly  segments  of  the  Lok
Sabha constituency of Bittoragarh, PP.
```

Begumbagh
GOBS (Greedy Oversmart Brahmins and Seths Area)
These people perceive jiji as too liberal, too close to the OBCs and tribals. They will vote for Vir Singh or for Dwivedi. Our chances here are minuscule.

Champapul
PADMA (Poor Dalit and Muslim Area)
Traditionally a Praggu area, but now people are restive. High voter turnout area because of joblessness. Jiji will probably retain Champapul – but the lead may be small, one-two thousand only.

Jummabagh
PUM (Poor Underemployed Muslim Area)
Craftsmen, carpenters and all. Traditional Pragati Party loyalties may retain them – but these areas are also loyal to the old royalty. So ZAK is a serious threat. Contacting local leaders and offering financial help could work.

Doodhiya
FUCT (Forest of Unemployed Christian Tribals)
Jiji is very popular here for her many good works. Lead of eight to ten thousand seems assured. This lead could clinch the election for jiji.

Durguja
THID (Thirsty Hindu Illiterate Dalits)

Water, electicity, roads are problems
here. And there are no schools. This is a
very backward area. People here told our
surveyors they will vote for change - for
ZAK, especially because he has got good
relations with Dugguji Sisodia, local
industrialist and landowner. However, if
jiji can manage to get Dugguji on our side
somehow, then we could win Durguja.

Sujanpur
THID
Same problems as Durguja. But traditionally
Pragati-loyal area. Pragati Party has
never lost here. We will definitely get
lead of eight thousand.

Tanki Bazaar
Could go to anyone. Hasina Behenji should
be contacted. People here will vote for
whoever she says. We should promise her
MLA ticket also, funds also. If Tanki
Bazaar is secured, victory for jiji is
secured.

Purana Bittora
ROMP (Rich Oversmart Muslim People)
It is a hopeless case. Don't even try.
They will all vote for ZAK, regardless of
which party he stands from. He will get
lead of forty thousand from here.

I read through the report, did the math, and instantly lost
interest in all Facebook friendship requests.

'Pappu,' I said, 'according to this, our lead will be maximum

8 + 8 + 2, which is eighteen thousand. But Zain's lead, *just* from Purana Bittora, is a full forty! So, according to Mr Urvashi, we have no hope of winning, is that right?'

Our Pappu beamed at me approvingly, like I'd said something extremely intelligent. 'Didi, main point of Mr Urvashi is that it will be a *close* thing, *very* close. At the moment, maybe IJP has the lead, but if we campaign with science, and put oxygen injections in the right areas, the areas that he indicates – *then* you *could* squeeze ahead with two--three thousand margin!'

Amma threw down the report with a snort. 'This Urvasi is a fool!' she declared. 'Last time he said there waj no way Dwivedi would win, and he did! And once before that he said we would lose and we swept! If this time he ij saying ki Sarojini will win, then let us all shave our heads and go into mourning now only!'

'Actually, he's saying I'll lose,' I pointed out mildly. 'So—'

'So *nothing*!' Amma said roundly. Then she turned to Our Pappu. 'We hope,' she said sternly, 'that you have commissioned this survey with your own funds. We are not going to pay for that fool Urvasi's so-called fieldwork and findings.'

Our Pappu ducked his head and nodded cheerfully, not at all fazed. 'Yes, jiji!' he agreed and quickly took back his spiffy spiral-bound folders from us. 'Okay, jiji! Sorry, jiji!'

I said, with slightly forced heartiness, 'Well! Does anybody else have any suggestions or advice?'

Total silence.

Amma stood up.

'Bhai, let us talk about the most important thing,' she said. 'When ij last date to withdraw nominasun?'

'In nine days' time,' wheezed Rocket Singh, suddenly looking wide awake.

'Will anyone sit down?' Amma asked.

It took me a minute to realize that she meant, 'Will anyone withdraw?'

Munni blinked her big long-lashed eyes and ventured doubtfully, 'I could *try* to persuade Vir Singhji to sit. He knows only Begumbagh is with him. No one else. He is just standing out of pride. But he'll ask for money, jiji.'

'De denge, little bit,' Amma said grudgingly. 'But tell him not to open his mouth too big – *and* he will have to campaign for us afterwards. Talk to him, Munni. What about Dwivedi? He is also strong in Begumbagh. Must be even stronger than before, after saying so many anti-Muslim things!'

There was an uncomfortable silence. It occurred to me that some of the people in the room, Our Pappu and Munni definitely, must have worked for Dwivedi in the last election – and had been gearing up to work for him this time too, till he screwed it up with his English-style commode and mossie-bashing on national TV.

'Jiji, I don't think so he will sit down,' Our Pappu said with finality. 'He is very upset, purey emosunal ho gaye hain.'

Amma just grunted. 'Find out what it'll take to make him pack his cards and leave the table, Pappu,' she said brusquely. 'We can't have all these nuisance-value people splitting the GOBS vote. Now go, all of you.'

Looking suitably cowed, the crack team took its leave.

Immediately, Gudia aunty leaned back in her seat, sighed, uncapped a plastic bottle of Himalayan mineral water, and took a hefty swig. The unmistakable odour of Absolut vodka filled the air. Amma and I exchanged glances.

'Baba re,' said Gudia aunty in a tired, slightly self-conscious voice. 'I am so tired, madam.'

'Hmmm,' said Amma, noncommittal. 'Don't drink too much water at night, Gudia, you will have to go to the bathroom again and again.'

'Only two-three sips, madam,' she returned in a slightly wheedling voice. 'Otherwise I wake up at night feeling *so* thirsty.'

Rolling my eyes at this entirely coded conversation, I climbed into the top berth and flipped open my laptop to see if I had hallucinated the whole Facebook email. But there it was, sitting prettily in my inbox.

Zain Altaf Khan wants to be friends with you on Facebook, it purred tantalizingly. *To confirm (or quietly ignore) this friend request go to www.facebook.com/in?reqs.php&midicea17d= jinnipande% 40gmail.com.*

There was a picture of him next to the message. A tiny one. But enough to get my heartbeat zooming. I squinted and thrust my face closer to the screen to see it better...

'Gudia, how much oxygen?' Amma asked abruptly.

I jumped up a few inches, almost hitting my head on the roof of the train.

Amma looked up crossly. 'What is *wrong* with you?' she demanded. 'Jumping like a crack. And your hair looks mad.'

The trouble with my life, I thought resentfully as I hunched behind my laptop screen again and sucked on a lock of my hair, is that I have no *standing*.

Gudia aunty recapped her Himalayan water bottle, took down an insulated red-checked Milton tiffin-carrier from the empty top berth opposite mine, and peered into it. From my perch above, I could clearly see, not parathas or sandwiches, but stacks and stacks of red-and-white thousand-rupee notes. 'It's not *so* bad, madam,' she said in hushed self-important tones.

'We have forty L and fifty T. Just enough to start us off. The main consignment will reach us through Shortcut.'

'Shortcut?' I asked, too intrigued to sulk.

Gudia aunty looked up, opening her eyes very wide, as if marvelling at my ignorance.

'Shafquat,' she explained in the sweet mango-laced-with-onion voice that always set my teeth on edge. 'Shafquat Haq. He's a local construction king. Old well-wisher of madam's. Our people drop off the consignment at his office in Delhi, and when we get to Bittora, his people release the same amount to us there. It's a quick, smooth and really *safe* system. Standard procedure.'

'Still, it ij nothing,' Amma said gloomily. 'Nowadayj you need six, seven, even ten crore to win.'

Gudia aunty tittered. 'Madam, you have been away too long!' she said. 'People are spending *much* more than that now.'

A heavy silence prevailed for a while as the elderly ladies unwound their saris and climbed into their nighties.

Then Gudia aunty said, 'Madam, do you want me to help you remove your shoes?'

Uff. So must the French bourgeoisie have grovelled before the aristocrats, before jumping on them one dark night and chopping off all their heads beneath the guillotine. Leaving her to suck up to Amma, I leaned against the 'To Stop Train Pull Chain' sign, feeling slightly stunned. *What* was I getting myself into?

I mean, obviously, Shortcut wasn't just a nice guy. He wanted something. Anybody who helped a political candidate wanted something in return. Could I handle where this whole thing was headed? The day Shortcut strutted into my MP's office (that is, *if* I won) and demanded his pound of flesh, would I have to cower and scrape and go 'of course, of course, you were my Shortcut, now *I'll* be your Shortcut'?

Cross that bridge when you come to it, I told myself. Right now, just concentrate on the present.

Which brought me right back to my laptop and the H-bomb fizzing gently there. *To confirm this friend request, go to...*

I clicked on the link, staring at the screen, my fingers drumming against the space bar nervously. The image flipped to my Facebook page, and there was Zain's profile picture. He was smiling right at me, dark eyes quizzical, all these cool, intellectual looking lines crinkling up his forehead.

I looked around quickly.

Amma was snoring lightly in the lower berth, but Gudia aunty was still standing, swaying gently, her extremely plump bottom wobbling rhythmically like the boot of an Ambassador car. She seemed to be having a problem unknotting the naada of her petticoat.

I sneaked a look at Zain's picture again. His eyes seemed to dance, they were positively conspiratorial.

I wanted to *hit* him.

They'd called him *what* in that newspaper article? Charismatic. Upright. Intelligent. And a 'scion'. Why hadn't they called *me* a scion? Bauji was thirty times more khandaani than Zain's psycho dad! *And* he was a freedom fighter! We were *the* Brahmin family of Bittoragarh. But no, they'd made fun of Amma and called me short and warm and eager and 'pretty'. Who the hell wanted a short, warm, eager and pretty MP? That too, in the cut-throat badlands of Pavit Pradesh.

Well, the scion of bloody Bittora could just go cuddle his string of trophy girlfriends. I swivelled my thumb to click the *Ignore* option. And stopped.

I had to be cunning.

Because if my life really had turned into a bad Madhur Bhandarkar film (called *Politics,* you know, like *Corporate* and *Fashion* and *Jail*), I had to play this smartly. If Zain could play Frenemy-Frenemy, then I could play Frenemy-Frenemy too.

The train tracks clicked *don't do it – don't do it – don't do it,* the 'To Stop Train Pull Chain' sign swayed before my eyes. I closed my eyes, took a deep breath and clicked *Confirm.*

You are now friends with Zain Altaf Khan, the screen informed me smoothly. *Click here to view his profile and see pictures like this.* And all these tiny tantalizing images popped up. So, of course (just to check that there were no pics of last night's Dark Doings uploaded there), I clicked.

Images of Zain filled the screen. Grinning through mussed-up, sweaty dark curls, standing with a cricket group in the mustard fields of Bittoragarh. Leaning against an ivy-covered wall at Winchester, arms crossed, wearing a grey sweater. Sittting behind the wheel of an open, mud-spattered four-wheel drive, looking exhausted but happy. In a white kurta and cap, pulling hideous faces at the backs of some laughing girls in salwar kameezes.

Next to his profile picture was his latest status update (Nine hours ago). *Zain is thinking that old friends are the best friends one can have after all...*

There were already seven comments in response to his status.

Hey! Who are you calling old? This from a hulking, grinning creature called Bunty Sisodia. Ugh, I remembered him vaguely from the old days in Bittora. He was always after Zain to open a *Sholay*-themed pub in London called The Thakur's Arms. He thought that was the height of wit.

So true... So true... from some random-looking gora who had a toddler sitting on his shoulders.

And *five* responses from various simpering bimbos saying cheesy things like *Time is relative* and *Bonds can be made in one eternal moment* and *It matters not how far you go back but how deep you go within*, which was frankly *obscene* if you ask me.

I took a long, long look at his home page, snorted and snapped my laptop shut.

(His relationship status said *Single* by the way, not that I was looking or anything.)

4

Bittoragarh swung into view at seven in the morning, looking dewy fresh and deceptively quiet. I sat on the steps at the door of the bogie, sipping tea, the wind ruffling my hair, watching the sun rise -- a shiny, translucent, well-sucked disc of orange candy in a sky as purple as jacarandas. I saw parties of birds swirl and dip and chase each other above the green fields, smelled the pungent odour of buffalo dung and counted thirteen dusty red bogies as the train curved round a bend and became briefly visible. Finally, I spotted, shimmering in the morning mist, the ancient, moss-covered bridge guarded by three rampant stone lions, hanging across the sluggishly flowing Bitwa river.

I felt a silly surge of happiness when I saw that bridge. When I was a child, sighting the bridge used to mean the end of square roots and logarithms and the beginning of good times for two whole months. I leaned out impulsively, hoping to see monkeys sitting on the low railings on either side. *If I see a monkey here, I will have a blast this year...* and then Amma was behind me, brandishing toothbrush, mug and towel in my face, insisting I do kulla, take snaan and make mosun immediately.

God, she is *so* irritating. She knows I *hate* 'making mosun' on the train – when I was a child I was convinced I would fall through The Hole in the pot and be crushed to death on the tracks. Amma always told me crossly that it was far more likely that I'd fall off the steps and die, but I ignored her – I loved sitting on the steps too much. You can hear the wheels sing, and smell the smoke, and fill the wind in your hair. Zain used to tell me that Bunty Sisodia and he always sat on the steps on their way to Bittoragarh, and when they spotted people squatting in the fields doing their morning job, plastic bottles of water beside them for washing up afterwards, they'd shoot stones from their catapults to upset the bottles and leave the squatters all high and dry.

But I mustn't think of Zain.

I got up and made my way to the rattling first AC loo, and when I came lurching back into the compartment twenty minutes later, adjusting the pallu of my simple pink and red cotton sari and finger-combing my wet hair, Amma was all dressed. She was tweezing little-little hairs out of her nose, peering short-sightedly into the mirror of a powder compact which Gudia aunty was holding up for her. They both turned to look at me when I entered. I realized with a slight start that Gudia aunty was wearing my watch. For safekeeping probably, I told myself. No need to panic.

'Jinni, you look lovely!' gushed Gudia aunty. 'Hain na, madam?'

But Amma shook her head.

'Kuch missing hai,' she grunted.

I could've told her kya missing hai. My high heels missing hain. Basically, I'd been reduced to my natural height of five feet two inches because Amma insisted I wear a pair of stupid Champapuli chappals for the campaigning. They're the main produce of the assembly segment of Champapul, and famous across India. I've always hated them. People from Champapul have been gifting them to Amma, Ma and me ever since I can remember. I have one in every size. They look like they're made out of buffalo scrotum and give me instant blisters.

'See is looking too *plain*,' grumbled Amma.

'Yes yes,' Gudia aunty agreed at once, eyeing me critically. 'I was also thinking that only. Perhaps… a little gold, madam?'

Amma brightened up immediately, rummaged through the oregano, saunf and chilli flakes sachets in her handbag and, much to my horror, produced a little red velvet box and flipped it open. Nestled inside were a pair of highly uncool, large gold 'tops' with thick grooved stems. I groaned.

'Perfect!' breathed Gudia aunty with evangelical zeal.

'No!' I said desperately. 'Amma, those stems are too thick, they'll never go through. I don't want to wear them, I *won't*—'

But it was of no use. At a signal from Amma, Gudia aunty *jumped* me. She held me down with a grip of steel, smiling apologetically, while Amma, after slathering dollops of ShaSmooth lotion onto the monstrous stems, thrust them through my ears and screwed them in nice and tight.

'These things are way too thick for my ears,' I wailed, my eyes watering.

Amma flashed her gap-toothed grin, panting slightly as she screwed. 'Well, what to do?' she said. 'You are very young, and so maybe at first,' her grin got all meaningful, 'the stick seems too big for the hole. But don't worry,' she cackled, 'if the stick is well lubricated it won't hurt, and in time the hole will expand and you will get ujed to it.'

I couldn't believe she just said that! No wonder she got along so well with that prince of perverts, Gaiman Tagore Rumi!

'That,' I said with dignity, massaging my throbbing ears, 'is a low-down cheap crack that does absolutely *no* credit to your grey hair and long years in parliament.'

She chuckled. 'Arrey, relax Sarojini,' she said, slapping my butt lightly. 'Sometimes you talk just like an old woman.'

Muttering abuses, I retreated to a corner of the compartment and watched, revolted, as she serenely unpacked a huge box of mithai, part of her Holi loot, and proceeded to eat an extremely ugly pink and green khoya barfi shaped like a three-tiered birthday cake. I didn't bother to protest. *Life is sort, Sarojini,* is all I would've got for my pains. I looked out gloomily at the scenery instead, the lobes of my ears aching fit to burst. About ten minutes later, the Pavit Kranti Express pulled into Bittora Junction and screeched to a slow, majestic halt. Amma came up from behind me, hissing, 'Get up and wave! Remember, nod, smile, point with the finger!'

I nodded, my heart slamming a military beat against my ribs, and stood up as the train's engines hissed and grunted, and a sea of white khadi and orange, white and green flags engulfed the platform to our left.

Gudia aunty peered out the windows, shuddered theatrically and declared in thrilled horror, 'Madam! It's like a swayamwar outside, madam!'

Sure enough, a battalion of grinning, kurta-and-jacket clad men, some tall and brawny, some short and scrawny, were lined up on the platform, armed with garlands as thick as pythons, encrusted with rose, chrysanthemum and silver tinsel. Behind them milled a large white kurta-pyjama-clad horde.

Amma gave a satisfied grunt, popped two silver-coated pods of elaichi into her mouth to ensure that her breath was daisy fresh, pushed past me, and stepped onto the platform, beaming. She was immediately swallowed up by the crowd and by the garlands which, piled one on top of the other, obscured first her neck, then her entire head. Immediately, Gudia aunty, swelling with self-importance, clutching the Milton hotcase containing forty L and fifty T in her hands, swept past me and surged to the side of the Amazing Headless Lady, her accented Hindi sounding slightly surreal as she scolded the crowd: 'Back jaaeeye, back jaaeeye! Crush mat kariye!'

Cries of

> *Aaee aaee Pushpa Pande!*
> *Phootey brashtachar ke bhaande!*

rent the air. Suddenly, a sturdy figure began to push the crowd back roughly, abusing them roundly. It was Munni. The rest of the crack team followed her lead. As they parted the crowds, Gudia aunty peeled the garlands off Amma one at a time, staggering under their cumulative weight, and gradually Amma's head emerged, dishevelled but smiling graciously. She raised one frail hand delicately for silence.

The crowd gave it to her, instantly.

'Arrey bhai, we have retired,' she said.

They protested loudly.

She shook her head. 'Nahin-nahin-nahin, we have retired!'

The protests got louder.

She shook head again, smiling an enigmatic half-smile, and beckoned to me to come forward. Feeling like I was about to throw up, I came forward, tripping a little on my sari pleats. 'Ab hum chahten hain ki you all bless this child, and give her the same love that you have always given us.'

Deafening applause. Cries of *Pushpaji ki jai*. And as the Pragati Party's pulsating *Jai Ho* anthem kicked in, we were borne towards a convoy of hectically stickered white Tata Sumos and bundled into a particularly spiffy one, with a massive pointing finger on its bum.

Amma promptly clambered up and stuck her head through the strangely proportioned, custom-made sky roof, which pretty much put paid to any attempt at air-conditioning. I hung on grimly to her sandalled feet, perspiring, worried she might do herself an injury, the driver was going so fast.

'Why is this taking so long?' I yelled up at Amma after about twenty minutes of sweaty, deafening driving. 'It's just a five-minute drive to Begumbagh!'

'We need to let people know we are HERE!' she yelled back, waving her arms wildly at the crowd. 'That we are filing aawar NOMINASUN! Why sould we take the sort way?'

And so we drove manically round and round the town, our speakers blaring. Jai Ho, we hailed the pink-palmed, blue-skinned Krishna, playing his flute atop the stone gateway of the Bittora temple. Jai Ho, we boomed at the statue of old Begum Raiza Ali Khan, standing in the midst of a circular fountain, a hawk on her wrist. Jai Ho, Kings Bakery, makers of the yummiest nankhatai and pineapple pastries in Pavit Pradesh. Jai Ho, laughing school girls with neatly oiled, red-ribboned hair and bright blue pinafores, sailing to school in gaily painted cycle-rickshaws. Jai Ho, pyramids of pale muskmelons and emerald green watermelons! Jai Ho, mangy street dogs! Jai Ho, plump street pigs!

Finally, Amma sank down beside me, her face glowing. I handed her a chilled bottle of water from the tiny icebox, she glugged it down and declared, shouting above the music, her hair wild: 'Pragati ki hawa hai. We are sure of it!'

I nodded, smiling. Her excitement was infectious.

'Get up there and wave!' she yelled.

'Oh, no.' I shook my head at once. 'I couldn't!'

Amma narrowed her eyes. 'Sarojini, get up,' she urged.

No way, I thought chaotically, I can't. I'm just a weedy kitaanu animator from Mumbai.

Amma leaned in and thrust her face right into mine. 'Get up now,' she hissed.

Okay, okay, no need to *push*.

I clambered to my feet and then, with the 'Jai Ho' music pulsating madly in my ears, surrendered to the call of the sky roof and stuck my head out. It was searingly hot. And the dust made my eyes tear up instantly. But the childhood scent of diesel and roses was electrifying. I filled my lungs and threw back my head.

'Jai Ho, Bittoragarh!' I yelled, raising both arms in a namaste over my head which would've left me dead if the Sumo braked too suddenly. The wind whipped my hair about and great canopies of brassy red and gold gulmohar whizzed past my head. 'Jai Ho!!!'

As we looped the main Begumbagh street for what seemed like the fourth time, I realized there was a plain black Maruti Gypsy trailing our cavalcade. It wasn't a press vehicle, but it bore some kind of sticker. I frowned, squinting, trying to read. 'On Election Duty', the sticker said, just like ours did, but it carried no party insignia.

I slid into my seat and asked Amma who they were.

She just sniffed disdainfully but Gudia aunty supplied the information. 'Election commission fellows,' she said, with a roll of her ping-pong-ball eyes. 'Get used to them, Jinni. They will trail you everywhere you go, like beggars, and record everything you say and do. See their cameras?'

Peering out the window now, I realized that the grey safari-suited dude in the black Maruti Gypsy did indeed have a small black camcorder held up to the right side of his face.

'They have a permit to stop you *anywhere* and search your vehicles *anytime*,' she told me. 'They record all the speeches you make, too.'

'What would they be searching my vehicle for?' I asked in confusion.

She goggled a little at this very stupid question, but answered it patiently enough.

'Oxygen,' she said. 'Obviously! The candidate's car is never supposed to have more than a lakh and fifty thousand rupees in it, you know. They seize it otherwise.'

'But what can you buy with one lakh fifty in this day and age?' I protested jokingly.

Gudia aunty and Amma nodded vehemently in agreement. 'Exactly,' they said. '*Nothing.*'

'We need to carry money for diesel for all the vehicles in the convoy,' Amma explained. 'For food. For alcohol. Arrey, there could be a temple or a mosque on the way, we may need to make a donation. There could be anything! How will one lakh fifty cover it?'

'And if you're caught with more than twenty-five lakhs in your car, they can actually disqualify you!' Gudia aunty continued. 'Also, they send all your speech recordings back to the election commissioner's office. To be checked for objectionable statements – bigotry, hate, inciting violence and slander of opposing candidates. Or pressure tactics or attempts to bribe the voters.'

'So there are seventeen teams trailing all seventeen Bittora candidates?' I asked in disbelief. 'And hang on, in all 546 constituencies across India? In some constituencies there are like thirty candidates! Wow, no wonder our elections cost a bomb!'

Amma looked at me irritatedly. 'That is completely besides the point, Sarojini,' she said. 'The point ij, be careful.'

When we finally got to the office, about an hour later, the returning officer sucked up to Amma shamelessly, but very subtly. It's a highly specialized art, sucking up subtly, and he had just the right touch. Then he led us to his office to file the nomination papers. I sat down nervously, fighting the urge to giggle.

'Age?' he inquired.

I opened my mouth to answer, but Our Pappu was in before me. 'Twenty-five years! Birthday seventh September.' He looked around triumphantly at the rest of the crack team, like he'd scored a huge point over them. He then proceeded, much to my humiliation, to tell the officer what my salary was, to the exact paisa. He rattled off my address in Mumbai like it was his own, listed my immovable and moveable assets, and the 73.2 per cent with which I'd cleared my class twelve and the grade I'd got at Tuck University. He added that it was ik-weee-wah-lunt to an MA here in India. He concluded by announcing that I had no criminal record or cases pending against me whatsoever.

I smiled weakly. My ears throbbed.

'What he said,' I told him.

We handed over our ten thousand bucks, signed an oath swearing to fight clean and fair and to abide by the Constitution of India, got it stamped and emerged from the office into the sunshine. Tons of local newspaper people were lurking outside. They clicked pics of Amma and me showing The Finger, our mustachioed kurta-pyjama-clad cheerleaders chanted a few slogans, and then we loaded ourselves into the white Sumos and drove home to Bauji's house.

Looking out the window, more relaxed now, I realized that Bittora *had* changed after all. There were fewer trees, and much more traffic. The stray cows looked thinner. Internet cafés had sprung up all along the old clock-tower area. More hoardings – for jewellery stores, pressure-cookers and insurance policies – crowded the roads. Piles of garbage dotted the streets. A lot of old houses had been displaced by multi-storied buildings with too much fussy, plaster-of-Paris work. But it was still, unmistakably, the Bittora of my childhood.

And the house itself hadn't changed a bit. It stood behind the low spear-tipped, bottle-green iron gate at the end of Pandit MM Pande Road, its weathered cream walls set off by glowing, deep red bougainvillea. The yellowing marble nameplate, a little more cracked and gunky than before, still proclaimed *Saket Bhavan – the Abode of Peace,* in ornate devnagari script. The drive was lined with dancing black-eyed sunflowers and trees full of riotous clusters of mango blossoms. The white pillared verandah was dotted with comfy looking moodha chairs. Creamy white champa flowers with butter-yellow hearts lay scattered in the deep green grass and the humming of bees filled the air.

Tears sprang to my eyes as I jumped out of the Sumo.

And then two heavy, hairy paws locked themselves around my neck. Horrible, grunting, panting noises assaulted my ears as I looked, petrified, into a pair of maniacal, liquid chocolate eyes, inches away from my nose. They seemed to be glazing over with pleasure as a huge golden body pumped away at me frantically. A drooling mouth, with teeth as large as fat pods of garlic and a lolling pink tongue, grinned at me in a friendly nothing-personal sort of way.

'Ponky!' shouted Joline Bai, her guttural voice making us jump. 'Don, Ponky, don! Bad dog, Ponky! Get *don*, Ponky!'

But Ponky wasn't paying attention. He was too busy thrusting his snout way too intimately between my thighs and making sure that I really *was* a girl and not, you know, a female impersonator or something.

'What a nice doggie, madam!' cooed Gudia aunty as she emerged from the Sumo behind me. 'Jinni, don't be alarmed – he knows, ha ha ha' – this as Ponky finished with me and thrust his snout between her legs instead – 'he knows we are family! Hello doggie... hello doggie... He looks so intelligent!'

'He looks demented,' I said firmly. 'Joline Bai, take him away. He's trying to make *babies* with Gudia aunty.'

Gudia aunty giggled coyly at this, like being violated by Pushpa Pande's golden retriever was a badge of honour of sorts. Joline Bai lunged at the protesting Ponky and hauled him away by the collar, but he shook himself loose, weaved right and left with a silly grin across his face, and then gambolled playfully across the lawn, scattering mynahs in every direction.

'When did you get a dog, Amma?' I asked, brushing off my kurta. Both Gudia aunty and I had two large muddy paw marks imprinted precisely over our breasts. The Mark of Ponky. I didn't know then, but I was to see a lot of that particular mark over the next three weeks.

Amma shrugged and emerged from the Sumo with rickety dignity. 'It waj a Diwali gift. From cabinet minister industry ke son. He ij a breeder.'

'Baby, do lakh ka kutta hai yeh!' piped up Jugatram proudly. 'He is worth two lakh rupees! His parents are the best sniffer dogs in the Delhi police!'

'That explains a lot,' I said weakly. 'I think he's checked out just about *every* crevice in my body for cocaine.'

'Oh, *mine* too,' Gudia aunty chimed in with immediate competitiveness.

Amma gave us both a quelling look. 'Let us all take snaan,' she said austerely. 'Then we will eat.'

'*You* snaan again,' I told her sunnily. '*I* snaanned on the train. I'll go check out my old petal room...'

I raced up the three shallow verandah steps, a tight feeling of anticipation bubbling up inside me. I used to call my room from the old days the 'petal room' because it had just one corner, otherwise it was completely circular. There were two petal rooms in the house, flanking each end of the pillared front verandah and they gave the house a slight castle-with-towers feel. The other petal room used to be Bauji's study. Both petal rooms had old-fashioned, bottle-green-and-white patterned tiles on the floor and big barred windows looking into the garden but mine also had a pink bougainvillea creeper looking into it, which used to make me feel like I'd scored one over Bauji.

I threw open the door and burst into the room.

There was the high bed with the lumpy mattress, upon which I used to sprinkle three mugs of water every night because the heat used to be so oppressive. There was the eccentric old fan that did either five or nothing because the regulator was broken. There was the dark teak wardrobe with peeling superhero stickers still stuck on it. And there, sprawled on the old tiled floor, propped up on his elbows and writing furiously, a lock of dark hair falling on his forehead, was sixteen-year-old Zain Altaf Khan.

'Buzz off,' I hissed at this extremely lustworthy ghost, but he didn't budge. He just flipped a page and continued to write, while all the summers I had spent in Bittora came flooding back to me in a searingly hot, mango-blossom-and-wet-earth scented rush.

Turning my back on him, I fled to the loo, and even though

I'd told Amma I wouldn't, turned on the stiff old copper taps for another bath. And it worked. Kind of. Not because the bath was cold and refreshing or anything. But because by the time I'd dealt with the window that wouldn't latch shut, the hot-as-tea water that hissed out of the rusty tap and the unbelievable amount of gunk blocking the drain, I had stopped seeing pulse-quickening ghosts lounging on the floor, following my every movement with dark, stormy eyes.

He's a *fremeny*, I told myself firmly as I jabbed at the blocked drain with the back end of my toothbrush. You are being stupid, you haven't thought about him for years, the world is *full* of attractive men dying to date a wannabe MP. What kind of loser are you, anyway, mooning over a guy when there's a whole parliamentary constituency to be won?

There was to be a huge shindig to kick off our campaign that afternoon, not for the voters, but for the party workers. This was a slightly unorthodox move, but Amma was very clear she wanted to clear up any confusion or bad blood caused by Dwivedi's ouster and my last-minute nomination.

'Basically, we need to tell our workers that we are *back*,' she said with relish, as she energetically mixed ghee into her dal and rice at lunch. 'And that their lauki-ka-chhilka eating days are *over*!'

By four o'clock more than a thousand workers had poured into the venue – which was the much put upon Normal Public School in Begumbagh. The crowds, the press, the election commission cameramen stalking our every move, all of it was pretty intimidating. As nobody had bothered to inform the school children or their parents, the kids, instead of going home, stood around curiously, watching the Pragati Party workers troop in. They were definitely a compelling sight, all grinning and swaggering and dressed to party, with Pragati mufflers tied around their necks and flashy Pragati tattoos on their biceps. Many of them were dressed in flashy tiranga T-shirts over jeans. Some, I realized with a start, even had a picture of *me* scanned onto their tiranga tees.

'Namaste, didi,' one such dude said, flashing a bright white grin as he scratched my right eye (which was covering his right tit). 'I will get you a lead of three-four, no *five* thousand, just from my area, didi!'

'Thanks,' I said, pleasantly surprised. Wow, if all these guys here could promise me five thousand votes each…

'Don't you believe him,' Amma hissed into my ear. 'No single person can guarantee you five thousand votes just like that! This is not SMS-voting for *Big Boss*, you know!'

'Oh, okay,' I said, wilting a little. 'Um… Amma, are some of these dudes *drunk*?'

'Of course they are not drunk, Sarojini,' she said, smiling and nodding busily as a couple of men, suspiciously red-eyed, staggered, tripped and almost fell before us. 'They are just happy to see us, that ij all!'

There was a garish, multi-coloured shamiana set up over a cemented platform, and with huge amounts of whooping and cheering, Amma, Munni, Our Pappu and I were ushered on to it. Garlands of thousand-rupee notes arranged like playing-card fans were strung around our necks and then we were seated on red plastic chairs behind a long white table. Plastic glasses of water stood before us, and two medium-sized storm fans blew vast amounts of hot air into our faces. Every now and then, a thin stream of warm water would spray out from a tiny tube attached to the fans, smudging the red bindi I'd painted onto my forehead. Soon, I would start looking like I'd taken a bullet in the head. No wonder Amma always wore stick-on bindis.

Still, I'd never sat at a political podium before! It was way cooler than sitting down below and looking up supplicantly. I could totally get used to this.

Intermittently, to keep the crowd stoked, somebody would yell into the mike at the lectern, 'Pushpa Pande ki?'

And the workers would obligingly yell back, 'Jai!!!'

'Sarojini Pande ki?'

'Jai!!!!'

'Pragati Party ki?'

'Jai!!!!'

Munni sat behind me, fidgeting endlessly. 'Sab bakwaas hai, didi,' she told me in a conspiratorial whisper. 'This is a rubbish congregation – these people, these *men* – they are all opportunists.'

I looked at her, intrigued. 'Oh, really?' I said, as I wrestled grimly with the thin plastic film over my glass of water.

She nodded emphatically, her chubby cheeks quivering. 'It is *all* up to us ladies eventually,' she said earnestly. 'Like jiji and you and—'

'And *you*,' I whispered back sincerely. 'You're fantastic, Munni.'

'Thenks,' she replied composedly. She peeled off the plastic film covering her glass in one smooth move and took a big sip, smacking her lips.

Abruptly, I asked, 'How am I doing? I… I mean… am I looking the part and all?'

She pursed her lips and studied me intently.

I fiddled with the film over my water glass, feeling absurdly self-conscious under her frank, assessing gaze.

Finally she said, 'You're super, didi, super. Only… you move your face too much.'

'Matlab?' I asked worriedly.

'Keep a still face,' she advised me. 'Don't react so much to what all the people say. If you smile so much, your cheek muscles will die of pain by the end of the second day, only. So save your energy. Make your face like a finks.'

'A finks?' I asked, stumped.

'It's a famous statue in Egypt,' she explained kindly. 'Ekchully, you must be careful because your mouth and eyes are big, no – which is good,' she clarified hastily, 'but if you show too much reactions, big big ones, then in photos you may look little bit crack.'

Basically, I had been grinning like a mentally deficient person the whole day.

'Okay, okay,' I said. 'Umm, can I have the rest of your water? This thing is refusing to open.'

She looked a little startled, then said, 'Of course, didi,' and quietly handed it over. I glugged it thankfully, though there wasn't much left.

Silence for a while.

Then Munni said in heartfelt accents, 'Ufffff, how much Our Pappu can *talk*!'

This was true. Our Pappu was standing at the lectern and doing a very fulsome introductory address for Amma, calling her a Jewel in the Crown of India and a Flaming Torch of the Freedom Struggle. He said that she had travelled to every country in the world and met Margaret Scratcher and Baraat Obama himself.

Munni shifted uneasily. 'When will he stop his Yaadon ki Baraat? I have to go to toilet.'

So did I, actually. I wished she hadn't mentioned it.

Amma's bladder, however, was obviously made of iron, because she just sat there, eyes half-closed, nodding gently and letting Our Pappu drone on about Rubies and Diamonds and every other kind of precious stone that she apparently was.

Suddenly, Munni twinkled at me. 'Shall I show you something?'

I nodded. 'Sure.'

She leaned into the table mike, balled both hands into fists, raised them above her head and, rudely interrupting Our Pappu, yelled in her shrill voice, 'Chacha Chaudhury ki?'

The crowd obligingly roared back, '*Jai!*'

'Michael Jackson ki?' yelled Munni.

'*Jai!*' roared the crowd.

I thrust my face into the mike and shouted, 'Pixel animation ki?'

'*Jai!*' roared the crowd again.

'Ponky doggie ki?'

'*Jai!*'

Wow.

She flashed me a triumphant grin. 'Dekha,' she said. 'I told you men are *stupid.*'

I nodded, both depressed and impressed.

'We should've tried *Zain Altaf ki*,' I told her gloomily. 'I bet they'd have cheered. Will you speak too, Munni?'

She shook her head. 'Not to *workers*,' she said, wrinkling up her nose. 'Now, if they were *voters*...'

Our Pappu, who'd restarted his speech like there had been no interruption, now got started on me. He said Amma was the Great Mother Cow, and that she had fed me from her breast and that I was the calf who had imbibed all the good values from her and now that I had grown up into a fine young cow myself, I was going to nourish all of Bittora from my juicy young br—

Amma opened one gimlet-like eye and barked out shortly, 'Pappu. Enough.'

He went 'Jai Hind! Jai Hind! Jai Hind!' immediately, bowed thrice very low and jumped off the stage to switch on music on the loud speaker systems.

I stared at Amma reproachfully. 'Amma, you could've made him stop *ages* ago.'

'We know,' Amma said. The five-rupee-coin gap between her teeth flashed as her face split slowly into a wicked grin. 'But he's *funny*, Sarojini. He makes us *laugh*.' She giggled heartily to herself for two whole minutes, her shoulders shaking, while I glowered at her with my new finks face on. Finally, she drew a long deep breath, wiping tears from the corners of her eyes. 'Oh, we love campaigning!' she declared. 'Nothing like meeting the people face to face, hai-ke-nahin?'

I wanted to tell her that these were not really *people*, just party workers with an axe to grind, but just then the music started blaring from the speakers. The raucous crowd roared with laughter as some workers, wearing masks with the faces of Zain and other IJP leaders on them, swung to a parody set to the tune of a song from *Rock On*.

Meri MP ki gaddi
Nana na na na, nana na
Meri kesari chaddi
Nana na na na, nana na
Mera pyaara Jummabagh
Nana na na na, nana na
Champapul aur Begumbagh
Nana na na na, nana na

Mera… das hazaar ka deposit!
Mera… bhagwan Ram ka locket
Pichhle saat dino mein, maine khoya
Kabhi khud pe hansa mein, aur,
kabhi khud pe roya!

And then, once everybody was fully stoked up, Amma took the mike and delivered a speech outlining all the points listed in the extremely predictable Pragati Party manifesto.

Only, when she said it, they stopped sounding hollow. Maybe it was the flawlessness of her Pavit Pradeshi, maybe it was the authentic throb of sincerity in her voice, maybe it was just that it was the cowdust hour, a beautiful early summer evening in the place where I'd spent my childhood. But Amma made me believe that the Pragati really was a grand old party, the party that had bought us independence, the only party for me to be starting my political career in. When she spoke like that, and the crowd – no matter that it was just a gathering of what's-in-it-for-me party workers – cheered with her, I believed that Ma and I were both wrong, that Amma's cynical veneer was just that, a veneer, and that she did have Bauji's principles close to her heart, after all.

After the meeting, Amma decreed that I should wrap up the day by putting in a spot of door-to-door campaigning in the nearby PADMA (Poor Dalit and Muslim Area) in Champapul.

'Just get a sense of which way the wind is blowing, Sarojini,' she said. 'Munni, you take her. We will go home and take rest. Tomorrow, offisial campaigning can start.'

There were no streets in Champapul, as I discovered, and we had to park the Sumos and walk everywhere, because the lanes in Champapul were about as broad as aeroplane aisles.

There were continuous lines of houses on both sides of these lanes, their front doors practically touching each other. Drains opened right into the lanes. You could smell Lifebuoy soap, or *arhar ka dal* or human potty, depending on what was being thrown down the pipes as you passed. The place was a total fire hazard, of course, but excellently constructed for door-to-door campaigning. The other good part was that the lanes were cool and shady, and very social too, with ladies shelling peas outside their houses and feeding the pods to the cows wandering up and down, dribbling dung at will, staring at the evening action with large, soft, long-lashed eyes.

The sign on the first door we happened upon read 'Chief Petty Officer Liaquat ul Haque'.

I hoped his loo would be fully shipshape – I was desperate to pee again – and rang the bell.

The door opened and a very ancient man peered out. He was meticulously clean shaven, had a gleaming dome-like forehead, and was dressed in a spotless white kurta over a checked blue lungi. His features were bulbous and his skin was the colour of darkest walnut.

'Namaste!' I said brightly. And almost added, *take it away, Munni!* Because that was Munni's cue to give a little speech on who I was. She pointed at me and rattled off shrilly, 'Aap hain Srimati Sarojini Pande ji, BA, post graduate from fillum school, Toronto, MP candidate for Bittora seat from Pragati Party, granddaughter of hamari jiji Pushpa Pandeji.'

'Namaste,' I said again, right on cue. 'Please give me your keemti vote.'

He gazed at me with rheumy, jewel-like eyes under *huge* sweeping lashes. I noticed a cluster of tiny brown warts upon one eyelid.

'Why?' he asked point blank, in a rich baritone, in pretty much perfect English.

I blinked. 'Uh… because I will do my best for the upliftment of this area.'

'How?' he asked. I got the distinct feeling he wasn't being rude. He looked genuinely curious.

I looked at Munni. She thrust out her ship-in-full-sail bosom, perhaps to appeal to his nautical mind, and said aggressively, 'Pragati Party is a secular party. We believe all religions are equal-equal.'

He looked a little bewildered. 'So?'

She said, extremely fluently, like she had learnt this off by heart, 'So, unlike other parties, we will protect your community and not let it be marginalized.'

'Sit down,' the old man said.

He had a voice you couldn't mess with. We sat down.

He said, 'So I will not be marginalized. Well and good. Now what are you going to do about education? Sanitation? The PDS? Ex-servicemen's pensions? Rural credit? Law and order? Employment? The state of the roads? Bipasa?'

'Who's Bipasha?' I asked, confused.

'Bijli-Paani-Sadak,' he explained patiently. 'Electricity-Water-Roads. What have you learnt in film school, Toronto that will help us with these?'

'All these things have been badly messed up by the IJP state gourmint,' smiled Munni instantly, with the assurance of one who knew her cue. 'But if you support us in the upcoming state elections also, we will fix all this, slowly slowly.'

The old man heard her out politely, then turned to me. 'You look like a nice enough girl,' he said kindly. 'But don't you see… the same old answers won't do any more. Thank you for dropping by.'

And before I could even *ask* if I could use his bathroom, he ushered us to the door and shut the door firmly in our faces.

'*Saala* Tata tea!' muttered Munni as a few giggles sounded from the street behind us. '*Bhaashan deta hai!* I'll just now make two phone calls and get his name cut off the rolls!'

'No, Munni,' I said, my cheeks hot with humiliation. 'He was absolutely right. Tell me, can I visit some schools and health centres in the area, anonymously?'

She shook her head vehemently. 'Uff… not now, Sarojini didi! After you win election, you can do all this surprise visits and upliftments and all! Right now, we are doing campaigning…'

We shuffled along to the next door where, after peering at the chipped plywood nameplate, Munni told me that we were about to enter a Dalit home. Gingerly, I enquired if they were of the same caste as she was, but she instantly drew herself up very tall and shook her head. 'Oh *no*,' she said loftily. 'These are very inferior type Dalit people. My family are very *high*-caste Dalits.'

Well, of course, what was I thinking, I thought resignedly. There *would* be a complicated pecking order amongst Dalits as well.

The house was full of giggling women and a few sleeping babies. One, two, three… five… seven… there were nine women in all, who looked over eighteen years of age. Nine votes for the Pragati Party, if I could convert them with sheer vim and wit!

They were sitting out in the shady, khus-scented aangan, where a desert cooler was keeping everything very cool indeed. So cool, in fact, that one of the ladies was knitting a remarkably ugly sweater.

This time, I decided grimly, I would get to the point straightaway. Before Munni even started off on the Pragati Party speil, I was going to butt in and say, 'Excuse me, behenji, *par aap ka gusalkhana kahan hai?*' I was quickly coming to realize that the two most important things about political campaigning were 1) loo access and 2) bladder control.

Asking for the loo seemed to break the ice. When I came back after washing my hands, wiping them dry on the pallu of my sari, the ladies looked me up and down appraisingly all right, but they also offered me a cup of hot adrak ki chai and a moodha to sit on.

I sat down, sipped my tea, and flashed around my extra-wide smile.

They giggled.

One of them reached out and fingered the folds of my cotton sari. 'Suti hai,' she sniffed, not very impressed. 'Cotton.'

'Blouj is very boring, but,' chimed in a third.

'Earrings nice hai,' another one declared grudgingly.

'TV serial type ka blouj, why don't you wear?' demanded one of the ladies, who was wearing a rather tight choli herself.

Munni cleared her throat and said with prim stridency, 'Sarojini didi Gandhian hain, simple hain. Isliye.'

I grinned at them, switched to Pavit Pradeshi, and said, 'Ammaji does not let me wear small blouses. She says if I wear small-small blouses, her nose will get cut into small small pieces also!'

They looked rather scornful at this.

'Why you listen so much to your Ammaji? Everybody wears like that nowadays.'

'She thinks we're fools. In Delhi, she must be wearing small-small clothes only,' someone whispered behind me.

'Oho, didn't you hear? She's from *Bombay*,' came another whisper.

The lady who was knitting promptly poked me with the end of her needle and asked me which Bollywood hero I liked best.

But before I could answer, an intellectual looking type asked bluntly, 'What qualification you have?'

I told her. She nodded, not very impressed, and asked me if my degree was equivalent to an M.Phil.

'No,' I answered truthfully. 'It's equivalent to an MA, actually.'

She sniffed in a rather superior manner, and the girl sitting next to her said triumphantly, 'Didi has an M.Phil.'

'Fantastic,' I said humbly.

Somebody repeated the Bollywood hero question again, so I gave it the deep thought it merited and decided to play it safe.

'Hrithik Roshan?' I swung a little on the moodha and sang tentatively, '*Dhoom dhoom come light my fire.*'

A chorus of giggles greeted this sally. But then a very frail old lady with thin hair and really thick glasses said in a quavering, yet combative voice, 'Hrithik toh ab uncle hai! Woh new boy – Ranbir? Woh kaafi chikna hai!'

I grinned. 'Ammaji, in front of *you,* Ranbir is an uncle also!'

More giggles. The old lady asked Munni if I was married yet. Munni said I wasn't. 'Engaged?' Munni shook her head, no.

'Why not,' the old lady enquired.

'Nobody asked her, Ammaji,' Munni told her, with a wicked smile in my direction.

The old lady clicked her tongue sympathetically and advised me to eat more amla. She said it would make my hair grow.

Meanwhile, the other girls were nudging each other and murmuring names. Every now and then, one of them would squeal a name out loud. 'Sunny!' 'Akshay!' 'Dhoni!'

Stunned by the extremely high level of this political debate, I sat back on my moodha and did a thumbs up for Akshay, a thumbs down for Sunny and a double thumbs up for Dhoni.

Then a rather sweet young girl leaned forward eagerly and asked if I could show her some of the latest dance steps from Bombay. Munni looked a little put out at this, but I glared her down.

'It's okay,' I hissed. 'Let me do girlie-bonding with them. It shows I'm not stand-offish. Besides, I happen to know all the steps to the Dhan-ta-nan song from *Kaminey*.'

Ten minutes later, flushed, panting and confident that I'd charmed the ladies and secured nine definite votes for the Pragati Party, I took my leave.

'So I hope I have your vote, then?' I said at the door, beaming around as I wiped the sweat off my face with my pallu.

No reply. Just bright smiles, nudges and lots of giggles.

'Your *vote?*' I asked again, a little squeakily.

Oh god, I sounded frantic. Quickly, I added a gay laugh and sang out *Dhan ta nan...* again, just to keep things light.

There was an awkward silence.

Then one of the ladies, a fat matronly one who hadn't spoken a word till now, stepped forward. 'Ekchully, baby, don't mind,' she said apologetically. 'We should have told you earlier, par the thing is ki we are all from Himachal – our voting is not here – we are visiting for two days for a marriage function only.'

Oh.

The sweet one added, very kindly, 'But your dancing was very nice.'

There was an outburst of uncontrollable giggling and then they shut the door on my mortified face.

After several depressing encounters of more or less the same nature, we decided we'd had enough of Champapul and headed home. But then Munni made the Sumo halt once again, very close to Saket Bhavan, just to 'cheer us up' by visiting a home in Begumbagh, a locality where the Pragati is relatively stronger.

The door here was opened by a freshly bathed little boy in a Ben 10 T-shirt. He was sucking solemnly on the head of a remarkably realistic flesh-coloured rubber lizard. So realistic that I screamed and lunged at him and tried to wrest it from his grasp.

He grinned, very gratified by this reaction, and invited us in with a wordless flourish.

'Why you are not in bed?' Munni asked him as he led us into a spic-and-span little drawing room. 'Don't you have school tomorrow?'

The child, fair, apple-cheeked and very sturdy looking, dislodged the lizard's head from his mouth long enough to inform us, in the confident tone of one who is sure of his facts: 'Only donkeys go to school.'

Then he sat down on the sofa and resumed sucking, swinging his legs.

'Achha?' I asked. 'And what do clever people do?'

He considered this question for a while. Then he hopped up, extracted the wet lizard from his mouth, carefully placed it inside a spectacle case on the coffee table, shut it with a snap, and sat down again.

'Business,' he replied vaguely, scratching an impressive looking scab on his knee. 'They talk on cell-phones. And if anybody gets oversmart with them,' he turned his angelic light grey eyes on me and concluded with relish, 'they cut off his balls.'

We heard a low moan behind us.

Munni and I turned around.

A young woman stood in the doorway, holding a basket full of groceries. She was pretty but careworn and a little too thin. A ghost of a nervous tic haunted her left eye. Living with this angelic little boy was obviously taking its toll.

'Rajul!' she remonstrated in a hopeless sort of way. 'Don't talk like that.'

'Namaste,' I said to her, standing up, folding my hands and smiling.

Munni reared up too and rattled off her 'Aap-hain-Srimati-Sarojini-Pande' speil.

'Please give me your keemti vote,' I chimed in at the end, right on cue.

'Of course,' said Rajul's mom, not very enthusiastically. 'My husband always voted Pragati. So will I.'

'Thank you,' I said, relieved. She sounded totally *whatever* about it, but I wasn't complaining. She was the first person I'd met today who'd promised to vote for me. Then I started agonizing about whether I should ask her sympathetically if her husband was no more or if that would be considered too intrusive a question… or even offensive, in case he was just out of town, or if they were divorced or something. I finally settled for murmuring vague, soothing noises.

Munni, meanwhile, much relieved at having secured a vote, mentally ticked Rajul's mom off her list, and started backing out of the doorway, intent on hitting the next house. But I said, 'So, Rajul!' and patted the seat beside me, not wanting to come across as someone who left as soon as her purpose had been served. 'Tell me a little about yourself.'

He plopped down obligingly enough and informed me that his name was Rajul Sharma, that he was ten, and that his class teacher had failed him in English yesterday. 'I have to take a retest after the vacations,' he said gloomily. 'But it is not my fault.'

'Oh?' I asked. 'How come?'

He leaned forward.

'The thing is…' he began. Then he stopped.

'What?' I asked curiously.

'Woh picture thi na, Aamir Khan waali..?'

Which one? I wondered as I nodded and smiled at him encouragingly. *Ghajini? 3 Idiots?*

'I'm dickless sick.'

'Huh?'

He rolled his eyes. 'It's a medical condition,' he explained patiently.

'You mean dyslexic?' I said carefully, trying very hard to keep a straight face. 'Like in *Taare Zameen Par*?'

'You're laughing at me,' he said accusingly.

'No, I'm not,' I said hastily.

'We dickless sick people can't *help* being bad in studies,' Rajul said confidingly. 'It's not our fault. You have to be nice to us – give us presents, special attention and *plenty* of pocket money.'

'But,' I pointed out reasonably enough, 'you've done well in Hindi. So you *can't* be dyslexic.'

'It's *selective* dicklessicka,' he said solemnly.

'Ohhh.' I arranged my face to look suitably sensitive. '*That* explains it.'

'Yes,' he said. 'So I will have to join the Naxals when I grow up. Or go to Bombay and become a Bhai. No one will give me a regular job, na.'

'You could always join politics,' I suggested wittily.

Nobody laughed.

'The state of education in this country,' said Rajul's careworn mother, her voice trembling with intensity, 'is *terrible*. You must fix that, Sarojiniji.'

'Oh, I plan to,' I answered quickly. 'I am extremely committed to education – especially *quality* education in the primary classes.'

'The foundation,' volunteered Munni, 'must be strong.'

We all agreed that the foundation must be strong.

Silence for a moment. Then a musing look entered Rajul's seraphic green eyes.

'If you taught me English, I'm sure I would learn fast.'

'Me?' I exclaimed. 'Umm, I'd love to but…' My voice trailed away. I'd just claimed to be passionately committed to primary school education, I couldn't very well slime out of this.

He looked at me. Steadily.

'Um… I'm not going to be home much, because of the campaigning,' I offered weakly. 'I wouldn't want your studies to suffer because of erratic tuitions.'

'When you're away I could watch English programmes on your cable TV,' he said. 'We hardly get electricity here in Begumbagh, you know.'

'The power situation in this country,' put in his mother intensely, 'is terrible. You must fix it, Sarojiniji.'

'Uh, sure,' I said, feeling fully pressured now. 'I will… But Rajul—'

'Is it because we're so poor?' he asked me, swallowing bravely. 'Will I make your beautiful house look untidy?'

Oh god, how many Hindi movies had this kid watched?

'The monetary differences in this country,' put in his mother inexorably, 'are *terrible*. You must fix it, Sarojiniji.'

'Okay,' I said resignedly. I knew when I was beaten. 'Bring your books and come on Monday.'

Immediately, he beamed. 'D'you get AXN channel?' he enquired, bouncing to his feet. 'And WWE Smackdown and Raw?'

'Bye, Rajul,' I said hastily and got to my feet.

'Really nice meeting you,' I added politely to his mother.

'Oh, really nice meeting *you*,' she returned, wiping tears from her eyes and clinging to my arm. 'I will definitely make sure he comes and studies with you, *every* morning. It will be,' her face worked painfully, 'it will be such a break for me! I will tell everybody is this neighbourhood how kind you are! Helping a troubled boy. They will *all* vote for you!'

'Uh, not every *day*,' I said uneasily. 'Like I said, I will be campaigning – we will be out early morning to late evening – maybe every fortnight…?'

Rajul's mother narrowed her eyes.

'Every weekday,' she said firmly.

I wilted. 'Okay,' I said.

'Now let me just give you my phone number,' she continued as she produced a cell-phone and fumbled across the table for her spectacle case.

An anticipatory grin stretched across Rajul's angelic face.

'No – wait,' I started to say.

But it was too late.

Rajul's mother's hand encountered the sticky, saliva-slathered lizard inside the case, she pulled it out by its rubbery neck and stared at it in horrified disbelief.

'Super didi, super,' said Munni gloomily as Rajul's mother flung the lizard across the room and screamed and screamed. 'Kya student acquire kiya hai! He will make us all dickless sick only.'

5

I woke up next morning to the sound of buffalo. They were lowing and blowing and stamping their feet as they ambled along the road outside Bauji's house, the bells around their necks going *tadung tadung tadung*.

As the rich reek of fresh buffalo dung assailed my nostrils, I sat up in bed in my Spiderman ganji and pyjamas and groaned.

Last night had been so demoralizing! I had visited ten houses in all. And in all but two, *nobody* promised to vote for me. They hadn't even been polite enough to lie to my face. They plainly told me that:

'Your party is full of thugs and thieves.'

Or,

'We trust the ex-royal family.'

Or,

'Your grandmother hasn't shown her face for five years, why the hell should we vote for *you*?'

Or,

'This area has seen absolutely no development for years.'

Or,

'Pay us and we'll think about it.'

I brushed my teeth under the rusty tap and staggered across to the kitchen to cadge a cup of coffee. Joline Bai, disconcertingly clad in a tatty old nylon negligée of Amma's, grunted and shoved a cup towards me. I took a sip and almost gagged.

She regarded me dispassionately. 'You don't like Nescafé?'

I lowered the cup from my lips. Oh, I like Nescafé, I thought. Only, this isn't Nescafé. It's *Bhains*café.

The coffee was made with a huge dollop of thick, oily, stinky buffalo milk. How could I have forgotten? There's no homogenized Mother Dairy milk in Bittora. You know, the civilized milk that comes out of a slot machine or a decent, hygienic packet. Oh no, this was straight-from-the-tit bhains ka doodh – the *ughhest* thing about summer vacations here.

I held my breath as unobtrusively as I could, gingerly took a sip, smiled and said, 'Excellent coffee.'

Her mouth did this very tiny weird twitch which, with a huge amount of optimism, could be taken for a six-week foetus of a smile. 'Amma still sleeping,' she deigned to say.

'Okay,' I said. Then I lowered my voice and asked, 'And Gudia aunty?'

Joline Bai rolled her eyes. She doesn't like Gudia aunty. She resents her constant attempts to 'help'. And she's never forgotten that her best copper cucumber peeler went missing after Gudia aunty came to stay once.

'Counting...' she said, a little obscurely. 'Whole day counting.'

Hmmm, it sounded like Gudia aunty was calculating how much oxygen we had. I picked up my cup and decided to check my mail and found a whole bunch of mails from the dudes at Pixel, bitching and moaning about how I'd left some three projects incomplete when I went on leave. I ignored them and got onto Facebook instead (not that I wanted to visit anyone's page in particular, oh no), where the News Feed informed me that *Gaiman Tagore Rumi has checked into shopaholic rehab after overindulging disgracefully at the Mango and Bizarre spring sales.*

That bastard, Rumi. Shopping up a storm while I sweated it out in Bittora. I'd been leching at this perfect little ivory crochet top at Bizarre for two months now. Not to mention a pair of stretch jeans at Mango which made my butt look all peachy. I'd totally planned to buy them when they went on sale!

Rumi was online so I messaged him and asked if he'd picked up my stuff too. Then, warily sipping my bhainscafé, I half-heartedly checked out what everybody was talking about on Facebook.

- Aamir Khan's new haircut
- A wonder squid which could predict which football club was going to win the premier league
- Who was going to win *American Idol*
- The glitches in the latest, just-launched Apple gizmo

Hello, people, there's a Lok Sabha election brewing in our country! How about giving it a little mind space?

Rumi replied just then.

Shame on you, thinking about couture when there are starving millions to serve! he'd written. *Assumed you'd eschewed everything but saris now that you're an actual umeedwar. When were you planning to break that bit of news to your best friend, huh?*

Rumi, I wrote back, gritting my teeth. *Just tell me if you got my stuff. And don't think I haven't noticed that you never claimed me as a 'best friend' till the day I became an umeedwar.*

Whyn't you pop into RCKC? he wrote back at once. *Or Karol Bagh Sari House? You should be able to find something there. And why the hell would I suck up to you, anyway? All the exit polls say you're gonna lose:)*

Bastard!

I flipped my laptop shut and walked out to the garden to feed my bhainscafé to the sunflowers. When I turned around after pouring out the contents of my cup, I beheld a big golden Behind sitting on the grass. The head belonging to the Behind had entirely vanished, as it was stuck between its own back legs, licking itself energetically.

'Ponky,' I said firmly, and the head emerged, grinning enquiringly, fat pink tongue lolling. 'This is positively unhealthy! You and I are going for a long walk, dude.'

He leapt up immediately, and the Mark of Ponky was soon imprinted across my pyjama top. Throwing on a thin shawl, I found his leash, a long, thick, leather patta, and we set off down the road.

It was just a little misty, and the peepul trees above us were busy with chattering sparrows. The few shops behind the trees were shuttered and still. Ponky, fat body quivering with the excitement of a million tantalizing scents, leapt ahead, dragging me past the central Begumbagh chowk, the polo ground, several stinking rubbish dumps, the ghanta ghar and the Bittoragarh High School gate. He was headed for the Company Bagh, and obviously had a much longer walk in mind than I'd intended.

I stumbled along behind him, panting a little, starting to feel a bit warm in my pyjamas and shawl. Then I realized somebody was jogging along beside me. I turned, still trying to keep up with Ponky, and beheld a familiar face.

A dark, lanky body, streaked corkscrew curls, demented looking eyes and round John Lennon glasses.

I wrinkled up my forehead. 'Aren't you...' I began.

He grinned. 'Nauzer Nulwallah from MTV,' he replied, beaming happily, and held out his hand.

'Hi,' I said, 'uh… look, if you want to talk to me, you'll have to keep walking. There's no way I can stop this dog.'

'Wokay,' he said obligingly. He ran ahead, turned around and started running backwards, facing me. 'Actually, I wanted to ask if you'd be willing to be featured on our new show.' He threw up his arms and wiggled his fingers dramatically. '*MTV Democrazeeee!*'

'Demo-crazy?' I panted.

'Yeah,' he said, glasses flashing in the sunlight. 'Basically, our viewers are kinda excited about the election here – you're the youngest Praggu candidate in India, and Khan is the youngest from the IJP. Did you know that?'

'No,' I admitted. 'Really?'

'Yeah.' He took a deep breath and rattled off: 'The objective of the show is to raise young people's interest in our democratic system, arouse a passion for this particular form of service to the nation, and help the young, first-time voter make an informed choice while exercising his or her ballot, sponsored by Tata Tea, Jaago Re, Jaago Re, Jaaago Reyyyy! There's an episode tonight, you can watch. Phew!' He stopped running abruptly. 'Your dog wants to take a crap, thank god!'

I stopped too.

'I'll have to ask my… er… campaign managers,' I replied evasively. I'd seen Nulwallah in action on MTV, and I wasn't sure I wouldn't end up looking like an idiot if he interviewed me.

His eyes gleamed. 'Oh?' he said. 'Well, Khan said yes *immediately.* He didn't have to ask anyone. Don't you take your own decisions around here?'

Wow, this guy was seriously cocky.

'Well, no offence,' I said snidely, 'but unlike Zain Altaf

Khan, I'm working with people whose opinions are actually worth asking for.'

'So your party machinery *is* tying you down,' he riposted.

I was starting to get a little annoyed. The fact that we were now being tailed by a group of giggling little Bittora kids, all pointing at him and going *Oye dekho, Nauzer! Hello, Nauzer!* didn't help either.

'Is this a sample of your interviewing technique?' I asked him. 'What do you want to be when you grow up? Karan Thapar?'

'Not exactly,' he countered, looking irritatingly pompous. 'But as all the so-called "intellectual" news channels have sunk to cheap sensationalistic reportage, we frivolous MTV types have to give the viewers the serious, in-depth coverage they crave.' He grinned suddenly. 'And what do *you* want to be when you grow up? Prime minister?'

'Sure,' I replied coolly. 'Why not?'

'What about Z-A-K?' he asked meaningfully. 'Where d'you think he'll end up?'

But Ponky was done. He bounded away towards the Company Bagh and I huffed after him.

'He can be... my... umbrella-carrying spot boy!' I threw over my shoulder. It was a slightly snide remark, I'll admit, but the *you're-in-love-with-him* conversation with Ma still rankled.

'You mean he's gonna shade you completely?' Nauzer Nulwallah grinned as he reappeared smoothly at my elbow and continued running backwards, facing me.

I stopped and gave him a really nasty look.

'Look,' I told him. 'Maybe Altaf Khan is desperate for publicity, so he's coming on your funny little show. I'm *not*, so I *won't*.'

'Hey, no worries,' he said easily. 'Free will and all that, you know! But promise me you'll watch an episode – you might change your mind. And if it helps, we have a common friend, Gaiman Tagore Rumi.'

Hah. The selfish shopper. It *so* didn't help.

'It doesn't,' I said as I started to run again.

'Anyway, so I know a little bit about the world you come from,' he continued, running to keep up with me. 'Don't you find all this a bit disorienting? Bittora, Pavit Pradesh? Bittora means Heap Big Pile of Cowdung, by the way, did you know?'

Damn. I'd been hoping to keep that a deep dark secret.

'Bittora is my hometown,' I retorted sharply. 'So it isn't the least bit disorienting.'

'And what about the strange animal that is the,' he threw his arms out theatrically, 'Grand Old Party?'

I stuck out my chin and said, 'Look, of course the party has its flaws. But it's the best we've got. I mean, can you show me one alternative to the Pragati Party in this country which actually *works?*'

He said, a little dubiously, 'Well, there's the new and improved IJP…'

'Oh, please!' I snapped. 'Go back to Mumbai and make a reality show about guys and girls riding through India on motorbikes, will you?'

'But don't you find your party's system of dynastic politics rather regressive?'

'I don't know about *regressive*,' I shot back. '*I'm* not the one running backwards.'

'Ah,' he said, 'but *you're* the one chained to an ungainly, overweight, incontinent animal.'

Over the next few days, our little team quickly fell into a routine. We left Saket Bhavan early, an hour after daybreak, tailed by the ubiquitous black EC Maruti Gypsy, and addressed ten to seventeen public meetings a day, of fifty to five hundred people each.

For the first week we concentrated on Jummabagh, Chamapapul and Begumbagh, which were geographically close. Amma had decided we would hit the rural areas a little later, after Zain – and sixteen other candidates from various parties – had finished campaigning there.

It was rigorous work. I developed a practically permanent line around my midriff, where the petticoat naada chafed constantly. My cheeks ached because of the non-stop smiling. My voice was beyond hoarse, my eyes felt gritty, and I was slowly working up quite a tan in spite of all the Banana Boat (SPF 120) that Amma kept slathering on me.

And that was just the physical discomfort.

My moral dilemma, silenced during the day by the part seductive, part threatening *but everybody else does it* argument, returned to haunt me late at night. On the one hand, I was worried sick about all the money we were spending, where it was coming from, and what I might be asked to do when people started calling in their favours. On the other, I was fretting about all the money Zain was spending and wondering if it was way more than what we were handing out.

In this context, Gudia aunty had totally earned my respect. Even though I was pretty sure she was helping herself to my Moroccan Rose Body Shop perfume every morning, and rather liberally at that, I had to admit she was a rather savvy campaign manager. Wise to the fact that party workers made major money when the candidate held elaborate meetings, marking up prices shamelessly to demand as much as five thousand rupees for firecrackers, five thousand rupees for garlands, ten thousand rupees for the stage, five thousand rupees for tea and refreshments, two thousand rupees for loudspeakers, all in all adding up to about twenty-seven thousand rupees per meeting, she'd decreed bossily that Amma and I would be keeping it simple.

'Shame on you for holding such elaborate meetings when the nation is facing such a severe summer!' she castigated the workers in her piercing voice. 'Top Brass has said that these are times of austerity! Have you forgotten Gandhiji and Shashtriji?'

Invoking these highly convenient icons of simple living, she ordained that Amma and I would conduct our twenty-odd daily public meetings from the Sumo itself – sticking our head and shoulders out of the skyroof. Tubelights had been rigged to the Sumo roof to light up our faces, and loudspeakers were attached to the front and back of the vehicle. Instead of strings of firecrackers to herald our arrival, we would use traditional tribal drummers. So we'd managed to get the costs down a bit, but Our Pappu confided to me that the workers were muttering that Amma's election agent was a stingy skinflint who was destroying Amma's goodwill in the area.

Amma remained unfazed by this. 'Thoj boyj are never happy,' she said dismissively. 'We cannot give them any more money – we need it for Mr Urvasi's surveys.'

She'd had a change of heart regarding Mr Urvashi. The man-with-the-name-of-a-woman had been assigned the job of sending us a list of 'issues' for every area before we visited it, so that the speeches we subsequently made were sharply pinpointed and locally relevant. I pointed out that he was probably peddling the same list to all seventeen candidates and making a killing as he did so, but she told me not to be Nave.

'Rocket, Pappu and the rest don't have the pulse of the grassroots now that they are MLA,' she said. 'Whole day jooming about in jeeps, too high and mighty to talk to the common people! And anyway, they only give us *their* version of things. We need The People's version. The unbiased version. It ij a mistake to become cut off from The People, Sarojini. Besides, everybody should make a little money during elecsuns. You think Urvasi has no children?'

Every night, after dinner, we would assemble in Bauji's petal room. The crack team would show up one by one, slip off their shoes and sit cross-legged on a violently colourful cotton thread dhurrie. Joline Bai would set out huge steel-and-black thermoses filled with hot tea and bowls of rock-hard shakkar padas. And then Amma would sit and add up the votes obsessively, again and again and again.

This evening, Our Pappu arrived early, all red-cheeked and beaming. He dived reverentially at Amma's feet, then clutched my hand, bowed his head and murmured hoarsely, '*Anything* for you, didi, anything for you! *Whatever* you wish! Just ask and see! *Anything* you desire! My mind and body are at your service! Remember, I will do *anything* to satisfy you!' With that, he plonked himself on the floor, looked around and announced impressively, 'Jiji! You will get a solid lead from Jummabagh! I will get you fifty thousand votes! Pukka promise!'

Amma snorted. Her voice, never very strong, had been the first to go with all the speeches she had been making. She sucked ferociously on a Vicks ki goli to clear the *khich khich* and said nothing.

'Poorey pachaas hazaar,' Our Pappu repeated loudly, thinking she hadn't heard.

'We are not sooting Solay here,' Amma snapped at him.

'How can one person claim to deliver fifty thousand votes? Can you read those people's minds? Foolis!'

Our Pappu tugged at his ear lobes in mock contrition, but the moment she turned her back he waggled five fingers at me and grinned reassuringly.

Amma started to do the math again. There was a total of eleven lakh people on the Bittora rolls. The turnout in Bittora was traditionally around sixty per cent. Which meant that about six-and-a-half lakh people would actually show up to vote. Out of which we needed to get about three-and-a-half to four lakhs to win.

'If we get fifty thousand from Jummabagh and forty thousand from Champapul,' she muttered hoarsely, wrapping her pallu a little tighter around her thin shoulders, 'and chalo, even just ten thousand from Begumbagh. Then we will have one lakh. And in the villages, we will get lead from Sujanpur – we *always* get lead from Sujanpur – and Doodhiya… mila-ke-ho-gaye two lakhs… and if we can get fifty thousand from Tanki Bazaar we will have two lakh fifty. Purana Bittora toh we can forget about. Somehow, we'll have to get more numbers from the villages only. Uff… it is impossible without Begumbagh… that Dwivedi is spoiling everything, we need to *settle* him…'

Our Pappu instantly piped up, 'Jiji, from Jummabagh, poorey pachaas hazaar! Guaranteed!'

She glared at him and he cowered, grinning, and slurped his tea loudly.

Then the next bunch of people walked in. Depending on the kind of energy they brought into the room, we would bloom or wilt. Sometimes Munni would march in, beaming, eyes shining brightly above the dupatta she wore swathed round her neck, bringing news of our strong following in Champapul. And sometimes she would drift in, shaking her head dourly, even her ponytail looking limp, saying ki hawa badal gayee hai, the wind had changed, workers from the other side had made everyone swear on the Holy Quran to vote for Zain.

Today, she was beaming. 'Sixty-five thousand from Champapul, jiji!' she declared, as she pumped the top of the chai thermos vigorously. 'Full sixty-five! This is my vaada to you!' she added grandly.

Amma bit into her Vicks ki goli with an ominous crunching sound. 'Kyun,' she grunted, 'are people planning to break the vow they took on the Quran?'

Munni shook her head. 'No, no, jiji,' she said, 'kya hai ki, those fellows were trying IJP tricks – swearing on holy books, only the IJP does that – but we found a sura saying that swearing on the Quran is haraam, a mortal sin, so now the people are going to atone for it by voting for Jinni didi.'

'Wow, are these people that god-fearing?' I asked, thinking back to the feisty ladies I'd met in Champapul.

Amma snorted. 'Of course *not*! They know this is the only time they have us by the throat. They will vote exactly the way they want to vote – no matter how many books we make them swear on, or what their maulvis say.'

Rocket Singh walked in just then. He was the one responsible for the vital FUCT (Forest of Unemployed Christian Tribals) area of Doodhiya and the THID (Thirsty, Hindu, Illiterate Dalits) areas of Durguja and Sujanpur. The people of Durguja, especially, were notoriously unpredictable. They had once made national headlines when a media poll revealed that, unlike the rest of rural India, the good people of Durguja would rather have a *bathroom* than a television in their homes. What could you possibly promise to people like that?

Rocket Singh looked gloomy. He sighed, stirred his tea and said 'Jiji, Altaf Khan took water tankers through Durguja today. Fifty of them. He even organized rain dances.'

Amma was popping another Vicks ki goli from a blister pack, but she looked up sharply at this. 'What happened to the wells we had sanctioned for the junglee people in Durguja on Bauji's birthday last year?'

'Amma, don't say junglee. Say *tribals*,' I remonstrated, appalled.

Rocket Singh looked a little shifty. 'Haan, those wells… they got made, jiji.'

Amma's narrowed her eyes. 'And were the wells dug *inside* the junglee colonies, Rocket?'

Looking even more uncomfortable, he muttered, 'Actually, jiji, the thing is ki the engineers, when they came to bore the wells, they said that the water table was too low inside the tribal colonies. So they recommended that the wells be dug in the village common – where the water table is much higher. And Dwivediji agreed.'

'Arrey wah,' said Amma, her voice dangerously dry. 'So now even the *water table* is discriminating against the junglees?'

'Yes, jiji,' said Rocket Singh sullenly.

'We sanctioned seven wells,' said Amma. 'Not even *one* waj built within the junglee colony compounds? Water table waj too low in *all seven* colonies?'

He answered, his voice very low, 'Yes, jiji.'

'So now, of course, the high-castes are not letting the junglees into the village common to uje the wells that were made for the junglees' benefit only?'

Rocket Singh gave an uncertain laugh. 'No no, nothing like that!' he said, trying to sound convincing. 'Aisa kuch nahin hai, jiji! All are using!'

Amma said, in a dangerous voice, 'We will *see*. It is high time we covered the rural areas. When can Sarojini go?'

Rocket Singh said, 'Whenever you want, jiji. Shortcut has arranged a bungalow, so no problem.'

Amma looked up with a frown. 'Why not at Dugguji's?' she asked.

'Who's Doggieji?' I asked curiously.

'Dugguji Sisodia,' said Gudia aunty. 'He's the big zamindar. Why will Jinni not stay there, Rocket?'

'Actually,' Rocket Singh looked around shiftily, 'Dugguji's son Bunty bhai is supporting Altaf Khan. So Altaf Khan is staying there. But the bungalow is good, jiji, it is having electricity and everything.'

Gudia aunty looked completely crushed at this news. 'Bunty *bhai* indeed!' she said, with a scornful laugh. 'He's just a sycophantic sidekick of that Altaf Khan.'

Amma looked outraged. 'That *snakling* Bunty,' she said bitterly. 'We went for his sixth-day ceremony... he did susu in aawar lap. And now he has no place for us in his houj...'

Then everybody started talking about the latest rumour that the IJP had started in the villages of Doodhiya. That all the electronic voting machines for this Lok Sabha election had a little camera built into them, which took a photo of you when you voted. This way, they could tell who you voted for, and if it wasn't for the party you'd *promised* to vote for, the party workers of that party would come back to get you and there would be hell to pay.

'Wow,' I said, impressed, 'they really believe India is that technologically advanced?'

Munni nodded solemnly. 'Yes, didi. They have been told ki machine mein chip hai. The chip will click a photo which will reveal who you voted for and that photo will go straight to Bittora Fort, and then the nawabzada will come and deal with each and every one of the people who'd promised to vote IJP and then didn't.'

'That's *sick*,' I said, thinking, so much for all the lectures on national integration Zain had given me, he was playing real dirty. Where was he getting all these sicko ideas from?

'Who is *hij* crack team?' Amma demanded. 'How come he haj become so smart suddenly?'

'He doesn't have a crack team, jiji,' said Our Pappu gloomily. 'He has a cricket team...'

Amma looked flummoxed. But I remembered the bunch of sweaty local boys (headed by Bunty the snakling) with whom Zain used to play endless games of cricket in the old days. I'd hated the lot of them. They were a bunch of rich local kids who were always sidling over and snatching Zain away from me, because his bowling was really good or whatever. They used to hang out in the Company Bagh, playing cricket and sucking on Mango Delights from the local Kristal ice-cream carts. They'd won a couple of stupid trophies too, which Zain had been inordinately proud of. Obviously, they were all grown up now, and were giving him crafty advice and the local perspective and had their ear to the ground and everything. No wonder he'd written 'old friends are best' in his Facebook status. Right next to the cricket group pictures too. And I, like a fool, had thought he was talking about me.

'Funtaastic,' Amma said gloomily, when Our Pappu and I had explained all this to her. 'But old friends alone can't make you win – where is hij oxygen coming from, Munni?'

Munni hesitated. 'Jiji, his pockets are very full. Jeeps, helicopters, expensive giveaways. It is IJP money... their people are taking him around everywhere, and all of them are eating room service in Zain Mahal every day…'

'Munni, any news of Vir Singh?' Gudia aunty asked suddenly. 'And Dwivedi?'

Munni looked glum. 'Vir Singh wants forty lakhs,' she said. 'Means twenty mein settle kar lega.'

Amma tch tched. 'What, Munni,' she said, looking personally let down. 'You are losing your touch.'

'Jiji, he started with *ninety*,' Munni returned indignantly.

Gudia aunty winced. She looked in a haunted sort of way at her Milton hotcase, which was almost empty now.

'Aur Dwivedi?' Amma asked.

Rocket Singh shook his head and said, with finality, 'Jiji, unka toh pukka hai. He said nothing would make him withdraw.'

At this gloomy point, Jugatram walked in.

He looked really chirpy. Apparently, everyone in Tanki Bazaar was gung-ho about Pragati Party.

'*Eighty* thousand votes,' he promised. 'Full eighty. As long as we can arrange the transport to and from the polling booths.'

'No one person can promise to deliver eighty thousand votes, Jugatramji,' I said sternly. 'You can't read people's minds.'

But Amma's eyes had brightened visibly. 'Hain?' she said eagerly. 'Sachhi? *Eighty?* Did Hasina say so?'

Jugatram nodded. 'Yes, jiji!'

Amma started counting off on her fingers.

'Eighty from Tanki, fifty from Champapul, ten from Begumbagh…'

'Fifty from Jummabagh,' Our Pappu piped up.

Amma's eyes glittered dangerously and we braced ourselves. But before she could disembowel Our Pappu, Munni suddenly went 'Shhhhhushhh!' and pointed at the spiffy little plasma

TV which was showing the news on mute on the wall. I looked up – we all did – and saw an image of Zain, quickly followed by one of Nauzer Nulwallah. I realized this must be the show he'd been urging me to appear on. It was running on the Star News channel; MTV must have a tie-up with them. That was pretty impressive, maybe it had been a mistake refusing to appear on it.

'These people don't even know the *spelling* of Democracy,' Our Pappu scoffed as the graphics for *MTV Democrazeee* filled the screen. 'What programme will *they* make?'

The graphics got over and the show cut straight to Zain in conversation with Nauzer. They were both sitting on deck chairs, at a poolside – which I recognized with some surprise as the refurbished central courtyard of Zain's horrible dad's hideous Bittora Fort. Only, it looked kind of different. Clearly the Taj people had managed to get rid of all the dead stuffed animals. And the pool! They certainly didn't have a pool nine years ago! How dare Zain smarm about acting all khandaani and cool and pool-owning? Like he'd swum in it since he was a baby! Like he'd never gone swimming with me in the sludgy Bitwa river!

He was lounging in the deck chair, wearing a crew-necked ice-blue T-shirt and white cargoes. Purple jacaranda bloomed on the weathered stone walls behind him. He was wearing sunglasses, but when Nauzer introduced him, he took them off, squinting slightly, his skin dark gold in the late afternoon sun. Then he sat forward, legs planted wide, and grinned into the camera. That was the way he always sat, I remembered suddenly, vividly. It looked so *inviting* somehow, like his lap was open to anyone who wanted to drop into it. Also, can I just add that sitting at that angle, his T-shirt got just a little taut across his chest.

Basically, he totally had my vote at that instant.

NN (waving his arms about dramatically): He's muscular! He's popular! He's spectacular! And… he's secular! [Turning to Zain] Speaking of which, dude, aren't you in the wrong party?

ZAK: No way, Nauzer! This party's done major introspection and set itself a whole new agenda. There's been a lot of churning and change. Change for the better. Today, it's the only place for someone young and unconnected like me.

NN: Duh, you're Muslim. The IJP isn't exactly famous for its love of Muslims.

ZAK: The prime minister is a Sikh. The Pragati isn't exactly known for its love of Sikhs.

NN: What made you join politics?

ZAK: Politicians. I couldn't believe how unbelievably venal they are.

NN (smirking): As venal as centuries of rulers in Pavit Pradesh maybe?

ZAK (a trace of hauteur creeping into his voice): I know my ancestors have a lot to answer for. And I'm here to answer for them.

NN: You come from a world where the only naked and starving people you know are supermodels. How does the voter know this isn't just a giant ego trip for you?

ZAK: He doesn't, really. Except, look, I don't want to sound obnoxious, but there are a lot of other things I could do if all I wanted was an ego massage.

NN: Like what? Date a movie star? Grace the cover of *People* magazine? Buy an IPL team?

ZAK (with a shrug): Yeah, something like that. Or I could just wait until I'm thirty and buy my way into the Rajya Sabha. It's very easy, from what I hear. You pretty much just bribe a bunch of MLAs to vote you in.

NN: Dude, that's libellous.

ZAK (nostrils flaring): So sue me.

NN (combatively): I put it to you that you are just a rich kid playing at being grown-up.

ZAK (calmly): I put it to you that you've just described yourself. [Choking sounds from Nauzer] And anyway, I'm not that rich. Definitely not compared to all the fat cat netas in Lutyens' Delhi.

NN: So you'll really miss your ten thousand-rupee deposit if you lose it?

ZAK (with a lazy smile and glittering eyes): I won't lose it.

NN (waving a paper about): We have all your declared personal assets and liabilities listed right here, Mr Not-rich Man. Should I start reading them out?

ZAK (throwing up his hands and laughing): I can't stop you, I can just *request* you not to embarrass me!

NN: You think you'll have enough time for the job? Don't the hotel and the hospital and the women's college [he managed to make this sound highly suggestive somehow] and the eco-drives and rally driving take up all your time?

ZAK (doggedly): I'll *make* time.

NN: What upsets you the most about politics today?

ZAK (simply): I don't like the way my community is being treated.

NN: Speaking of which, the Christian, the serd and the lady in the burqa went to rent which DVD at the rental store?

ZAK: That is *such* an old one. *The Minority Report.*

NN (abruptly): Do you think you're a good Muslim?

ZAK (after a long pause): I'm trying to be a good person.

NN: So this is not about your religious identity?

ZAK (frowning): Look, I'm tired of being treated like a second-class citizen in my own country.

NN (nodding understandingly): Yeah, that sucks. Personally, I always fly first class.

ZAK (ignoring this very lame crack): Nobody's doing the Muslim a favour by being 'nice' to him. [suddenly adopting a squeaky pidgin accent] Oho, you're a *Muslim*? Never mind, what's there? We are very broadminded! God is One! So, do you whip yourself all the time? No? Can you read and write? Well done! In *English*? Fantastic! Do you have twenty-seven brothers and sisters? Do you have three stepmothers?

NN (completely deadpan): Do you?

ZAK's eyes blazed with pure anger for a moment, and then he burst out laughing. 'No man, but you see what I mean?'

NN: Yeeeahh... kinda. But that brings me back to my very first question. I mean, the IJP? They're the *Hindi, Hindu, Hindustan* brigade, dude!

ZAK (steadily): That's all in the past. I believe this is a genuine re-invention. They're trying to provide a solid option to the corruption-ridden Pragati. Getting clean people in. That's a good thing.

NN: You're a champion for the underdog. Muslims, Dalits, OBCs. A more natural ally for your beliefs would have been the Pragati Party, surely? Or the KDS? Did you never consider contesting on their ticket?

ZAK: Well, I hate clichés, but unfortunately, the term pseudo-secularist springs to the lips. Besides, I'm deeply uncomfortable about how... *centralized* the Pragati Party power structure is. Coming from an ex-royal family, I distrust any kind of rule by [he made inverted commas in the air] divine right.

NN: And the KDS?

ZAK (dismissively): The KDS is just a bunch of opportunist thugs.

NN: Wow. Okay! Tell us something about your plans for your constituency if you win.

ZAK (eyes lighting up): My constituency, in the heart of the historic district of Bittoragarh, is an eight-hundred-square kilometre stretch that includes the town of Bittora and 600 surrounding villages. My plans for the constituency are pretty much the same as the plans *every* other party claims to have for the constituency. Education. Jobs. Bijli-Paani-Sadak. Except that I am actually going to implement them.

NN: Who's funding your campaign?

ZAK: My party, obviously.

NN: The helicopter? You can get that in twenty-five lakhs?

ZAK (calmly): It's a friend's. All perfectly above board, I assure you.

NN (pursing his lips in disbelief): Hmmm! Can we talk a little about your opponent, now?

ZAK (looking all haughty): You must mean *opponents*. There are seventeen candidates standing in this election.

NN: Well, your *closest* opponent. Sarojini Pande. With whom you make up the Youngest Political Face-Off India's Ever Seen. Surely she proves there's place for youngsters in the Pragati ranks? That things there are not quite so – *centralized*?

ZAK (lightly): Sarojini Pande is just a mask. A very pretty, appealing, youthful mask for the ancient, canny political animal that is Srimati Pushpa Pande.

NN: And Srimati Pande's politics?

ZAK (jaw hardening): Are not mine.

NN: Zain, d'you really think you can win this thing?

ZAK: Look, whether I win or lose, I'm doing what *needs* to be done. I'm done with talking loudly from the sidelines. I'm here, I'm involved, I want to contribute. Bittoragarh is not just a political constituency for me. It's my home. My past. My future. My whole life.

NN: What's your political ambition?

ZAK: I told you, I want to be a first-class citizen.

NN (nudging him meaningfully): Not the *first citizen*, eh?

ZAK: I'd like to see a Muslim prime minister. Or a Dalit prime minister. Definitely.

NN (belligerently): Or a Parsi? Why not a Parsi, huh? Your party got issues with Parsis?

ZAK (laughing): Yes, a Parsi, or a Christian, or even just a below-fifty honest, educated, intelligent Indian from a non-political family, of any religious denomination!

NN: Okay. And here's the final question. As this is a music channel, you have to tell us your most favourite patriotic song of all time, and we'll play it for you.

ZAK: Um, well… [pausing for thought] that would have to be 'Desi Girl' from *Dostana*.

NN: Hmmm… cheesy choice, dude! Okay, coming up next,

right after the ad-break for all our viewers – sorry, *voters* – out there – *dekhi lakh lakh pardesi girls, aint nobody like my desi girl!*

———

We sat through the stupid *Dostana* number, and then they showed a quick montage of Zain riding the footboard of a black Scorpio, waving to the crowds as he drove past, flashing his quick, compelling grin. They rounded it off with one of his campaign speeches. I don't know exactly what I thought his campaigning style was, but after the very 'swayve' interview, I'd expected something pretty slick. Witty and clever and poking fun at Amma, you know. And so, I was really surprised by his speech.

He stood before a row of mikes, his dark hair tousled, the sleeves of his white kurta rolled up, giving him a very hands-on, ready-to-work appearance. It was a still day, very hot, and you could see a steady flutter of pamphlets in the audience. Zain spoke in fluent Pavit Pradeshi and his appeal to the people was simple, straight-up and unabashedly sentimental.

'My relationship with the people of Bittoragarh is a very old one. It is not a relationship *I* began, it began long before I was born, long before even you were born, about six hundred years ago. It is a relationship built, not on votes, not on politics, but on love.'

Oh please, based on six hundred years of exploitation, you mean.

A little breeze stirred, tousling his hair, making a rattling noise in the mike. He waited for it to die down, then leaned forward, resting his elbows on the podium, and continued steadily, his dark eyes glowing.

'Maybe you know, maybe you don't, but most members of my family chose to go to Pakistan after independence, while my grandfather decided to stay here. Because *this* was his home. *You* were his family.'

Dramatic pause.

In the drawing room, Jugatram cleared his throat and said rather randomly to no one in particular, 'I taught him how to drive when he was twelve years old.'

On TV, the twenty-five-year-old Zain continued. 'Maybe you know, maybe you don't, that my mother died when I was just three years old. I do not have many memories of her. The women of Bittoragarh have told me that she was beautiful and kind and brave. I feel very proud when they tell me this.'

Another pause. There wasn't a *choon* or a *chaan* from the crowd. They were quiet. Clearly, he was holding them in the palm of his hand.

'But do not for a moment think that I felt alone or abandoned as a child or when I was growing up. Because I *had* a mother.'

The ultimate pause.

'Bittora was my mother.'

Okay, excuse me while I throw up here.

This shamelessly Bollywoodish sally was greeted with huge applause by the crowd. And by Munni, who went all tremulous and moist-eyed and clapped until Amma glared at her.

'In her lap I played and was nourished and slept and grew strong. Now that I am grown up, I simply want to do what all sons want to do – look after my mother. And make her proud.'

Tumultous applause. Cries of *Zain Bhai ki jai!*. He waited for it to die down, smiling a little, his dark eyes glowing with emotion. I had an uneasy feeling that he actually *meant* what he said.

'I will not ask you for votes, one does not ask one's family for votes. One simply loves and is loved back. And so I ask you to shower your love on me and give me a chance to serve you. Jai Hind.'

He smiled and folded his hands with boyish, idealistic intensity. The superhit 'Sasuraal genda phool' song from *Delhi 6*, A.R. Rahman's unwitting gift to the IJP election campaign – which the party had lost no time in converting to 'Sarkar genda phool' – kicked in from the massive speakers. In response, the crowd leapt to its feet and cheered like it was at a heavy metal concert. I half expected the screaming village girls to stick out their tongues, rip off their cholis and bare their breasts.

In the drawing room, Amma snorted and zapped off the TV.

'Whatever you say, jiji,' declared Our Pappu, and the entire crack team nodded mistily as he spoke, 'banda kaafi cool hai!'

Amma muttered and grumbled and made rude snorting noises about Zain until she went to bed. She couldn't understand why he had his knife into her. She'd always been so nice to him, she said, given him big fat lifafas full of money on his birthday and on every festival. 'Arrey, he did not feel alone and abandoned as a child because *we* were hij mother!' she fumed. 'Ungrateful pilla! Alwayj coming over and eating and drinking here only. How could he insult us on TV? What did we ever do to him, Sarojini?'

'Nothing, Amma,' I said wearily. I was so not in the mood to talk.

It rankled that Zain had come across as so sincere and sorted out. He'd looked like he knew what he was doing – unlike me,

I wasn't even clear *why* I was standing in the first place. It was also pretty obvious that he thought I was some little puppet on a string, doing what I was told to. Well, I *wasn't*. I had a plan for Bittoragarh too, and the first part of the plan was to win the seat from under his haughty, muscular-and-secular nose.

Amma, meanwhile, was still on her own trip.

'But we fed him with our own hands when he was small!' she said, sounding perplexed. 'Such nice dark curls he had. Why is he so bitter? You two were childhood friends! Your *grandfathers* were childhood friends! The Altaf Khans have always been Pragati Party supporters! *Why* has he become so bitter, Sarojini?'

I sighed, patted her back and went into my petal room to sleep. She really had no clue, and I was *so* not in the mood to tell her…

I forget now how the whole thing started. What he said, what I said. But somehow it had been clearly understood by both of us. It was the last day of the holidays and when our game of carom ended, we were going to kiss.

I'd been dragging the game out all afternoon. Partly just to play hard-to-get, and partly because, though I would never admit it, I was lousy at carom.

We were down to one black, one white. He'd potted the queen ages ago. It was his turn. He smiled a slow lazy smile as he bent over the board, a lock of dark hair falling forward on his forehead. His long, lean fingers, slightly dusty with carom powder, tensed behind the striker. He hit it gently, there was a soft whfffuft sound and a blow of powder as the striker made contact with the white and slid smoothly home.

He looked up, grinning, and held out his hand.

'Chuck me the striker.'

I threw it at him, rolling my eyes.

He caught it rather cockily, placed it on the board, and started aligning the black for the last shot, whistling tunelessly between his teeth.

I waited until he had actually hit the shot and then, as the striker began its slide across the board, I leapt up, knocked the board over, and ran into the garden, laughing, expecting him to follow me.

But he didn't.

Instead, he stacked all the pieces back into the box, put away the board neatly and went home.

Leaving me with no option but to come racing out and stand in front of his cycle as he wheeled it out of the driveway.

'Hey!' I gasped.

He stopped. Was he relieved? I couldn't tell.

'What?' he asked.

'Don't you want to… I mean, where are you… I mean, are you going?'

He put the bike on its stand and said slowly, like he was talking to a moron, 'Yes, I am going.'

'But don't you want to…' My voice trailed away.

He leaned forward, a little pulse jumping at the base of his throat. 'Don't I want to what?'

'Uh… play another game?' I said lamely.

He glared at me. Then he took the bike off the stand and started wheeling it out again.

'Don't you want to kiss me?'

I said it in a rush, my cheeks flaming hot.

He dropped the bike.

It just keeled over and fell on the cemented drive with an awful clatter. There was a bunch of CDs hanging off it, hard rock compilations that Zain has spent ages recording, and they rolled about everywhere, adding to the pandemonium.

I started giggling at once, and now he was the one rolling his eyes and shushing me as we ran back into my room, slamming the door shut behind us. He pushed me gently against the wall, one hand on either side of me, almost as if he expected me to run away again. Then he lifted my chin and looked into my eyes, his own dark and stormy and very, very intense.

'Yes. I want to kiss you, Jinni. I want to kiss you very much.'

We were still kissing a good five minutes later, when Amma's car drove up and she stormed into the house, cursing her tailor loudly. Apparently, he hadn't even started work on the six silk sari blouses she'd planned to wear over the next two weeks.

Zain and I looked at each other in total panic.

Amma and Ma had both become very weird about Zain and me being home alone during these holidays, now that we were both sixteen and 'haarmoanal'. I bundled Zain into the cupboard and he let me shut him in, still grinning, his eyes dancing, pressing his finger against my lips, going shhhhhhhh dramatically just before he vanished from sight. I bolted it shut hurriedly just before Ma and Amma came into my room. Amma then proceeded to sit on my bed and hold forth blisteringly on Master Kamruddin of Saheli Boutique.

She began by saying that it was her own fault for trusting a Muslim. She should have known better – all Muslims are dirty, stupid, constantly breeding, election rigging, Pakistani-cricket-team-cheering rapist-murderers who should be packed off to Pakistan. She said that Master Kamruddin with his 'perfect fit, ready whenever you want it' claim, should be given a perfect kick in his circumcized crotch.

Then she changed gears and started holding forth on the carnage in Godhra, saying that what the IJP was doing to the Muslims there was absolutely right. They had totally asked for it. Instead of being grateful that we let them live here at all, they had started all the trouble. They had set the rail carriage on fire and now it served them right that they were being butchered in thousands. She said the chief minister of Gujarat was a genius, and that she would make him prime minister of India if she could. She bemoaned the lack of such brilliant people in her own party and said it was a shame that her party was saddled with this stupid idealistic secular agenda that nobody believed in anyway.

Then she said, 'You can't really blame the Muslims actually, look at the example they are set! Zaffar Ali Khan, the so-called ruler of these parts, is a lecher and a waster and a drunkard – half the village brats have kanji-kanji eyes, just like him!' She snorted loudly and continued. 'In fact, he is truly secular, he has left no pretty girl, Muslim, Hindu, Sikh, achhoot, bhangi, chamaar alone! Everyone knows that Zain's young mother almost died of shame when she found out where-where, in which-which dirty garage Zaffar had been parking his car! She never let him near her – that boy, Zain, everybody knows he is not his father's son, but his grandfather's son! Bhai, it is a fact. Everybody knows! It is not a big secret, Sarojini, why are you hushing and shushing and telling us to be quiet be quiet be quiet, again and again and again!?'

I had tears of helplessness in my eyes by then. Somehow, I managed to hustle them both out of my room, telling Amma to look in Ma's cupboards, perhaps she would find some blouses there to wear with her new silk saris.

When I blundered back into the room and unlocked the cupboard, Zain's eyes were like chips of stone. He stalked out of the room without saying a single word, picked up his bike and cycled *home. He didn't answer my frantic phone calls for the rest of the evening. The next day, I left for Delhi to take my tenth class board exams, and then Ma and I moved to Canada. That was the last I saw of him, till I met him making galouti kebabs at a wedding, nine years later.*

6

The next morning, I came down to breakfast after a night of the weirdest dreams. Rumi and I were being chased around the bottom of a dirty Indian-style potty by kitaanus with faces like the Top Brass and his minions. Meanwhile, Joline Bai was cooking a massive meal because Zain was coming for lunch. And the Rapist was asking my head to dance as it hung from a wall in the old Bittora Fort, mounted on a shield like something Zain's dad had shot dead with a gun.

Really sicko stuff.

Feeling slightly ill, I wandered into the verandah in my shorts and Spiderman ganji, collapsed on a wooden chauki, and dimly registered the fact that it was obscenely early in the morning. So early, in fact, that Joline Bai was in the driveway, talking to the milkman, who was doling out our daily quota of yucky buffalo milk.

Shuddering, I lay back on the chowki, rubbed my eyes and stretched. The verandah was very peaceful in the slanting early morning sunshine. The mali was watering the lawn and the air smelled of wet earth. Bees hummed among the sunflowers, a pleasant cawing of crows rose from the mango grove. There was the homely clatter of morning vessels being cleaned, and from a distance, way down Pandit MM Pande Road, came the sound of both azan and aarti.

I was relishing the early morning quiet, when a sudden hoarse shout from behind made me jump so hard I bit my tongue and yelped.

'Good morning, didi!' yelled Our Pappu in a loud, false, hearty voice from the gate. There were only about eighty-three people with him.

Swearing under my breath, I ducked back into the petal room.

When I emerged some fifteen minutes later, decently dressed, Our Pappu was still at the gate, waiting patiently. Again, in exactly the same false, hearty voice, he called out, 'Good morning, didi!'

'Uh, good morning!' I called back uncertainly.

'It ij a delegation of Muslims from the Jummabagh assembly area, we think so,' supplied Amma, who had just emerged from her room, resplendent in a dressing gown embroidered with red, turquoise and yellow tulips in Kashmiri crewelwork.

Obviously, Our Pappu, tired of us campaigning just in Begumbagh and Champapul, had taken matters into his own hands.

There was a loud chanting at the gate.

Jab se ayee Pushpa Pande,
Chud gayeen IJP ki gaande!

'Arrey bhai, somebody make Our Pappu understand,' said Amma austerely as I struggled to achieve a finks-like face. 'We are such a senior politician. We have saken hands with Hilary Rodham Clinton. Why ij Our Pappu alwayj putting aawar name in these crude, immodest slogans?'

It was almost like he'd heard her, because there was the sound of a hard slap, a smothered curse and a whimpered protest. A whispered confabulation followed, and then the voices rose hoarsely in another slogan.

> *How should aawar leader be?*
> *Just like Sarojiniji!*

'Well, that's slightly better,' Amma sniffed. Then she covered her head with a random dupatta that clashed horribly with her dressing gown. 'Come,' she said resignedly.

We approached the gate warily, where Our Pappu was beaming at us, flushed, excited and visibly nervous. This was a pro-active initiative on his part and he was obviously worried that Amma might bite his head off and destroy his standing amongst his flock. He called out, in the same loud, fake voice, 'Jiji, maulvi saab has come to invite you for milad-un-nabi celebrations in Jummabagh.'

Amma smoothly switched on her gracious smile for the maulvi saab. I quickly switched on one of my own. The crowd regarded us with unblinking curiosity, peering through the bars in the gate.

Looking at Our Pappu's uncertain, grinning, shiny-with-sweat face, I felt a pang of fellow-feeling. Motioning the guard to open the gate, I smiled and said, 'Pappu, call everyone in, give them some tea.'

Immediately, Our Pappu puffed up self-importantly to about twice his size and started shouting bossily, 'Come in, come in, didn't you hear? Come in and take tea.'

Amma smiled serenely as the motley crowd trooped in, and did not so much as raise an eyebrow when a large black-horned billy goat wandered past, attached by a thick jute rope to a gangly teenaged boy in a white lace cap and a shiny white kurta.

'We want you to just touch the bakra once, jiji,' said the maulvi saab to Amma in impeccable Urdu. 'Then, when we feed him to the poor, your blessing will go to all the people in the area. And god will bless your granddaughter's candidature.'

'Haan haan… of course, kyun nahin!' said Amma. 'But pleaj sit down first. Arrey bhai, Sarojini, chai kahan hai?'

The maulvi saab sat down with rickety dignity on one of our moodha chairs, very careful with the creases of his achkan, and Amma sat down next to him. I had just opened the door to the passage to ask Joline Bai to bring the tea, saying smilingly to our guests, 'Tea is coming. Actually, the milk came just now, she must be boiling…' when a flash of gold streaked past me at lightning speed.

'Ponky – no!' I shouted, whirling around in panic, fearing the worst – that I would find the old maulvi saab's achkan branded with the Mark of Ponky – and sighed in relief when I saw the dapper gent still unmolested and uncrumpled, ensconced upon his moodha, chit-chatting with Amma in a statesman-like manner.

But then a busy clicking and a popping of flashbulbs alerted me to look elsewhere.

The bakra was loose.

And Ponky was chasing it, barking enthusiastically, huge tail wagging frantically.

They circled the lawn thrice, splashing through the sludgy duck pond, the bakra snorting and *maai-eh-eh-eh*-ing loudly. Ponky, in high spirits, leapt from here to there, lunging and retreating alternately.

Finally cornered, the bakra lowered his head and pawed the

ground. Ponky charged, the elegant little carved tea table we'd placed before Amma and the maulvi saab went flying – and then, there it was, at centre stage, a sight that was truly mind-expanding.

Ponky, tongue lolling, eyes glazed over, idiot grin in place, was atop the sacrificial billy goat, thrusting away inaccurately but busily in the general erogenous zone, while the entire Jummabagh delegation, a perspiring Pappu, ecstatic press people and an appalled Amma watched in unqualified horror.

'Didi, coffee?'

I shuddered inwardly at the thick, sickly beige cupful of bhainscafé staring me in the face. It was being offered by a skinny child of indeterminate sex, with a cheerful smile and neatly oiled and combed hair, at the milad-un-nabi celebration in Jummabagh.

'Arrey, why did you make coffee?' I protested. 'I would have had Pepsi like everyone else!'

'Nahin, didi!' beamed a large woman from behind the child, her frilly pink burqa framing a plump, friendly face. 'We have done poora-ka-poora homework! We know ki aap coffee like karti hain!'

I smiled weakly and took the cup. 'Thanks, buddy,' I said solemnly to the child, who sped away, giggling, obviously thinking I was some kind of big city joke.

I touched the cup to my lips, then put it down sneakily without taking a sip, hoping no one would notice. Fat chance. I was sitting bang in the centre of a huge open courtyard, surrounded by a crowd of – if one were to believe Our Pappu's claim – seventeen hundred prospective voters. I was perched on one end of a hideously carved bottle green velvet sofa, which, I had a nasty feeling, clashed horribly with my sky blue and orange sari. Elaborate strings of electric lights – pink, green, purple, yellow – *much* more elaborate than any I'd seen at Diwali, twinkled, whirled and dipped in complicated loops and series around me. There were laughing children, three rows deep, at my feet; very pretty children with delicate features, kohl-darkened eyes and shiny clothes. There were some babies too, hanging off burqa-clad hips or running around in squeaking shoes, bundled in the striped red-and-white knitted bonnets that babies wear, and sporting the inevitable runny noses. The men were seated a few feet away from my sofa, in a sea of green, blue, purple, all topped off by the same lacy white skullcaps. The maulvi saab, however, had taken an armchair right next to me. So had Our Pappu, who was beaming from ear to ear, relieved that the whole fracas with the bakra had ended without rioting or curfew or calling in the NSG. (The newspaper captions the next day had been bitingly wicked, though. And they had been *national*. The photographer who snapped the iconic shot went on to win some major awards for the picture later that year, with juries gushing about its honesty, the perfect capturing of the decisive moment, the open mouths of the onlookers, the consternation of Amma, the blush on the cheeks of the maulvi saab, the frank, crinkly-eyed, gap-toothed enjoyment of Jugatram, the virility of Ponky, the confusion of the bakra, and for the way in which the picture summed up the spirit of 'The Times of India'.)

Mindful of the watchful eye of the lady who'd organized the refreshments, I gritted my teeth and took a big gulp of the bhainscafé. Swallowing smilingly, I looked at the stage in front, wondering what the next act would be.

There had been a qawaali and a kathputhli puppet theatre

already, plus a magic show for the kids (during which one of my stumpy thick-stemmed gold earrings was swallowed by a small boy and then recovered from his stomach, after his arm had been worked up and down like the handle of a waterpump). Amma left after that, pleading old age and fatigue, but when I made to follow, she made big-big eyes at me and said that I *had* to stay for dinner. 'And eat a lot!' she'd hissed. 'Nahin toh maulvi saab ko bad feel hoga!'

So now, I had to stay on for the finale and the biryani and jalebis and be dropped home by Our Pappu, who would, as usual, pin me with his hypnotic eyes and repeat his fervent, suspicious sounding offer of doing *Anything! Anything! Whatever you wish! Just ask and see! Anything you desire!*

There was a roar of jeep engines and a slight commotion from behind us, and I turned and looked at the scrum of gas-balloon and ice-cream sellers outside the gaily decorated gate, wondering who the latecomers were. Maybe Amma had come back, I thought hopefully, and I wouldn't have to eat large quantities of food by myself.

But when I saw who had entered the courtyard and was being warmly embraced by the maulvi saab, first to the left shoulder and then to the right, even as he looked around admiringly and exclaimed appreciatively at the rocking intezaam, I almost dropped my bhainscafé.

Actually, I wish I *had* dropped it, all over the wretched sofa, because that would have made what happened next impossible. Which was that after embracing just about every man in the courtyard, and flashing a rakish grin at the giggling women, Zain Altaf Khan trod lithely up the aisle to the garish bottle green sofa and, after the briefest of hesitations, dropped himself down *right next to me*!

I pretended not to notice, and stared at the stage intently, as if the dudes who were clearing away the magic show props were putting on the most interesting act in the world.

Zain leaned back a little and a lean, muscular forearm, with a black thread tied tightly around the wrist, came into view. I shifted a little, picked up the printed programme that they had given me when we arrived, and pretended to read. But it was tough, especially since he was sitting the way he always sat – like he was waiting for someone (me! me!) to drop into his lap.

Rough velvet sounded caressingly in my ear. 'Um… that's *Urdu.*'

'I know,' I returned carelessly. 'Pretty, isn't it?'

'Oh?' He sounded amused. I could smell marigolds and attitude. 'So you're admiring the calligraphy? You once told me it looked like piles of rat droppings.'

I turned to face him. He was lounging back in the sofa, wearing faded jeans, the mandatory genda phool garland and a short white collarless kurta. A little white prayer cap was perched on his head. It was a sprawling, rather combative stance, rather in contrast to his disturbingly warm smile. I was hit again by how much taller and stronger and hotter he'd grown. Had he spent all these years drinking hormonally enhanced Horlicks?

'Well, I'm older now,' I told him witheringly, 'and I find that my tastes have changed. A *lot.*'

He looked at me. '*Really?*' he said, sounding deeply sceptical.

'Yes!' I glared at him, thinking it was disgraceful how the V-neck of his kurta left the golden skin at the base of his throat freely visible to all. Didn't he realize it was blatantly soliciting kisses? 'And can't you go sit somewhere else?' I added. 'This is stupid.'

He grinned. 'No way,' he countered. 'People might say I lost my seat to you.'

'Well, they'll be saying that soon enough, anyway,' I returned sweetly.

His eyes glittered but he didn't react, just accepted a chilled glass of Pepsi from the child who'd handed me my coffee earlier, and thanked him solemnly.

Meanwhile, I sat there, seething. What did he think he was doing, barging in on what was clearly *my* event? Okay, so it was a public celebration and everyone was invited, but he could've showed up a bit later or earlier. That was just good manners. Especially after he had been so dismissive of me on Nauzer's show and so nasty about poor Amma, who had always been really nice to him when he was little. So what if she dissed his community just a little behind the closed doors of her home? How could he sit next to me so calmly, and try and make me feel unwanted at an event where I was the chief guest? Why the hell didn't he just go home and cuddle his *mummy* Bittora?

I sat there, getting angrier and angrier, while the object of my indignation sipped his Pepsi and conversed courteously with the old men to his left.

After a while, a long row of children, all dressed in white, trotted onto the stage. They were followed by an old gent with a bright orange beard and a harmonium. Somebody adjusted the mikes, and they launched into a slow but soulful milad-un-nabi classic.

They sang well and were met with enthusiastic applause, but just as they got ready to file out afterwards, Zain leaned forward and called out in his deep, pleasant voice, without even a trace of Winchester marring his chaste Urdu, 'Will you sing one more song with me?'

The children nodded, wide-eyed.

He leapt up, strode lightly across the courtyard to the stage and commandeered the harmonium from the old man with the orange beard. He strapped it to himself and then, standing with his legs planted wide and his head thrown back, flashed that quick, infectious grin and flooded the courtyard with the jaunty, lively strains of 'Aao bachchon tumhe dikhaaen jhaanki hindustaan ki'.

Of course, it was disgustingly cheesy, but what else do you expect from a guy who calls his hometown his *mother*?

Still, I had to say this for him. The mood did change instantly.

And I'm pretty sure it wasn't just me, though I'm a total sucker for patriotic songs from the fifties. I start blubbering the moment small children raise their piping little voices and bravely lisp out any one of them, and this particular song is number one on my tear-jerker list. Sure enough, I could instantly feel the beginnings of ugly, nose-reddening, free-flowing, snotty bawling coming on. And no way would that go down well in Pavit Pradesh. People wouldn't go, *So sweet, she's so naram dil, she's crying.* They'd think, *Ufff, just look at that amateur loser, she'll never be tough enough to nail all the thugs, fundamentalists, rapists, murderers and vigilantes running amuck in this place. Better not vote for her, the weakling.*

But tonight, the ruff-and-tuff Bittora types seemed to be as sentimental as me. The kids sang away lustily and soon the mummy-jaans joined in. By the time we hit the first 'vande-mataram, vande-mataram', the singing had swelled to about a thousand throats, and the vibrations seemed to shake the ancient courtyard. The dipping and whirling series lights seemed to twinkle brighter and the very air seemed to pulsate with something I couldn't quite define, but which hung over us all, huge, hopeful and brimming with promise.

As Zain's deep, not-very tuneful voice led the singing into the third stanza, the lyrics of which nobody else seemed to know, Our Pappu sidled closer to me and hissed, 'This is *Indian Idol* or what? What cheap band-baajaa tack-tricks, Sarojini didi! He is trying to steal your thunder.'

'Don't worry, Pappu!' I replied, still clapping away. 'Just get me the mike before he finishes singing.'

He scurried off and managed to get hold of a hand-held mike... so that right after the song got over and everyone was standing around, looking all pumped up and teary, I spoke into the sudden hush that had fallen: 'Wah! What wonderful singing! Children, today, I, Sarojini Pande, granddaughter of sabki jiji Pushpa Pande, give five lakhs to your school building fund and promise to secure CBSE recognition for all the Muslim schools in Bittoragarh.'

There was a startled silence. Like something seriously out-of-syllabus had happened. But then a thunderous applause broke out in the courtyard and the maulvi saab came forward, took both my hands in his, squeezed them hard, and declared that I had his vote.

'Hey, you pretended in Delhi about your Urdu being bad!' I said, trying for a casual note.

We had been ushered into the 'VIP' area, a deserted shamiana of the most lurid colours possible. Huge plates of food sat before us. I picked up a flimsy white plastic fork, stared hopelessly at the mound of flourescent orange biryani on my plate, and resigned myself to losing this particular contest to Zain.

'I wanted to make you laugh,' he said shortly, picking out large sticks of cinnamon from his biryani and chucking them aside in a business-like manner.

I looked at him uneasily. His accent had gotten all clipped, the way it used to get whenever he got into one of those brooding moods I used to dread when I was a child.

But I wasn't a child any more.

I sat a little straighter and pointed an accusing fork at him.

'You're manipulative,' I said.

He flashed me a quick, derisive look.

'And you're not?' he enquired mildly, shovelling the rice into his face at a rate I could only admire. He swallowed, his eyes not even watering, and said, 'Is this how you're planning to win the election, by the way? By handing out large sums of money left, right and centre?'

'Well, you know, what to do,' I answered coolly. 'All of us don't sing as well as *you.*'

His lips tightened, but all he said as he pushed away his plate was, 'A word of advice. The EC goons taped you. They'll be after you if you go around making these donation announcements so publicly. Watch out.'

'And a word of advice to you too,' I returned, feeling slightly sick and clammy because I knew he was right. And also because the extremely spicy biryani on top of the bhainscafé was playing havoc with my system. 'I don't know if you picked the right song tonight. It may have a bit of a backlash. Lose you some votes. It was probably a bit too nationalistic for tonight's audience.'

He flicked a glance at me, his fork arrested halfway to his mouth.

'*Really,*' he said. 'And what would you even *begin* to know about tonight's audience?'

I shrugged. 'Oh, I know enough. I learnt everything I know right here in Bittoragarh.'

'At your grandmother's knee?' he returned. 'Give the Muslims money, they will give you votes? That totally figures.'

Oops. Touchy subject. But he was still talking.

'For your information,' he said, 'the people of Jummabagh will take the money you give them, but on polling day, they will go in there and vote for *me*.'

'In which case,' I said, banging down my glass, 'they will prove that they essentially are a treacherous race.'

The silence that followed was positively murderous.

A little unnerved, I said, 'Look, I find this idealistic we-are-all-one-big-Indian-nation attitude rather thick coming from someone who's standing on an IJP ticket.'

He slammed his glass down hard and said, his eyes blazing, 'And I find your cynicism revolting, considering it's coming from the nation's only so-called secular party.'

'Okay,' I said, my voice wobbling a little. 'Since I'm so *revolting*, I'll just say goodnight to you right now. Happy milad-un-nabi.'

'Oh, typical!' he said, throwing his hands up in exasperation, 'Let's take all this extremely personally, shall we?'

'And you're not being personal?' I shot back. 'Are you honestly going to claim that all this isn't happening because I locked you into a cupboard, what, *nine* years ago?'

His eyes shuttered over. 'Goodnight, *Saro*jini.'

'Goodnight, *Zain*!' I snapped back immediately.

'*Altaf Khan*,' I added for good measure.

Silence.

Neither of us made a move to leave.

'*Pande*,' he said after a pause.

A little snort of laughter escaped me.

He flashed me the quick, contrite grin I knew so well.

I grinned back.

He put a hand to his heart and staggered back into his red plastic chair. 'Whoa. Smile impact.'

He was doing it again. The just-kidding voice with the disturbingly serious look in his eyes. I looked uneasily around the hall.

'Look, Kaka Nagar,' he said peacably. 'I'm sorry I gate-crashed your party. It was stupid, but I just wanted to see you so badly.'

'Well, next time just *call*, okay?' I said primly as I stood up, desperately trying to pretend that the change in tone hadn't caused my heart to thud madly against my ribs. 'And it won't cost my campaign fund five lakhs. Now, good night.'

He looked up. 'Don't go,' he said simply. 'God knows when I'll get to meet you again.'

Which was so true that I sat down again, a depressing, leaden feeling settling into the pit of my stomach. Around us, the celebrations continued, people ate and drank, lurid qawaalis blared muddily from massive speakers.

Chehra chhipa liya hai kisi ne hijab mein
Ji karta hai aag laga du naqab mein...

Finally, I said, 'How can you possibly get along with all those sicko Hindutva types?'

His lean cheeks flushed. But all he said was, 'You've been in Canada far too long. The party's changed. It had no option but to change. And anyway, at least they aren't hypocrites. I abhor hypocrites.'

Stung by this snide reference to Amma and by his pompous

choice of words (I mean, *abhor*? Who the hell says *abhor*?), I said heatedly, 'You're just some stupid *kid*! Don't you *get* it? They're *using* you! They just want you to be their token Muslim boy in parliament. Surely you realize that?'

He shrugged. 'So? As long as I can bring progress to Bittora, I'm game. I'll make damn sure it's a mutually exploitative relationship, never fear.'

I shook my head. 'It's just so disorienting to see you in the IJP.'

His jaw tightened.

'Quit worrying about *me*,' he advised, 'and start worrying about your ex-party man, Dwivedi.'

'Oh, I know,' I said gloomily. 'He's standing as an indy just to shaft Amma. God, talk about harbouring a snake in your bosom!'

Zain set down his glass.

'Can we *please* not talk about your bosom?'

I blushed bright pink.

'Okay,' I said happily. 'Though it's quite something, huh?'

'Yes,' he agreed, sounding a little strangled. 'Yes, it's something all right.'

There was an awkward silence.

Then he asked, 'How's Saket Bhavan?'

'Huh? Oh, the same,' I said with a shrug. 'The lights keep tripping, and there's a *huuuge* beehive in the garden.'

His eyes lit up.

'I love that place,' he said. 'Are you staying in the old petal room, then?'

'Yes!' I laughed. 'And my campaign office is in Bauji's petal room.'

'Hey, wow,' he said and he really did sound impressed. 'That is *so* cool. Bauji's study was always out of bounds for us brats! Are those ducks still around?'

I frowned.

'I have no idea, actually,' I admitted. 'Maybe Ponky ate them.'

'A dog of peculiar but broad-minded tastes,' Zain remarked drily.

I giggled.

And almost inhaled a whining mosquito, which was *bhinnn bhinnaoing* right in front of my nose.

'There are tons of them circling over your head,' Zain said, raising one arm and waving it about graphically, as I blew my nose and spat. 'Moving in a giant, cyclonic formation. Bittorawallahs would say you'll have a very big wedding.'

I grabbed some yellow paper napkins from the table and waved them about vigorously above my head, hoping to scatter the swarm. 'God, I hate these bloody mossies,' I said fervently.

His face tightened, almost imperceptibly.

'Mosquitoes, I mean,' I said hastily.

At this inopportune moment, Our Pappu bounded in, all bright-eyed and smiley faced, obviously determined to get me out of this highly irregular tête-à-tête as fast as possible. He shook hands with Zain, and informed him in one well-constructed sentence that he was MLA-Jummabagh, a science graduate, a bachelor, an only son, a trained yoga instructor, from a business family, and totally at his service. Then he turned to me. 'Didi, let us go,' he said with sunny firmness. 'Early start tomorrow.'

'Of course, Pappu!' I replied. Then I turned back to Zain. 'Well, goodnight, then,' I said graciously. 'Nice meeting you.'

He nodded formally. 'Likewise,' he said, his expression unreadable.

I stood up, folded my hands into an elaborate namaste, and

made my way out of the function, a grinning, nodding Pappu scurrying in my wake.

—

Our Pappu was very tight-lipped the whole way home. I think he was trying to make some kind of point, but I didn't particularly care. I was too busy playing back my conversation with Zain in my head and wondering if there was any truth in what he'd said about the IJP not being as dreadful as I, brought up in a hard-core Praggu home, had always assumed it to be.

At least, that's what I was *trying* to focus my mind on. Unfortunately, it kept looping back to all the non-intellectual elements of our conversation – like how he'd said *Don't go* with that glowing look in his eyes and how sinewy his forearms had looked below his rolled-up sleeves. And how he apparently couldn't *bear* to talk about my bosom because it was so oomphy. Surely that meant I wasn't the only one constantly flashbacking to that night at the wedding, right? Right?

Of course, Amma managed to pull me out of this happy haze the moment I entered the front door. She was still awake, huddled with Gudia aunty in her bedroom, discussing the depleting levels of oxygen in the Milton hotcase.

I hurried to her room and told them about my evening as matter-of-factly as I could. She pursed her lips when she heard that Zain had showed up so soon after she left. 'Bhai, it ij obvious,' she declared. 'He can't face us. He doej not have the gurrts.'

Gudia aunty gave a low involuntary moan the moment she heard about my five lakh donation to the Jummabagh school, but Amma wasn't too hassled. 'Doejn't matter, Gudia,' she said. 'The fellow was being over-smart. Singing and all. Of course Sarojini had to give him a tit!'

'Excuse me?' I looked at her, dumbfounded. 'I had to give him a *what*?'

'A tit,' Amma repeated patiently. 'Arrey bhai, you had to give him a tit for his tat, no?'

With that, she heaved herself out of bed and walked into her loo.

Really, sometimes when I think that Amma has travelled all over the world and met Bill Clinton and Margaret Thatcher, my blood runs absolutely cold.

The sound of a mineral water bottle cap turning and the familiar reek of Absolut reminded me that Gudia aunty was still in the room, hyperventilating. According to her, our campaign was in danger of death by asphyxiation.

'We need more oxygen to buy out those two spoilers,' she fretted feverishly, as she bent down and placed the bottle back on the ground next to the bed. Her blouse fell away from her shoulder, and I caught a flash of light purple and did a double take. Was she wearing my *bra*? 'I've tried to catch hold of Mr Suleiman, but he's just not taking my calls. I think he's avoiding me.'

'Why would he do that?' I asked soothingly, even though I could think of at least seven good reasons, including the fact that he didn't want to be robbed of his underwear. 'He's the AIPC General Secretary for Pavit Pradesh! Surely he'd want Amma to win?'

Gudia aunty shook her head.

'Jinni, Tawny Suleiman may not be all that thrilled about a Pande dynasty taking root right here, so close to his own turf. You in Lok Sabha, madam most probably in the Rajya Sabha... Have you ever thought about *that*?'

'He's my grandmother's oldest friend and ally,' I reminded

her coldly, thinking, *and that's probably the reason you dislike him. You can't stand people being closer to Amma than you are.* Wow, was she complicated.

She looked at me with obvious dissatisfaction.

'Madam is right,' she said, 'you are just like your grandfather.'

I flushed. 'I'm very proud of my grandfather,' I retorted. 'In fact, I'm *proudest* of my grandfather.'

'Oye hoye!' Gudia aunty sniffed. 'Madam is fifty times the politician he was.'

'You never met him,' I pointed out. 'Besides, he wasn't a politician, he was a *freedom fighter.*'

'Oh, I know you think I'm just an outsider who knows nothing of your family ideals,' she said defensively, her voice trembling. 'But let's be *practical.* The fact remains that we need at least two more bursts of oxygen to see this campaign through. A big chunk now, to buy off the spoilers, and one more towards the end, for polling day. We'll need to give kits to workers in every booth across the constituency. Two hundred booths in all. Five workers per booth. They'll need food, money, T-shirts, petrol money for buses to ferry people to and fro, maybe even a little extra money to buy out voters on the day itself… so that's at least a thousand a day to each worker, *ideally* two thousand – that's twenty lakhs straight. Just for that one day.'

'Fuck,' I whispered, stumped.

'Also,' she continued, 'we should have money to buy alcohol, at least one bottle per voter, and distribute it on the eve of voting day.'

'But if people get drunk they'll be too hungover to come and vote!' I pointed out.

Gudia aunty's smirk got smirkier. 'So we distribute the alcohol, not amongst our supporters, but amongst *IJP* supporters,' she said. 'By the time they stagger in to vote, somebody else will have already voted for them.'

'*Booth* capturing?' I asked, round-eyed.

She looked at me impatiently. 'Of course not,' she said mildly. 'Why would you say that?'

'Doesn't *anybody* out here vote without asking for money?' I asked, almost desperately.

Gudia aunty thought about it. 'Well, they do in Sujanpur,' she offered finally. 'We always sweep in Sujanpur.'

'Because of the good work Amma's done?' I asked hopefully.

'That *also*,' she replied evasively, 'but it's mostly because they all think Top Brass's mummy is a goddess. They think ki if they don't vote for Pragati it won't rain and their crops will fail and they will all die. So they vote.'

Served me right for asking.

'But there's no need to panic,' Gudia aunty muttered, more to herself than to me, as she glugged from her bottle of Himalayan and wiped her mouth. 'I mean, we've been *promised* a lot of oxygen. It's just that it isn't here yet. It's a question of liquidity. We are in dire need of *liquid* oxygen.'

I couldn't resist saying, in a nasal Ajit-the-gangster voice, 'Liquid hume jeene nahin dega, oxygen hume marne nahin dega.'

'Exactly,' she said in a preoccupied voice. 'After your donation tonight, I have only three lakhs left, Jinni.'

'We've spent thirty-seven?' I exclaimed. 'In what, four days? How? On what? Isn't the EC limit twenty-five lakhs?'

Amma returned from the loo, just in time to deliver her favourite admonition, which was, of course, 'Don't be Nave, Sarojini.'

Gudia aunty drew herself up.

'If you are suggesting,' she said stiffly, 'that there is some hanky-panky going on in the accounting…'

'No, no!' I said hastily. 'Of course not.'

'God has not given me much,' she continued inexorably, 'but He has given me Integrity.'

'Yes!' I said. 'I know. *We* know! Amma, it's all Tawny uncle's fault, isn't it? *He's* the weak link here!'

Amma grunted. 'Tawny did warn us that he won't be able to do too much for us,' she said. 'Besides, he must be sending extra funds to hij son Titu in Tiloni. Can't blame him, we would do the same.'

Oh, so the Rapist *had* managed to get a ticket then. Good for him. Hopefully, his father, being an AIPC General Secretary and all, had got him a constituency from where he actually had a chance of winning. Unlike me.

'Anyway, we will be meeting Tawny at the Numaish ka mela tomorrow. We will prejent a status report and explain how, if we are given funds to buy out Dwivedi and Vir Singh, we can actually win. That ij really all we can do.'

And with that, Amma reached for Gudia aunty's bottle of mineral water and took a deep, morose swig.

7

I had a throbbing headache. My right eye had developed a nervous tic. My hands were itching to close around a certain scrawny neck and squeeze. I stared at the Normal Public School English reader on the desk, open to Chapter Number One, and took several deep breaths. The name of the chapter was printed at the top of the page in big, bold, black letters.

RULES FOR READING

Rajul wrinkled his nose for what felt like eternity, a vague faraway look in his eyes. He made circles in the dust with one grimy pointed toe and finally said, with agonizing slowness, 'Aaaar?'

'Yes!' I said, almost weeping with relief. 'Yes! It's R! Now, what's after the R? What is it? *What is it?*'

Rajul, who had brightened up a little, immediately looked hunted again. He hunched over his English reader, small whistling voices emitting sporadically from his lips. 'Ya... ya... yooooo?'

My eyes misted over with joy. I beamed at him, thrilled beyond belief. 'Yes, Rajul!' I said, sniffing and blinking back sudden, stupid tears. 'Yes. It's U! Well done!'

He grinned proudly. 'Can I go now?' he asked.

My tears dried up immediately. I grabbed him by the collar

of his shirt. 'You're not going *anywhere*,' I grated. 'Now join the two sounds together. R plus U. What noise is that?'

He looked around shiftily. '*Aaar… Yoo?*' he said, sounding hopeful. '*Aar* plus *Yoo* is *Aaryoo?*'

I shook my head patiently. 'No, baba, think a little! We have done this many *many* times. Fine, I'll help you, okay?'

'Okay, okay.' He nodded obligingly, hunching over his reader again.

'*Bee* plus *Yoo* is *Boo*,' I said. '*Em* plus *Yoo* is *Moo*. So what is *Aar* plus *Yoo?*'

Something seemed to click in Rajul's light-grey eyes. They brightened. His little chest puffed up. He raised one chubby, assured arm up in the air. He grinned.

'*Aaryoo?*' he said.

I banged both fists on the table between us and shouted like a madwoman. 'No, Rajul! R plus U is *not Aaryoo*. It's *Roo*! *ROOO! ROOO!*'

His face crumpled. He cringed and started to emit a low snivelling sound.

'Oh god, don't *cry*,' I groaned.

He shot me an injured look, grabbed his notebook and ran into the garden, leaving his sandals behind, his snivels getting progressively louder the farther he got from me.

'Come backkk!' I yelled. 'Sorry! Let's start over!'

He ignored me at first, but when he crossed the green gate and reached the safety of MM Pande Road, he wheeled around and bellowed: 'I'm going to tell EVERYBODY in Begumbagh that you TORTURE me! That you GOUGED out my EYES! That you BROKE my BACK! NOBODY WILL VOTE FOR YOU!'

'*What?*' I gasped, bounding up from my chair.

He gave a little yelp when he saw me rise, and scurried down the slumbering street, yelling shrilly and waving his arms about. 'DON'T vote for her! DON'T vote for her!'

'Fine!' I yelled back dementedly from the gate, my hair in my eyes, as I hurled his forgotten sandals at him, one after the other. '*Don't* vote for me! See if I care!'

'Err... Pandeji?'

I spun around and saw Nulwallah looking at me quizzically.

'Shit.'

'Yeah, whatever.' He grinned and draped his lanky body against the green gate comfortably. 'Nice campaigning style. Very... *different*. Hey, Ponky! Dude, you're a star!'

This, because Ponky had rushed up noisily, planted his front paws against the gate and hauled himself up to grin gormlessly at Nulwallah through the spear-tipped bars at the top of the gate.

Nulwallah reached for the soft spot between Ponky's eyebrows and scratched. Ponky's large golden body quivered and he let out weird, squeaky moans of delight.

'So will you be dropping in at the Numaish ka mela today?' Nulwallah asked as he scratched.

I looked up, a little surprised he knew my schedule. But then, maybe it was just an educated guess. Because the Numaish ka mela is a Big Deal in Bittora. It's a crazy one-month-long excercise in hedonism that starts a few weeks after Holi. It began more than four centuries ago as a cattle fair, but it has mutated over time into a massive Woodstock-like gig, PP-style of course – very hot and dusty, packed with smelly animals and people dressed in wedding finery, all running around and 'enjoying' with the single-minded intensity of traders at the Bombay Stock Exchange.

'Yes, I *am* going, but just as a regular person,' I was careful to clarify. 'I won't be campaigning there.'

'Of course not,' he grinned. 'That would be against the law.'

'Yes,' I said demurely. 'And I have great respect for the law.'

'Like you showed at the milad-un-nabi celebration last night?' he said knowingly. 'The IJP has filed a complaint with the election commission because you used a religious occasion to push your agenda, by the way.'

'I am aware of that,' I replied coolly, a sinking feeling gripping my innards. I was aware of no such thing. Obviously, my so-called childhood friend had struck like a snake last night, while I'd been hugging my pillow, dreaming about his stormy eyes. More fool I. 'It's a baseless accusation, of course.'

Nulwallah nodded.

'I'm just going because I have great childhood memories of the mela,' I told him. 'Taking the day off, you could say.'

He raised his eyebrows. 'Confident,' he remarked. Then he cracked his usual demented grin. 'Well, see you there!'

Which sounded pretty non-combative. For Nulwallah, that is. Still, there was no way I would've confessed to him that I had *no* great childhood memories of the Numaish ka mela. I like my melas during Diwali or in early winter, when the weather is deliciously cool – not in April-May, when everything is sticky and stinky and sweaty. Besides, I defy anyone with breasts – male or female – to visit the Numaish and emerge unmolested. The place is packed with frantic gropers, out to pinch, probe or bite every fleshy body part within reach.

Amma and I were going to the mela to be seen and heard, of course. Over seven thousand people visited it every day, it would be silly to miss such a huge captive audience. We couldn't *campaign* there obviously, but we could smile and be charming, and give some small sum of money to the organizers. More importantly, we were hoping to close in on Tawny Suleiman and talk to him about our rapidly depleting liquid oxygen stores. Tawny uncle was the chief guest at the Bittora Annual Wrestling Day, a big event at the mela, and Rocket Singh had promised Amma that she would be seated next to him, so they could have a frank, open discussion without worrying about their phones being bugged or whatever.

A couple of hours later, we drove up to Gate No. 3, the one closest to the wrestling enclosure and, with one eye on the black EC Maruti Gypsy trailing us, humbly bought tickets like regular people. After an elaborate frisking which we underwent graciously, we walked in and proceeded to look all surprised and embarrassed as an announcement blared from the Ahuja loudspeakers stuck on wooden poles all over the four-square kilometre area.

'Ladies and gentlemen! Please welcome into our humble midst, our sister, no, our *mother*, national leader and three-time MP from Bittora, ex-MP Shrimati Pushpa Pande jiji! And her granddaughter, Pragati Party candidate from Bittora, Kumari Sarojini Pandeji!'

We folded our hands above our heads in humble greeting as, bang on cue, bare-chested tribal dancers appeared out of nowhere, beating their drums deafeningly. Pretty women in tricolour saris sashayed up and placed the inevitable thousand-rupee garlands around our necks. Finally, a bunch of oily men walked up coyly, hands folded, with Rocket Singh at their head, smiling constipatedly. He was dressed for the occasion in a bright red tracksuit and was wearing all three of his Asian Games medals. They clinked majestically as he walked, the sound reminiscent of the buffalo bells I heard outside my window every morning. He held up one hand, and the drumming stopped instantly.

'Jiji!' he said dramatically, diving at Amma's feet.

She strategically let him grovel there for a bit before stretching out a hand to lift him up. She placed a hand on his head to bless him, and he indicated the hordes behind him. 'Organizing committee, jiji,' he informed her.

The head of the organizing committee thrust himself forward and told us, in ringing accents, that we had to patronize every one of the thousand stalls at the mela, buy whatever we liked and pay for none of it.

'Thanks so much!' Gudia aunty said breathlessly. 'I'll just-now start...'

But the invitation turned out to be purely rhetorical. Because, right at that moment, Rocket Singh gestured, the tribal dancers restarted their defeaning drumming, and Amma raced ahead, hands held in a namaste over her head. She sped through long lines of seated spectators to the podium in the centre, smiling and nodding, her pallu fluttering like a banner behind her. Everybody jumped to their feet as she passed and then sank down again in a blissful *omg-I-saw-Pushpa-Pande-now-I-can-die-happy* swoon, so that she ended up creating a huge Mexican wave in her wake.

Tawny Suleiman sat on the podium, behind a long white table, looking sleek but cornered. His three moustaches (*You always know what I mean, Jinni*, I remembered with a pang) were drooping in the sweltering heat.

'Tawny!' said Amma loudly, flashing her gap-toothed grin. 'We are *so* happy to see you!'

Looking infinitely unhappy, Tawny said resignedly that he was ecstatic to see Amma too.

She sat next to him, bent her head and began a whispered conversation.

I turned to Rocket Singh.

'What's the next event?' I asked him, peering down at the mud-floor circular wrestling ring below us. The whole scene had a vaguely gladiatorial feel.

The ring was huge, and empty for now, cordoned off by thick jute ropes. Beyond the ropes milled a massive crowd – among them Gudia aunty, looking distinctly disgruntled because, on top of being done out of a complimentary shopping spree, she hadn't been invited to sit on the dais with Amma. I smiled down at her, hoping meanly that the gropers in the crowd would be unable to resist the lure of her bulbous posterior.

'This is the free-style final!' shouted Rocket Singh, his mud-coloured, bubblewrap textured skin gleaming in the sun. There was a huge roar from the crowd below. I looked down and saw a smooth, hairless, spectacular specimen of manhood striding into the ring, clad in a red chaddi, festooned with a golden rocket over the crotch.

'My best boy,' whispered Rocket Singh. 'You'll not believe it – I used to look *exactly* like that when I won the Asiad in '82.'

'He looks very... uh... well-developed,' I said faintly as Red Underwear slapped his humongous thighs, causing them to ripple impressively in the bright sunshine. He also let out aggressive cries of *Ghheeeaaah! Ghheeeaaaah!* and flashed large tombstone-like teeth.

Another roar rose from the crowd as a guy in black underwear strode into the ring from the other side. He was bigger, brawnier and hairier than Red Underwear. There was a huge, droopy-eyed python wrapped around his cliff-like shoulders. It was not a pretty sight.

'He is from the Purana Bittora akhada,' Rocket Singh bellowed above the roar of the crowd, little bits of saunf flying out of his mouth and peppering the lobe of my ear. 'Altaf Khan's area.'

'He looks pretty mean,' I yelled back.

Rocket Singh grunted dismissively, 'Andar se phat rahi hogi. Such WWE stunts means he is actually feeling scared inside. You just wait and see.'

Black Underwear strutted around the ring, stroking his python, waggling his tongue and hissing threats at Red Underwear, who responded by yawning deliberately and cleaning the inside of his ear with his pinky finger. Finally, Black Underwear handed his snake to a sidekick and the referee, attired in a Kolkata Knight Riders T-shirt, blew his whistle. The two lunged at each other instantly. Black Underwear wrapped both arms around Red Underwear in a crushing bear hug, while Red Underwear grabbed Black Underwear's neck and rotated firmly in an anti-clockwise direction.

'Go, Red!' I shrieked out of solidarity with Rocket Singh, who smiled in a gentle I'm-too-buzurg-to-take-sides manner.

They stood locked thus for a while, Black Underwear's grip getting tigher and tighter while his face got redder and redder. Then suddenly, the referee blew his whistle and the two disengaged. As the roaring of the crowd died down, I realized that somebody was talking into my ear.

'I've been trying to explain to your stubborn grandmother, but she is just not listening,' Tawny uncle was whispering loudly. 'The party is reluctant to sanction you more funds. They are asking why to throw good money after bad?'

My heart sank.

'Never mind the party, what do *you* think?' I whispered back fiercely.

He spread out his hands helplessly. 'Arrey dear, who am I? I have to do what I'm told. All local reports – you know I don't trust the surveys – clearly say that IJP has the upper hand. Khan's chances of winning are ninety per cent. My advice to you, frankly…' He turned to look me in the eye.

'Yes?' I asked, squaring my shoulders.

He blew out his cheeks, making first one pop out, then the other. Then he shook his head and pursed his lips. 'My advice to you is to quit,' he said. 'The IJP has made this seat a prestige issue. They are spending money like water.'

Down in the ring, Black Underwear, displeased with the referee's alleged preference for Red Undie, had grabbed him by the scruff of his Knight Riders T-shirt and was shaking him violently. The referee was screaming, his limbs fluttering about like prayer flags in a high Himalayan wind.

I knew exactly how he felt.

'I'll never quit,' I said vehemently, my voice trembling. 'And if the hawa is so anti-Pragati, whyn't you get Tits to withdraw from Tiloni, huh?'

'Titu is not facing a tough candidate. *You* are,' said Tawny uncle gently. 'Jinni, you are like my daughter, so I am telling you – don't make this an ego issue.'

'Why?' I demanded.

He blew out his cheeks again, contemplatively, turn by turn. *Pop* swelled up one, *pop* swelled up the other. He swung the air from cheek to cheek, *pop pop pop pop*. Then he exhaled gustily.

'My dear, I know you are very idealistic, that you want to contribute. So why don't you help my Titu, hain? Together, you will be unbeatable.'

I blinked. 'What?' I said blankly.

He leaned closer to me. 'Let me announce your engagement,'

he said eagerly. 'People will love it! Then you and he can *both* campaign from Tiloni. Let Bittora be.'

'So Titu's in love with me?' I said in disbelief, my head spinning.

Tawny uncle looked a little shifty. 'Oh, yes,' he said.

I snorted. 'I don't believe you.'

'Well, he thinks you are nice. That's a start. And *I* think ki you are *too* cute,' he said loyally.

I couldn't help laughing. 'Uncle, that's neither here nor there!'

His eyes twinkled, but just for a moment. Then he sighed, lowered his voice and said, 'Arrey Jinni, try to understand. Your seat is hopeless. If you withdraw, nobody in the party will hold it against you. Especially if you convince *her*,' he nodded exasperatedly at Amma, 'to fake a heart attack. And in Tiloni, you could help Titu score the Brahmin votes.'

I looked at him. He'd always given me good advice. Looked out for me. Gotten me my first cell-phone. Talked Ma into letting me do animation.

'Tawny uncle,' I said, taking both his hands in mine, 'you're seriously telling me to *quit*?'

He looked at me. 'Yes.'

'In fact—' he began and stopped.

'What?'

He shrugged. 'It could even be *profitable* for you to do so.'

I stared at him, stunned. What was he suggesting?

He smiled, stroking his third moustache, the one above his right eye, with his index finger. 'You have well-wishers *everywhere,* dear,' he said meaningfully. 'Even in the IJP camp. They will look after your financial interests if you withdraw. Think about it.'

Oh.

Like *that*.

Down in the ring, Red Underwear had just shoved a hand straight at Black Undie's crotch. And was now proceeding to squeeze as hard as he could, his face frozen in a wide, toothy rictus of unadulterated pleasure. Black Undie howled in impotent rage, hopping about, slapping Red Undie on the head to no avail.

'Surely that's unfair?' I leaned over and shook Rocket Singh, who was dozing gently in the heat. 'It's against the rules. He can't do that!'

Rocket Singh shrugged. 'He should have thought of that before beating up the referee. Now the referee will take a nice long time before blowing the whistle.'

'Still…' I muttered. 'Rules are rules, right?'

'It is free-style wrestling.' Rocket Singh winked at me. 'No holds barred. No rule-shool. Anything goes.'

Hmm. I looked at the ring, mulling over what Tawny uncle had just said. Maybe it was time I tried a little free-style too…

'You look like you are *marrying* the wrestler in the red chaddi, Sarojini,' Amma said in disgust over the early morning papers the next day, as she sucked on a kalmi mango. 'Why are you putting a garland around his neck?'

I looked up.

'I'm awarding him a medal,' I said. 'You *know* that, Amma, you were there.'

She sniffed and turned a page.

'See, here is the pilla's photo, cutting a ribbon at a computer centre in Durguja,' she pointed. 'Which candidate would *you* vote for, hain?' The one marrying a naked man or the one inaugurating an internet café?'

'Amma,' I said, rolling my eyes. 'Chill, okay?'

She'd been spoiling for a fight ever since her chat with Tawny. Luckily, some old associate of hers, who owed her for god-alone-knows-what favour, had sent us a decent chunk of money. Gudia aunty had driven to Shortcut's place and picked it up last night.

We were splitting forces today. I was headed for the deep dark interiors of rural Bittora, with Munni and Rocket Singh for company. Amma, who'd been looking rather wan, was staying behind to work the urban areas on my behalf. Gudia aunty was staying put in Begumbagh too, because the district commissioner's office was here and, as election agent, she had to visit it every two days with all our fudged expense accounts. According to her official accounts, we'd spent a modest seven lakhs in campaigning so far. In reality, we had spent over seventy. I tried not to think about it – it gave me nightmares.

'We don't know what you will do there without us to watch over you,' Amma muttered direly as she threw aside one efficiently sucked mango heart and started on another. 'Start some scandal or get yourself disqualified.'

'I'll be fine!' I told her bracingly, feeling a little guilty about how bubbly I was feeling. It had gotten too claustrophobic in Saket Bhavan. 'Don't worry, Amma!'

It was a two-hour journey by train. We boarded at six, and we would reach by eight, in time for a long day of campaigning. It was faster than travelling by the roads – which were particularly disastrous in these areas. The train moved at a good clip and I peered out the murky AC window as well as I could, trying not to slosh my tea about. The jungle outside seemed beautiful.

'Durguja has some of the lushest jungles in north India,' Rocket Singh told me proudly. 'The tribals here guard their forest like tigers. If you do poaching here, they pick you up by your navel with an iron hook, yeh… *aisey*,' he raised his bush shirt, hooked his finger into his flabby brown belly button and demonstrated graphically while Munni winced, 'then they shave your head with a knife and leave you hanging upside-down from the trees.'

'Wow,' I said, 'they sound really fierce.'

Rocket Singh shook his head. 'No no… they are very gentle people. They go to church every Sunday. And they sing so soothingly, like angels.'

The jungle passed only too quickly, and soon gave way to flat farmland. Munni fell asleep, her little pink mouth wide open, and when Rocket Singh got up to go to the loo, I stretched out my legs in the space he had vacated, leaned back and anticipated a glorious sunrise. Peering out, I realized the sun would rise from the other side, so I got up and went to the corridor. But suddenly, and with no station in sight, the train started slowing down.

Wondering what was up, I knelt down to window level and flattened my nose against the dingy tinted glass.

And saw a surreal sight.

There was a little army of people outside, swathed in grey blankets and white dhotis, carrying empty pista green and dirty pink plastic buckets, glass bottles and aluminium vessels.

As the train slowed to an almost halt, they leapt onto it gracefully. Six of them entered our bogie, three from either side. They didn't enter the corridor but headed purposefully for the loos instead.

Wondering what exactly was going on, I made my way to the loos closer to our bogie, the ones into which Rocket Singh would have gone.

It was quite dark in the corridor, a blue light burned overhead, and the waiter who'd brought our tea was fast asleep, curled up with his face to the wall, in the little alcove before the loos. I stepped past him, opened the door into the loo area near the doors and smiled uncertainly at the mustachioed men-with-buckets. None of them smiled back, but one of them did raise an imperious arm, as if asking me to wait my turn. So I waited.

I then realized that they were doing the strangest thing. They were standing in the Western-style loo and *filling their plastic buckets with water from the train taps.*

As I watched, open-mouthed, they filled one, two, four, *seven* buckets, three two-litre plastic Pepsi bottles and a small black Sintex tank. All this, while the train moved along, really slowly, never stopping completely, but so slow that I saw a herd of cows overtake it from the left.

When the taps started to cough and splutter, and all that came out of them was a dry hissing sound, the three dudes picked up their loaded containers and leapt smoothly off the train, barely spilling any water in the process. I saw more of them emerge from every door of the train, all lugging filled baltis and bartans, moving quickly and economically, and with the ease of long practice.

They melted away into the high jungle grass that lined the tracks on both sides, even as the sun came bursting out, a cheerful ball of red in a sky the colour of turmeric.

And then Rocket Singh's aggravated voice floated out from the Indian-style loo.

'Abbey, who finished the water, behencho—?'

We reached Doodhiya station around eight. There'd been total mayhem on the train when everybody woke up and discovered that the tankis on the train had been drained dry. People wandered about, toothbrush in mouth, constipated expressions on their faces. Especially the people who were going all the way to Delhi – they were truly, literally, up shit creek.When we got off the train, the loos (and even the bogies) had started to stink.

We disembarked to the cheers of a thousand-member reception committee, all shouting Pragati Party slogans with full gusto, and were ushered into the ubiquitous Tata Sumos. I looked closely at the people who'd come to pick us up, but they all looked well-washed, not at all like they had been languishing for water for weeks. Maybe they bathed in water purloined from trains too.

'How's the mood?' I asked Munni, peering nervously through the banners draped over the windshields. Suddenly, my cockiness had drained away and I was feeling very lost without Amma.

She beamed, her big cheeks glowing bright. 'Super, didi! Super!' she said heartily.

I looked at her, irritated. What was with the constant Super Didi thing? Now I was what, Wonder Woman?

'Munni,' I snapped. 'Tell me the truth.'

She wrapped her dupatta vigorously round and round her neck, avoided my eyes, and said glibly, 'We have distributed a thousand EVM mockups to the workers. They are taking them everywhere, explaining them to the people.'

I frowned.

'But shouldn't we talk to them about all the other THID things? The ones Mr Urvashi said are a big issue here? Like thirst and healthcare?'

She nodded vaguely. 'Of course, didi. You have to promise them water and public health systems. But more importantly, you have to explain how the EVM works – this is the area where the rumour has spread that the EVM takes your photograph. The IJP workers have told the people that if they don't vote for Zain bhai then he will come to know and burn their houses. The people are completely convinced of it. What to do?'

Like I had the faintest idea. I knew how tough these rumours were to shake off once they started. We could take apart the EVMs and show the dour Doodhiya dudes there was no camera till we were blue in the face, and they still wouldn't believe us. They were positively ox-like. Amma would say it was the lack of iodine in their diet.

'We'll think of something,' I said inadequately. 'And Munni, tell me, how come things are so bad here that people are stealing water from trains?'

She looked at me in frank bewilderment.

'This is not a fact-finding mission, didi,' she said. 'Never mind *why* they don't have water. Just *promise* them water. And doctors.'

Just then the Sumo stopped and, armed with this bit of advice, I rose to my feet to be welcomed into the 'low caste' Ambedkar colony for an informal breakfast meeting. The entire village had turned out to meet me. There were people sitting everywhere, in the courtyard, on top of the courtyard walls, in a tractor trolley parked nearby; all looking at me and my outgrowing half-blown rosebud cut with big-big eyes. Big mommy buffaloes, tethered to the walls, chewed cud impassively. Three little kids with black threads tied around distended bellies, one of whom was picking at a pus-encrusted purple sty in his left eye, were seated in front of me. Everybody had these large fake smiles pasted on their faces as two small giggling girls ran up to me and handed me a big, tight posy of desi gulab framed in a fan of mango leaves while a gaggle of eleven-year-old boys, out to prove that their village school teacher was no slacker, sang 'Twinkle Twinkle Little Star' to welcome me.

'Namaste,' I said, smiling as I flashed the Pragati Party finger symbol. The kids pointed back good-naturedly. 'Helllllo!' they chorused. Except for one little girl who was squatting in the mud, painstakingly sticking on tiny, shiny red 'Finger' stickers to each of her fingernails. She wiggled her fingers so that they glittered in the light and smiled in delight.

I fiddled with my rose bouquet, sat down on a folding aluminium chair, beamed at everyone, took a deep breath and said, without preamble, in my rather crappy Pavit Pradeshi: 'You guys have heard right. There *is* a camera inside the EVMs.'

There was a stunned silence, and a small choking sound from behind me – probably Munni, strangling on her own dupatta.

And then everybody started talking at once.

They were so glad I was telling the truth! They weren't fools, you know, they understood today's modern techonologies! There was a 'chip', they said knowledgeably. It recorded everything!

I nodded and inhaled my roses as everybody around chattered away, and then held out my hand for a plastic EVM mockup. Munni handed it to me with trembling hands. I bet she didn't think everything was super-didi-super now.

'Wanna know where the camera is?' I asked the crowd. They nodded, all agog.

I held up the mockup, drawing out the silence for as long as I could. Then I pointed dramatically at a little black hole in the top left hand corner of the EVM. 'There!' I announced. 'The camera is there!'

Major sensation!

That's exactly where they had thought it would be! The angle was perfect, the camera would capture the face of the voter and also which particular button he or she was pressing! It was a marvellous mechanism! And the photos would go directly into the air – via *Blue Truth*, they informed me knowledgeably – right onto Zain bhai's TV screen in the Fort. So now they hoped I would understand why it was impossible of them to vote for me and that there were no hard feelings, right?

But I shook my head. 'This is not about whether you vote for me or not,' I said loftily. 'This is about your *freedom*, under the Indian constitution, to exercise your right to vote safely and anonymously.'

They all looked a little wary at this.

'See, it's very simple,' I told them. 'All you have to do when you go in to vote is lift your thumb and place it firmly *like this*, right over the little black hole. That way you cover the camera, see? The picture will come all dark-dark. And then just press the button – on whatever symbol you like – with your other hand!'

Everybody mulled over this. Munni handed out more EVM mockups and some of the people tried to practise the manoeuvre, covering the little black hole in the top left hand corner (god only knows what it was) and pressing on a symbol (the Finger, mostly, I noted with a quickening heart) with the index finger of their right hand.

Finally, a few of them started nodding. 'Haan,' they said, 'camera mein picture black aayegi. Blue Truth will send back a black picture only!' People started grinning and slapping their hands on their thighs. Munni, sensing the change in mood, instantly started explaining the how-to-cover-the-camera manoeuvre to the slowpokes in the back who hadn't caught on as yet.

I grinned around happily. A lot of people grinned back – not so fixedly this time, I thought. 'Now tell me,' I asked, finally finding the gumption to get off the aluminum chair and sit cross-legged on the floor with the ladies in the front row. 'What exactly is the cause of the water problem here?'

'Jin?'

It was 11:16 p.m. The chat box on my Facebook page had popped up with a little *boinnng* sound. Frenemy Altaf Khan wanted to chat online with me.

I stared at it in horrid fascination, then finally typed out: *'What?'*

'I dig your pic with the naked wrestler. Very sexy.'

I gave a little snort of laughter and typed back: *'And I don't dig your snaky move, complaining about me to the EC goons.'*

'Nothing personal,' came the glib reply. *'Where are you?'*

'Where are you?' I asked right back.

'Very close by,' he replied. *'At Bunty's. Listen, stop stalking my Facebook account.'*

'Excuse me?' I wrote, puzzled.

'Yeah...' he wrote back. *'I've got a Visitor Monitoring Program installed, and it reveals that you've visited my homepage sixteen times since day before yesterday. You're constantly, stealthily browsing through my pictures and my posts. It's creepy. Stop it.'*

For one sinking moment I thought it was true. That he really *knew*. How long I had stared at that picture of him laughing as he leaned against the sun-dappled wall in his grey school sweater. Or the one in which he looked all preppie and cool.

And then the other one in the black achkan with his hair all slicked back. But then I figured he was bluffing. I mean, no way. He couldn't possibly know. There was no such software.

'*You stop stalking ME!*' I blustered back aggressively. '*I've got the Visitor Monitoring thingie too, and it reveals that you're ALWAYS on my home page, composing pathetic, needy messages on my wall and then quickly deleting them without posting.*'

'*Bullshit,*' he wrote. '*You're lying.*'

'*YOU'RE lying,*' I retorted.

'*Well, yes. I'm lying in bed. And you're lying in bed too, aren't you, Jinni?*'

My mind and my body split cleanly into two. I rolled over on my stomach and watched as my fingers typed back an answer dreamily.

'*Yes, I'm in bed. Are you still wearing that nice white kurta?*'

But he was obviously not in the mood to answer questions.

'*So, technically, we're lying in bed... together.*'

My mouth went dry.

I slowly typed back: '*Technically... yes.*'

A very long pause followed.

The 'Zain is typing' message started flashing and I stared at it like someone hypnotized.

Finally,

'*You feel soft. And... buttery. And you smell like roses. And you're begging to be kissed. Shall I kiss you, Jinni?*'

I gazed stupidly at the screen, a moronic smile on my face. Then gave a sudden start of horror, pulled my fingers away from the keyboard like they'd been burned and slammed the laptop shut.

I really didn't know what was happening to me. At one level, I was campaigning through the FUCT and THID areas, promising water, jobs and healthcare to the common man. At another, I was in a permanent state of hyper-awareness, constantly hoping to hear the *khatakhatakhata* of the blades of Zain's low-flying chopper.

I've turned into Jaya Bachchan in *K3G*, I thought, disgusted with myself. The way she quivered and got major shivers of anticipation at the very *sound* of Shah Rukh's helicopter…

No way could I deny that I was a hopeless, seething mass of frenemy alerts and pheromones. Which was not only loser-like but also supremely shallow. Seriously, what kind of a sicko was I, wandering through the homes of malnourished and suffering people in a state of continuous, feverish lust?

Munni and Rocket Singh didn't seem to notice anything amiss, though.

Rocket Singh reported that Zain's workers had come round to Doodhiya again, still talking about the camera in the EVMs. The canny villagers had apparently nodded and promised their vote to Zain bhai, all the while slyly laughing up their sleeve about how they were going to block the camera with their thumb.

We'd got Gudia aunty to lodge a complaint with the election commission about Zain's helicopter, saying it was violating both air traffic control and the twenty-five lakh budget constraint, but it hadn't worked. Apparently, they had all the permissions in place, and it was a personal chopper, belonging to his buddy Bunty's steel company, and he was letting Zain use it free of charge.

'But didi, statistics of helicopters crashing during political campaigning is very high,' Munni said encouragingly. 'Let us hope for the best…'

And then there were all these pictures which kept coming out in the local paper, of Zain emerging from the chopper, looking like some kind of concerned, idealistic rock star in his dark glasses, white kurta and sleeveless bomber jacket. He definitely looked the part of new-age politician much more than me, who was always being photographed with snotty children, swathed in an amateurishly tied crumpled sari, all mouth and Half-Mad Full-Crack haircut. He looked powerful and 'swayve' and like he could get things done. I looked, well, *Nave*.

Nave versus Swayve, I kept thinking all the time. Any bets on who would win this thing?

I remembered how I'd said *they'll be saying I stole your seat soon enough, anyway* to him that night in Jummabagh, and how patronizingly he'd smiled at me, and the blood rushed to my cheeks, hot and angry. He was trying to play me for a loser, I thought, distracting me with all that guff about how *buttery* I was. Well, I was *not* going to let anything shift my focus away from rocking the FUCT and THID areas of Doodhiya-Durguja and Sujanpur.

We were headed for the Good Friday mass in the tribal jungles of Durguja today. I had spent most of the drive explaining to Munni that it was in very bad taste for her to go *Happy Good Friday! Happy Good Friday!* to all the Christians we would meet in the welcoming committee. It had been hard going.

'But didi, it is called Good, how can it be good if He *died* that day?' she'd protested. 'It should be called Bad Friday… or Sad Friday or Black Friday…'

But she finally piped down when, after driving for hours through thick, dark forest, we reached the church and she was faced with a giant blowup of the tortured, suffering face of

Jesus, sweating blood beneath his crown of thorns. 'Hai Ram,' she gasped and subsided, awed.

There was a massive turnout. Durguja had been at the centre of a huge 're-conversion' attempt four years ago. Weird Hindutva outfits – all offshoots of the IJP – had descended and taken possession of the church. Armed thugs had patrolled the boundaries while a 'yagna' was performed inside the building, the padres were bundled out, and about two thousand terrorized tribals were forcibly reconverted through some random 'ghar waapsi' or 'homecoming' ritual.

Amma had been very hassled about it, especially since Bauji loved the tribals of Durguja – the two of them had shared a rather me-Tarzan you-Jane type honeymoon here, some sixty years ago. She'd protested that the Pragati couldn't stand by and let something like this happen – but the morphed photo scandal broke out right after, and she got distracted. Still, her outburst had drawn the attention of journalists, NGOs and international experts to the problem, and a parliamentary committee was set up to look into the matter. Since then, things had quietened down, the church had been reconsecrated, cleansed and blessed with holy water, and the tribals had re-re-converted.

'See, didi,' Munni told me above the din of the inevitable welcoming tribal drums, as we walked towards the church, 'the missionaries believe in educating the tribals. And they provide them with basic healthcare also. And the district administration doesn't like that. If the tribals get too educated, too organized and too healthy, they start demanding their rights and protest that their forests are being looted and want a bigger cut of everything. That's why they wanted them to become Hindu again! To kick out the missionaries. It is not about Ram at all, it is only about Rupees.'

This was true. Amma had told me that if you map India's richest forests and mineral reserves and then map India's poorest tribal areas, you will get a perfect match. The tribals have absolutely no access to the riches beneath their feet, and are constantly booted out and shifted around instead.

At the moment though, things looked peaceful. The biggest issue here now, I remembered, sneaking a look at the FUCT written with a ballpoint pen on my palm was U – for Unemployment and everything that went with it.

You wouldn't have thought it, looking at the church. It was sparkling and everybody had neat, combed and oiled hair and scrupulously clean clothes. We hadn't come for the Mass, though, I realized as I looked around. Rocket Singh had got it wrong. We had come for the Stations of the Cross.

There were fourteen stations in all, starting with the first, where Jesus is condemned to death, and continued inexorably, with horrific, graphic gruesomeness, to the fourteenth, where Jesus is laid in the tomb after being crucified. Munni got more and more upset by the vividness of the depictions and even I had to admit that the tribals were enacting the scenes with a raw, powerful relish I had never seen in Loreto Convent. They actually had a thin, tragic looking kid in a loin cloth, wearing a crown of thorns, who kept moaning realistically as he was bashed up and dragged along. The high point of the whole show was when they 'nailed' him to the cross. They banged a long, rusty nail into his palm with a large, showy hammer and all this 'blood' came gushing out. Munni totally freaked, even though I whispered to her that the kid was obviously holding little balloons filled with red-coloured water in his hands.

Besides, all the standing, sitting, turning and kneeling during the stations really confused her. 'Uff, why can't they make up their minds?' she grumbled, shifting her bulk between the pews on creaky knees. 'Up and down, stand and sit, bend and kneel. These Muslims and Christians are all the same. Why can't they just sit and clap? Like us? Poori PT karaadi…'

The singing was lovely, though, just as Rocket Singh had promised, and the scent of frankinscense and the swinging of the chalice hypnotic. Afterwards, we had tea with the priests.

'We can't thank your grandmother enough, Miss Pande,' the chief padre, a short, earnest dude, bespectacled, clean shaven, with slicked back, black hair and a slight lisp, told me over Parle-G biscuits and chai. 'She has a very long association with this church.'

I nodded, feeling a warm glow at this glimpse of the Amma I used to idolize – the one who didn't kowtow to anybody and who just wanted to serve the 'pure' people in the best way possible. We had an unofficial public meeting after tea, where I talked about Amma and Bauji spending their honeymoon here and then shamelessly went on to compare IJP rule in the state with the darkness and suffering of Good Friday, and urged the tribals to claim a glorious Easter resurrection by voting for Pragati.

Then we played some Pragati Party versions of the latest soulful Bollywood songs. Nothing flashy, it was Good Friday, after all. They gifted me a really cool woven basket, the kind Bauji had learned to weave in prison. We handed out our usual goodies – stickers, T-shirts, scarves – and moved on, hoping we had retained Durguja.

Ballot Boxing
Number 19 in a continuing series of reports from
Lok Sabha constituencies across India

Marigold Wilts in Bittora?

A poll conducted by this paper reveals that while Zain Altaf Khan is still clearly ahead of his nearest rival Sarojini Pande, granddaughter of maverick politician Pushpa Pande, the gap seems to be narrowing, and that too, quite rapidly.

Two close contenders, Vir Singh of the KDS, and Pandit Dinanath Dwivedi, who is standing as an independent, are tied in third place.

Khan has stated that he has been preparing for this election for at least a year, but Sarojini's last-minute nomination seems to have upset his careful calculations.

The Pande offensive, though haphazard (itineraries change at the last minute, the rattletrap-white Sumos break down almost every day and the giveaways are tacky) seems to be gathering momentum.

This could be because grandmother and granddaughter have split forces, with Pande senior covering the urban areas while Sarojini tours the rural areas, thus doubling their impact.

It could even be because Sarojini exudes a certain candid, heartwarming, womanly sympathy that seems to be charming her constituents. Her campaign managers have been quick to cotton onto this and are setting her an exhausting pace. 'We want didi to visit every single village in Bittoragarh,' declared Pappu, a member of her crack campaign team. 'Anyone who meets didi wants to vote only for her.'

According to our poll, the Pragati Party seems poised to retain its traditionally strong bastions of Doodhiya, Sujanpur and Durguja. Khan will probably sweep the predominantly Muslim urban areas of Purana Bittora, Jummabagh and Champapul. The Brahmin area of Begumbagh will most likely plump for independent candidate, Dwivedi. The eighth assembly segment, Tanki Bazaar, is undecided and could swing to anyone.

The IJP camp, however, scoffed at our poll findings. 'Your so-called poll features 2077 people across the eight assembly segments,' a spokesperson told this journalist. 'The total number of registered voters here is almost eleven lakh. How can you call this a representative sample?'

Morale is still high in the ZAK camp, where a convoy of black Scorpios works on a tight, almost military, schedule. The campaigning is high-tech, with video-conferencing and walkie-talkies and the giveaways are glitzy, toy cell-phones with 'Sarkar genda phool' ring-tone. Khan himself, with his intense good looks, aristocratic background and seemingly earnest desire to do good, appears almost Bollywood-heroic.

At the time of going to print it does seem that the Marigold's days in the sun are numbered. But stranger things have happened. Either way, the Battle for Bittora seems to be heading towards a photo finish.

I woke up early the next morning, and walked downstairs to ask Munni and Rocket Singh what the plaan for the day was. We'd all taken to saying 'plaan', Pappu style. To rhyme with darn and yarn and barn. It was a kind of tribute to Our Pappu's enthusiastic approach to everything.

I found Our Pappu in the flesh downstairs. The moment he saw me, he leapt to his feet, saying, 'Anything, didi, anything! I will do anything you ask, anything for you! Your wish is my command!'

'What're you doing here, Pappu?' I asked, blinking a little at the suddenness of this assault.

'Didi, Zain bhai is doing Sujanpur today… So we thought, instead of clashing, we could go to Tanki Bazaar instead.'

Hello, there were seventeen people contesting this election! Obviously, we would all keep clashing into each other. Was I supposed to make my campaigning plans after checking with Zain's gang?

'But what about the Sujanpur meetings?' I asked. 'Won't those people get hassled if we don't show up?'

Our Pappu shook his head. 'Didi, they are *very* loyal people!' he said. 'They won't mind! They *always* vote for us.'

Hmmm… an urban area would make a nice change actually. They might even have electricity. And clean loos.

'How far is Tanki from here, Pappu?' I asked.

'Two hours' drive, didi!' he said. 'The road is smooth as butter.'

Yeah, *right*.

Tanki Bazaar… what was Mr Urvashi's abbreviation for it? I frowned. There had been *no* abbreviation for Tanki Bazaar. Odd.

'Okay,' I nodded. 'But that isn't really one of your areas, is it? Who will take us around, organize meetings and all that?'

As if on cue, a large lady with muscular forearms, clad in a printed nylon sari, strode in and grabbed my hand in a business-like manner. 'Hasina Behenji,' she said crisply.

As I shook hands with her, Munni hissed into my ear, 'Watch out, didi. Hasina Behenji is Hard Core. When her husband died, ten years ago, his younger brother raped her in front of her small-small children two days after the funeral so she would leave the house and not ask for a share in the family property. But she fixed him *good*. Now he is behind bars and she owns the whole house and works tirelessly to improve the lot of the underprivileged women in Tanki.'

Wow.

But Munni wasn't done.

'She doesn't go to any parlour-shalour to have her underarms waxed,' Munni whispered. 'She just lifts up her arms, aisey, and *bites* the hair off with her teeth...'

Again, wow.

'Tanki Bazaar mera ilaka hai!' Hasina Behenji announced with aggressive bonhomie, flashing large, white, armpit-hair-biting teeth.

Our Pappu piped up with, 'Yes, yes, Hasina Behenji does excellent work in Tanki, didi. Her NGO is very well known. She has brought even Akshay Kumar and Ashlee Simpson to Tanki Bazaar; people love her there.'

I smiled, genuinely awestruck, at Hasina Behenji, and meekly let her lead me to the back seat of the Sumo.

———

Tanki Bazaar turned out to be a massive water pump market. Huge black Sintex tanks, motors and pipes were stacked high on both sides of the main street. Traders sat around, sweating profusely and gesticulating loudly, swatting at flies, and occasionally raising one bum cheek slightly off their gaddis to let fly long, loud, hopefully odourless farts. I peered at them from the car as we drove into Tanki and parked the Sumos in a highly illegal manner, inches from the traffic policeman's island, bang in the middle of the main chowk.

Hasina Behenji emerged from Jugatram's Sumo, elbowed past the garland-bearing party workers milling around me and grabbed my arm hard.

She led me to the dais, a wondrous thing of gleaming steel, rexine chairs and red shaneel carpets. Mouldy looking rajnigandha flowers stood at attention in brass vases on a plastic tablecloth. Our Pappu and Jugatram went to sit in the front row, while the EC crew set themselves up at the back of the shamiana.

I sipped a glass of water and looked around at the crowd curiously. For such a business-like neighbourhood, there seemed to be a lot of women in the crowd. The split was practically eighty-twenty.

There were cries of

> *How should aawar leader be?*
> *Just like Sarojiniji!*

and everybody cheered lustily. It was a brightly dressed, rather giggly crowd, and it looked all set to party. The intezaam was really good too. Red cardboard boxes loaded with fat, yellow, black-pepper-pod-encrusted boondi ka laddoo and chunky, greasy kachoris were being handed out at the back. My mouth started watering instantly.

When Our Pappu brought a trayful of goodies to the dais, I nodded graciously and grabbed a laddoo. Biting into the heavenly, crunchy, sugar-coated boondi, I slid back into my chair and tuned in slowly to what Hasina Behenji was saying.

'And so, ladies, I would like to tell you, once again, how the march of ill health has been stopped cold in its tracks in this ancient area of Tanki Bazaar by the work done by the Samaj Sevika Forum! Before I hand over to the honourable Sarojini didi who will tell you about the Pragati Party's plan for you, I would once again like to remind you that Health is Wealth, ladies, especially for *you* in the social service that you do. If you are not a Healthy, you cannot be a Wealthy. Today, I would like to give you a revision lesson on how to ensure Health and Wellness in your daily business. Sarojini didi, please will you do the honours...'

I looked up, startled. Opening addresses were usually much longer than this. My mouth was still full of laddoo. I swallowed mightily, got to my feet and staggered to the mike, where Hasina Behenji stood, beaming a friendly muscular welcome.

As I approached hesitantly, wondering what I was supposed to do, as there was no lamp-to-be-lit or ribbon-to-be-cut in sight, she reached into her capacious black rexine handbag and, with the air of a skilled magician, whipped out a wonderfully lifelike, flesh-coloured wooden penis, complete with scrotum and foreskin.

I choked.

The ladies in the crowd didn't seem too put out or anything, though. Hasina Behenji held out the model invitingly, obviously expecting me to take it from her. I reached for the contraption – there was a smooth brown handle attached to its base – and grasped it gingerly. The ladies of Tanki Bazaar giggled a little and I heard whispers of *oh, look, sharma gayee... she's blushing!*

Hasina Behenji proceeded to pull out a pack of lubricated

PP state-supplied condoms. She pinched the top firmly (to avoid air bubbles, which could cause rupture during rapture, she explained) and with an expert flick of her wrist, proceeded to roll it snugly over my (as in, because I was *holding* it) penis.

I held the sheathed model high up in the air for all to see as she called out, 'Okay? Everybody understood? Any questions? Health is Wealth, after all!'

One of the ladies, a pretty, young, slightly oriental-looking girl, raised her hand.

'Yes?' I smiled at her encouragingly.

'Didi…' she asked hesitantly, pointed at the sheathed phallus. 'It is all suited-booted now and looking very smart, but can you tell me… because I am very innocent… where do I *put* it?'

Raucous laughter broke out. My questioner laughed the loudest, tears in her eyes. 'Put it in your *ear*,' I told her sweetly, demonstrating by pointing the model at my own ear. They shrieked with mirth.

'You must make sure they keep it on right through,' instructed Hasina Behenji seriously. 'And afterwards, make sure their tanki does not overflow or spill! If there's no spill, HIV can't kill!'

The women nodded, accepted the free condom packets that were handed out and then, finally, I was allowed to make my speech. That bloody Pappu, I thought, as I put down the wooden penis and picked up the hand mike testily. Why didn't he just tell me that Tanki Bazaar was a red light area?

After the meeting, I went to the houses on top of the water pump shops, where the shady ladies lived. They were really hospitable, pressing extremely sweet tea and more boondi ka laddoo on me, turning the table fans to face me, and exclaiming admiringly at my heavy gold earrings.

A number of snotty babies were playing about in the flimsy

balconies upstairs. They all seemed very fond of Hasina Behenji, crawling into her ample lap and yanking at her lower lip so that her pink gums flashed in the afternoon sun.

'Where are your children now, Hasina Behenji?' I asked curiously.

'Oh!' She tossed her head. 'They are big now – sixteen and fourteen. I can leave them alone at home.'

'It must have been awful for all of you when your husband died,' I said awkwardly.

'Oh, no, it was quite a relief,' replied Hasina Behenji unexpectedly. 'You see, my husband was not a good man. Always wanting to consume.'

'Really?' I asked, intrigued.

She nodded. 'Sometimes, he would consume seven-eight times in one day!'

'Wow,' I breathed, my eyes now as round as saucers.

'Then one day he consumed so much he died of it.'

'He died of *consuming*?' I asked in disbelief. 'Is that even possible?'

She looked at me in surprise. 'Of course! Cirrhosis. Excessive alcohol consumption can do that to you.'

Oh.

'So, how did you get interested in politics?' I asked her next.

'Bhai, after the haadsa at my husband's funeral,' she looked up enquiringly to see if I knew what she was referring to; I nodded, giving her large hand a heartfelt squeeze, 'I became very sympathetic to the plight of girls like these. Once my problems were sorted, I decided I must help them.'

I looked at her a little blankly. 'How could helping girls in a red light area get you interested in politics?'

She smiled. 'Many different different party workers come here to Tanki. And they like the girls to role-play.'

'Like wigs and stuff?'

She shook her head. 'No no, they want the girls to pretend to be *real* people. Celebrities. Bollywood actresses. That old Doordarshan newsreader, the one with a rose in her hair, she was very popular once. They like Draupadi's cheerharan too. Then they like girls to dress like Missionaries of Charity in white-and-blue saris—'

'No!' I cried out, revolted.

She nodded. 'But I got interested in politics because the lady impersonation they found the most exciting was...' she leaned in and whispered into my ear.

'No!' I gasped in horror. 'That's like, blasphemous!'

She giggled a little. 'Oh, ya,' she said. 'And they didn't stop there – they like the girls to dress up as *all* the lady political leaders. Like...' She whispered into my ear again.

'No!' I said weakly. 'Eww.'

She nodded, her eyes dancing.

'Also...'

I gasped again.

'And international lady leaders too – like Hillary Clinton and Candee Rice. So I helped the girls find recordings of the speeches made by these ladies. And then I got interested in the things they said.'

Wow. What a political induction.

A tiny baby crawled up to her just then, caught hold of her massive, cliff-like midriff, pushed itself up, and stood, beaming proudly with the triumphant air of one who has scaled Mount Everest. It had an unnaturally distended belly, mosquito bitten arms and hollow dark eyes, and its head was still a little unsteady upon its neck, but the smile it bobbed at both of us was extremely sociable.

Hasina Behenji said, 'Pata hai, didi, this little one is HIV-positive, such a sweet baby, na?'

There was something challenging in her kind eyes and in her tone, almost as if she were daring me to touch the baby. But hello, I was a woman who had just held a hideous, disembodied, rubber-smelling, condom-encased wooden penis in front of five hundred people! What was one tiny HIV-positive baby?

I swung the little girl? boy? – I sneaked a peek under the loose shift it was wearing – boy, into my lap and gave him a wet smacking kiss on the cheek. He chuckled at me in a good-humoured, gummy way, drooling and clutching at my hair with tiny, sticky brown fingers. 'Yes, Hasina Behenji,' I agreed, my voice a little squeaky because the baby's fingers were now gripping my nose and squeezing thoroughly. 'Such a sweet baby!'

Suddenly, she reached out and grabbed my arm. 'Didi, can I talk to you?'

I looked at her blankly, as the baby's tiny hands yanked at my hair. Weren't we already talking?

'Zain bhai's people were here two days ago,' she said. 'They were very nice, I suppose. Gave money for the school and all. But the ladies here, they don't like the nawabzada's family. Especially his father. So this is what I want to say to you...'

She paused while I wondered where this was going. Meanwhile, the baby stuck a finger up my left nostril and rotated it anti-clockwise.

'I am saying that our hearts are with you, didi! And with Pushpa jiji. You understand us, you will look after us. So we will vote for *you*.'

'Thank you!' I said, genuinely moved.

Hasina Behenji reached out, grabbed both my hands in her hefty ones, looked deep into my eyes and said earnestly, 'Didi, they gave us two lakhs for the school. But on the twenty-third, I swear to you, *all* of us will go and put our finger on the Finger!'

'*Thank* you,' I said again, even more gratefully. The baby hit the top of my head vigorously and grinned. My eyes watered.

'But *please* understand, didi,' she said, 'don't mind, but can you also give us two lakhs?'

8

'Duuuuude! Don't you wish you were where I am?'

I sighed. I was inside a bumpy, rattling vehicle. I had just promised Hasina Behenji two lakhs for a guaranteed lead in Tanki Bazaar. There was a line of fire around my midriff, where the naada of my sari petticoat was chafing against my skin. I was longing to pull the damn thing off, *burn* it and never wear one again. I *so* did not need this conversation.

'No, Rumi,' I snapped. 'I do not wish to be at a smoky bar, sipping sour white wine and speculating about the sexuality of the people around me.'

'Dry, Jinni,' he said above a lot of humming and crackling. 'The word is *dry* – not sour.'

'I can barely hear you,' I said crabbily. 'The signal sucks.'

'I know!' he yelled. 'This place has practically no network! I had to climb up to a crumbling balcony to call you.'

'Where are you?' I asked incuriously.

'I'm in Buttora,' he shouted.

'*Bitt*ora,' I said, irritated. 'I've told you a hundred times, it's – wait, hang on, you're *where*?'

Rumi chuckled happily. 'I'm at Dugguji's haveli. At a dinner party with my bro Nauzer. You met him, I heard?'

'Rumi, slow down,' I said. 'What are you doing here? And why are you *there*? That's the *enemy* camp!'

'Be civilized, Jinni,' he drawled. He obviously had a *lake* of sour white wine sloshing inside him. '*Frenemy* camp. They invited Nauzer and I piled on! Besides, speak for yourself – *my* political affiliations are my own.'

'Is Nulwallah, like, your *partner*?' I asked, momentarily diverted.

'Is your mind, like, a *sink*?' he retorted. 'He's my friend, Jinni. My buddy. My bro.'

'Hmmm….' I said sceptically, massaging my raw, burning midriff. 'Watch out, you're sounding almost *macho*, Rumi!'

'No *way*, darling.' Here, Rumi lowered his voice confidingly. I could practically smell the wine fumes. ''Coz I just met the opposition. And he's *hot*.'

My heart gave a sickening lurch.

'Zain's there?'

'Yeah, and we've just shared a deep meaningful conversation. About poetry. He loves my namesake's work.'

He would, I thought in disgust. The poetry of Rumi. Bloody pseudo.

'And the host is one of your old buddies, Bunty something. A rather dull, homophobic human bhatura who doesn't seem to have even *heard* of the amendment to Article 377 of the Indian Penal Code. Anyway, he wants you to come over—'

'Why's he a bhatura?' I interrupted.

'Because he looks like one,' Rumi explained. 'Fried and fair and swollen-up-tight-and-asking-to-be-burst. So, will you come?'

'No, thanks,' I said hastily. 'I'm totally exhausted. It's late. And besides, I have nothing to wear.'

'Oh, yes you do,' said Rumi. 'I got your Mango jeans and Bizzare blouse.'

'You *didn't*!' I said, genuinely moved. 'That's really sweet of you, Rumi.'

Then I added, just to be sure, 'It was on sale, na?'

'Yes, you cow. Forty per cent off. Now come.'

'But Rumi, I…'

'Bunty's *dying to* meet you!' he interrupted, suddenly upping the gushiness by a notch. 'Oh, look, here he comes! *Talk* to him!'

'Don't you *dare* put him on the line, Rumi, you bastard!' I hissed.

But of course he handed over the phone to bloody Bunty Sisodia. I could've killed him!

'Hello, Jeanie?' said a fruity, over-friendly voice. 'Kahan ho, yaar? Come over, na.'

I rolled my eyes. 'Hi, Bunty,' I said awkwardly, inwardly groaning. 'Sorry, ya, but I'm on the road, bahut late ho jayega…'

'Where are you?' he asked, in an irritating I'm-taking-charge manner. 'Let me talk to your driver.'

'He's driving,' I said evasively. 'There are cops on the road. We're near the Durguja turnoff, I think.'

'Fantastic! That's five minutes from my place. I'll come and pick you up!'

Oh god, what was this?

'I'm really tired, Bunty… some other time, okay?'

'No way,' he said, all bossy bonhomie, 'we're childhood friends! Just pull over, I'm coming there right now.'

Bloody! Why was he being so overfamiliar? I couldn't stand the guy. All he'd done when we were kids was sneak Zain away from me to bowl to him.

He must've handed the phone back to Rumi, because the next thing I heard was Rumi's voice, hissing like a temptress in an old Bollywood flick: 'Jinni… they have *AC. And* power backup.'

I sat there in my damp, sweaty sari, in my rattling hot iron box, wiped my grimy face and sighed with pure longing. He'd known exactly which button to press.

And besides, who was I kidding? Zain was there. I was desperate to see him again.

'Tell Bunty I'm waiting at the turnoff,' I said and hung up.

Bunty drove up self-importantly, about ten minutes later, in a white pyjama and an orange T-shirt, all fair and fried and silver earringed. He wasn't content for me just to follow his car but insisted I get out, embrace him and get into his car, which smelled strongly of Pan Parag and Drakkar Noir.

I *hate* Drakkar Noir.

I told the Sumo driver to follow and let Bunty drive me to the haveli, feeling rather disoriented.

'Great to meet up, ya,' grinned the bhatura from Bittora, his silver balis flashing. 'And you're looking so good, ya!'

Sitting this close to him, I noticed that his T-shirt had MOJITO ERGO SUM – *I drink, therefore I am* – emblazoned across the front.

Dad sending him abroad to work had been the making of him, he informed me as he drove us down the muddy road, which was flanked by tall snake grass on both sides. 'Dad told me ki sitting here, doing nothing, tu bhi Manu Sharma, Sanjeev Nanda ban jayega. Go work, stand on your own two feet…'

I let him prattle on, but when he tried to hustle me into the drawing room as soon as we reached, I dug my heels in. 'Bunty, I'm sorry, I need to have a bath first.'

He looked a little taken aback, then looked me over carefully and nodded. 'Actually, you do,' he said with a grin. 'So of course ya, no formality, please have bath, shower... have,' he laughed expansively, '*everything*!' Then he bustled me into a massive room with a fancy loo. The mattress looked so plump and inviting I almost wept.

He stood around, kicking the edge of the bed coyly with a Gucci sandalled foot, and then said, with awkward gallantry, 'I wish you could also stay with us during your campaigning, Jeanie. After all, *you* are my childhood friend too, it's just that...'

'Zain is closer,' I said, as I edged him towards the door. 'It's cool, Bunty, I'm happy with just the bathroom, believe me!'

When I emerged, scrubbed and tingling, twenty blissful minutes later, I found a Mango packet on the bed. I swooped down on it with delight and soon discovered that the Mango jeans *did* make my butt look peachy. And the crocheted blouse was gorgeous. My scruffy Champapuli chappals looked a bit strange with them but all I could do about that was go back into the loo and clean out the grime under my toenails scrupulously.

Feeling quite high on my new gear, fresh soap and Ponds Dreamflower talc, I finger-combed my wet mop of hair and padded into the drawing room to Meet the Sisodias.

It was a very imposing home. Huge, gilt-framed oil paintings hung on red walls. I walked down a corridor patterned with fading mustard yellow and green tiles and pushed open the door which Bunty had tried to hustle me through when we arrived.

It opened into a large, beautifully lit, glass conservatory. There were about twelve people – Rumi, very much the political tourist in a crisp white kurta-pyjama with a massive Canon camera slung around his neck, Nauzer Nulwallah, Bunty, his dad Dugguji, a sexy, kohl-eyed girl in a hijab, some random bureaucratic types... and, of course, Zain, casually exuding gorgeousness in a worn Deep Purple T-shirt and faded jeans, talking intensely to some old dudes. My heart jerked upwards almost painfully, like a hooked fish, and then sank slowly into my scruffy Champapulis.

Squaring my shoulders, I sketched a tiny hi to Rumi and walked over to greet old Dugguji.

'Namaste, Duggu uncle,' I said. 'Thanks for inviting me to dinner!'

'For dinner *at least*, you mean,' boomed Dugguji. 'We should have invited you to stay, but kya karen, this politics is drawing boundary lines across our heart!' (This, with a dramatic sawing gesture and a roguish look at the sexy girl in the hijab, who tapped his knuckles with her cocktail stirrer and said, 'Really, uncle!' in a husky, amused voice.)

'Jinni!' chirrupped Rumi, bouncing up, looking hugely pleased with himself. 'You're so thinny!' He drew back a little and pursed his lips, considering me. 'And you've become as kaali as the "before" of a fairness cream ad, but we won't go into that.'

'Hey, Gaiman Tagore,' I said grudgingly. 'I never thought I'd say this, but it's really nice to see you!'

'Thanks.' He grinned.

'So, how's everything at Pixel?'

He pulled an expressive moue. 'Oh, the same...' He yanked at the neck of his T-shirt and peered down at his scrawny chest. 'Phew, this town is *hot*. I think I'm getting ghamoriyan.'

'Who's getting gonorrhea?' asked Nulwallah, appearing at my elbow.

'Ha ha,' said Rumi coldly. 'Okay, I'll catch you in a bit. I want to check out your rather cute opponent for loser stench.'

Nulwallah looked intrigued. '*Loser* stench? What's that?'

Rumi instantly stopped looking haughty and started looking evangelical.

'Oh, it's a foul, *foul* miasma,' he said earnestly. 'It hangs over losers, or losers-to-be. It's not discernable to the naked nose – but keen sniffers like me can sniff it out.'

'What rubbish you talk, Rumi,' I said, laughing.

'So, what does it smell like, then?' persisted Nulwallah the press hound. 'Loser stench? To the discerning sniffer, that is.'

'Ah,' said Rumi solemnly. 'It smells like... an impotent mixture of disappointment, fear, rejection, urine, sweat and Indian cricket team.'

'Do I have it?' I asked, fearful in spite of myself.

He swooped in for a good long sniff, looked arch for a moment, and then shook his head. 'Nope,' he said. 'You're clean. Now lemme go sniff up six-pack Zak.'

He bounded away, taking Nulwallah with him, while the sexy girl materialized by my side. She held out a long graceful hand and said, 'Jinni, pleasure to meet you, I'm the only Praggu at the party!'

'Hi, err...' I shook her hand, a little taken aback.

'Meet Pinky, Zak's cousin,' said Bunty, looking a little pink himself.

'Hi, Pinky,' I said with a laugh. 'Wow, well done. You should try talking some sense into your friends!'

She shook her head. 'Oh, that's impossible. These two are completely insane.'

'We're not,' said Bunty, rocking on his heels. 'We're completely *normal*.' He threw a dark glance in Rumi's direction as he said this, which made me feel like hitting him.

'Do you know,' Pinky said to me, ignoring Bunty completely, 'that whenever these two got fed up with the snooty society girls in England, they'd start speaking pidgin English, just to shake them off? It was so embarrassing!'

'You-so-fair,' Bunty said, grinning. 'Touch-you-I?'

'That's obnoxious, Bunty!' I said.

'*They* didn't think so,' said Bunty stoutly. 'They couldn't get enough of us!'

'They couldn't get enough of Zak, you mean!' Pinky pulled a face at him, then looked towards Zain.

He was conversing with an old bureaucrat type, but he looked up just then and smiled, almost like he'd felt her eyes upon him. 'Hey, it's a free country, Pink!' he called out, obviously thinking we were talking about something else. 'You're welcome to vote for Jinni, if you like!'

His dark eyes met mine for just a moment – *Shall I kiss you, Jinni?* – and just that tiniest of contacts was enough to make my heartbeat zoom.

'Oh, I *will*!' Pinky called back. 'Don't worry.'

He rolled his eyes, shrugged good-naturedly and went back to his conversation with the prosy bureaucrat.

I caught a few stray bits of it.

'Missed calls were invented in India,' the old gent was saying. 'They're a completely *free* way to communicate. You dial a number, let it ring, then hang up before the other person picks it up, see? Just like a pager. You get the message across but you don't have to pay anything to do it!'

'That's ingenious,' Zain was saying all politely, like he'd just got in from another planet so he didn't know what a missed call was.

'Pakistan, Sri Lanka, Africa… *all* have started making missed calls now,' the gentleman continued. 'It is India's gift to the developing world!'

Just then Dugguji started moaning about how Pinky had ripped him off while playing teen-patti earlier in the evening. 'Humko kahin ka na chhoda!' he said, sounding quite thrilled. 'Heart and sleep toh she had stolen already, now she has stolen our money also!'

'You've become a Praggu campaign fund provider, uncle!' Pinky told him laughingly. 'Whether you like it or not!'

Then Bunty hustled me over to the bar to make me a very elaborate mojito, in a fancy frosted glass. I watched him, my back to the other guests, and slowly my heartbeat climbed down to something remotely approaching normal.

'Nice T-shirt by the way,' I told him. 'Are you a Descartes fan?'

He looked at me blankly. 'Who?'

I indicated the slogan on his tee.

'Oh, that,' he said. 'It's a present from Zak. He knows I like mojitos.'

'Oh, but it's—' I started to say but he looked beyond me and said hurriedly, 'Uh, excuse me, Jeanie…' and headed towards the door.

Looking on curiously, I was a little appalled to discover the new arrival: Karan Sethie, a Rajya Sabha MP and a big noise in the IJP. He's a famous lawyer and one of the intellectual 'secular' faces of the rabidly right-wing party. You know, the ones whose main job is to keep the IJP from busting the modest green corset of secularism to reveal the heaving Hindutva breasts beneath.

Bunty, after much bowing and scraping, ushered Karan Sethie to Dugguji's side and came back to the bar, looking self-important. Feeling rather flustered, I pretended not to recognize his very important guest and merely said, as Bunty handed me a surprisingly professional-looking cocktail, 'What *is* it with you guys, anyway? Zain makes kebabs and you make drinks?'

Bunty put down his cocktail shaker in surprise. 'Arrey, how do you know?' he demanded. I looked at him blankly. 'Ke Zak is a solid kebabchi?'

Uff. Me and my big mouth.

'We met recently at a wedding in Delhi,' Zain's voice sounded easily from behind us. He strolled up, lithely straddled the barstool next to me, and said ruefully to Bunty, 'But Jinni didn't taste anything I cooked.'

'How come?' demanded Bunty of me. 'He's fantastic, yaar, you should have had!'

'Because...' said I to Bunty, cheeks very hot. 'Because... uh, because everything was over by the time I met him.'

'How strange,' said Zain, continuing to address Bunty. 'I felt everything *began* when I met her.'

'My memories of the evening are obviously very different from yours,' I threw at him tartly, as I reached for the last olive in the bowl.

'Well, I hope yours are good,' he said carelessly, as he reached out and nicked the olive smoothly from under my fingers. 'Because *mine*,' he popped the olive into his mouth, chewed, and raised intimate dark eyes to meet mine, 'are incredible.'

I choked. And suddenly remembered how, when we were eight, he'd spent ages teaching me how to blow bubblegum. I had been hopeless, making puffing noises, spewing out little bits of spit, producing pathetic little bubblets. Zain thought it was vastly entertaining. One day, blowing with rather too much enthusiasm, I dropped my pink wad of Boomer on the table. He laughed so hard his gum fell out too, and I, by mistake, picked up *his* wad and popped it into my mouth. Realizing what I'd done, I spat it out instantly, acting like I was fully grossed out. But I *wasn't* fully grossed out. Boomer is still my favourite gum ever.

Now, I glared at him, torn between two primal urges. To stab him in the eye with the cocktail shaker or to rip off his Deep Purple T-shirt and cover his toned, honey gold chest with fervent kisses.

'Are you two fighting?' Pinky called out gaily from behind us.

'Yes.' I smiled at her, as I made room for her to join the group. 'But nothing major. Just a Lok Sabha election.'

I don't think she heard me. She sat down, glared at Bunty and hissed, 'I can't *believe* you invited that weasel Sethie to your house for dinner!'

A red-faced Bunty said, 'Shhh! Softer, Pinky. He's a great man, very broad-minded, and you know Zak likes him.'

Zain turned to her. 'I'm sorry if you're upset, Pink. But he's a real harbinger of change in the party. Karan Sethie believes in democracy.'

'*Please!*' I snorted, and knocked back my mojito. 'I know their kind of democracy! Democracy means the majority rules – Hindus are the majority – so Hindus rule. Spare me that crap.'

'Yeah,' said Pinky, looking at me approvingly, 'and Zak, don't say you're sorry I'm upset. You don't give a *damn* that I'm upset – and you know it!'

Zain stared at both of us, pretending to look alarmed. 'Oops,' he muttered ruefully. Then he walked away.

Pinky looked after him in frustration. 'Typical,' she said, 'he doesn't even think we're worth a debate. I *hate* him.'

'Yeah,' I agreed with feeling.

I looked around the room. Zain was talking to Nulwallah. Rumi had buttoned up Dugguji and was explaining to him earnestly exactly what the lyricist meant by the phrase *ishq di gali*, in the hit Bollywood number 'Ishq di gali vich no entry'. Then he moved on to the multiple oral sex insinuations involved in lighting a *beedi* from your *jigar*. 'You know the shape of a beedi, right?' he was telling the old man seriously. 'It's blunt and cylindrical. Now imagine it placed on a young nymph's chest. I'm telling you, sir, the Bollywood greats are nothing but a bunch of dirty old men...'

I shuddered and looked away.

The old bureaucrat who'd been talking to Zain wandered up. 'Hello,' he said animatedly. 'Do you know that the COAI, the Cellular Operators Association of India, is conducting a study to understand the revenue implications of the missed call phenomenon in India?'

'Err... no, sir,' I said blankly. 'Have they?'

He nodded vigorously. 'They estimate that the loss of revenue due to people communicating through missed calls is as much as thirty per cent.'

'That's incredible,' I said politely.

'Yes,' he said. 'Excuse me, beta.'

He wandered off again and I turned back to Pinky.

'Why don't I know you?' I asked abruptly. 'I mean, I knew Zain when we were kids but you...'

'I grew up in the UK,' she said. 'I've come down to set up an

NGO. Just moved here a couple of months ago. I'm working with underprivileged women.'

'Awesome,' I replied automatically, but my mind was on something else. 'Uh, tell me, Pinky, d'you know when Zain got started on this whole IJP trip? It just doesn't add up.'

She looked thoughtful. 'I don't know,' she said finally. 'He'd been wanting to do something for Bittora for years and he fell in with that Karan Sethie at some mountain rally – he's a rallyist too, you know that? Anyway, they did some major male bonding and Sethie managed to reel him in. He told him the party is introspecting madly after the last debacle at the polls. They're going to change the system from within, become more inclusive, provide a genuine alternative to the Pragati, yada yada yada – Zain wants to be part of that change.'

'It's completely insane,' I muttered.

'Yes, it's definitely strange,' she agreed. 'When Zain was a kid, all he talked about was the freedom struggle and the Pragati Party. It used to upset his dad – he hated the Pragati for taking away the privileges of the royal houses.'

Just then, Nulwallah popped up again. 'Pandeji,' he demanded. 'Have you heard the latest outrage in Hyderabad?'

'No,' I said warily. Nulwallah's questions were always trick questions. 'I hardly get time to watch TV. What happened?'

He grinned. 'It's quite bizzare. A Muslim cleric has exhorted all young eligible Muslim males to go forth and marry into other religious communities and thus slowly turn the world Muslim. Conversion through love, he's calling it.'

'That's silly,' I said, 'because it cuts both ways. I hope he realizes that his young men could end up getting converted through love themselves?'

'Can I quote you?' Nauzer asked eagerly.

'I don't see why not,' I told him. 'So, is there a fatwa out on him yet?'

'Of course.' Pinky laughed. '*And* the IJP's after his blood too!'

'Whose blood is the IJP after?' a deep baritone enquired behind us, and we turned to see Karan Sethie, flanked by Zain.

Pinky stiffened. 'Sarojini Pande,' she introduced me formally. 'Mr Karan Sethie.'

'Charmed!' he exclaimed, all silver-haired and debonair, holding out his hand.

I folded my hands. 'Namaste!' I said primly.

He looked amused. 'Namaste,' he said good-naturedly.

I flushed, feeling a little churlish.

'So, Pinkyji,' said Karan Sethie combatively, 'whose blood are we after then?'

''Most everybody's, sir,' she said demurely. 'But specifically, we were talking about the Hyderabadi cleric.'

'Ah!' Karan Sethie looked thoughtful. 'Personally,' he said slowly, 'I feel marriage should have no agenda but love.'

'Is that why you've had three, Karan?' said Zain with a grin.

Everybody laughed, like this was really witty or something. Except me. I was finding the sight of Zain being so charmingly deferential to an IJP frontman faintly nauseating.

'Mr Sethie.' This was Nulwallah at his Karan Thaparish best. 'I hear the latest from you guys, after a Maharashtra-for-the-Marathas dictat, a no-girls-in-pubs order and a no-Pakistanis-or-Aussies-at-the-IPL firman, is a no-mixed-marriages order. Is this true?'

'Listen, *dude*,' said Karan Sethie trendily. 'The pub thingie was a Sri Ram Sena initiative, the other issues you mention are MNS and RSS affairs. Nothing to do with the IJP!'

'And the demolition of the mosques?' I asked, knowing I sounded Nave as hell, but not caring. 'And the persecution in Gujarat?'

He looked at me properly for the first time. 'How young you are,' he said. It sounded really patronizing.

I flushed.

'So's your electorate,' I retorted.

'True... You know, Sarojini, lovely name by the way...'

'It's for Sarojini Naidu,' Zain supplied, smiling slightly, because he knew I hated my name. 'Her grandfather named her.'

'Ah, great man, your grandfather, great man,' said Karan Sethie gustily. 'How sad he would be to see the state of the Pragati Party today!'

I glared at him, irritated. He was talking like he'd known Bauji *personally* or something. Fat chance – he must've been in diapers when Bauji first became MP.

'But you didn't answer Nauzer's question, Karan – is the party really against mixed marriages?' said Zain.

Karan Sethie furrowed his broad, intellectual-looking brow and sighed heavily. 'We in the IJP,' he said self-importantly, 'believe in Hindu-Muslim unity. We believe Hindus and Muslims should be close, *very* close, like brothers and sisters.' He paused, letting this admirable sentiment sink in. Then he added, 'And you don't marry your brothers or sisters, do you?'

He laughed loudly. Bunty joined in, chortling away. Nobody else did.

Zain said, with good-natured resignation, 'And that's typical IJP doublespeak for you.'

I looked at him.

So what are you doing in this stupid party? I asked silently.

He flushed a little, almost like he'd heard me.

'Anyway, all this Hindu-Muslim, jaati-paati stuff is old hat now!' continued Sethie, waving his hands fastidiously, like his party hadn't lived off Hindu-Muslim and jaati-paati its whole life. 'The young generation care tuppence about it! They just want a clean, intelligent government that delivers progress to everybody.'

Zain brightened visibly.

I wanted to shake him.

Instead, I said politely to Sethie, 'So, basically you're saying that all these years you were pursuing the Hindutva agenda not because you *believed* in it, but because you felt it could get you votes. Wow, at least in *my* party we stay loyal to our beliefs, no matter how popular or unpopular they might be!'

Karan Sethie's shoulders shook with silent laughter. He leaned in till we were practically nose to nose.

'Oh, no, young lady,' he drawled, looking irritatingly superior. 'In your party, you just stay loyal to the *family*, no matter how popular or unpopular they might be!'

Everyone laughed appreciatively.

Except me, of course.

'You know, someone young and fiery like you will just get extinguished in that den of sycophancy. They'll turn you into a yes-woman, you wait and see. You'll soon be tap dancing to the Top Brass's every whim.'

'Excuse *me*—' I began hotly, but he didn't stop to listen.

'What I always ask is,' he said in a louder voice, appealing to all of us with a practised sweep of the arm, 'how can a party that hands down its top post from father to mother to son, a party that is entirely *not* democratic, deliver to a country that *is*?'

He sounded so rehearsed, I thought sourly as I shut my

stupidly open mouth. Like he said this every day. And how galling to know that he was absolutely right.

'And of course, in *your* party everybody gets an equal opportunity,' I said sweetly. 'I mean, you've given a ticket to a political novice simply because he's an ex-prince. That's *really* democratic.'

'Uh, a *Muslim* ex-prince,' Bunty clarified, like that made it slightly better.

'Yeah... whatever,' I said, rolling my eyes.

'Besides,' Bunty went on doggedly, 'he doesn't even behave like a prince. He never did. I mean, when we were kids, he used to *bowl*.'

Everyone looked blank.

'Matlab ki, he was the only one who actually *didn't* mind bowling! All the other rich kids only wanted to bat, and made their servants bowl to them.'

'How egalitarian,' I murmured snidely.

'Shut *up*, Bunty,' muttered Zain. 'You're not helping.'

'We've given him a ticket,' said Sethie, refusing to be diverted, pointing an emphatic finger at me, his eyes flashing with passion and good white wine, 'because he's a *fantastic* vote-puller. As you're shortly about to find out.'

'Boooooo!' whooped Pinky, looking all feisty and cute.

'Boooooo!' whooped back Bunty, looking like a total choot.

I realized that everyone had formed a kind of circle around Zain and me, and we were standing in the middle, toe-to-toe, like boxers.

Or like people who were just about to kiss.

Raising my chin to look up at him, I found him looking puzzled.

'You feel... *shorter* tonight,' he said.

'It's my stupid Champapuli chappals,' I muttered, scowling, sticking out one foot to show him.

'Ah...!' He grinned. 'You've been taken down a couple of pegs!'

I just glared at him. He was wearing Champapulis too. But of course, they hadn't made him shrink magically, like mine had.

'Well, get *used* to the feeling...' He folded one large hand into a fist, reached out and biffed me gently, very gently, on the chin. ''Coz you're going down, Bapa Nagar.'

'In your *dreams*, baby,' I snapped, so pissed off, my heart forgot to skip a beat at his touch.

'Now *that's* a picture,' declared Rumi, appearing from nowhere and clicking away. Then he asked briskly, 'I hope you cross-party types are being mature enough not to squabble?'

'Naah, they're squabbling, all right!' reported Nulwallah happily. 'About which is the good party and which is the evil one.'

'Well, darlings, everybody knows that absolutes like Good party and Evil party don't really exist,' said Rumi, busily clicking pictures of Pinky now. 'Every party is usually a mix of both.'

'Yeah...' piped up Nulwallah. 'Most parties are *Govils*. Like Arun Govil.'

Karan Sethie cleared his throat and said, 'Bachhon, instead of bickering about who's Good and who's Evil and other rhetorical, irrelevant things – if you concentrated on the difference you could make right here in the eight-hundred-square kilometres of Bittora itself, you'd feel a lot more empowered. Most MPs waste too much time in Delhi, at the durbars, as you yourself put it, politicking about. It's a waste of time. You'll be amazed at what you can acheive, if you are a focused, committed and on-the-spot MP.'

'That's what *I* want to be!'

Zain and I had spoken in unison. We looked at each other, startled.

'Incredible,' said the IJP frontman wryly. 'It would seem that the Bittoragarh voter is spoilt for choice.'

After dinner – which was disappointingly uneventful, Zain sat way down the table from me – I picked up my phone to call Jugatram to ferry me home.

'Oh, you'll never get network here,' Rumi informed me. 'Wherever-you-go-our-network-follows my *ass*. It's a total scam. I tell you, if I see a small, black-faced, brown-assed pug anywhere, wriggling its stumpy little tail, I'll *strangle* it.'

He was right, I realized as I looked down at my phone. There seemed to be no network in Casa Sisodia. Idly, I wondered if that could be a campaign issue.

'So where did you call me from?' I asked.

He nodded at the dark courtyard. 'If you walk across and climb those stairs, you'll reach these two lacy stone balcony thingies, one floor up. They jut out, kinda like the boobs of the building. Get onto one of them, face the fields, stand on one leg and you might get two little bars of signal.'

'You can't be serious!' I said, laughing.

At this, Zain leaned back in his chair, three seats away. 'Oh, he's serious, all right,' he called out, smiling ruefully. 'I could show you the spot, if you like. I need to make a call too.'

His voice was casual, but something in it made my muscles go limp. Setting down the monogrammed silver spoon, which suddenly felt too heavy, I managed to say, my voice very demure, 'Thank you. That would be most kind.'

The dark eyes gleamed wickedly for a moment, but all he said, in the same noncommittal tone was, 'Don't mention it. Come.'

So I picked up my phone and followed him.

He held the glass door of the conservatory open for me in this very chivalrous manner, but I couldn't meet his eyes as I passed through. We walked across the large courtyard without speaking, the muggy heat somehow underlining the utter quiet in the dark fields that stretched out in every direction beyond the haveli. The stars above were bright and the scent of the raat-ki-rani was almost oppressive. Our shadows against the old stone steps were inky black and sharply etched.

There was a flight of stairs, and then, next to the top branches of an ancient neem tree, I saw the twin protruding, latticed balconies. They hung a good three feet above us, with no steps in sight.

Zain mounted one lightly, then turned around and held out his hand to haul me up.

Hah! No *way* was I falling for this. He'd hauled me up a mango tree once, and what good had come of that?

So I took one step back, put both my hands firmly behind my back and shook my head.

I thought he'd let his hand drop, but he kept holding it out, looking down at me. His expression seemed... friendly. And a little amused.

'You'll never get any signal down there, you know.'

Oh, he was *so* wrong. I was getting signal all right. All kinds of signals. And they were all radiating out of *him*. And I knew I was signalling right back. The music from the old harmonium was deafening. Couldn't he hear it?

Apparently not.

Because he just stood there, smiling, head cocked to one side, hand held out, looking nice and harmless.

Come on, his dark eyes seemed to say. I won't bite. Besides, it's just my *hand*. An entirely non-controversial, non-erogenous body part. What could possibly happen?

I didn't want to be rude. Or prim. Also, I didn't think I could clamber onto that balcony unaided. At least, not without getting my prized new clothes dirty. And I *did* need to phone the driver.

So I shrugged, gave this light, sophisticated laugh and placed my hand in his.

Bad move.

His fingers closed surely over mine, he pulled me up, and then somehow, smoothly, effortlessly, and with no fuss at all, I was standing within the circle of his arms. Two large hands rested possessively on the small of my back, and because I'd landed on a low boundary wall, I was directly at eye level with him. Through his Deep Purple T-shirt, and my thin crocheted top, our navels were totally kissing.

'Sorry,' he said as he steadied us. I could feel his chest vibrate as he spoke. 'I thought you'd be heavier.'

I realized dazedly that my hands had come to rest on the face of Ian Paice, the Deep Purple drummer, right over Zain's chest. And that Zain's heart was thudding hard, like he'd just run a marathon.

'Oh, no,' I said, somewhat incoherently, as I snatched my hands away. 'You're just... really strong.'

It was a pretty vacuous thing to say. But I don't know, it was just what my brain had been registering. That he *was*. Really strong, I mean. Six-pack Zak, as Rumi had put it. He must be fully narcissistic to work out that hard, I thought. If not gay.

'How's your network?' he asked, his hands still clasping me to him with disturbing intimacy, seemingly unaware of the whole navel-to-navel situation.

'Oh, yeah, lemme see,' I said, peering down at my phone, while he, supposedly in order to examine my phone screen, pushed me up even closer against him, exploding my gay theory instantly and unequivocally. My knees practically buckled, but I also made a pleasant discovery. 'Hey, I'm getting *full* signal now!'

'Great,' he said, laughing a little, his lips brushing my collarbone. 'Now give me a missed call, I'll save your number.'

Hello, no way was I going to give him my phone number! It was bad enough that he was totally psyching me out on Facebook!

So I said, pretending not to notice that his hand had slid up my front and was now deliberately undoing the tiny, mother-of-pearl buttons on my blouse, 'Did you know that Pakistan, Sri Lanka, Africa... *all* have started making missed calls now? The missed call is India's gift to the developing world!'

'Yeah,' he agreed smoothly, as the last button fell open gently. (I suppose I could've slapped his hands away and told him to cut it out. But I couldn't. I just *couldn't*.) 'In fact, the COAI has instituted a study to understand the revenue implications of this social phenomenon in India.'

'That's right,' I said shakily to the stars, as he bent to trail kisses along the soft skin his fingers had uncovered. 'They estimate that the loss of revenue due to missed calls is as much as thirty per cent.'

'That's beautiful.' He sighed.

'Yeah,' I agreed. 'It's—'

Huh?

I yanked his head up by his messy hair. 'How,' I asked pertinently, 'is that beautiful?'

He blinked, his eyes just a little glazed. 'Sorry, what?' he said softly, one rough, slightly shaky hand coming up to touch my cheek gently.

My mind went blank.

A stupid little sigh escaped me.

'I missed you,' I whispered.

His eyes darkened. His breath caught. He bent his tousled dark head and kissed me.

It was like we'd never stopped kissing at the wedding. We took up exactly where we'd left off. And at the wedding, I remembered, it had felt like we'd never stopped kissing since we were sixteen. We were sixteen year olds, kissing for the first time. He sank down to the dried neem leaf-strewn stone floor, taking me with him, and then, suddenly, incongruously, the unofficial IJP theme song *Sarkar Genda Phool* rang loudly in my ears.

I blinked in disbelief.

It was Zain's phone.

He was sitting up, answering it, talking to his party people, and my hands were still under his shirt! I withdrew them hastily and sat up.

'Yeah… okay,' he was saying, a little dazedly, into the phone. 'I'll be down in five.'

He put down the phone and looked at me. 'I have to go,' he said slowly (regretfully?). 'Bunty and I are driving to Tanki tonight. I have meetings in the morning.'

My face was red. Not that he could tell in the darkness, I hoped.

Suddenly I felt incredibly cheap.

'Okay,' I managed to say airily. 'Run along then. Suck up to Karan Sethie. I'll stay here. I came out here to phone my driver, anyway.'

He frowned, shaking his head. 'I didn't...' he began, then stopped. 'I wasn't...' He stopped again, and all these hot, brooding lines appeared across his forehead. 'You mustn't...'

But I was too busy dusting the neem leaves off my Mango jeans to answer.

Silence.

I was idiotically close to tears.

'Jinni,' he said finally, half-affectionate, half-exasperated. 'I know how you think. So I want to you to know that *this*,' he made a sweeping hand gesture which I assumed was to symbolize our recent excesses, 'has absolutely *nothing* to do with the election, okay? They are two separate things. Have you got that?'

I nodded. 'Of course,' I said lightly. 'The election is the main thing, I know.'

He frowned again. 'That's not exactly what I...'

But I didn't let him finish.

'Go do your worst in Tanki,' I said dismissively, fingers busily dialling Jugatram's number. 'Though I'm warning you, I'm *so* gonna sweep there.'

Jugatram drove up promptly enough, but just as I was leaving, old Dugguji called out to me. He was sitting alone in a curved armchair at the head of the dining table, looking a little like a Sufi saint, with his long beard and glowing white clothes.

'Kitni badi ho gayee ho!' he said. 'How big you have become.'

I smiled vaguely, my mind still on Zain.

'That Rumi told me you are very good at your work? Making very good animations, vaghera?'

I flushed with pleasure, happy that he had not used the word *cartoons*. 'I'm okay,' I said modestly. 'Not *that* great. My...' I cleared my throat a little self-consciously, 'my kitaanus for Harpic toiletbowl cleaner won an award for best animation at the Goafest last year.'

He nodded kindly. 'Good, good. Very good.' Then he said, 'You don't feel bad, beta? That your Amma is pulling you out of the work you are so good at and pushing you into politics?'

I shrugged my shoulders. 'No, it's okay actually, Dugguji,' I said, only half-truthfully. 'Koi zabardasti nahin hai.'

He said, thumping the ground with his walking stick emphatically, 'But the world needs artists! They are much, much more important than MPs! Aur waise bhi, you know, Zain is a good boy, he's your childhood friend. He will take care of Bittoragarh. It's not like you will be leaving your grandfather's constituency in the hands of a crook like Dwivedi.'

I liked that he had called Bittora Bauji's constituency. I felt, sometimes, that even Amma forgot that part. Still, what was he trying to say?

'You know, beta,' he said, 'we have a good survey man, recommended to us by Karan Sethie. His name is Mr Urvashi. It is a woman's name, but he is a man. Very sound fellow!'

I nodded, wishing the old dude would get on with it.

'He is not like those ghatiya newspaper surveys, which interview four-five people only. It is thorough, in-depth, his people are everywhere. Khair, he has done a full survey and it is saying that Zain's chances of winning are eighty-twenty.'

I felt like I'd just been sandbagged.

He's lying, I told myself. Don't be fooled by his grandfatherly air. He's just trying to psyche you.

Old Dugguji continued inexorably, killing me with unsolicited kindness: 'So, here is what I say to you... you are also like my grandchild, no?'

I nodded. I had to hear this one out quietly.

'As your *grandfather*, then, I am saying to you ki, beta, why to fight a losing battle?'

I just stared at him blankly.

Seeing he was faced with a moron, he spelt it out. 'Two days mein withdrawal date hai, withdraw kar lo.'

Wow.

It was all a Plaan.

They had lured me in here, bathed me, fed and fêted me, rendered me incoherent with lust, and now they were closing in for the kill. I continued to look at him, expressionless.

'I know you must have spent a lot of money on this election already. It is not fair that you should lose that. So what I am saying is this – we will compensate you for all the money you have spent. Let us say... what... two crores?'

'That should cover it,' I managed to say faintly.

'But so much money we can't arrange that quickly, so,' old Dugguji paused like he was really thinking about it, 'suppose we give you one now, right now, before you go home tonight, and one in a few days' time – chalo, right after the withdrawal date, then it should be okay, no?'

'It should be,' I agreed.

He leaned forward. 'You are a big girl now, beta, you don't need to ask anybody's permission. And Ammaji is so unwell nowadays, why to give her trouble, no?'

'No,' I said. 'I mean, yes, why to give her trouble?'

'I will instruct them to put a bag inside your car when everybody is still in the conservatory. Nobody will know.'

'Um… okay, Dugguji… put it in the car. And… is it fine if I go to the bathroom? I need to wash my hands before I leave.'

Saying which, I got up and stumbled out of the dining room and into the loo where I'd bathed so happily barely two hours ago. My ears were ringing. I needed to do some serious thinking…

The next day was easily one of the worst in my life.

First, I was disgusted with myself for dashing across rural Bittora to get a little Zain-fix. I mean, I'd managed without seeing the guy for nine whole years! Why then, this sudden, desperate conviction that if I didn't have a one-on-one encounter with his smooth, muscular, honey coloured chest every few days, I would die?

Second, I was horribly deflated by the mysterious Urvashi's predictions about how my chances of winning were just twenty per cent.

Third, I was sick with fear about Amma's reaction when she found out I had accepted money from Dugguji.

And fourth, I woke up with a headache from hell.

As we drove drearily through the most depressing, dusty, desolate countryside on our way to Sujanpur, my temples were throbbing so hard, I was almost seeing double. I could've told Munni or Rocket about it, but I'd learnt by now that they tended to fuss too much. If I mentioned a headache, they'd probably embarrass the hell out of me by kidnapping a doctor to tend to me immediately. Who, in turn, would advise an emergency CAT scan because I was such a VVIP. They'd never do something as simple as getting me a couple of aspirin.

So I just sat in the back seat, doused the pallu of my sari with a bottle of water, covered my head with it, and tried to sleep.

But then the Sumos lurched to a halt. I sat up gingerly, wondering what was going on. We were at a level crossing. Grinning children thrust their heads in through the car window and offered me glowing, deep purple, just-off-the-tree shehtoot. I bought some, while Munni hopped out of the Sumo and headed off somewhere with a purposeful air. Rocket Singh was dozing gently. I scanned the shop signs around us, looking for geographical clues. A cycle repair shop sign informed me that we were on the main Dhoodiya-Sujanpur road. And then I saw a sign for a medical clinic. The board was festooned with a big red cross and proudly read 'Dr J.C. Bhoopendra Singh, MBBS, MD'.

Oh, good, I thought. I'll just nip in there and hopefully, he'll give me some aspirin.

Patting the driver's shoulder, I slid out of the Sumo and zipped into the clinic.

It was a small, peaceful room, whitewashed a pale medical green. A large desert cooler kept the place cool and fragrant with khus. A fair, plump, genial looking man, who was sitting behind a smart aluminium desk, looked up with a smile when I walked in and asked, 'Yursss?'

'Yursss… matlab, uh, namaste,' I said, suddenly realizing how shabby I must look in my mustard yellow sari with its damp, wrinkled pallu. 'Actually, I have a very bad headache. Can you give me something for it?'

'Front of the head or back?' asked the doctor.

I thought about it. 'Temples actually,' I said.

'Hmm,' said the plump, genial doctor. Then he looked me up and down and asked abruptly, 'Periods regular hain?'

Huh? My extra large mouth gaped open for a moment. We were speaking in Hindi, and he had used a word I'd only ever heard in Mala-D ads – *mahavaari*. 'Yes,' I said, bemused.

'Hmmmm,' he said again, this time softer and longer. 'On the first day, do you see brownish streaks on the pad? Before regular flow commences?'

'Err… yes,' I said, slightly grossed out. Was he a pevert or something? 'That's normal, right?'

'No no *no*,' exclaimed Dr Bhoopendra. 'That is *not* good, yursss… not good at all. You could be having cancer and all. In your baby-basket and all…' Then, beckoning me closer, he held a plump, fair thumb to the soft skin just below my left eye, pulled it down and peered inside. 'You need to take a strong syrup to build your strength,' he declared, 'then only the brown streaks and these headaches will go.'

He reached down and opened a cupboard below his desk. It was obviously refrigerated, because a lot of white frosty air billowed out of it creepily. He pulled out a large brown bottle, decorated with the silhouette of a magnificently well-endowed lady, her bosom and butt swelling like the bulbous bits of a sitar, and said, 'Two spoonfuls morning-evening. Taakat ke liye. For strength. Keep taking it until your period is normal. Then headache will also go. Seven hundred rupees, please.'

I stared at him, totally gobsmacked. All I wanted was a two-rupee Saridon pill for my headache, for heaven's sake. What was this?

He smiled at me genially. 'Don't have enough money?' he asked sympathetically.

I stared at him, practically hypnotized. 'Uh… no, actually,' I ventured, wondering what was coming next.

He opened his frosty refrigerated cabinet again, this time to retrieve a shiny steel tablespoon. 'Then I will give you one spoonful, just for now,' he said kindly. 'Only seventy-five rupees. It will make the headache go, at least. That will be good, yursss?'

'Actually, I have a *better* idea,' I hissed. 'Why don't you give me the whole bottle, for *free,* and then I'll get it analyzed in a lab in Delhi for, you know, *addictive drugs* of any sort and human ash and cow dung or whatever. And then, when it tests positive, I'll come back here and take a good hard look at your *licence*, Dr *Quack Quack* Bhoopendra!'

I lunged forward, grabbed the bottle from his suddenly slack grip, and bounded out of his little green 'clinic' before he could get another word out of his smooth fat mouth.

Munni was waiting for me in front of the Sumos, looking completely fed up with the heat. 'Where did you go, didi?' she scolded me. 'Train went past ages ago. Get in quick before they shut the gate for the next one!' She bustled me into the Sumo and we managed to scoot across the tracks just before they closed it down. Flopping back in my seat, I realized I still didn't have anything for my headache. Damn.

'What's this?' Munni asked, eyeing my bottle of Taakat Syrup warily. She probably thought the electioneering had driven me to drink like Gudia aunty.

I told her.

She pursed her lips and tut-tutted and professed to be really shocked. 'Want us to turn back and get the boys to bust up his shop?'

It was a tempting offer but I shook my head.

'Not now, Munni,' I said. 'He's not the main problem. The main problem is that both law and order and the public health system are in shambles here – that's why a weed like him is flourishing.'

She murmured something incoherent involving 'this terrible IJP local gourmint' and I closed my eyes, utterly depressed. I was so tired of that particular excuse.

But there was worse to come.

And that was Sujanpur.

When we drove through the arid, dusty villages, our convoy was greeted with wide, skeletal smiles from girls of twenty who looked like old women. We met men with skittering eyes and restless movements who seemed to smirk at everything I said. We met little children with jutting collarbones and unnaturally large, listless eyes, who looked indifferently at the shiny stickers and bandanas we had to offer. The only thing they seemed half into was our orange-white-and-green cellophane wrapped candy.

Even Munni, usually so brash and bold and hearty, was subdued.

'If there's such terrible hunger here, why haven't we seen it in the papers?' I whispered to Rocket Singh as we sipped watery tea at a villager's house that afternoon. 'I've never heard anybody talking about Sujanpur in Delhi!'

Rocket Singh looked at me wryly. 'It's not bad enough, that's why. These children are not photogenic – yet. When they start looking like those African children from Somy-ali-ya, then only the BBC will come. Or if one of the mothers sells a child, or *eats* it, or something like that. Then toh all the news channels will come. But because these people still have a little grain, a little gruel, a little self-respect… no one cares. Do you know, bitiya, this is the most loyal area in this entire parliamentary constituency? They have always voted for Pragati. And look what pragati they have made!'

'Amma?' I asked. 'Why didn't *she* do anything...?'

Munni said quietly, 'These people are not Dalits. Or Muslims. Or any special group. They are just... poor. Poor, uneducated Hindu people in an area of barren soil and no industry. Who, for some reason, believe that if they don't vote for the Top Brass's party, they will get no rain for their crops. They think Top Brass's mummy is a goddess. A devi. Some of them don't even know she is dead. Others think that after she died, she became even stronger, and closer to god. So on polling day, we put up big images of her with incense burning before it, and they all come in one after another and press the button on the Finger. They have no schools. No healthcare. And because they treat Pragati Party like a goddess, nobody in it does anything for them. Madam is so busy... she forgets also.'

That was true. The only thing Amma had said about Sujanpur was a careless, confident, 'We'll get a lead from Sujanpur, at least. We always get lead from Sujanpur.' And Ma! When I told her I was going there she said she'd never heard of it. How horribly depressing.

'Don't they get cable TV?' I asked desperately. 'TV serials and all that? I though *everyone* got that in this day and age.'

Rocket Singh shook his head. 'They're too poor,' he said simply. 'Advertisers – even the multinationals who sell one-rupee shampoo and fairness cream sachets – are not interested in them. This man whose house we're having tea in? He is seventh fail and the most educated man in the area. He has no job either.'

I slumped in my seat, feeling sick.

Zain was right, I thought miserably. The Pragati *really* sucks. They grab the votes and run away and don't show their face for five years. What was the guarantee that *I* would do anything for these people? I'd probably forget them the moment I got back to Bauji's house, pulled off my chafing sari and put on the AC.

We're useless, I told myself as we drove away, waving with pointed fingers at the small, dispirited crowd. Me and Amma, we're both useless. Two nagins, as Vir Singh had recently said in a passionate speech, an old white nagin and a young black nagin who were sure to give the kiss of death to Bittora if we were elected.

Munni continued, the explanation tripping off her tongue a little too effortlessly, 'Didi, Bittora is geographically one of the larger constituencies. It is much easier if the area is smaller and more densely populated. Then one school can help many children. One hospital also. Or one PHC. Par yahan, everything is scattered. And MP funds are limited. Besides, Dwivedi did absolutely *nothing*. So what to do?'

But it wasn't that simple. We couldn't blame Dwivedi for everything. The people in Sujanpur clearly had been neglected for a long, long time. Some of it had to be Amma's fault. Clearly, she didn't think that the people who'd voted her in, not once but *thrice*, had claim to her time. After all, hadn't she told me back in Delhi that: 'Afterwards, you can go back to your job and make your keeda-makoda all day. Go to Parliament on the first day of every sessun – budget sessun, summer sessun, monsoon sessun, winter sessun – milaa-ke-bana four times a year. Wearing a nice sari, of course. And go to Bittora every Diwali.'

It was exactly like Karan Sethie had said, I thought as the Sumo rattled along the bumpy kachha roads. There was no way I could get anything done without *living* here. Otherwise, the moment I left, things would get slack, the schools I commissioned would never be built, nor the roads or hospitals or anything else. Wells would be dug where the tribals couldn't access them. Or people in the middle would pocket the money and that would be it. Oh god, maybe I should risk a quick swig of quack quack Bhoopendra's Taakat Syrup. My head was threatening to split wide open.

Next to me, Munni rattled on and on about the flaws in the PDS. About how there were a gazillion bogus ration cards in circulation in Pavit Pradesh. How lakhs of above-the-poverty-line households had been included in the PDS list – inclusion errors, she called them. And lakhs of below-the-poverty-line families had been left out – exclusion errors, she said. But I wasn't listening.

I was the inclusion error, I thought gloomily as I wiped the sweat off my grimy face. I had no business being here. Suddenly, everything Dugguji had said last night made perfect sense. These people were Zain's family's responsibility. Everybody's money was on him. Bowing out of the race and leaving him a clear field was perhaps the best possible thing for me to do...

9

I decided to head back to Bauji's place that evening. Munni and Rocket Singh were finally satisfied that we had done as much as we could here. This was a huge relief, as I was frantic to get back to Amma and tell her about the deal I'd cut with Dugguji.

The train had left for the day, so we figured we'd just drive back in the Sumos. It would take only a few hours longer by road. I got Jugatram to close the skyroof, crank up the AC and then we hit the road. I had the back seat of one Sumo all to myself; well, except for my deep, dark secret: the suitcase stuffed with Dugguji's money that I'd told no one about. Oxygen was Gudia aunty's department, and I hadn't thought it wise to burden the team here with the knowledge that I was carrying a suitcase laden with lovely lolly. As our convoy turned onto the bumpy Dilli-Bittora highway, I lay back, propped my feet up against the bulging bag and fell into a fitful sleep.

I woke up with a start for no reason in particular. Maybe the Sumo jolted over a particularly bad pothole or something. Whatever. I sat up groggily, all stiff and cramped, peered out the window, and saw a sight that froze my blood solid.

A black Maruti Gypsy stood parked in the middle of the road – with two grey safari suited dudes inside it, motioning for us to stop.

They have permits to check any vehicle, any time, I remembered Gudia aunty telling me in what now felt like another life. *If you don't have a good explanation for why you're carting around more than one-and-a-half lakhs, they confiscate it. And if it's more than twenty-five lakhs you will be instantly disqualified.*

Using a very foul Pavit swear word that made Jugatram's head whip around in surprise, I leapt forward and grabbed the wheel. Ass in the air, hair in my face, stomach shoved painfully against the headrest of the front seat, I swivelled the Sumo to turn into a dirt track that had mercifully appeared on the left.

'Baby, what are you doing?' Jugatram bleated, wresting the wheel back from me.

'Never mind,' I told him grimly, 'just drive as fast as you can, and no stopping for anything, okay?'

He scratched his head.

'But the others?'

'Never mind about the others,' I said tersely, as I slid back into the back seat. 'They'll catch on. Now *move.*'

Hopefully, Munni would be smart enough to figure out why I'd suddenly changed course. After all, she must've noticed that I'd suddenly acquired a spiffy, heavy, new suitcase in the poorest part of rural Bittora!

We hurtled down the dark dirt track for what felt like forever, Jugatram mumbling about his nightblindness. Finally, the road broadened out and hit a three-way fork. As neither of us knew which way to go, we were immensely relieved to spot a dhaba, and stopped with a showy squealing of brakes, spinning huge amounts of dirt into the air. I jumped out, thankful for my jeans and sweatshirt instead of the usual cumbersome sari, and asked for two cups of tea, as casually as I could, even though my heart was still pounding hard.

The tea would take a while, the sleepy-looking guy behind the counter told us as he rubbed his gummy eyes, pulled a pair of striped pyjamas over skinny, hairy thighs, and tied the drawstring dazedly. I averted my eyes, opened one of the huge thick glass jars on the counter and helped myself to a cream roll. After giving him ample time to execute a neat double bow on his naada, I asked him, 'Yeh… Bittora ka raasta batayenge, bhaisaab?'

'Hain?' His voice was a nasal twang. He looked at me vacantly, rubbing the tops of the glass jars with a filthy rag, making them progressively dirtier. Then his slopey bovine eyes skittered away from me to the tiny TV screen hanging above the stove. He had obviously decided to ignore me.

'Bhaisaab…' I said, louder this time.

'Hain?' he said again, his eyes glued to the TV.

'Bittora ki sadak?'

In response, he just looked at the TV, where a fat man in a tight kurta was running into the arms of a coy, busty babe in a ghagra-choli with a cone on her head and a large black dot on her chin.

'Bittora–Dilli Highway?'

His gaze flickered to me for just a moment, then swivelled right back to the TV, where the fat man had the busty chick up against a haystack. She was squealing loudly.

'Dilli ki sadak?' I bellowed.

'It's right in front of you,' said an amused voice behind me. 'Are you running away, Jinni?'

Startled, I spun around, spraying crumbs from my crusty cream roll all over Maruti Zain's chest.

'Whoops,' I said automatically, 'I've spoilt your nice white kurta. Sorry.'

His dark eyes lit up appreciatively. 'And you *like* my nice white kurta,' he said grinning. 'You *said* so.'

I started to grin back foolishly, but then recovered my wits. I was not going to be suckered and practically seduced again, I told myself firmly.

'I am not running away,' I said coldly. 'I'm just… a little lost. That's all. What are you doing here?'

He raised one quizzical eyebrow. I wasn't impressed.

'I'm driving back from Tanki,' he said mildly.

'Alone?' I asked.

'Yeah.' He shrugged. 'I wanted to think – and I do that best when I hit the road alone.' Then he added, his eyes dancing, 'You were on the front page of the *Tanki Times* this morning, by the way. Holding some kind of adult sex toy.'

I winced.

'You looked pretty, though,' he added consolingly. Then he grinned. 'Pretty *professional.*'

'I'll have you know that AIDS awareness is a *huge* issue in Tanki,' I said loftily. 'And it's really juvenile of you to poke fun at hard-core educative initiatives—'

'But you were the one doing the *poking,*' he pointed out, straight-faced.

I glared at him, at a loss for words.

'Chai,' said the dhaba guy, slapping down two steaming glasses, half filled with bright orange liquid, on the counter.

'Hey, thanks, Jinni,' Zain said as he picked one up and began to slurp noisily. 'I really needed this!'

'It's not for you,' I said crabbily as I picked up the other glass. 'It's for Jugatramji.'

'Jugatramji?' Zain said, looking around eagerly. 'Wow! Hey, Jugatramji!'

This, because Jugatram, *ratondhi* notwithstanding, had spotted Zain after nine long years and was stumping up to say hello, grinning in delight.

He tried to shake hands but Zain, all enthusiastic, manly affection, drained his tea in one long draught and swung the old man into a warm hug. As they embraced, doing that whole, peculiar, macho-emotional thing, I stood around grumpily, feeling extremely redundant, dipped my cream roll into my tea and bit into it resentfully.

'Zain baba, good you have come,' announced Jugatram, when they had finally disengaged and stopped slapping each other on various parts of their anatomy and exchanging compliments on what good shape they were both in. (*Top ki body banayee hai, baba! Bilkul James Bond lag rahe ho, Jugatramji!*) 'Now Jinni baby can just follow your car home.'

'Jugatramji, your baby will never follow me home,' said Zain, shaking his head.

But I wasn't listening. I could see a pair of headlights behind him, a long way down the road, too indistinct to be identified as yet, but every instinct I possessed screamed that it was the EC Maruti Gypsy.

'That's right,' I said distractedly. 'Jugatramji, can I talk to you for a bit?'

He nodded, looking solemn, then leaned over and stuck his ear right next to my lips.

'There's a suitcase in the back seat,' I whispered. 'Take it out and keep it *anywhere* – in the dhaba, on the road, in a ditch, just not in the vehicle. The EC are coming to check.'

He nodded unhurriedly, his expression unchanged. Then, yawning lightly, he plodded towards the Sumo.

I turned back to Zain with a smile. Behind him, I could

see the headlights of the Gypsy getting closer. The luminous *On Election Duty* sign was now clearly visible between the twin beams, gleaming ominously, like teeth in the dark.

'Cream roll?' I proffered, holding up my tin plate.

'Why, yes,' he said, looking pleasantly surprised. 'Thanks, just one, I don't want to eat up Jugatramji's share.' He turned to the dhaba guy, who was happily engrossed in the TV again. 'One more tea, please.'

As Zain bit into his cream roll, I saw Jugatram stagger into the channa fields, lugging Dugguji's suitcase. And that was when a plan of true, evil genius bloomed in my brain.

'Hey, could I drive back with you tonight?'

Zain looked up in surprise, chewing absently. As his dark eyes locked into mine, I suddenly wondered how nice it would be to kiss him now, to taste his mouth, all mixed up with sweet, crumbly vanilla cream. My stomach executed a slow, perfect belly flip at the very thought.

I shook my head to clear it.

'Isn't that… highly irregular?' said Zain. 'I mean, wouldn't the esteemed Pappu disapprove?'

I shrugged defiantly, my cheeks hot. 'I feel like doing something highly irregular.'

One mobile eyebrow flew up at this. 'Cool,' he drawled, grinning.

The poor fool. His mind must've rewound to our steamy encounter in the boobs of Bunty's building. Unlike mine, which was rewinding back to how that steamy encounter had only been a calculated, softening-up technique to coax me into withdrawing my candidature.

Anyway, I'd got him all excited. He quickly wolfed down the rest of the cream roll and dusted the crumbs off his kurta. 'C'mon!' he said. 'Let's go.'

'Grrrreat!' I purred. 'Jugatramji, please put my clothes' suitcase in Zain's vehicle, he'll drive me home. You take the Sumo and come tomorrow.'

Jugatram looked a little confused. 'This one?' he said meaningfully, being careful to heft Dugguji's extremely heavy suitcase like it was filled with candyfloss.

'Obviously,' I replied sunnily.

He swung the suitcase lightly into the back of the Scorpio, then staggered and sat down rather suddenly, slightly breathless.

'Are you okay?' Zain asked, taking a step forward.

'Oh, he's *fine*,' I said, panicking a little. 'It's a very light bag.'

Jugatram shot me a killer look from under his grizzled brows. 'But I am a very old man,' he said austerely.

'Sorry,' I said, not very attentively because the black EC Maruti Gypsy had finally rolled up.

Two suited dudes alighted from it and smiled all around. 'Hello, hello,' they said, in low, matching gravelly voices.

'Hiiiii!' I practically sang back at them, like we were meeting at a cocktail party.

'Stopping for tea, officers?' said Zain.

'Oh, no,' they replied in unison, shaking their heads. 'Actually...' they managed to sound both wheedling and menacing at the same time, 'we would like to search the vehicles.'

Zain's nostrils flared. He started to say, his pleasant voice just a little haughty, 'But this is ridicu—'

But I interrupted him graciously. 'No no, Zain saab. Of course the officers have to do their duty!' I gestured towards my now squeaky-clean, purged-of-all-oxygen Sumo. '*Please*, go right ahead!'

They nodded and strutted over to the Sumo. One of them recorded everything with his camcorder, the other meticulously searched every possible nook and cranny in the vehicle. Dashboard, seats, under the mats, inside the suitcases, on top of the luggage carrier, under the chassis. Finally, they came back and regarded me sulkily.

'All clear?' I said breezily.

'All seems to be clear,' they acknowledged grudgingly.

'Now hurry up and check my fellow candidate's vehicle,' I said bossily. 'I'm sure he's in a rush, too.'

'Oh, that won't be necessary, madam,' they said, sliding a hesitant, appeasing smile in Zain's general direction. 'We checked that vehicle only fifteen minutes ago. That is why sir was getting angry. But he misunderstood. We won't trouble you again, sir. Goodnight.'

And with that, they turned around and sped away, leaving behind a huge cloud of dust.

Come back, I wanted to yell. Come back and *disqualify* him! This dude has one crore in the backseat of his car! This discovery could make your career! It could make your life! It could make *my* life, actually!

But of course, I didn't.

Instead, somehow managing to swallow my chagrin, I turned to Zain and said, as politely as I could, 'You know, you were right, this *is* highly irregular. I think I'd better go home in my vehicle only. I'll just unload my bag—'

But he took one step closer, looming disconcertingly over me.

'Oh, no,' he said, his voice pure velvet. 'No *way*. You are going to drive home in *my* car. Like you promised. But,' he added, his dark eyes dancing, 'I'll let you unload your "clothes" bag,' (he actually made inverted quote marks in the air, how humiliating!) 'and put it in your car, and Jugatram can drive it right behind us. So that if we're stopped again, there's no confusion about which bag belongs to whom. All right?'

'Oh, all *right*,' I snarled with bad grace, deciding to be thankful I hadn't been caught with large sums of money on my hands. Getting him disqualified had been a bit of a long shot, anyway... and I would've lost all the money too.

But it *would* have been money well spent.

We didn't speak for the first twenty minutes. Me, because I was sulking. And he, I realized after about five minutes, because he was struggling not to laugh.

'Fuck you,' I said finally, just to get the conversation going. For some reason, this made him burst into loud, guffawing laughter. I ignored this uncouth behaviour in as queenly a manner as I could, till finally, he managed to control himself long enough to gasp out, 'It *is* money inside that suitcase, I hope, not a couple of dead bodies or something?'

'As if you don't know,' I said darkly, 'considering it was your Uncleji who gave it to me!'

He stopped laughing abruptly. 'Duggu uncle?' he asked. 'Why'd he give you money?'

'To withdraw, of course!' I said. 'Don't pretend you didn't know.'

'Oh, I know,' he admitted with a frown. 'I mean, I know he meant to make you an offer. Pretty cheeky of him, I thought. But I was sure you wouldn't accept it. Don't tell me you did?'

I nodded. 'I did.'

'Amma hasn't been too well,' I continued, 'and I... well,

everyone seems to think you'll win in any case… so I thought I'd just cut my losses, you know.'

He flashed me a quizzical look.

'Somehow, that doesn't quite add up with your trying to get me disqualified just now,' he remarked drily.

'Oh, that was just a knee-jerk thing,' I assured him serenely. 'An automatic reaction to your generally insufferable manner.'

He frowned.

'But I'm not insufferable,' he said. 'At least, not intentionally. Is that how I come across?'

Now what? Of course he wasn't insufferable. Just that, every time I looked at him, I felt so vulnerable, so smitten, so *exposed* somehow, that I had to be nasty to him to preserve some kind of fundamental internal balance.

Then his frown deepened. 'I'm sorry your grandmother's unwell, Jinni. But… are you sure about this withdrawing thing?'

I nodded sombrely. 'I'm sure,' I said. 'It's the only thing to do.'

He absorbed this for a moment, and then said, 'But what about ethics? Taking money to withdraw? That's not a very principled thing to do, is it?'

'Hello, you're the one *offering* money,' I pointed out at once. 'You think that's ethically sound? Besides, what about all the money I've spent already? Someone has to make that good, right?'

'Fair enough,' he commented wryly. 'Spoken like a true granddaughter of Pushpa Pande. So you're going to leave Bittora to the mercy of the IJP, is that it? Suppose we run amuck, re-re-converting the Christian tribals in Durguja?'

'You won't,' I said confidently.

'But what would Bauji have said?'

'Bauji would've been cool,' I said lightly.

His lips curled. 'Because he was a hypocrite too, just like his wife?'

'No,' I replied steadily, my voice like ice. 'Because it's *you*. He trusted you.'

He flushed. 'Are you being sarcastic?'

'No, you're being defensive,' I said shortly.

He sighed. 'Are you *sure* about this?'

I shrugged evasively and said, 'Zain, you're a good, clean guy – it's not like I'm leaving my hometown to Dwivedi or Pant. Frankly, if I'd known you were standing, I probably wouldn't have agreed to stand in the first place.'

'Really?' he asked, reaching for my hand and grasping it, his grip almost painful in its intensity. 'Wow, Jin, it means so much to me that you're saying that. I *really* want you on my side.'

I couldn't quite bring myself to respond to this.

He continued eagerly, 'I have so many plans for Bittora, so many things I want to get started! All the stuff we talked about when we were kids, what we wrote about in those Enforcer 49 comics. Come home one day, I'll show you.'

I nodded as animatedly as I could. Then, not just to change the subject but also because I badly wanted to know, I asked casually, 'Why'd you never get in touch with me? After the cupboard thing, I mean?'

Silence.

Like, a *long* silence.

'You're driving too fast,' I said.

His glance barely flickered to the speedometer. 110.

'No, I'm not,' he said shortly.

'Okay,' I said with a shrug.

'Honestly?' he said after a while, finally glancing my way.

'Well, *obviously*.'

He said, slowly, thoughtfully, his eyes still on the road, 'Well, to tell you the truth, at the time, I didn't know how special it was.'

A long silence followed.

He was right, of course. That was it, exactly. I hadn't known how special it was either. At sixteen, I'd thought that the next guy I met would be nicer. Older, taller, Canadian, whatever. But none of them had really matched up.

I didn't say anything, just shifted in my seat a little and regarded his slightly aquiline profile as he drove steadily through the darkness. I knew my face was wearing the smug expression you see on the face of a Sarojini Nagar Market T-shirt seller when you don't buy a tee, claiming it's too expensive and then come back, red-faced and perspiring, after two hours of rootling through a gazillion stalls and say sheepishly, 'Woh T-shirt phir se dikhana, bhaiyya.'

'Don't ask me the obvious question, Jinni Pande,' he said warningly.

'I don't need to,' I answered, reaching across and tweaking his rather large ear smartly. 'I know that *now* you know how special this is.'

He groaned.

'I know no such thing,' he protested. 'I have a bevy of trophy girlfriends, don't you read the papers?'

'Your life has a gaping hole right in the middle of it, that only I can fill,' I said triumphantly.

'Listen, Rajindar Nagar,' he said, looking right at me, really hassled now. 'Stop putting words into my mouth!'

'Oh, let's not talk about your mouth,' I told him huskily, reaching over and touching it lightly. 'It's wayyy too distracting.'

Then I giggled. Snorted, actually.

He looked away again, shaking his head.

'If I didn't have Jugatramji on my tail,' he said ruefully, 'I'd stop this car *right now* and let you have it.'

'Your tail?' I guffawed.

He choked.

Hah! Rumi would've been proud of me.

I fell asleep after that, cuddling up to a sweatshirt he produced from somewhere. I dreamed that as I slept, he put out a hand every now and then and touched my cheek. I don't know, maybe he even did.

When I woke up, the sun was rising over the Lion Bridge on the Bitwa. And the winking lights of the rest of the Sumo convoy were coming up on our left. I caught a flash of Our Pappu glowering at me as he whizzed past with a snoring Munni, totally ignoring the cheery wave Zain gave him.

'Well, we're back,' Zain stated the obvious as he pulled up outside Saket Bhavan. 'Hopefully, all this high drama will end once you withdraw. I can't wait to meet you without that dude looking daggers at me, Jinni.'

'Yeah…' I replied.

Before I could say anything else, Jugatram came up and started giving Zain a verbal report card on his driving. 'Not bad. Speed achhi thi, par you should not use brakes to slow down, you should use gears,' he said sternly. 'Also, overtake karna hai toh bas overtake karo! Don't waffle about! What did I always say? Lead, follow or get out of the way. I think there is too much air in your back tyres also…'

Zain gave him a patient hearing, lounging against the Scorpio, looking exhausted but tranquil. He mouthed a bye at me as I walked past the two of them and opened the green gate.

'Bye.' I waved back, smiling sweetly as I shut the gate. *And if you believed any of that withdrawing bullshit I fed you tonight, you're a bigger fool than I ever took you for, Zain Altaf Khan!*

Ballot Boxing
Number 22 in a series of reports from Lok Sabha constituencies around India

Withdrawal Pangs

Yesterday was the last date for the withdrawal of nominations for the first phase of the fifteenth Lok Sabha elections. High drama marked the offices of magistrates across four states in north India. And nowhere was the drama more intense than in Bittoragarh, the high-profile constituency which is home to the redoubtable Pushpa Pande the shady Dinanath Dwivedi and Zain Altaf Khan, the new face of young, election-savvy India.

Rumours were thick that Sarojini Pande, Pande senior's granddaughter, was withdrawing her nomination. Spokespersons from the IJP camp, Bunty and Duggu Sisodia, gave statements, hinting that they were expecting her to withdraw in Zain's favour. Our sources say that both the Sisodias were even in place, close to the offices, to accompany Pande when she went to tender her withdrawal officially. 'Ms Pande knows she can't possibly beat the nawabzada,' they asserted. 'She vowed to withdraw and even campaign for him, since they are childhood friends, and she knows that constituency unke haathon mein mehfoos rahegi – he will take good care of the constituency.' Much was made of a close friendship between the twosome's grandfathers.

But Sarojini never showed up. Instead, very unexpectedly, Vir Singh, the venom-spewing wonder from Begumbagh, drove up and withdrew. Speaking briefly to press people outside the offices, Vir Singh said, 'Yes, it is true, I am withdrawing. There is no coercion-worshon. It is because we are having too little time to do preparation… that is all. KDS Party jindabad. Jai Hind.'

When asked if he was going to campaign for anybody now, Singh merely spat, swore and slunk away.

Hardly had the drama of this withdrawal subsided, than another contingent drove up to the electoral office. Lucky journalists were shocked to see emerging from the unmarked vehicle, not the petite, fresh-faced Ms Pande, but the portly Dinanath Dwivedi instead.

'Dwivediji! Dwivediji!' the reporters shouted, thrusting mikes and cameras into his face. 'Are you withdrawing?'

'Nahin,' replied Dwivedi, in his classic understated style, 'hum yahan *facial* karane aaye hain.' He shouldered through the mass of reporters and emerged fifteen minutes later, looking exceedingly grim. When pressed about the reason for his withdrawal, he said, 'We are giving no statements! You people have done enough damage already! First, you made that tampered tape with our footage – talking all lies about our attitude towards our Muslim brothers. Then you printed a photo of us making motion. And now you are trying to trap us again. Please let us go, we are just a humble servant of the people of Pavit Pradesh.'

And with that, he too, drove away.

The press waited agog for the arrival of Sarojini Pande, thinking that now, Zain Altaf Khan would have a virtual walkover into the seat. Local experts, however, were quick to point out that if Sarojini did not withdraw, she had more to gain from the two withdrawals than Altaf Khan. 'Dwivedi was essentially going to weaken some Pragati Party loyalist groups,' they explained. 'Pragati will gain all that back now. And both Dwivedi and Vir Singh had followers amongst the Brahmins of Begumbagh. Now those votes will definitely go to Sarojini.'

After the offices closed, and the no-show was confirmed, journalists thronged to the gates of Saket Bhavan, the Pande residence in Begumbagh, where they were greeted by an extremely smug grandmother and granddaughter duo. Asked if they knew about the two withdrawals before they happened, both demurred.

'We are so busy with our own campaigning, who has time to see what all the others are doing?' said Pande Sr. 'It's good that Dwivedi has bowed out; who knows, one day he may even be received back into the Pragati Party with full honour...'

On Vir Singh, she said tolerantly, 'He is young, he will get many turns to stand. we are so old, let us see our granddaughter win before we die.'

When queried, Pande Jr said, 'Yes, I think our chances look a lot better, the battle lines have definitely cleared. It's just Zain and me now, and I'm looking forward to a close finish.'

When asked if there was any truth to the rumour that she was supposed to have withdrawn today, Sarojini replied unhesitatingly, 'None whatsoever.'

He was already online when I switched on my laptop that night. I'd kind of expected him to be.

You evil evil person.

I grinned. I was on top of the world.

That would be me, I wrote back cockily. *How's Dugguji?*

Apoplectic, he wrote back.

I giggled.

Tell him, I wrote, *that he can have his money back really soon*

– it was just a question of liquidity. I'll drive over personally and drop it off.

He doesn't want your money, he wants your blood, Zain wrote. *So you doled out the contents of his suitcase to Vir Singh and the Peel-Eater, did you?*

I gurgled with laughter. *Of course not! Whatever gave you such a sick, twisted idea?*

Jinni, I salute you, he wrote. *You are truly an opponent to be feared and respected.*

I giggled some more. Then he wrote:

You know, I knew there was something a little off-key last night. You were much too... nice.

More fool you, I wrote back. *I can't believe you actually thought I would pack up and go home that easily. Don't you know me at all?*

I guess not, he wrote. *Didn't you mean anything you said?*

I stopped giggling abruptly. Then I wrote, *I meant some stuff.*

Good, he wrote back. *I meant some stuff too. Now go away and let me think about how I'm going to crush you.*

I couldn't resist writing, *In your arms?*

No, you maniac, came the exasperated rejoinder. *In the election.*

10

It was like Amma had received a second lease of life. She was glowing, looking way younger than her official eighty-seven and unofficial seventy-four years, there was a spring in her stride, and her cheeks were russet-red like apples.

She'd been really kicked by the way I handled the liquid oxygen crisis. It was supposed to be a sign or something, that her cunning polly blood flowed in my veins. She even called Ma and gloated about it, causing Ma in turn to phone me and enquire if I realized that I was slowly, inexorably turning into Arun Govil.

'And soon all the Good will go and you will be pure Evil,' said my mother virtuously. 'Don't say I didn't warn you.'

'Ma, I have to do whatever I can to win this thing,' I told her earnestly. 'It's vital.'

'Why?' she asked. 'Will Zain make such a horrible MP? Do you have to save Bittora from a fate worse than death or something?'

'Look, you're not *here*!' I snapped. 'You have no idea how high the stakes are!'

'How high are they, Jinni?' she asked mildly.

'They're *very* high! Our family legacy, Amma's political future, her standing, her *aukaat* is at stake, okay?'

The moment the word was out of my mouth I knew I'd made a mistake. She pounced on it at once.

'Aukaat?' Ma hissed slowly, vengefully, the way environ-mentalists hiss 'disposable diapers', personal trainers hiss 'cellulite' or Indian censor board officials hiss 'liplock'. 'Wow, I haven't heard that word for a while. So basically, it's all about *aukaat*. Is that what you're saying, Jinni?'

I squirmed uncomfortably. 'Sorry,' I muttered. 'Silly word to use, I know.'

'It's *not* just a silly word!' Ma said vehemently. 'It's an *evil*, *egotistical* word – it means *proper pla*ce. It pigeonholes people, stacks them higher or lower in an extremely rigid social pecking order. It's—'

'—a word that sums up *everything* that's wrong with India today,' I finished tiredly, rolling my eyes. 'I *know*, Ma you've only said that like a million times. But things are tough here. You can't understand it sitting over *there*.'

'You know what?' she said cryptically. 'I'm starting to think so myself.'

And then she hung up.

Whatever. At least my grandmother seemed proud of me.

The Rapist showed up the next day, lugging a small suitcase half full of liquid oxygen.

I said hello as nicely as I could, and crossed my arms firmly across my chest, trying not to think about how his fond father had asked me to marry him.

'Hello!' he replied brightly. 'Please tell, how can I help you? Papa has sent me for that only!'

Yeah, *right*. Papa must've figured that we had half a chance because Vir Singh and Dwivedi had thrown in the towel, that was all.

'Arrey, no need ya, Titu,' I assured him breezily. 'Tell me how we can help *you*. How's it going in Tiloni?'

Amma came in just then and he dived for her feet. She patted his head with uncalled-for violence and ordered him to sit down and give us the news. He sat down obediently, fixed his eyes on my chest and started talking.

'Mood is very positive!' he informed my breasts. 'All are saying Pragati can get two-third majority and form the government at the centre without anybody's help even!'

I nodded, smiling brightly, knowing this wasn't as good news as it appeared to be. Because if the party did really well, but we lost here in Bittoragarh, we couldn't blame it on a 'trend' or an IJP wave or anti-incumbency or anything. It would be our very own personal screw-up.

Amma didn't seem very impressed either. 'Arrey, what do you know?' she replied rudely. 'Who ij saying? All thoj survey people? They alwayj get it wrong!'

'Papa is saying,' Titu said doggedly to *Amma's* breasts. Really, the guy was unbelievable.

Amma snorted, making it clear she didn't think too much of Papa.

Titu cleared his throat self-importantly, and locked large lustful eyes with mine. 'Shall I give you some *really* big news?' he said.

'What?' I asked uneasily.

'Top Bra is planning—' he began.

'Top Brass,' I corrected him, slightly blown away by the vision he'd caused to spring to my mind. 'Top Brass, Titu.'

'Call me Tits,' he said invitingly.

I choked.

'Top Brass,' said Titu, picking up the thread again, 'is planning a rally in Tiloni…'

'That ij not fair—' Amma started.

'*And* Bittoragarh!' finished Titu with the air of one delivering Christmas to the Durguja orphans.

'Really?' Amma exclaimed delightedly. 'Are you *sure*? Pukka? How do you know?'

Titu shrugged modestly. 'Daughter-of-Top-Bra told me. She's taking special interest in this state, you know, Ammaji.'

'Is she also coming?' Amma asked breathlessly, while I suppressed a groan. My grandmother is like the Pragati Party Top Brass Groupie Number One.

'Ya ya,' said Titu sweepingly. 'It's all done! Arranged! They will call you from Top Brass's office anytime, today, tomorrow! Ammaji, their charisma is electrifying! You will be bundling out that good-for-nothing kebab cook for sure!'

Amma beamed. 'See, everybody is coming around because the hawa has changed,' she crowed. 'The two withdrawals have turned the tables in aawar favour! Arrey bhai, Titu,' she said, turning to him impulsively, 'come campaigning with us today! We have eleven public meetings in Begumbagh. Come – send home a good report to Papa!'

I glared at her, exasperated. Just because she wanted to show the Begumbagh types that Tawney's son was under her thumb, I would have to spend a whole day with the Rapist.

I smiled politely at Tits, willing him to refuse.

He hesitated, somehow managed to tear his eyes away from my neckline and nodded. 'Okay, chaliye,' he said obligingly.

We swept through the eleven public meetings as smooth as butter, and I was pleased to see that Titu was starting to look less lecherous and more impressed. And this was Begumbagh – the stronghold of the snooty GOBS aka Greedy Oversmart

Brahmins and Seths – where Amma was traditionally known to be not-so popular. Titu's eyes widened when Vir Singh and Dinanath Dwivedi joined Amma, Munni and me at the podium and said glowing things about my youth and cleanness and about how much Pandit Madan Mohan Pande had done for the country. (They couldn't quite bring themselves to say nice things about Amma, though.) Amma behaved most cordially, and didn't make one rude comment about lauki-ka-chilkas the whole day. I was very proud of her.

In the evening, Titu went into a huddle with his cell-phone for a while, and then slunk away, declining our invitation to stay for dinner, saying he had to hurry back to Tiloni.

'I can't believe he had the gurrts to come here!' said Munni, shaking her head as we sipped our evening tea. 'After being so uncooperative before! Chalo, at least he brought a little oxygen. Why did he come anyway, jiji?'

'He came to tell us that TB is fully behind us and is positive we will win,' said my grandmother regally if not entirely truthfully.

The crack team left soon after, and Gudia aunty said, as we headed upstairs to sleep, 'Jinni, I'll drop off Dugguji's money tomorrow. I'm going to tell him that we were *just* about to withdraw, like you'd promised, but when Vir Singh and Dwivedi withdrew, we changed our mind, thinking that perhaps *now* we may stand some small chance of victory. So thank you, but no thank you.'

'You think he'll buy that?' I asked sceptically.

'No,' she said serenely. 'But he'll *pretend* to buy that. And one hundred per cent, they'll dream up some dirty way to get back at you.'

'You're right,' I replied gloomily. 'I wonder what it will be.'

All around the country, things were getting dirtier as India hurtled closer to the first stage of the elections. The news channels were full of it.

A leading Muslim cleric standing on a KDS ticket in northern Pavit Pradesh had taken up the agenda of the Hyderabadi maulvi. He went around exhorting all Allah-fearing Muslims to marry and impregnate Hindu women and turn all of India slowly Muslim. The EC cameramen, who were lurking about everywhere during this election, recorded it, and now the EC had slapped a show cause notice on the guy, but not before his remarks sent shockwaves through the state. There were rumblings within the supposedly 'purged', newly 'secular' IJP, which was angered at these anti-Hindu sentiments and was doing a lot of sword-rattling of its own, making incendiary remarks and cracking down on 'mixed' families, wherever it could find them in rural PP.

And because the EC had banned large, colour-coded political party buntings, flags and posters, there was a lot of confusion. A prominent Pragati Party leader had strutted into a large public meeting in a north Indian state, surrounded by gun-toting security guards, stood on the podium and delivered half a speech, filled with stinging criticism of the IJP, before the booing of the crowd alerted him to the fact that he was in *the wrong public meeting*. He had to flee to his car, leaving half his entourage behind, even as irate IJP supporters pelted him with empty water bottles. This particular incident had affected me deeply, because I sometimes got the sneaking suspicion, when I watched tapes of Zain's speeches, that some of his workers looked rather familiar. They were probably organizing rallies for both of us, I thought uneasily, and earning large sums of money all round.

In Tiloni, an independent candidate, bald, transvestite and much given to flashy nylon saris, with a pair of fleshy, swollen red lips as his symbol, had topped the exit polls for two whole weeks. He promised he would open a Bollywood-style film school in the constituency and, as proof, organized a rally which would be 'packed with stars from Bollywood and Hollywood'. People turned up in thousands, but when they found nobody but Mac Mohan aka Sambha from *Sholay*, a fat blonde woman with suspiciously dark roots, and a monkey-faced Shahrukh Khan look alike, they grabbed hold of the hapless hijra, pulled off his sari in a manner reminiscent of Draupadi's vastraharan, beat him up mercilessly and sent him scampering off, bare-bummed.

And Salmon Khan, maverick movie star and shirtless crowd puller, who was campaigning for whichever candidate took his fancy, regardless of party or ideology, made a speech urging people to vote for 'good purrsons', which got five thousand hits in two hours on YouTube. Wearing a tight, sleeveless, salmon pink T-shirt and a wire hairband, he declared that 'it didn't matturrr what kind of clothes you worrre, as long as you were a good purrson with a purrre heartt – and that if you wurrr a pooorr purrson, and couldn't afforrrd good clothes, then you should at least wearr clean clothes. And drrrive carrrefully. Without drrrinking. Jai Hind.'

Totally disgusted with these bizzare goings-on, the news channels on TV were hailing this election as the most lowbrow Indian election *ever*.

The psephologists were moaning that, this time round, there had been no issues or polemics or higher levels of debate whatsoever. 'It's basically just a bunch of greedy, opportunistic people, running helter-skelter, frantically trying to make up the numbers,' they moaned on news channel after news channel. 'Anybody is getting into alliances with anybody. The manifestos are a joke. Sab kuch chalta hai. This entire election is ideologically bankrupt.'

The dirt entered our life too, the very next day. When I took Ponky out for an early morning walk, it literally flew up and hit me in the face. A flimsy, luridly pink pamphlet, covered with thick black type. Begumbagh was awash with them. They stated, in the most graphic, explicit Pavit Pradeshi, that I had managed to get a ticket to contest the election only because I had sexually serviced practically the entire Pragati Party working committee in just about every position. They also said that I was a shameless wanton man-eater who had recently had an abortion. As to the father, it could be any one of my endless list of Canadian, Chinese and African clients, none of whom could satisfy my slavering, raging lust.

Reading the shrill, gloating, self-righteous words, I suppose I should've been angry. I should've been furious and vengeful and out to screw whoever had done this. But somehow, I couldn't summon up these strengthening, focused emotions. I just felt... ill. All sucked out. Like I wanted to sit down, right there in the middle of the dusty street, like a cow, and never get up again. Very poor-spirited, I know, but I couldn't help it.

I just couldn't get over the fact that somebody disliked me enough to do something as vicious as this. Because I tend to go through life operating under the assumption that, basically, people *like* me.

Holding the pamphlets in my hand, out on the streets of Begumbagh, with the loo swirling around me, I came very close to crying.

Somehow, I managed to follow Ponky home and handed the pamphlets, in all their lurid pinkness, to Amma.

She took it pretty stoically. She said, wrinkling up her patrician little nose in disgust as she read them over a breakfast of hot fried paranthas and mixed fruit jam, 'Chheee, what ghatiya tactics. We will have to turn this into an *opportunity* somehow, Sarojini.'

I looked at her hopelessly. What was she talking about?

'Of course it's an opportunity, madam,' said Gudia aunty at once. 'It's our chance to have that boy put behind bars!'

'Amma, Zain couldn't have done this,' I said automatically, not sure if I really meant it.

Amma pushed her chair away from the table and glared at me.

'Why?' she demanded. 'Because he went to that Windcheater school? Don't be Nave, Sarojini.'

'Because...' I paused. 'Because, well, he's my childhood friend... Surely Zain wouldn't stoop to something like this?'

Gudia aunty tittered. 'Jinni, don't talk like a child. Madam and I are political veterans, we *know*. Besides, Jugatram just informed us that thousands of these pamphlets have been circulated. Somebody has clearly spent a lot of money. It *has* to be Khan – we've bought off all the others, haven't we?'

'Maybe Dugguji did it without Zain knowing,' I said, a little desperately.

Her large watery eyes looked scornful. 'Dugguji is not that smart,' she said. 'Arrey, he gave you all that money just like that! Better face the fact that it's your great *friend* Zain who's really calling the shots. What did you think? That you had him under your thumb?'

I flushed. 'That's a little uncalled for,' I said.

She laughed. 'You young girls, you think everything will go your way always.'

I said, a little more snidely then I should have, 'Look, why don't you sit down and drink some *Himalayan* mineral water?'

She made a sudden movement but Amma was beside her in an instant.

'See's crack,' she told Gudia aunty soothingly. 'My granddaughter ij a crack. See doesn't realize that all musalmaan men think this way about Hindu women – that we are all nympho. See thinks all this is a game, with rules and *times-please* and good manners. Arrey bhai, this is politics! It ij free-style fighting! No holes barred!'

'That's no *holds* barred, actually,' I said wearily. God alone knows what she was thinking of.

Gudia aunty grabbed a pamphlet and stood up, breathing hard. 'Madam, this stuff is *filthy*! They've slandered your family. And so, just for *your* sake, I'm going to see the DC and make sure somebody's head rolls for this.'

She blundered out of the room without a look in my direction. Amma promptly turned reproachful eyes on me. 'Sarojini,' she said, 'you must be *kind*. Remember she had a hysterectomy at twenty—'

'And her husband left her, and didn't even hook up with anybody else, I know, I know,' I said sulkily. 'But could you cut me some slack here? I'm reeling from the shock of my nymphomania having been made *public*.'

Amma chuckled, walked over and poked me chummily in the ribs. 'When you got all those modest sari bloujej made, you sud have ordered a thicker *skin* too, Sarojini. Arrey, how many allegesuns have we withstood in aawar time! Now don't take tensun. Chalo, we will also go to the DC. If we can make him feel guilty enough, he may give us permission to hold a rally in the Company Bagh for free.'

She went off, and I sat heavily on a moodha. Ponky wandered in, collapsed at my feet, and nosed his way into my lap. I read and re-read the pamphlets morbidly, my ears burning, and then let them drop slowly to the floor.

Now go away and let me think about how I'm going to crush you.

They were right, of course, I thought miserably. Zain had printed the pamphlets. The fight had gotten real dirty. He would obviously stoop to anything to defeat me. There was no gaping hole in his life that only I could fill. On the contrary, *I* was the raging nymphomaniac with the gaping hole that nobody could fill. What a bloody con.

I reached down violently, startling Ponky, grabbed the pink pamphlets and tore them systematically into little strips. Then I got up and walked out to do the day's round of public meetings, white-faced and tight-chested and finally, blessedly, seething with rage.

———

Zain denied printing the pamphlets. I heard him say so on the local channel Thumka TV – clearly, steadily, no hint of laughter in his dark eyes. 'I completely deny any involvement with these pamphlets,' he said. 'I respect all women, I respect the election commission and its rules and regulations. I have instructed my workers to scour the streets of Begumbagh for the pamphlets and destroy as many as they can. My heart goes out to Sarojini Pande, who is a good human being and my childhood friend.'

The bile rushed, bitter and strong, into my mouth just looking at him. I don't need a character certificate from *you*, you bastard, I thought tightly. You might fool the EC with your goody-goody act, you might fool the voters, but you'll never fool me again...

The EC officials served a show cause notice on him but, much to our disappointment, they didn't make him spend a single night in the lock-up. He walked out of the police station, looking all troubled and concerned in his white pyjama-kurta and went back to campaigning with a vengeance. Two dogged EC cameramen and about a million journalists immediately started following me wherever I went, obviously hoping for a vitriolic outburst against Zain in one of my public meetings.

But I'd decided I wasn't going to do that. Along with a bladder of iron, I was also quickly developing nerves of steel. I did the rounds in Begumbagh with as much dignity as I could summon, and our workers reported that the smutty pamphlets had not spread to the other areas.

'And anyway, Sarojini didi,' Our Pappu told me, 'as it is half the voters in Doodhiya-Durgaja and Sujanpur are illiterate. They won't understand all this! So you don't worry, okay?'

Fortified with this rather depressing logic, I soldiered on through Begumbagh, Vir Singh and Dwivedi alternately by my side. The public meetings had become a bit of a blur, full of promises and exhortations and, of course, hugs, kisses and blessings from women of all ages. Hasina Behenji, having discovered a new affinity with me because of my 'scarlet woman' status, showed up by my side wherever I went, constantly promising me the support of the women of Tanki Bazaar. And then, just when I was congratulating myself on weathering the whole pamphlet thing with so much dignity, Amma went and lost it at some stupid meeting in the heart of the Muslim quarter in Jummabagh, lashing out directly at Zain and the entire Altaf Khan clan, regaling the crowds with tales of their debauchery, telling them that no woman would be safe under their stewardship.

The EC promptly served Amma a show cause notice, and banned her from making any more public speeches. She was apoplectic with rage at this, and so was poor Pappu, who knew she'd done us no end of harm in Jummabagh, because the people there loved Zain so much.

'Didi, hawa is changing again,' said Munni morosely during one of our nightly conferences. 'It's blowing for Zain bhai now, I can feel it. We will have to do something, otherwise he will pull this election away from under our nose.'

'Maybe we should print some pamphlets too?' ventured Rocket Singh hesitantly.

'Saying what?' Amma snapped. 'That that ujless Maruti Zain ij homo with hij darling elecsun agent Bunty?'

Gross. Really, Amma's mind was like a sink.

Our Pappu giggled. 'Jiji, that may actually bring him *more* votes in Jummabagh.'

Amma chuckled at this, while I stared at the two of them in disgust. What was I doing in the midst of this totally politically incorrect gang of thugs, anyway?

'We need... something symbolic,' Amma said slowly. 'Kuch *drama* chahiye. I wonder what it could be...'

Nulwallah showed up the next evening, swinging on the green gate, grinning ingratiatingly, asking me if I wanted to clear the air regarding my supposed nymphomania by issuing a statement of some sort. I told him I didn't, but invited him into the aangan for a chat, realizing suddenly that he would be a great guy to hand over Dr Quack Quack Bhoopendra's

Taakat Syrup to. Besides, it would be quite therapeutic to talk to someone who didn't have a Pavit Pradeshi accent and who wasn't urging me to release doctored pornographic CDs of Zain in bed with Bunty Sisodia.

'So how come you're still in Bittora?' I asked him, after he'd duly admired the contours of the lady on the Taakat Syrup bottle. 'Don't you have to cover, like, loads of stories?'

He shook his head and stretched his lanky, praying mantis-like legs on the moodha, his teeth and glasses flashing.

'We're following this particular election very closely,' he said. 'Right till the grim end. Youngest contestants in India, you know.

'And,' he continued, his eyes gleaming dementedly, 'cutest.'

'Me or Zain?' I demanded belligerently.

'You,' he replied promptly. 'Zain's not really my type.'

'Thanks,' I said. 'So how many minutes have you devoted to his latest offensive against me?'

He perked up instantly. 'Are you saying he printed the pamphlets?'

I raised my eyebrows. 'Well, *obviously*,' I replied. 'Surely you didn't fall for his cheap stunt, asking his workers to destroy them? That was pathetic!'

Nulwallah wrinkled his forehead. 'I don't know… I kind of like the guy… *and*,' he lowered his voice, 'he seems really fond of you. You guys have a solid vibe – I felt it that day, at Casa Sisodia. You seemed very friendly.'

My heart gave a bump.

'Please!' I managed to snort dismissively. 'With friends like that…'

'Who needs enemas?' Nulwallah finished, his eyes glinting.

I couldn't help chuckling. 'Exactly,' I said.

'Good! In that case, when all this is over and you're a big shot MP, will you *finally* do an interview with me?'

'You think I'm going to win?' I asked excitedly, beaming from ear to ear.

He winced. 'Little less smile, Pandeji, little less smile. I'm not wearing sunglasses.'

'D'you think I'm going to win?' I demanded again.

He shrugged evasively. 'The latest polls show you're catching up... but slowly.'

'But those were conducted before the pamphlets broke,' I pointed out gloomily.

'Yeah...' He looked a little grim. 'Still, you'll have to do something quick to remedy the character assassination. So whatchha gonna do, Pandeji?'

'No idea,' I replied.

There was a scratching at the door and Rumi poked his head in and eyed me warily. 'Friends?' he asked.

I scowled. I was mad at Rumi.

He'd been driving me crazy, moaning on and on about the *smells* and the *mosquitoes* and the *heat,* like some city-bred diva. He complained that the AC hissed hot gas and the shower had no pressure. He carped constantly about his *ghamoriyan.* But when he turned up his nose at Hasina Behenji and alluded to her in a not-very soft voice as *Pasina* Behenji, I snapped and told him that the sooner he got his pampered ass back to Mumbai, the better it would be for everybody.

Now he rolled in, all meek contriteness, looking like an ad for Incredible India. Elaborate, deep orange mehendi adorned his forearms, striped pyjamas encased his willowy legs and a traditional Bittora weave kurta graced his slim torso. He had a tilak on his forehead, and there was a tinsel-fringed Pragati Party muffler slung around his neck, almost obscuring his faithful camera.

'I've been at the Begumbagh temple, praying for victory for you and ignominious defeat for your foes,' he announced virtuously as he produced a little tin box of holy ash and rubbed some on our foreheads. 'It's beautiful,' he added ingratiatingly. '*All* of PP is beautiful! So...' he paused, searching for the right word, '*unspoilt.*'

'Uh huh,' I said, noncommittal.

Nauzer looked at him in disgust. 'D'you even *know* what's happening in the election, Rumi?'

Rumi looked up, all offended. "Course I know,' he said. Then he added mysteriously, 'I know more than *you* know, Mr Smarty pants Reporter Guy,' and threw down a thick bundle of A4-sized sheets on the table with a flourish.

'What's this?' said Nulwallah, pouncing on the papers at once.

'Those are *personal*,' I said sharply, because I had an inkling of what the papers were. 'Off the record, Nauzer, okay?'

'Okay, okay,' he said, nodding distractedly as he scanned the sheets. 'Wow, these are really good.'

I sneaked a peek at the pages. Yes, they were what I'd thought they were. Bugger.

'Duuuuude,' gloated Rumi happily. 'You are *so* busted! This is conclusive *proof* that you and six pack Zak used to be an item!'

'Oh, for heaven's sake, these aren't love letters,' I said dismissively, as I picked up a bundle and slowly turned the pages. 'They're just a comic book series we used to write.'

The
Incredible Case Files
OF THE
Amazing Incendiary Enforcer # 49
MP by day, Enforcer of the Indian Constitution by Night

Art	Text
Jinni Pande	Zain Altaf Khan

Rana Thakur, scion of one of the richest families in Pavit Pradesh, was a lonely child. Orphaned at an early age, Rana was brought up by an elderly trustee, who had been a legendary freedom fighter in the 1920s. Now crippled, living in obscurity and deeply mistrustful of all material success, this trustee told tales of idealistic days to fire young Rana's imagination.

Years later, propelled by a fervent desire to serve the people of India, Rana rides on family name and fabulous wealth to join the leading political party of the day, and gets sworn in as a Member of Parliament in the all powerful Lok Sabha.

But just one session in Parliament reveals that an MP's hands are tied. Because 90 paisa out of every 1 rupee that is sent to the states by New Delhi is eaten up by a nexus of venal middlemen. Only 10 paisa trickles down to the common man. Hobbled by the twin chains of corruption and sycophancy, an MP can achieve virtually nothing.

And so Rana decides to achieve Freedom at Midnight. By day, Rana is the quintessential bribe-taking MP, hand-in-glove with the Nexus. But come midnight, and Rana takes to the skies as Enforcer 49, to ensure that the Nexus's plots are foiled and all government policies that exist on paper are actually implemented. The Enforcer ensures that schools actually run, that roads are really constructed, that jobs are properly created. Until the break of dawn, Rana patrols the country tirelessly to enforce Justice – Social, Economic and Political; Freedom – of Thought, Action, Belief, Faith and Worship; Equality – of Status and Opportunity; and ensures amongst all Indians Fraternity – assuring the dignity of the individual and the unity and integrity of the nation.

In short, everything that was promised in the original, 26th November 1949 draft of the Indian Constitution.

'These drawings are really good,' said Rumi condescendingly. 'The framing is excellent too. How old were you when you did them?'

'Fourteen,' I said, shortly, not looking at him. Knowing the mind that had scripted this idealistic, though purple, prose had also scripted the obscene pink pamphlets circulating all over Begumbagh was making me feel physically ill.

'Is Rana a boy or a girl?' Rumi asked next, squinting down at the drawings.

I bit my lip.

'We couldn't decide,' I said. 'So we kept it kind of vague.'

I'd wanted Rana to be a girl, of course, but Zain said that would be unrealistic. He said Rana had to be a guy to do all the cool stunts he'd put into the stories. We finally agreed to leave it to the reader to decide.

We started the series one sultry summer afternoon when I'd been gushing on about how Bruce Wayne aka Batman and Don Deigo de la Vega aka Zorro didn't really have any superpowers – they were just regular guys battling a bunch of crazy villains in a corrupt city with nothing but intellect, gadgets and physical prowess. And large sums of money, Zain pointed out, which, I had to admit, was true. I'd been telling him how Batman had been co-created by artist Bob Kane and writer Bill Finger when he had said suddenly, 'Big deal, I bet we could make a comic book series, too. You draw and I'll write.'

'Where'd you find these?' I asked Rumi, a little shaken by the memory.

'I told you,' he said. 'In the old desk.'

Of course. I used to study at that desk. For my boards. Amma must've had it moved out of my room and into the guest room at some point.

'What were you poking and prying about in the desk for?' I demanded crossly.

'There's no need to yell,' he replied sulkily, rolling his eyes. 'You've just dumped me in your guest room and you never have any time for me. I have to do *something* to pass the time!'

'Rumi, I'm fighting a Lok Sabha *election*!' I said in exasperation. 'I hardly have time to hang out with you! I thought you wanted to help? To take pictures?'

'You leave too early,' he muttered. 'I never get up before eleven…'

Nulwallah, who had been poring over the comics, suddenly said, 'What an idealistic pair of kids you must've been! Why didn't you just watch TNT and Cartoon Network like regular kids?'

'Power cuts,' I said shortly. 'You have no idea.'

He whistled.

'Well, these are *great*, Pandeji! How many did you guys do?'

'Eight.'

They'd taken *ages* to do – and it was especially hard on me because I had to painstakingly draw every single frame by hand. Zain used to lie around on the floor and watch me as I worked, reading, scribbling, constantly eating. We had a couple of huge fights, when he would go over everything I'd done really carefully, and then insist the storyline needed changing and expect me to redraw everything. I'd thrown all the papers at him and stormed out, fuming, any number of times.

And now here they were.

Enforcer 49 and the Dam of Death
Enforcer 49 and the Fertilizer Farmer Suicides
Enforcer 49 and the Midday Meal Scheme
Enforcer 49 and the Paved Road to Nowhere
Enforcer 49 and the Inter-caste Love Story

Enforcer 49 and the Nuclear Deal
Enforcer 49 and the Rural Employment Guarantee Programme
Enforcer 49 and the Universal Immunization Drive

'Must've been great fun doing them?' Nauzer the newshound asked in a carefully casual manner I didn't like at all.

'Umm, yes,' I said awkwardly. 'Actually, it wasn't—'

Thankfully, Amma sailed in just then, talking nineteen to the dozen. 'Sarojini, where ij Ponky? Still not back? We are *telling* you that that no-good boy ij taking him to mate with all kinds of unsuitable, mixed pedigree, low-quality bitches for pocket money. He'll get dog-AIDS, wait and see.'

We all blinked at her blankly.

Realizing I had company, she acknowledged Nauzer, who'd leapt to his feet, with a resigned sniff, but smiled benignly at Rumi, who had become quite her favourite.

'Hello hello,' she said with vague bonhomie. 'Must be talking all Bombay things, hain? Where ij aawar dog, but?'

Rumi instantly lunged forward to smear her with holy ash from his little tin box and just then, an extremely chirpy looking Rajul walked in, with Ponky bounding along behind him, a happy lolling grin on his face. He fell upon Amma happily, while Rajul looked up at me, and asked, all chubby, ingratiating charm, 'Didi, can I be absent from evening class today?'

'Why?' I asked perfunctorily, thrilled that I wouldn't have to tutor the little git.

He raised his angelic hazel eyes to mine.

'I want to see the panchayat meeting in Ahri village,' he said eagerly. 'Everyone is saying there will be a stoning… maybe even a hanging!'

'*What!*' Rumi, Nulwallah and I exclaimed all at once.

Rajul nodded virtuously. 'A Brahmin girl was caught with

an achhoot boy. Naturally, her family beat her and beat her and beat her. She screamed all night – just like a peacock. *Keeeaaayon! Keeaaayon!* But she's gone quiet now. Today, her father is going to *kill* the boy. Behind the threshing field. At least,' he added conscientiously, 'that is what he is *saying*. But my mother says he doesn't have the gurrrts.'

Rumi just stared at Rajul, hypnotized, like he had never seen anything like him in his whole pampered south Mumbai existence. And he probably hadn't.

But Nauzer leapt to his feet. 'Is he for real?' he exclaimed. 'Is this happening?'

Amma spread out her hands, not looking too perturbed. 'We don't know, might be true, might be a rumour,' she said. 'These girls are getting completely out of hand nowadays, they watch too many TV serials…'

'I have never seen anybody hang,' Rajul continued excitedly. 'I want to shoot a video of it – will you give me your cell-phone? They say the tongue sticks out and the face goes black…'

I gave him a shove. 'That's enough, Rajul!' I hissed. 'Don't talk about things you don't understand! Go home now, and *stay* home. No running into Ahri, okay?'

'But everybody is saying it's the boy's fault,' he said mutinously. 'They're saying his whole community needs to be taught a lesson! Bloody low caste! He should've stayed within his aukaat.'

The blood rushed to my head.

I lunged for him.

'Jinni!' Rumi cried out. 'He's just a kid. He's only repeating what he's heard his elders say.'

I shook my head.

'Go. Home. Now,' I thundered at Rajul.

He slunk away, looking sulky, and I turned to Amma. 'What do we do now?' I asked. 'Go there and tangle with the Aukaat police of Ahri?'

She sniffed. 'And lose the Brahmin vote? As it is, everybody thinks you are nympho. You want them to think ki you are mad also?'

I stamped my foot. 'Didn't you hear? They're hanging him *now. Tonight!*'

'Sarojini, it could just be a rumour,' Amma said, looking completely exasperated. 'But we will phone the district magistrate and the police! Pleaj understand, Ahri is in the heart of Begumbagh! We are not going to rush in there like a crajy person and read out the Equality of Status and Opportunity clauj from the Indian Constitution to a mob of Ahri duffers! This is not *Aap ki Kachheri*. It would be most foolis!'

I glared at her.

She glowered at me.

Nulwallah and Rumi shifted awkwardly on their moodhas.

'Fine.' I shrugged, backing down. 'Don't. You're right, that boy does have a lurid imagination...'

'Good,' she said, turning to leave. She stopped near the door, her gaze sweeping over the two figures cowering on the moodhas. 'And get some sleep. We have sixteen public meetings tomorrow.'

'Okay, okay,' I said, yawning. 'Goodnight, Amma, sleep well.'

I stretched in my moodha sleepily. And the moment she cleared the corridor, I lunged for the stack of *Enforcer 49s* on the table.

I fumbled through them, flipping pages until I found the one I wanted. I stared at it, my palms sweating, the hair at the back at of my neck standing on end, singing the '*Jana Gana Mana*'.

Enforcer 49 and the Inter-caste Love Story.

No way was it a coincidence that it had showed up here tonight.

'Rumi,' I said, turning to him. 'You go in there and chat with Amma. About her youth. Her cleansing-toning-moisturizing routine. The *Avatar* porn flick. Anything. Just keep her distracted. Nauzer, c'mon, if we hurry we can still catch Rajul and scoop him into the Sumo to show us the way to Ahri...'

Twenty minutes later, a drowsy, over-excited child was seated between Nulwallah and me, snivelling loudly because we hadn't let him bring along his mother's cell-phone.

'It has enough memory for three pictures,' Rajul fretted. 'I would have had to delete the pictures of papa and Durga mata and me, but it doesn't matter, I would've been the most popular boy in my class, even though I've failed in English!'

'Chill, kiddo, chill,' said Nauzer, waving Rumi's huge Canon camera at Rajul. 'We'll get it all on this, it's got a big flash, we'll need it in the dark – and then I'll give you copies of the photos.'

'Don't *encourage* him,' I snapped. 'We're going to stop the hanging, not film it. And Rajul, stop making such a racket or they'll see you and know it was *you* who raised the alarm! Now tell me, do I go straight here or do I take a right?'

'Ruh... rrrrighhht!' wailed Rajul. 'And I'm going to tell EVERYBODY that you're EVIL! That you TORTURE me! And I want to VOMIT!'

And he did. Never having sat in a moving vehicle in his life, he puked his guts out, sticking his head out the window so he wouldn't 'spoil the sofas'. I tried to tell him I'd rather he stain the seats than die by banging his head into a passing tractor but he wouldn't listen, and I ended up feeling like a total monster as I patted his little hiccupping back and asked him for directions to Ahri.

It was pitch dark by the time we drove into Ahri. We passed all the standard village spots: the buffalo pond, the big peepul tree, the school, the temple. They were all deserted. The main 'road' (if you could call it that: it was basically a dirt track with a series of front doors and a drain running along either side) died out after a while, and still Rajul kept telling me to go straight.

Soon, there were fields on both sides – flanked by the tall, straw-covered cowdung stacks that give Bittora its name. There was a clearing up ahead, where we could spot the flickering flames of torches. I stalled the engine and sat for a moment, considering my options, when Rajul gave my jeans a sudden, urgent tug and pointed wordlessly in front of us.

'Go run and hide, Rajul,' I whispered as I peered, heart thumping, palms sweating, into the dark heart of the clearing. I could make out a circle of people, all men, I think, in white dhoti-kurtas and turbans, facing inwards, in a rustic travesty of a cricket huddle. They had very solid looking, iron-topped lathis in their hands and they were talking animatedly. I could hear voices, garbled grunts and exclamations but I couldn't make out what they were saying. There was a tree in the middle of the clearing. A neem tree. And from there hung – my stomach lurched at the sight – a long white rope, as yet unknotted.

Fuck, I thought, my heart in my mouth. It really *is* the Aukaat Police.

'Um... Pandeji,' whispered Nulwallah next to me. 'Honoured as I am to be assisting you on this guerilla expedition, I must ask: Do you, like, have a Plaan?'

As I could hardly tell him I had a plaan right out of a comic book written by a fourteen year old, I just nodded confidently, and continued to look at the daunting, inverted circle of shadowy dirty-white backs. The dudes didn't look like they were in the mood to listen. I could hear wails from the heart of the huddle now, high-pitched, animal-like wails, and they were making my hair – such as it was – stand on end.

'Yes, *yes*, Nulwallah,' I whispered back. 'I have a Plaan. Just lemme think it *through*.'

And wow, was my brain thinking. It was in think *overdrive*.

C'mon, you drove all the way here, my brain thought at me. That's more than anyone else would have done! It's a big crowd, they all have lathis, it's clearly impossible to stop this atrocity now... just get Nulwallah to click some pictures, then phone the police, give them the location and slip away home. No point in trying to pull that stunt from Enforcer 49. It'll never work in real life, anyway...

I sat there, frozen, for hours or seconds, I don't know which. And then the circle parted, and I could see the cringing, bloody, blanket-covered bundle on the ground.

One of the men brought a lathi down on it, hard.

Beside me, I heard the camera whir to life and start clicking.

Okay. This *had* to be my cue. I had *so* not come here just to click pictures.

I raised my chin, squared my shoulders and put the Sumo into gear. Then I drove the vehicle right into the heart of the clearing. The mob parted, shouting aggressively. I realized that Nauzer and I were shouting too.

I stopped with a dramatic squealing of brakes, churning mud. Then I leapt out, walked straight up to the writhing blanket, yanked it off, pulled the boy up by the filthy tattered scarf around his neck and spat in his face.

'Filth!' I shouted. 'Scum! How *dare* you look at a Brahmin girl, you dirty, untouchable, toilet-cleaning vermin?'

The boy couldn't have been over sixteen. Practically a child. His eyes were glazed over and puffy, his face black with bruises, his lips so dry and cracked that they seemed made of tree bark. He didn't even blink in reaction to all my shouting. A thin stream of my spit dribbled down his totally blank face. I felt my stomach heave.

'Yaaah, filth!' Nulwallah shouted suddenly from behind me, making me jump. I spun around, saw his frantic eyes telegraphing *Are you fucking nuts?* at me, and noticed that he'd found time to hide Rumi's huge camera somehow. Good scene, at least Enforcer 49 was working with a capable sidekick tonight.

I nodded approvingly at Nulwallah, thrust out my chest and faced the crowd aggressively. Most of them probably had no idea who I was, but I recognized one turbaned, leathery-looking man with a single earring and a cleft lip. I'd had tea in his house and asked for his keemti vote not two days ago. He looked a little stunned to see me here.

'This... *thing*,' I gestured at the sagging figure, now being held up by two muscular dudes with holy threads slung across their shoulders, 'deserves to *die,* for his impudence! Kill the bastard!'

'Kill the bastard!' echoed Nulwallah with gusto, looking wonderfully Brahminical with his holy ash tilak.

'Kill the bastard!' shouted the leathery cleftie.

'Kill the bastard!' roared the crowd and surged forward.

I leapt up onto the bonnet of my jeep and held out one hand dramatically. 'But not by hanging!'

'Why?' called out the cleftie pertinently.

'Why?' echoed Nulwallah, missing his cue like an idiot.

'Why? Why? Why?' demanded the crowd.

Dhung Dhung Dhung.

My heart seemed to have relocated between my ears. I could hear it thumping there, as loud as a military drum. Swallowing hard, I managed to produce a malignant sneer.

'Hanging is too good for the likes of him!' I shouted. 'Bhagat Singh was hanged! Sukhdev was hanged!'

The crowd looked at me, confused, suspicious, murmuring a little.

Realizing I had to reassure them that I was on their side, I quickly spat on the boy again. It was much more contemptuous than a slap, and much less painful. God knows he needed to be spared the pain. Especially with what I had planned for him.

Villainous sneer in place, I held up one dramatic finger. 'Let us have a bit of fun with him first! So his death can be a lesson to his whole wretched community. Let them know their place is *there,* with the dirt below our feet. Let us tie him to the bumper of my jeep and drag him around till he dies!'

'Drag him till he dies!' shouted Nulwallah, finding the thread again.

A roar of approval went up from the crowd. I quickly slid into the driving seat and commanded the muscular dudes: 'Tie him! Hard!'

'Hard! Hard!' shouted Nulwallah, capering around madly.

The crowd dragged the boy, who'd regained enough consciousness to buck and curse and struggle, and lashed him with ropes to the back of the Sumo.

The cleftie, maybe suspecting something, made to climb into the front seat beside me, but Nulwallah was too quick for him. He leapt in, I quickly put the Sumo into gear and pressed the accelerator hard, spinning dirt into the eyes of the crowd.

Then, with a mighty bloodcurdling yell, I drove the Sumo the hell out of there.

Thankfully, it was a dirt track, not a cemented road. I didn't dare stop too soon, in case they caught up with me. I went up the dusty track about two hundred metres, and then, fervently praying I hadn't *killed* the guy, I flipped off the headlights, and scrambled out, leaving the engine running, feeling about frantically for the ropes that bound him to the bumper.

'Is he dead?' asked Nulwallah in panic.

'Bhaisaab!' I whispered urgently. The rope felt long. Thank god. He could get into the back of the jeep without my having to untie the rope. 'Hello, bhaisaab! I can't put on the lights, or they'll see us! Are you okay? Can you walk?'

The boy gave a low, unearthly groan that froze my blood solid. He's going to die, I thought in blind panic. I've killed him, oh god, and there were about fifty witnesses! I'm going to go to prison for life!

Then I heard shouts and running footsteps coming down the dark path. Torch flames flickered. Someone shouted. And hang on, were those *gun shots?*

'Nauzer, you fuck, come here and help me haul him in!' I shrieked.

'No way,' he replied, his voice suddenly very calm. 'I'm getting some great pics here on the long lens. Of the whole, fucking, unbelievable crowd.'

Cursing, I shook the motionless, prone figure hard and said urgently, 'Listen, loverboy, if you don't want the crowd to *hang* you tonight, find the strength to haul your ass into the back seat now. *Understand?*'

As I watched tensely, my stomach balled up into a hard little knot, the boy moved and reached out with one hand. Almost weeping with relief, I gave him a shove, so that he managed to clamber into the back seat and collapse into it, moaning softly.

'Well done!' I said as encouragingly as I could, and ran back to the driver's seat.

As I switched on the headlights and the Sumo jumped ahead, the crowd, close behind us now, set up a loud, angry yell of thwarted bloodlust.

'I've got ALL your faces on camera!' Nulwallah yelled out in broken Pavit Pradeshi as we sped away. 'So keep your mouths SHUT, okay?'

'Oh, good thinking, Nauzer! Now they'll chase us till the day we *die*,' I muttered as I drove as fast as I could, praying fervently that I would remember the way back, when a small head reared up from under my legs and regarded me with reproachful hazel eyes. 'You spoilt all the fun!'

I almost slammed the brakes in shock.

'Rajul! You're still here?' I gasped. 'I thought I told you to run and hide?'

'Did you get good pictures?' he asked Nauzer. 'I couldn't see much from under the back seat.'

Oh my god, he'd been in the back seat! I'd endangered his life too!

'Rajul,' I said carefully. 'Don't tell your mummy what we did tonight, okay? She'll just worry.'

He sucked on his knuckles. 'You're just scared she'll shout at you,' he said sapiently.

I opened my mouth, and shut it.

Rajul cast a distinct look of disapproval towards the back seat. 'Achhoots can't keep going off with Brahmin girls,' he declared. 'If achhoots take all the Brahmin girls, what will be left for good high-caste boys like us?'

'You're too young to be thinking about girls,' Nulwallah told him roundly. 'Too ugly, also. Now show us the way back.'

'First I thought ki, arrey wah, you are very cool, dragging the achhoot to death!' Rajul continued, ignoring Nulwallah. 'Just like in a movie! I hid and watched him bump along, moaning and groaning; it was fun. But just as he started bleeding *properly*, you stopped! You shouldn't have stopped, didi.'

I glared at him, gripping the wheel hard. 'You are one *sick* kid,' I told him. 'When we reach home, I am going to *whack* you many times, *very* hard.'

'You're not taking the achhoot *home*?' Rajul asked, his eyes very wide. 'To *Saket* Bhavan?'

'Why not?' I asked, confused.

'Everybody will get angry with you,' he said. 'Your Ammaji. And all the Brahmins.' Then he started on his usual chorus. 'NOBODY will vote for—'

'Okay, okay, I can't take him home,' I snapped. 'So *where* do I take him?'

But before either of them could answer, there was a stirring and a moan from the back seat. The loverboy was asking for water. Of course, there was none in the Sumo.

The groans grew louder.

Rajul, Nauzer and I looked at each other.

'Everyone will say you killed him,' Rajul said, not without satisfaction.

I glared at him. 'And you *helped*,' I pointed out. 'They'll put you in jail, too.'

That shut him up for a bit. He sucked on his knuckles pensively, while the groans from the backseat grew steadily fainter.

'Let's just throw him down on the road and go home,' Rajul said finally. 'He'll crawl off and hide somewhere.'

The groaning from the back grew more agitated instantly. I caught a muttered swear word or two.

'Isn't there, like, a *hospital*?' asked Nauzer desperately.

Silence.

Finally, I said with grudging decisiveness, 'Yeah, there is. The RAK. We'll take him there.'

Nauzer looked at me, puzzled.

'So let's *go*, then,' he said. 'What are we waiting for? And kiddo, chill, we'll drop you off on the way.'

The Raiza Ali Khan hospital is the main hospital in Bittora. I was born there. So was Ma. It had been recently refurbished and, as the brand new neon signs informed me, boasted a Coronary Care Unit, a Neonatal Intensive Care Unit, a Tuberculosis Centre, a Trauma Centre and a 24 hour Emergency Unit.

I hurried towards the Emergency area, hoping to get some people to help carry the unconscious boy inside.

There was just one sleepy looking woman sitting at the reception. 'Patient's name?' she asked without any preliminaries, as I burst in.

Damn. I couldn't quite say achhoot loverboy.

'BR Ambedkar,' Nulwallah blurted out, trying to help.

She looked up suspiciously.

'Uh, it's Babu Ram, actually,' I said hastily. 'He's an accident victim. We found him lying by the side of the road.'

She looked even more suspicious. 'And he told you his name?' she asked.

I nodded desperately. 'Yes! Before he passed out. You'd better admit him, he looks pretty serious.'

She said, 'Madam, if it is a police case, we cannot treat him until the police come.'

'But he'll die!' I cried out. 'He's very badly wounded.'

She tightened her lips and looked at a point a little beyond me. 'I'm sorry,' she said distantly. 'My hands are tied.'

Cow. I would have to do a bit of name-dropping here.

I leaned in and said persuasively, 'Look, if bending the protocol can help save a life, why don't you? I'm sure my grandmother, Pushpa Pande, three-time MP from this constituency, would really appreciate it.'

She didn't seem to know Amma's name. It was disgusting. I tell you, the common person's apathy to politics is the reason why India has never become a global superpower.

'I'm sorry,' she said. 'The hospital rules are very strict.'

Stupid cow.

Looking straight into her calm, unimpressed eyes, I knew what I had to do.

'Perhaps I could make a donation of some sort?' I murmured.

She drew back, looking extremely disdainful. Oh, fabulous, she had ethics and stuff.

That was when Nulwallah, who'd been gazing thoughtfully at a portrait of Begum Raiza hanging above the reception area, said suddenly, 'Oh, just *tell* her, Jinni!'

'What?' I looked at him blankly.

Nulwallah looked around conspiratorially, then leaned in and beckoned the receptionist chick to come closer.

'Your trustee, Zain Altaf Khan,' he murmured into her ear in dulcet tones, much to my horror, 'is a very close... err... *friend* of my friend here.'

The chick went very still.

'*Very, very* close,' said Nauzer again, for good measure.

'Everybody says that,' she said finally, with a shrug.

'It's *true*,' I said fiercely, sensing her cracking. 'I'd call him right now if I could, but I happen to know that he's... umm...'

'On a flight,' supplied Nulwallah.

'Yeah,' I said, smiling at him gratefully. 'Zak – we call him *Zak*, you know – is flying right now. In his *helicopter*.'

The chick said, looking slightly impressed now, 'Madam, it is against procedure. But if you can give me some *proof*, then we can expedite it, little bit...'

And that's when Nauzer yanked up Rumi's camera and showed her the picture of my sicko pamphlet-printing frenemy in his Deep Purple T-shirt, cuffing me fondly on the chin in Sisodia's conservatory. Looked at out-of-context, it was really quite an intimate picture. His thumb was practically touching my extra-large mouth.

She peered at it for a long time, then gave a decisive nod and jerked her head at some loitering orderlies picking their noses nearby. They leapt to their feet, and in about three minutes, our patient Babu Ram had been wheeled into the Emergency. I filled out the forms they gave me, more or less truthfully, and then, sagging with relief, slumped into the Sumo and drove home.

Nulwallah was uncharacteristically quiet on the drive back to Saket Bhavan. I didn't mind, I was too busy feeling nauseous about the effortless way in which I had managed to sabotage my own election campaign. But as we neared Begumbagh, he finally spoke.

'That wasn't particularly smart, was it, Jinni?'

Oh, so I wasn't Pandeji any more? Well, I guess we *were* kind of friends now.

'What?' I asked miserably. 'Pissing off the Brahmins or claiming to be having an affair with the IJP candidate?'

'Uh… both, I guess,' he said. 'Sorry for getting a bit proactive there, but I'm pretty sure that if he hadn't been admitted right away, he'd have died.'

'You're right,' I admitted. 'It wasn't very smart.'

One lanky brown hand closed comfortingly over mine on the gear stick. 'But it was *very* brave,' he said encouragingly. 'Even though,' he added ruefully, 'it was what my soccer coach would've called a Self Goal.'

I laughed weakly.

'How many Brahmins are there in Begumbagh, anyway?'

'*Millions*,' I said tonelessly. 'You have no *idea*.'

A gloomy silence prevailed for a bit.

Then he said resolutely, 'I'm going to get to the bottom of this whole pamphlet thing for you.'

'Why bother?' I said listlessly. 'I know it was Zain.'

His jaw shot out. 'But I'll get you *proof*. Proof you can use to get the person who did it disqualified.'

'You *still* don't think it was Zain, do you?' I asked him. 'You keep saying *the person*, not *Zain*.'

'I have my doubts,' he admitted. 'I also have my own theories. But hey, Jinni—'

'What, Nauzer?' I asked, feeling a sudden surge of affection for him. He really was a nice guy. I would never have been able to pull it off without him tonight.

'If I *do* get you the proof, will you go out for dinner with me?'

I blinked. 'Like on a date?' I said stupidly.

'Sure.' He grinned. 'Why, don't MPs date?'

'I don't know what MPs do,' I mumbled, going a little red. 'I've never been one.'

'Hey, c'mon!' he said, giving my hand another squeeze. 'We live in enlightened times! Look at what we witnessed tonight! If a Brahmin girl can dare to date a so-called untouchable boy, why can't a Parsi VJ dare to date a young MP, huh?'

I could've pointed out that things hadn't ended too well for the couple he was invoking but I didn't have the heart. I just looked at him, a little stunned at this turn of events.

He chanted softly, looking at me, a curious, musing smile on his face:

> *Jinni Pande, she's hot stuff,*
> *Outside sweet but inside tough.*

'So, you like me now, is that it?' I said.

'Yes!' He nodded emphatically, his eyes disturbingly warm behind his John Lennon glasses. 'I *like* you now, Jinni Pande. Deal with it.'

But I had bigger things to deal with than Nulwallah's sudden infatuation with me. Even though, thankfully, there seemed to be no direct fallout of my excursion into Ahri as yet, the poison from the pamphlets was spreading steadily. Our public meetings were sparsely attended the next day, and there was some muttered sloganeering as we drove through the streets.

> *Jinni Pande thu thu thu*
> *Decent people spit on you!*

Munni got really hassled by that. 'It's so easy to do this to women, didi,' she said bitterly. 'Oldest trick in the bloody book. How to shut their big fat mouths for good?'

That was the question on my mind too, when we drove to the big Begumbagh temple for the Ramnaumi puja the next day, decorously draped in pretty saris with our pallus covering our heads. The Ponga pandits received us cordially enough, but I could tell they were smirking behind our backs. Maybe they knew about the stunt I'd pulled last night, I thought fearfully. I could only pray that they didn't tell Amma.

They received us in the 'community' courtyard, which was a major sore point with Amma. She had sanctioned the money for it from her MP's fund, and it was supposed to be a secular space for all Begumbagh residents. But the pandits had got the enormous pillared courtyard built right next to the temple compound, with the result that nobody but high-caste Hindus actually got to use it.

'And *they* never vote for us, anyway,' Amma muttered now, as she smiled, bowed and namasted to the reception committee. 'Useless, good-for-nothing *educated* people!'

The gig kicked off with an aarti in the main temple. It was a festive affair, all the ladies resplendent in Benarasi saris and oodles of fake (according to Munni) gold jewellery.

I couldn't help thinking, rather reluctantly, as I inhaled the familiar scent of incense and burning ghee, and gazed at the chubby marble statue, that it was really progressive of Zain's great-granddad to have allowed this temple to be built in the 1920s, right here, in such close proximity to the statue of his late wife, after whom Begumbagh is named. He'd probably done it because, like Bauji, he'd replaced overzealous religion in his life with overzealous patriotism. Boy, would he have been disappointed in his pamphlet-strewing grandson!

I clapped along sedately during the aarti, constantly making sure my pallu stayed over my head, but somehow, I couldn't get myself to pray. The fact that there was a definite smell of toejam lurking below the incense didn't help. Behind me, Amma wasn't even trying. She dozed off discreetly, waking up only on the third 'Sia Pati Ram Chandra ki jai' at the end of the aarti, which signalled the move to the courtyard, where the food was laid out.

The food was *awesome*. There was steaming rasedaar aalu – a hot red curry of broken potatoes with lashings of hing, jeera and desi ghee, hot sitaphal ki sabzi, and a rocking yellow dal tadka. There were moong-ki-daal ki pakodis, with ringlets of cold white radish and, of course, steaming hot-n-sweet suji ka halwa. Supressing a moan of pure ecstasy, I sat down at a table next to Amma and proceeded to eat myself sick.

Amma was, as usual, eating with gusto, accepting puri after piping hot puri. 'Food ij excellent,' she told the servers. 'Get us some more halwa, pleaj.'

'Amma,' I said, looking up uneasily. 'It's very rich food, you shouldn't—'

But she just cracked her slow, sweet smile, and said, 'Life is sort, Sarojini.'

After everybody had eaten, and Amma was biting into an aromatic saada paan, I realized I'd better take a quick precautionary leak before the drive back home.

'Amma,' I whispered to her, 'I have to go to the loo.'

She wrinkled up her straight little nose. 'Arrey bhai, how many times do you go in one day, Sarojini. Go then! God knowj what it will be like! One thing we know for sure is that the bigger the temple, the dirtier the toilet.'

I stood up, adjusted my sari pleats and wove my way between the tables.

It took me ages to find the loo. I wandered through large musty parts of the temple complex and through a courtyard full of placidly chewing moonlight-white cows, before spotting the loo at the end of a long corridor of pillars. It wasn't too bad, clean even, but when I came out to wash my hands, I realized that the tap was dry.

Really irritated, I yanked at it hard. It hissed, burbled, dripped and suddenly fell off with a clunk while a huge jet of water hit me straight in the chest, soaking me from head to foot.

I gasped and held up my hand involuntarily, trying to block the flow but it was useless. The jet just forked into two sprays and they wet me in parts the first jet hadn't reached.

I picked up the tap and tried to screw it back on but the gush of water was too strong. Finally, I just shrugged, dropped the tap and simply moved out of the way. The jet of water was now hitting the opposite wall, running down to the floor and flooding the loo, but there was nothing I could do about it. Deciding I'd just tell one of the temple pujaris about the faulty tap, I tried to towel-dry my sopping wet hair with my sopping wet pallu, gave up, finger-combed it, and resignedly made my squelchy way out of the loo. The tap had done a thorough job. My petticoat, my blouse, even my undies were drenched.

I decided to head straight for the Sumos. It would look a little odd if I didn't say bye, but not as odd as it would look if

I showed up looking like a Bollywood wet-sari sequence, going *Bye ji, Thank you ji, Happy Ramnaumi ji.*

When I finally found the corridor leading to the community hall, I suddenly realized that everything was eerily quiet.

Then I heard an odd, rushing sound.

An odour that reminded me of freshly ironed clothes filled the air. Air which, when I inhaled, seemed to scorch my lungs.

I turned the corner and my heart almost stopped.

The hall was on fire. The tables at which we had been eating not twenty minutes ago were aflame, the ornate gateway we'd admired when we entered was blazing and *everyone* but me was on the other shore of the fiery river, screaming my name.

'*Sarojini!*' I could hear Amma's hoarse voice. I could see her hazily. She was trying to push people into the inferno, imploring them, 'Arrey, kuch karo!'

I whirled around. The fire was behind me now. It was before me, it was everywhere.

I stood there, panting a little, feeling oddly calm. Last night's Enforcer 49 experience had helped.

It's just ten big steps, I told myself. Just ten. If you take a deep breath and run, you'll make it. You're sopping wet, in any case.

I took a deep breath, pulled my pallu over my head and, feeling rather like Johnny Storm from Fantastic Four, rushed right into the heart of the fire.

A strange roaring sensation. Unbearable heat. And then I was through. Barely singed, actually.

There was total silence on this shore of the fiery river.

Everybody was looking up at me, open-mouthed, as I stood at the head of the steps.

Well, except for the cameras, which were clicking away busily.

I grinned my extra wide grin.

'Wow, lucky escape,' I said shakily.

And then Amma spoke up. 'It was not a lucky escape!'

There was a sudden hush. Everyone turned to look at Amma; there was an odd edge to her voice, and she seemed to be on the brink of making some momentous accusation. Behind me, the fire continued to roar, something crashed and fell. I stood uneasily at the head of the steps, looking down at the gawping crowd, wishing they would move back a little.

Amma hurried up the steps towards me. 'Theek ho na, tum?' she demanded in an urgent undertone, grabbing both my shoulders and looking me up and down for injuries. 'Thank god!' Then she frowned. 'Sarojini, you are *wet*.'

'I know,' I said eagerly. 'Amma, so lucky, you won't belie—'

'Sssssss!' she hissed. 'Keep quiet! Don't tell now!' She turned to face the crowd, her hand gripping my elbow hard, too hard.

'It was *not* a lucky escape,' Amma repeated, as all the cameras lapped up the sight of her, small and fierce in her grey and silver Benarasi sari. 'It was an Agni Pariksha, a Test by Fire. And my pure, good, virtuous girl has passed it with flying colours!'

The losers actually bought it. Really. God, how dumb were they? Simply because I'd walked through fire, I was absolved of all the dark deeds Zain's pink pamphlets had accused me of. Maybe the Ponga pandits of Begumbagh Ram Temple were petrified of being accused of arson and attempted assassination of a Lok Sabha candidate. Or maybe they thought it would boost tourism and increase donations to their temple or something. Either way, they gave interviews to every possible newspaper and news channel, making the story sound more and more miraculous with every retelling. The verdict was clear. I was a nymphomaniac no more. I was Pure. I'd been given a clean chit by Agni, the God of Fire himself, and all the Begumbagh ki junta bought the story with gusto.

'Hawa phir badal gayee,' chuckled Munni, avidly lapping up the headlines in the next day's Hindi newspaper. A picture of me emerging from leaping orange flames graced the cover. 'The wind is blowing for *us* now! Super didi, super! Phuntaastic!'

'What bullshit, Munni,' I muttered, secretly pleased, despite knowing better. Really, if I ever became MP of this place, the first thing I'd do is eradicate blind faith and religious mumbo-jumbo in bloody Begumbagh. It was ridiculous.

Amma was as pleased as punch with her fast thinking. She went chuckling from meeting to meeting, smiling and nodding and telling everyone about the Top Brass rally, which was only six days away now.

'Arrey bhai, Sarojini, we were *thinking*,' she said, as she handed me a big mug of yucky buffalo milk in my petal room that night, 'that everything that happens, happens for the best!'

I looked at her warily. 'Why?' I asked.

She said, with a smug little toss of her head, 'We were so disappointed when aawar movie *Saadi, Khaadi aur Azaadi* was delayed. But now we are thinking, your Agni Pariksha and victory in this election will make *such* a good end for the movie, na? Grandmother passes on the baton to granddaughter. Superb, it will be!'

'Amma,' I groaned. 'You're spending too much time talking to that idiot Rumi. *Please* don't take anything for granted! Anything could happen in the next eight days!'

'Seven, actually,' said Gudia aunty as she busily counted fat wads of money. 'We have enough oxygen. The last consignment will be coming to Shortcut's tomorrow. You drive down and get it, Jinni, and then we need to make the envelopes.'

I nodded, glad we were on talking terms again. I couldn't help noticing though, that she was smelling of my Moroccan Rose Body Shop perfume again and that the scrunchie in her hair was Amma's.

'Yeah, sure,' I said unenthusiastically. 'Envelopes.'

I knew all about stuffing envelopes. It was one of the few things Amma had let me do during election time when I was a child. Ma and I used to do them together, before she got fed up and left for Canada.

Basically, all the trusted people sit in a big circle and put two thousand rupees into an envelope that already contains a badge, a sash, a cap and, in the old days when the EC wasn't so omnipresent and omnipotent, a T-shirt. The envelopes – one for each worker, so that's one thousand envelopes in all – are then sealed and delivered by trusted crack team members to the workers on the day of the voting. The workers set up tables outside the polling booth and help the voters as they come in to cast their vote. They help them find their names on the rolls and make *parchis* – the little white voter's slips – for them. They show them EVM mockups and explain which button to press. Sometimes, they ferry them to the booth in tempos or buses and drop them back afterwards. If there's any hanky-panky going on at the booth, they call the crack team. It's an exhausting, vital job, and that's why the whole 'envelope' system is so important. Of course, the going rate had gone up a lot since I did my first stint of enveloping. Back then, we used to put just two hundred rupees inside each envelope.

Driving back from Shortcut's early next morning, an innocent looking Wonder Woman rucksack on my shoulder, I was surprised to see a lot of reporters outside Saket Bhavan. There were a couple of OB vans too, one of them was just the local Thumka TV, but the other one was NDTV. I honked my way past the crowd of journos at the gate and demanded of a rather subdued looking Jugatram, 'Why so much crowd, Jugatramji?'

Looking a little shifty, he said, 'Baby, Zain baba has come.'

I almost dropped my twenty lakh Wonder Woman rucksack. What was the bastard doing in *my* house?

'And you let him in?' I asked in disbelief.

He shrugged uncomfortably. 'Baby, it is *Zain* baba – and the press were taking so many pictures of him in front of our gate. Maine socha, better inside than outside.'

'Well, I'm going *inside* to throw him *outside*,' I told him. 'You and your Zain baba! If you're so fond of him, Jugatramji, why don't you go campaign for him only!'

Steaming gently at the nostrils, crushed cotton pallu streaming out like a banner behind me, I stormed into the courtyard.

Zain, who had been lounging in one of the moodhas, listening to Rajul read aloud from his blotchy English notebook, leapt up when he saw me and came towards me, his eyes dark with concern.

'Are you okay?' he asked urgently.

'Why?' I demanded. 'Why shouldn't I be okay?'

He frowned. 'The papers said you were in a fire. In the Ram temple at Begumbagh. Some kind of dumb purity test. Is your crazy grandmother pushing you around, Jin?'

I gasped. I just couldn't believe the gall of the guy.

'Get out of my house,' I told him, my voice very level.

'Jinni, listen,' he began again as Rajul looked at us from one to the other, his hazel eyes wide.

I cut him off.

'Get out for *ever*,' I told him. 'How *dare* you...' My voice shook, my chest was so constricted with anger I had to stop to breathe. The sight of him oozing fake, noxious concern made me want to hurl. I managed to suck in some air, and then I let him have it, all in a rush.

'How can you imply that my grandmother would hurt me? How can you ask if I'm *okay*, after circulating vile, filthy rumours about me? After your sicko Doggieji offers me – me, a Pragati Party candidate – money to withdraw from the election? Are you *nuts*?'

'Aar plus Yoo is Roo,' Rajul volunteered suddenly. 'Bhaiyya taught me. He's very good in teaching.'

'Shut *up*, Rajul,' I snapped.

There was a long, tense pause.

Then Zain shrugged, shook his head and said, 'We didn't print those pamphlets, Jinni, you have to believe me. I wouldn't do that to you! We're childhood friends—'

'Friends!' I exclaimed. 'You think that stuff matters?'

He looked up, a lock of dark hair falling onto his forehead, his dark eyes glowing strangely.

'Doesn't it?' he asked lightly.

I stood up and crossed my arms across my chest. 'Of course *not*!' I snarled. 'It doesn't matter a jot! Look, I'm not a fool... don't think I can't see through your great Plaan—'

'Plan,' he corrected me, looking mildly pained.

I choked.

'Whoops, sorry,' he said immediately, looking like he was trying not to laugh. 'That was totally uncalled for.'

I wanted to *hit* him.

He saw the intention in my eyes, I think, because he backed away a little.

'If *any* of this comes out,' I said, very low and fast, '*I'll* be the one stuck with the bad reputation while *you* come out looking like a stud. All the chauvinists – and that's *everybody* in Bittora – will be maha-impressed and vote for you! So *I* would like to focus on my campaign and not on whatever old *connections* you're trying to revive. And, by the way, speaking of *friendship,* I can't help noticing that you never bothered to get in touch with me – for *nine whole years* – until you found out I was standing from here.'

He heard me out quietly, his face unreadable. Then he said, with that slight trace of hauteur I hated, his public school accent suddenly very prominent, 'Incredible. You sound just like your grandmother.'

'And lay off Amma!' I snapped. 'She has the prejudices typical of her generation! So what? I am *not* ashamed of Amma!'

'All right,' he said, his lips tightening. 'I get it.'

'Good,' I said dismissively, and sat down on a moodha, picked up Rajul's English notebook and started to correct the dictation.

Zain loomed tensely above me but I ignored him. Let him find his own dumb way out of the house. God knows he knew it well enough.

'I didn't circulate those pamphlets.'

I laughed a low, incredulous laugh. 'Save it for the EC,' I advised him, making large red cross marks in Rajul's notebook.

'I'm *warning* you...' he began, his voice thick with a suppressed violence that made tiny hairs stand up on the back of my neck. But I still didn't look up.

'I was holding back,' he continued. 'Not letting it get too nasty. But now I won't.'

I finally put down the hideously untidy notebook, stood up and met his glittering dark eyes.

'Well, watch out, *Zak*,' I said. 'Because neither will I.'

Ballot Boxing

Number 27 in our series of reports from Lok Sabha
constituencies across India

India's Youngest Opponents
Shed 'Kid' Gloves

The 'kid' gloves are off in Bittoragarh.

The contest between the two youngest Lok Sabha candidates in India, which started with civilized we-are-childhood-friends statements and pious let-the-best-person-win noises has deteriorated into a bloody no-holds-barred brawl, where anything goes.

Confused locals are struggling to keep up with the constant onslaught of allegations and counter-allegations. Starting with 'issue-based' charges of corruption and negligence, the two candidates moved on to squabbling over who is to be credited with the 'progress' Bittoragarh has recently made and have now graduated into the far more sensational space of immorality, homosexuality and insanity.

The war began when anonymous pamphlets revealing graphic tales of young Sarojini's lusty immoralities flooded Begumbagh, an undecided assembly segment that neither candidate is sure of securing. This was followed swiftly by allegations of debauchery and incest levelled at Zain's father, the recently deceased Zaffar Ali Khan, made by Sarojini's grandmother, the formidable Pushpa Pande.

Zain's camp responded by claiming that Pushpa Pande was a certified lunatic, even procuring a certificate of insanity from a highly respected local specialist, Dr Bhoopendra, which they circulated in the Doodhiya-Durguja area.

Sarojini Pande promptly denounced Dr Bhoopendra as a mercenary quack.

At the time of going to press, rumours are rife in Bittoragarh that Zain Ali Khan is in a homosexual relationship with Bunty Sisodia, a local landowner and industrialist. Videos of the two of them together are circulating in the area.

In retaliation, Zain has alleged that Sarojini Pande is a tenth class fail with faked certificates, reduced to 'making drawings' for a living as she is a 'total duffer'.

The EC has served show cause notices on both parties.

'I can't believe I have to leave just when things are getting so deliciously low,' moaned Rumi as he packed his rucksack. He'd been summoned back to Mumbai to work on a UNICEF project, making 3-D mosquito models for a series of anti-malaria ads. 'It's so *unfair*!'

'Then *don't* go!' Amma sang out blithely. 'Stay! Take more pictures!'

She seemed to be getting into a recklessly good mood even as things came inexorably to a boil. She'd gone all *Hello? Hellloooo? Uff, so bad signal, can't hear anything...* and then actually *cut the phone* when the TB had called to lecture her about our dirty dancing campaigning tactics last night.

Rumi sniffed.

'Well, Nauzer took the best pictures,' he said sullenly. (He was rather put out that he'd missed the opportunity to click the raving mobs of Ahri.) 'Still,' his face brightened a little, 'I suppose some of my pics aren't bad either.'

'Yours are great,' I told him sincerely. 'And you really *helped*. I think your coming here turned the tide, no, Amma?'

Amma nodded. 'One hundred per cent,' she said assuringly. 'You brought us good luck, Rumi! We are finally surging ahead. The hawa is with us! Arrey, Bhagvan Agni himself ij with us! The pilla haj run out of tricks. Besides, he doej not seem to have any understanding of The People's minds. Otheriwise he would not say ki you are duffer. Arrey, who *cares* if you are a duffer, as long as you are a *pure* duffer?'

And so, Rumi left, more or less satisfied. But not before offering me all kinds of solicitous advice, and urging me to be kind to his buddy Nauzer. 'He's not a *prince*,' he said meaningfully, making me want to hit him. 'But he's a great guy. And he really likes you, Jinni. Ever since your Enforcer 49 stunt, he's gone fully boinnng on you. Give him a bit of a test drive, will ya?'

Like I was even thinking about test driving men! My heart had taken up permanent residence in my mouth because I was so worried that, any moment now, the news of the Ahri incident would break out, losing me all the upper caste votes in Begumbagh, and causing my grandmother to strangle me till I was dead.

And of course, news of the Ahri incident *did* break out. Two days before Amma's big Top Brass rally. But not in the way I had been dreading. In a way that was much, much worse.

Ballot Boxing

Number 33 in our series of reports from
Lok Sabha constituencies across India

Neck-to-Neck or Necking?

The youngest ever Lok Sabha election is getting curiouser and curiouser. The two opponents – who have been at each other's throats for the last week, making the vilest of allegations – are now rumoured to be embroiled in a steamy affair themselves, and may have been laughing up their sleeves at the electorate all along.

The rumour, which has sent shock waves through the IJP, because it violates their pet anti-mixed marriage stance, has emanated from unnamed staff members of the Raiza Ali Khan hospital, who claim to have spotted the two opponents holding hands, hugging and talking intimately into the wee hours of the morning in the hospital lobby.

Both sides have denied the involvement.

'Can we please be *serious*, we're fighting a Lok Sabha election here,' said a visibly irate Altaf Khan. 'I've no time for this rubbish. Yes, she's my friend on Facebook, but I have 630 friends on Facebook – are you implying that I am having an affair with all of them?'

Pande's reaction was even more biting. 'It's obviously the latest in a long series of puerile attempts to discredit me and demoralize my workers,' she said. 'The fact that it's coming from the RAK hospital staff proves this. Khan practically owns that place. Anyway, it's no more than I expect from the IJP, they've taken election campaigning to an all time low. But the electorate are not fools – they will show what they think of such tactics on polling day.'

I tried to laugh off the whole thing as a crazy rumour but naturally, Amma managed to worm the truth out of me. Backwards. I started by admitting that I *had* flashed a pic of Zain and me at the RAK – but only in order to get a grievously injured man admitted. And that, of course, totally begged the question she asked next. *Why* did I have a grievously injured man on my hands in the first place?

And so, the whole sorry tale tumbled out, complete with cleft-lipped Brahmins and MTV VJs and desperate drives in the dead of night.

Amma was predictably livid.

She swore she'd had the whole thing under control, that she'd spoken to the DC, and that the Brahmins had just been frightening the boy, that they had had no intention of actually hanging him. She said I'd overreacted big time, that my small sleight of hand with Dugguji's money had made me too cocky.

Maybe she had a point there, I thought despondently. Three days later, in the bright sunny daytime, it did seem that perhaps the Brahmins had just meant to torture Babu Ram a little, not actually murder him. What had Rajul said exactly? 'The girl's father *says* he's going to kill him, but I don't think he has the gurrrts.' And he hadn't been *so* badly injured when I first saw him. Just totally traumatized. Oh god, *I* had probably done him the most harm, dragging him along the ground for two hundred metres while doing forty kilometres an hour, acting like I was the amazing, incredible, incendiary Enforcer 49.

'They were going *to kill* him, okay,' I told her angrily, with less conviction than I felt. 'You weren't there – you didn't see – they're bullshitting you, Amma! I saved his *life.*'

'And finished *us* off,' Amma, never one to miss an opportunity, said with full dramatic gusto. 'You should have just tied *us* to the back of the jeep, Sarojini, and driven till we died. Bas! We, Pushpa Pande, three-time MP, have been sacrificed for one miserable achhoot teenager with more haarmoans than sense!'

She was probably right again, I thought gloomily. As Mr Urvashi was constantly telling us, the Begumbagh assembly segment was *critical* if we wanted to win Bittoragarh.

'But Amma, nobody's talking about it,' I told her earnestly. 'They're too scared about the footage Nulwallah's got.'

It was like she hadn't heard me. 'And what was the need to take him to RAK,' she demanded. 'And boast about being friends with the pilla?'

I squirmed. 'That was… um… kind of Nauzer's idea,' I said cravenly.

I think she ground her teeth. 'Bloody Parsi,' she said and retreated into a disgusted silence, leaning back in her moodha, her eyes closed.

I sat there and looked down at her, worried she might take ill or something. Her face was paper white.

'Is that all?' she asked, through gritted teeth, her eyes still closed. 'You are just friends with him on facing-book? Or is there anything more?'

I thought back miserably to the sofa in the study at the wedding in Delhi, to the encounter in the boobs of Bunty's haveli, to the long drive home from the rural areas. And shook my head.

'No, Amma,' I said steadily. 'There's nothing more.'

'Bhool jao Begumbagh!' she intoned suddenly, in sepulchral accents, making me jump. '*Forget* Begumbagh! Forget Bittoragarh, forget family legacy, forget India's youngest MP! Start remembering your Pixie Animation. Only they will give you job now!'

'You want some tea?' I said inadequately.

'Why not?' she gestured martyredly. 'Tell Joline we will take it with two teaspoons of rat poison.'

'It's ridiculous,' Gudia aunty told me as I pottered about with the tea things in the kitchen, a little later. 'Where do these people get such stories? Are they mad?'

For once, I was in complete agreement with her. The story was a gross, all-out exaggeration. All I'd done was flash a picture, that too, a pretty non-raunchy picture, of Zain and me together. So where had they got the bit about us cuddling together in the bloody hospital? What kind of sicko perverts cuddle in a hospital, anyway? It was typical media sensationalism.

'Luckily, it's a story no one will believe,' Gudia aunty continued, adjusting her housecoat. I caught a flash of a light purple bra strap.

'Hello, it's not *that* far-fetched,' I said, just a little piqued.

'Oh, I know you played together when you were kiddies,' she tittered. 'But a romantic involvement? That's just bizarre.'

I put down the tea strainer and looked at her.

She hadn't actually come out and said that Zain was hot and ex-royal and foreign educated and rich, while I was this unhot, uncouth loser. But she'd totally implied it. She had. It was there in the toss of her head, in the gleam in her watery eyes, in the curl of her thin upper lip.

I saw red. I was overworked and underlaid and bitter and messed up, but that's no excuse. I should've known better.

But I didn't.

'Oh, I don't know, bizarre things happen,' I said coolly, looking her straight in the eye. 'I mean, why would you wear my bra? That's pretty *bizarre* – but you're wearing it, aren't you?'

I regretted the words the moment they were out of my mouth.

She looked stricken. Her large watery eyes filled up like enormous goldfish bowls. Her enormous nose wobbled. She turned an extremely unattractive shade of puce, gave a weird grunting sob, flung down the paper and blundered away, not to be seen for the rest of the day.

I remained standing in the kitchen, appalled.

How could I have been so unkind?

I *knew* that she couldn't control her kleptomania, that she had a hysterectomy at twenty and that her husband had left her and not even for anyone else. I knew the whole sad story. And still I'd snapped at her, me with my perfect life and my famous grandmother and my intact ovaries and my alleged ex-royal admirer.

I sucked.

I sat down on Joline Bai's kitchen stool, picked up the quilted tea cosy and pulled it over my head.

I should just stay put here, I told myself gloomily. Inside this nice, dark tea cosy tent. I'll inhale this stale smell and keep my stupid mouth shut and emerge after six years, when both this election and the next are safely over...

The tea revived Amma.

She took a long sip and sat up, her eyes all beady-bright.

'Bhai, only Top Brass can save us now,' she declared. 'Sarojini, we had better make sure *everything* is on track for the rally...'

Oh, not again. We'd already discussed the arrangements for the TB rally some fifty times. It was all Amma talked about now. She'd made up her mind that the only way to change the hawa once again was to give the teeming masses of Bittora a solid dose of Top Brass charisma.

I told her, 'Amma, we *all* know the arrangements by heart.'

'Phir se batao,' she insisted. 'Tell us again!'

Ufff.

'The TB will first be addressing a rally in Tiloni,' I rattled off, 'to give Tits a solid headstart against the Hijra. Then he and his daughter will drive over to our constituency, bringing Tawny and Tits with them. Our Pappu will be driving the Sumo containing Top Brass, you and Tawny, while Tits and I will follow in the one behind. Our Sumo will be driven by Jugatramji. Munni and Rocket Singh will follow in a third Sumo, travelling with some important Top Brass aides, who go everywhere he goes. A garland of fragrant roses and pure, finest quality jasmine, weighing forty-seven kilos and costing one lakh rupees has been organized for you, me and TB to be photographed in. Full-page spaces have been taken in all the Bittora papers for a photo the next day. The podium is fully air-cooled, the chairs are of the finest leather and the catering is being done by the Oberoi group, arch rivals of the Taj Bittora. There is even to be, for the first time in Bittora, a fine, almost invisible, state-of-the-art mosquito netting set on the podium, to keep the mossies at bay.'

I stopped, a little out of breath.

'Good, good.' Amma nodded. 'It all seems good. And if TB wants to go to toilet?'

'A fancy porta-toilet has been ordered from the guys who supply them for the most expensive Bollywood outdoor location shoots,' I informed her.

'Excellent!' She grinned. 'Now…'

Just then, Our Pappu, Munni and Rocket Singh trooped in,

copies of the '*Neck to Neck or Necking*' piece in their hands, eager to commiserate and confabulate. I quickly deflected them.

'What's the latest on the rally, team?' I asked brightly. 'Everything under control?'

Munni frowned. I could tell that she wanted to drop in on the journo who'd written the article and make him eat about two thousand copies of it. *After* dipping them in hydrochloric acid.

'Didi...' she began, her voice strident.

'Let's just talk about the crowds for the rally, Munni, okay?' I said pleasantly, cutting her off.

The protuberant, doll-like eyes blinked.

'Okkkay,' she said, adjusting rapidly. 'So then... the crowds. Let's discuss tempos, buses, fetching, dropping, clapping at the right time – all that.'

They all started talking together. We had to have a big showing tomorrow. If the crowds failed us, Amma's nose would really be cut – but apparently, everything was under control. Money, drivers, diesel, people, everything seemed to be in place.

And that's when Jugatram rushed in, all dramatically, and said in a low, fast, double-oh-seven type whisper, 'Jiji, baby, Zain baba is also having a big rally day after tomorrow.'

Amma sniffed, unimpressed, very much the M to his James. 'So what? He can't compete with our rally. *Top Brass* is coming to our rally.'

Jugatram shook his head. 'Didi, just listen, pay attention! You know that movie, *Jeevan Apnaa Saara, Sanam?* Which was shot at the Bittora Fort?'

'Yes, I do, Jugatramji,' I said impatiently. It was this totally cheesy movie. About a princess and an auto-rickshaw driver. They fall in love and elope in the auto, and are shot dead by her autocratic brother in the end, leaving behind a curly-haired baby to be brought up by the girl's jilted, good-hearted ex-fiancé. It had been a super-duper hit. 'What about it?'

'Zain baba became great friends with the stars when it was being shot,' said Jugatram. 'So now…' He paused.

'So now *what*, Jugatramji?' we chorused.

He shrugged and said, his shoulders drooping, 'So now, *Salmon Khan* is coming for Zain baba's rally.'

11

I woke up on the day of the rally with a sense of foreboding. There was a hard knot in my stomach and a dull ache between my eyes. It's today, a voice whispered inside my head. The rally to which no one will come.

I groaned, threw off the covers and got out of bed, while the buffaloes stamped their way down the street, blowing and lowing, their bells ding-dinging softly.

I sipped my bhainscafé gloomily in the aangan, with no one but Ponky for company. Amma was already at her snaan, Gudia aunty was still sulking at me and the crack team obviously had a million things to do today. Even Joline Bai wasn't around. She was probably getting a facial and a manicure to look pretty for Salmon Khan.

We had all tried to convince Amma to cancel the Top Brass rally, pleading that it would be career-destroying for her if the TB showed up and the crowd didn't, but Amma was adamant. She insisted that we were panicking for no good reason, and that it just was a case of calling a bluff and making the other guy blink.

'Arrey, no Bollywood actor-shaktor will have the gurrrts to hold a rally on the same day as a TB rally!' she had declared, with typical Praggu delusion. 'They also know whose gourmint is coming! They know that if they get too big for their boots, TB can get them put into jail like *this,* because of some chota tax evasion or drug addiction or immorality or something else! Wait and see, once that Salmon finds out *who* is coming here tomorrow, he will cancel himself!'

Such had been her confidence that I'd fallen for it, even sleeping well last night. But now it was morning, and I was convinced the people of Bittora had been up since five, pumping iron, stripping down to their waists and pushing their hair back in wire hairbands, getting ready for the wonder and the weirdness that was Salmon Khan. And who could blame them? Bollywood stars hardly ever came to Pavit Pradesh. It was just too far out.

But Our Pappu bounced into the aangan, brimming with confidence. 'Hello, didi!' he said brightly. A shiny silver digital camera, suspended from a nylon cord, was bouncing against his chest, which, in turn, was encased in a horrid blood-red and Burnol-yellow checked bush shirt. 'What can I do for you? What is your wish? Anything you want! I will do anything! I will do *everything*!'

'Err... nice shirt, Pappu,' I said faintly.

'Thenks,' he grinned. 'Aisa hai ke, I want to look *smart* in the photu with Top Brass, na!'

He seemed very confident that huge hordes would show up for our rally, and insisted that everything was under control. He wasn't at all fussed about Salmon Khan and said, large-heartedly, that there were more than enough people in Bittoragarh to fill two measly maidans – Company Bagh, where our rally was, and the Purana Bittora park, where Zain's rally was supposed to be held. He also reassured me that Bittora had seen Salmon before, when he'd come for the *Jeevan Apnaa Saara, Sanam* shooting. So he wasn't *that* big a deal, really.

Which did make me feel a little better.

'But tell me the truth, Pappu,' I asked him. 'If you had a choice – who would you rather go and see?'

He frowned. 'As Pragati Party MLA, of course I would want to see TB,' he said finally, 'but as common man, perhaps Salmon bhai would be my choice… But don't worry, didi, their rally will *definitely* go housefull, so all the extra people will come for our show!'

Fortified with this tepid reassurance, I went to my room to get ready, taking a vigorous mugga-balti bath and slipping into a white sari with an orange and pink border and a firoza blue blouse. I slipped the tri-coloured Pragati Party scarf around my neck, ruffled my hair until it regained its Bombay rosebudness and sighed at my reflection in the mirror.

My life was such a mess! My grandmother – my only blood relative who gave a damn about me, because my mum obviously didn't – was barely speaking to me. My oldest friend had turned out to be a complete snake. My career was on hold, my reputation was in shreds, I badly needed a haircut, and I was reduced to depending on the bloody Pragati Party Top Brass, an entity I've always felt vaguely resentful of, to bail me out of the sorry mess I found myself in.

Tawny uncle had told Amma that the TB would be speaking at eleven in Tiloni and would arrive at Begumbagh by one. They'd be here forty whole minutes before driving on to the three other constituencies they would be speaking in today. Obviously, they too, were trying to pack in as much as possible on the last day of campaigning. So we set off for the venue at twelve, to get the crowds nicely stoked with music and dancing and a couple of fiery speeches.

My spirits rose when Jugatram drove us into the Company

Bagh grounds – the place was packed. Amma and I walked triumphantly down the aisle towards the podium, amidst deafening cheers, and took our places behind the long white table. Our name cards had been placed at the two extreme ends of the table. I was next to TB junior, Amma was next to TB senior. Tawny uncle's name card had been placed bang in the middle.

I quickly realized Our Pappu wasn't the only one who wanted a photo with TB. Almost as soon as we sat down, a perspiring old man in a wheelchair pounced on me, crying eagerly, 'Didi, I want a photu with Top Brass. I am HIV-positive! You must make sure I get a chance!'

'Okay, okay,' I promised sympathetically.

A truculent looking dude in a turban roughly swung the wheelchair out of the way. '*I* want a photu with Top Brass,' he said aggressively. 'I won a bronze medal in the 1992 National Games! For wrestling,' he added, flexing his muscles.

'I am a Kargil widow,' said a thin reedy voice from behind the bronze-medallist. 'My husband laid-down-his-life-for-thee-country. *I* demand a photu with Top Brass.'

They circled me and started yelling threateningly, all at once. Which was when Munni sailed in and told them to beat it.

I would have expected them to start lashing out at us, but they took it rather well. The guy in the wheelchair actually got up, folded the wheelchair, and limped away. Probably to Zain's rally where he might have better luck with Salmon Khan.

Meanwhile, Amma had popped two silver-coated elaichi pods in her mouth and was smiling at the crowd benignly. She looked perfectly composed, if a little pale, not at all like someone whose moron granddaughter was out to destroy her life's work and reputation. I felt a sudden, fierce urge to hug her. Maybe sensing my glance, Amma looked up just then, caught my eye, and winked, flashing her gap-toothed smile. I smiled back, and then Rocket Singh launched into a long speech, extolling the virtues of me, Amma, the TB and the party. I tuned out, looking dreamily at the three garish red rosebuds surrounded by the inevitable *morpankhi* in the brass vase in front of me, sure that everything would be fine now. The crowd was here, they hadn't ditched us for the Salmon Khan gig, and soon the Top Brass would arrive. I thought idly that I should be revising my speech, but I'd learnt it by heart and there was tons of time yet. Besides, the Oberoi catering team had just sent up the first tray of refreshments from their mobile kitchen and it smelled divine. Sucks to you, Maruti Zain, I said to myself as I bit into a crisp, delicious canapé. Bet you aren't serving anything half as fancy at your rally. I took a long luxuriant pull at my Pepsi, safe in the thought that there was a fancy porta-toilet parked right outside. Campaigning like this was a piece of cake.

Behind me, people were scurrying about, giving the busy ones. Munni and Rocket Singh, staggering under the weight of the forty-seven kilo, one lakh rupee garland, were at the base of the podium. I could smell the roses and jasmine from my seat on the podium. Our Pappu, looking nervous but extremely excited, was talking to a little knot of workers, his spiffy digital camera still dancing against his chest. Probably telling them about how he was going to escort Top Brass to the venue, I thought snidely. Then I frowned. Hey, how come Pappu was still here? He should've left to receive TB at the border half an hour ago. Were they running late?

I turned around to ask Amma why Our Pappu was still here, when I saw Gudia aunty rush up from her place in the front row to whisper something into Amma's ear. Amma heard her out, her face set. Then she nodded and beckoned me, and hissed, 'It's your speech now, Jinni, get up and make it.'

I looked at her, perplexed. 'Already? What about Top Brass, Amma?'

She said, her voice unnaturally calm, 'Tawny's rally was running late, so TB decided to fly here instead of driving. But now the helicopter haj engine troublej. They won't make it in time, Sarojini. *They are not coming.* Now go and make your speech.'

I don't remember a word of what I said that day. I'd revised my speech so many times, I probably just rattled it off like Rajul rattling off the five times table. My palms were clammy with ice-cold sweat, my heart was sick for Amma. The crowd, plied with alcohol and snacks, clapped at the right moments and cheered me gamely. The only bit of my speech I do recall, word for word, is the bit right at the end, where I had to say pretty much this:

'Beloved, respected brothers and sisters, it is with great regret that I have to tell you that our great leader and his daughter who were coming to meet you today, will not be able to make it. The young lady took ill and had to be rushed back to Delhi. They send their deepest love and regrets to you and beg you to forgive their absence and hope that you will vote for the progressive, democratic Pragati Party so that we can all make progress. Jai Hind.'

There was a stunned silence when I sat down, as though the crowd hadn't quite internalized my last remark – and then they started muttering. Ominously. The news of the no-show seemed to sweep through the rows of seated people and across the grounds like the shadow of a huge cloud rolling in and blotting out the sun. Then the thunder started. Roars. Boos. Hoarse cries.

Our Pappu appeared like a genie behind my chair. 'Didi, chalo,' he whispered urgently. 'Jiji and you had better get out of here.'

He whisked Amma and me off the podium even as the hired dancers came on to sing a funny, anti-Zain parody. They didn't make it past the third line of the song. The crowd started throwing things at them and the dancers, instead of exiting like sensible people, chose to stay on stage and hurl abuses at the crowd instead.

I marched out quickly to the Sumos with my head down, letting Our Pappu and Jugatram lead the way, while the dancers pleaded cordially with the crowd (*Sit down, maadarchod, Show some class, behenchod*).

Engine trouble, my ass, I thought bitterly. Karan Sethie was right, this party *was* a joke. We were all at the mercy of the whims and fancies of the Top Brass who acted like some kind of pre-independence royalty. He must've just thought that Bittora was a lost cause, so why bother showing up. Or that the weather was too hot. Or that Salmon Khan was coming, why risk going and being photographed in an empty ground.

The moment we were back in the Sumo and honking madly to get through the chaotic parking lot, Gudia aunty burst out, 'What is this, madam, this is just not done! They owe you an explanation!'

But Amma remained silent, head bowed, saying nothing. Nothing at all. She looked like she wasn't hearing a word Gudia aunty was saying. She looked every bit of her supposed eighty-seven years.

'Leave it, Gudia aunty,' I said hesitantly. (She still wasn't talking to me.) 'Amma doesn't want to talk. Let her be.'

'She *always* wants to talk,' Gudia aunty snapped at me. She reached out and shook Amma's shoulder. '*Say* something, madam!' she beseeched. 'You're scaring me.'

'Duck,' said Amma suddenly, very loud and clear.

I frowned. 'What?' I asked. 'Why should I duck?'

She shook her head impatiently. 'Duck,' she repeated. 'We need Duck.'

'To eat?' I asked, puzzled.

She shot me a baleful, completely exasperated look and glanced beyond me at Gudia aunty, who gave a sudden loud, dying-turkey gulp and gasped, her voice all panicky, 'Oh, madam, do you want your *doctor*?'

Amma nodded. 'Duck Saab,' she said faintly, looking at Gudia aunty gratefully. 'We want aawar Duck Saab.'

Then she fell forward and we noticed how laboriously she was breathing. And the nightmare really began.

———

'Didi, coffee.'

I took the proferred cup of bhainscafé and cradled it between my hands, blowing on the yucky thick skin on top. I might as well drink it – it would be the first thing to go into my stomach since the Oberoi canapé I'd had at noon.

It was almost midnight. We were back at the RAK, in the new Intensive Care Unit. Amma's Duck Saab was here, airlifted from Delhi by Tawny uncle. He had just been telling me and Tawny uncle things that were making us feel like the victims of a particularly savage hit-and-run accident.

Amma was dying.

She'd known for a month.

Suddenly, the whole fried-paranthas-and-mixed-fruit-jam diet made total sense.

Life is sort, Sarojini.

She'd had a series of tests done because she hadn't been feeling too well and she had got the results just one day before Dwivedi's Pottygate photos popped up in the papers. But as soon as that happened, and she knew there was a chance of her getting the ticket, she decided to get me nominated instead. Duck Saab had told her clearly that she didn't have too much time, so she didn't want to risk being the candidate – if she died before the polling, the election would have to be cancelled. So she'd bullied Duck Saab into keeping his lip buttoned – he'd been sucking up to her to get his niece admission into the All India Institute of Medical Sciences and she said she'd do it only if he kept mum – so he hadn't said a word to anybody.

Thinking over it as I sipped my coffee, I realized she must have had to move fast to secure the 'succession'. She'd suggested my name to the AIPC, and the very next day, she'd come running to Mumbai to talk me into standing. She hadn't dared to break it to me too suddenly, worried I would start acting like Ma, harping on her corrupt ways and her morphed photo scandal and the filth and mess of politics, so she merely told me she wanted me to help with her campaigning. She must have been sure that once she got me to Delhi and presented me with a fait accompli, telling me that the TB had asked for me *specially*, I would capitulate. She must have put my name on the electoral rolls too, somehow. And when the IJP announced Zain's name and the TB decided he wanted a young candidate too, it was as though god himself was on her side. As though he was rooting for the Pandes.

'You should have informed *me* that she was sick,' Tawny uncle said as he rested one hand heavily on the shoulder of the hapless Duck Saab. 'You should have informed *somebody*. It was too bad of you!'

Duck Saab, a thin, hunted-looking man with an indecisive mouth, murmured that it hadn't been his place to say anything.

Tawny uncle glowered at him. '*You* are responsible for her being in this situation.'

The man looked miserable. 'Yes, sir,' he said faintly.

I sighed.

'It's okay,' I told him. 'I'm sure you did your best. My grandmother can be a complete bully, I know.'

Tawny uncle didn't look too thrilled about my absolution of Duck Saab.

'It's all *my* fault,' he declared next, clearly in the mood to blame somebody. 'If my rally hadn't ended so late, TB could have driven to jiji's rally! Now, if she dies of disappointment, her blood will be on *my* hands.'

'Oh, for heaven's sake, Tawny uncle,' I snapped. 'Stop being so bloody melodramatic!'

His eyes blazed out under moustaches No. 2 and 3, and for a moment I thought he was going to yell right back at me. But then he just shook his head, patted my back gently, and walked away.

Gudia aunty looked even more devastated than Tawny uncle. I'd expected her to beat her chest and make a big show of grief, or to rail dramatically at Amma for keeping this big secret from her, but she just sat there, silent and still, tears flowing down her cheeks in a constant stream, only her fingers moving as she dialled Ma's number in Canada again and again.

'If only I had known,' she kept murmuring manically. 'If *only* I had known!'

There was no response, though. Ma's phone was switched off.

I sipped my coffee and looked through the glass walls, at the scene outside. The crack team plus over three hundred Pragati Party workers were milling around inside the gates, like a subdued, murmuring hurricane. They looked stricken, in shock, a lot of them were praying – counting beads, kneeling on prayer mats, standing with folded hands. A long line of TV channel vans were parked in the driveway, and their anchors were standing near the hospital entrance, gesticulating dramatically into their cameras.

I frowned.

'Munni, the workers and those TV channel vans are blocking the drive. Make them move. People won't be able to get into the hospital – Amma isn't the only patient here, you know.'

She nodded. 'Yes, didi,' she said, laying a hand briefly on my shoulder. Then she raised her chin and stomped away, yelling bossily, 'Yeh drive clear karo! Drive clear karo! Hospital ko Numaish ka mela bana rakha hai! Move, people, move!'

Gudia aunty looked up from her non-stop dialling and said gently, 'Jinni, why don't you try and sleep for a while?'

'I'll sleep when we get through to Ma,' I told her fretfully. 'I don't get it, she never switches her phone off. And I've no landline number for her. Just the two cell-phones. Do you think I should send her an email?'

'Great idea,' she said encouragingly. 'Jyoti's always online, no? I'm sure these people have internet here. This place looks very high-tech.'

I rushed off to the nurse's room, intent on getting my hands on a computer. I just *knew* everything would be fine once I got hold of Ma. She always managed to pull Amma together. She'd done it the last time, after the morphed photos affair. She would come down here, we would have a long crib session about how badly Amma had behaved, slyly hiding her illness from us, and then Ma would bully, cajole and nurse Amma back into the pink of health, never mind Duck Saab's gloomy prognosis. Everything would be fine.

The guy at the reception desk directed me to an office upstairs and I hurried towards it. As I was crossing the corridor, I heard a voice, Our Pappu's voice, speaking in a hoarse whisper.

'If jiji dies now we will hundred per cent win on a sympathy vote.'

I felt like somebody had slapped me hard across the face.

Rocket Singh's dour voice replied, 'But if jiji dies won't they call off the election?'

'No, no,' Our Pappu's voice said excitedly. Then there was a pause and a slight puffing sound. The two of them had stepped out for a ciggy break. Then Our Pappu's voice continued. 'Because jiji is not really the candidate – *didi* is the candidate! EC rules only call off the election if a *candidate* dies! It's brilliant! It is a lottery! We will get the sympathy benefits of a candidate's death without the candidate dying!'

Rocket Singh, voice heavy with emotion, said, 'Yes, but it is still very sad…'

Our Pappu's voice grew lugubrious instantly. 'I know,' he replied.

Two long drawn-out, gusty sighs.

Then Rocket Singh asked, somewhat wistfully, 'Do you think the sympathy wave will stay till the assembly elections? And help us win that too?'

'I'm not sure,' Our Pappu's voice said somewhat flatly. 'Effect may not last that long. But we should definitely increase the size of jiji's pictures on the posters. And add a thick golden halo...'

His voice seemed to be coming from farther off, they must have stubbed out their cigarettes and walked away. Giving myself a little shake, I started walking again.

Then Gudia aunty hurried up to me. 'Jinni, what took you so long?' she demanded. 'Madam wants to see you. Go in and talk to her. No, wait, you need to wear these sanitized bags over your shoes...'

'Amma?'

'Hmmm?' She twitched slightly, then opened her eyes. There were huge shadows, purple as jamuns, under them. She looked a little strange, unfamiliar somehow, probably because they'd removed the gold naakphool from her nose. She was propped up against the pillows, and there was a pipe going up into her nose. She was wearing a long, loose white hospital nightgown that was tied up with a string to one side of her chest and there was a green surgical cap on her head.

'We look like *khwaja mere khwaja*,' she said resignedly, waving the loose, flapping sleeves of her white nightgown around. 'Like a Turkis dervis. Why are we in this stupid Mohammedan hospital? How could you do this to us, Sarojini?'

'It's a standard hospital gown,' I told her, as I sank down on the bed next to her. 'And anyway, how could you do this to *me*? Why didn't you tell me you weren't well?'

There was a long pause, broken only by the steady *beep beeping* of the vital signs monitor hooked up to her left index finger.

'We are fine,' she murmured finally, reaching out to hold my hand, but not quite looking me in the eye.

I stroked her silver hair gently. 'You should've been getting treatment in AIIMS,' I said reproachfully. 'Not bullying poor Duck Saab into giving you a clean bill of health so you could eat like a pig and gad about bloody Bittora in the heat!'

She winced. 'But we wanted to *settle* you properly,' she said, 'then we could relax and feel that chalo, our duty is done.'

I gave an incredulous, tearful laugh. 'Then you should've just found me a *boy*, Amma,' I said. 'That's what settling a girl usually means.'

Amma snorted. Weakly, but it was unmistakably a snort. 'What are boys?' she said dismissively. 'You will get many many boys! Just grow out your hair, that is all. We wanted to settle your *career.*'

'Well, you've settled it all right,' I said, as cheerfully as I could. 'We're going to win this election for *sure.*'

This drew a faint twinkle and a reluctant half-smile, but then she was wracked by a sudden bout of coughing. Her shoulders shook, her eyes watered. I realized again, painfully, how frail she was.

'Don't *bullsit* us!' she managed to gasp out finally.

'Okay, okay,' I said, then added, lying glibly, 'Hey, Ma will be here any time now. That's nice to know, isn't it?'

'Yes,' she sighed, patting my hand and then resting hers over mine. 'It will be good to see her before we d—'

'Before you sleep?' I broke in with a little laugh.

She snorted again. 'Before we *die,*' she said firmly. She felt around under her pillow for her prayer beads, fingered them meditatively for a while and then said suddenly, 'I wonder what He will have to say to us when we meet Him?'

'Who?' I asked, bewildered. 'Bhagwanji? God?'

One more snort. A tiny one. 'No, you foolis,' she said mildly, 'your grandfather. Hamare hujbend. Panditji Madan Mohan Pande.'

'He will say,' I said gently, 'that you are one sassy, kickass babe and he's very proud of you.'

She gave a rather tremulous laugh. 'Aisa?' she said. Then she sighed. 'We tried to do our best, Sarojini. We struggled. One-two things we have done we are asamed of, rest everything, we can hold our head high.'

'You did good,' I told her earnestly.

She said, 'If you get confused about anything, read your Bauji's diaries. Your mother always does.'

'Okay, okay,' I told her, 'now rest, Amma.'

'He left them to *her*,' she added, somewhat irately. 'Not to us.'

She closed her eyes and started to lie back against the pillow but then, abruptly, she snapped them open and smiled. 'You are going to win now, you know,' she said, her voice suddenly, vibrantly, powerfully alive. 'We have *settled* it, hundred per cent.'

'I know, Amma,' I said, blinking back tears. 'Thank you. Rest now.'

She nodded, closed her eyes and sank back into her pillow.

I sat there, holding her hand, looking down at her, so tiny in the huge hospital bed. Her chest was barely rising and falling. Her eyelids were as thin and veined and translucent as new leaves uncurling.

Then abruptly, they flicked open again. She tried to sit up. Her lips twitched. Her small gnarled hand clutched mine compulsively, her eyes locked into mine, urgently appealing.

'Don't…' she gasped. 'Don't let…'

I bent down, hugging her frail shoulders. 'Don't what, Amma?' I asked, fighting back tears, my voice breaking.

'Don't let that fat Katrina play us in the movie,' she said.

Then she dropped back against the pillow and very quietly, so quietly that I didn't realize at first that it had happened, she died.

—

By noon the next day, the Begumbagh mandir community hall, scene of my 'test-by-fire', was chock-full of crowds shuffling past in darshan, as Amma lay in state, while they chanted:

> *Till the sun and moon remain*
> *Pushpa we will say your name.*

I'd spent the morning getting her ready. Joline Bai and Gudia aunty and me. We'd laid her out on the floor of her room on white bedsheets, and sponged her down, using all her Sha-this and Sha-that products. I'd always thought this ritual extremely barbaric, but doing it had actually felt deeply satisfying.

I combed out her silvery hair, braided it into a single long plait and laid it along her left shoulder, so her head could rest easy. I screwed in her dainty gold naakphool and her heavy earring tops. I sprinkled her with *Anais Anais,* her favourite perfume, and then, as she lay there, regally swathed in a kora, never-before-worn-or-washed purple Benarasi sari, I got Munni and Joline Bai to carry in the one lakh rupee, forty-three kilo, desi gulab and jasmine garland that we'd ordered for the no-show TB and lay it around Amma's frail form.

It suited her tremendously. She looked like a queen, smiling peacefully, like she was having pleasant dreams of me kicking major IJP butt.

I sat on a cotton dhurrie, dressed in a white sari, with a silently weeping Gudia aunty by my side. The musty dhurrie, with its inevitable pattern of intertwining bright cotton threads in every colour imaginable, whirled and swam before my eyes. The weather was almost unbearably oppressive and the constant clicking of newspaper cameras didn't help.

People walked up to me, endless lines of people, all muttering vaguely consoling things. The women bent down and kind of hugged my head silently. Some kissed my forehead or held my hand. I got a peep into about a thousand cleavages. Withered old ones, massive matronly ones, perky young ones, you name it. I sat stoically, numb, cauterized, like somebody playing a part, and mechanically whispered thank you after every encounter.

I could sense a mutedly jubilant mood emanating from the crack team, and everything inside me recoiled against it. To my newly cynical eyes, every mourner, every single one of them, was insincere. None of them had loved Amma, none of them meant what he said. They were *happy* Amma was dead, that she had died when she did, with such impeccable, obliging timing, so they could win the election.

Our Pappu, who kept rushing up to ask if I wanted coffee or juice: Fraud.

Rocket Singh: Ditto.

Munni, tears leaking uncontrollably from her eyes, her face a red, blotchy mess: Hypocrite.

Jugatram, stoic, soldier-like, with ravaged eyes: Oscar winner.

Gudia aunty, all fights forgotten, asking me with gentle concern if I wanted to pee: Sycophant.

Tawny uncle, harassed, hovering protectively over me: Fake.

I hate all of them, I thought bitterly. I have no friends here. None.

'Jinni?'

I looked around and saw Nulwallah. He'd tied his wild hair

into a ponytail and was wearing white. There was a mournful expression on his long face, probably the kind he thought suitable for meeting bereaved people, I thought with a twinge of irritation.

'No interviews,' I said, without looking at him. He nodded vigorously several times.

'Of course! Of course!' he said, looking all sensitive. 'I wouldn't intrude at a time like this!'

Then he glanced around and added, his voice oddly gentle, 'Listen, I know it's none of my business, but where's your *family*? I mean, was it just you and your grandmother against the bad old world or what?'

'My mother lives in Canada,' I informed him tightly.

He nodded sympathetically. 'Well, if there's anything I can do, just holler, okay?' he said, reaching out, grabbing my shoulder and squeezing it firmly.

'Okay,' I said.

He stood there looking at me uncertainly for a bit, like he was thinking about maybe lunging down and attempting to hug me, but then he ducked his head and walked away to where Amma lay in state.

I continued sitting there, watching everybody pay their respects, my mind a chaotic, angst-filled mess. Incense burned, the smoke rose straight up into the air in the stillness of the muggy afternoon. A sombre attendant dressed in white wheeled an ancient gent on a wheelchair around the pedestal where Amma lay. The old man was hunched low in his chair, drooling slightly, clutching a rose garland in claw-like fingers. His attendant parked the chair and tried to take the garland from him to lay it on Amma's body, but the old gent shook his head firmly. He leaned forward, hands shaking, lips tight in concentration, and sort of *threw* his garland at her. It landed more or less around her neck and he gave a satisfied grunt. Then he looked around the square triumphantly, almost like he expected an applause, like he'd won first prize at the hoopla stall at the Numaish ka mela or something.

And then, suddenly, Our Pappu gave a loud, involuntary squawk. An electric current seemed to pass right through his body. He sat up very straight and hissed at me in an urgent, excited whisper, 'Didi, didi, *Top Brass* is here!'

I looked up and saw that Top Brass, obviously recognizing campaigning manna from heaven when he saw it, had rolled in to offer his condolences, dressed in white.

Gudia aunty snapped, 'Theek hai, Pappu, she's not going to get up and *receive* him, you know, she's in mourning. Take TB to do darshan of madam first!'

Our Pappu nodded and hurried away, his white kurta crackling with starch. Should've brought your shiny little digital camera today, baby! I thought sourly, as I shredded little cotton threads from the dhurrie before me.

Rocket Singh cleared his throat and said, 'Didi, TB is here, I think so we should do the cremation now.'

I didn't reply.

I knew what was on his mind. On *all* their minds. They were thinking that if the funeral took place *now*, the pictures in tomorrow's papers would be fantastic. Flames burning in the background. The nation's most charismatic leader in the foreground, his expression sombre, perhaps with one avuncular arm around me. The kind of images money couldn't buy. The kind of images that would send voters out to the hustings in droves to put their finger on the pointing finger. Well, I wasn't in the mood to oblige them.

Meanwhile, TB had finished his reverent little perambulation around Amma and was now headed towards me. Years of Praggu indoctrination made me rise to my feet involuntarily. He came up, grasped both my hands and murmured some meaningless platitudes, which I answered with a polite thank you. Then he started holding forth about Amma and Bauji, and what *stalwarts* they had both been, but I wasn't really listening. As far as I was concerned, he'd showed how much he cared for Amma by not showing up yesterday.

He finished off his piece by saying he deeply regretted not attending her rally yesterday, that the idiots on the organizing committee had messed up the schedule – and that I needn't think he would flinch from accepting total responsibility during this tragedy.

I could find nothing to say to this monumental piece of conceit, but Gudia aunty stepped forward and said, with a magnificent toss of her head, 'Excuse me, sir, but please don't think that Pushpa Pande died because *you* let her down so badly, in front of over ten thousand people! Madam was too tough for that. She died because she was medically ill, *grievously* ill.'

To do him credit, TB flushed instantly, looking intensely embarrassed. He started to say something but there was a slight commotion at the gate just then, and I turned around wearily, wondering which other VIP had showed up to milk this highly photogenic situation for all it was worth.

Then I heard a hissed whisper.

'*Hain?* What's *he* doing here?'

'Come to do afsos, of course,' said a voice behind me. 'To offer his sympathies. It's good manners. But he could have avoided, especially after the latest rumour.'

The scrum at the entrance parted to let the tall, lithe figure through. He came striding in through the temple square, a white rumaal tied around his forehead, the sleeves of his kurta rolled up to just below his elbows, a large leaf pattra, heaped high with marigolds in his hands. Behind him scurried Bunty Sisodia, talking shadily into his cell-phone, looking around suspiciously, like some kind of hired bouncer. What was he so worried about, that his buddy was going to get *stabbed* to death in the enemy camp? I thought resentfully, even as my heartbeat started its familiar military beat of *dhung-dhung-dhung, dhung-dhung-dhung*.

Zain stopped at the centre of the square and looked around, his eyes tense under the white bandana. There was a resolute, almost defiant set to his jaw. He looked a little haughty as he stood there, scanning the crowd, refusing to acknowledge the whispers around him, which were now really loud.

And then, all at once, he spotted me.

He started forward, his eyes glowing almost painfully, but before he could say anything, the wizened old gentleman in the wheelchair cut in neatly and spoke up, his voice rather shrill as he addressed TB and me.

'Bibi, we are very sorry to hear of your loss. We loved Pushpa jiji like an elder sister. She was so loving to our children! Got them all admission in good schools – even the girls! And last year, we needed a loan for our grandson's nikaah, no small sum, and she gave it to us, and would not hear of us repaying it! She was chief guest at the wedding. A great lady – a great loss.'

'Uh, thank you, sir,' I said faintly. 'I didn't get your name?'

The little old gent adjusted the cuffs of his exquisitely tailored achkan and said, 'We are Master Kamruddin of Saheli Boutique.' Then he added, almost automatically, '*The perfect fit, ready whenever you want it!*'

I choked, my eyes going instinctively to Zain's to see if he remembered. From the faintly amused, rather rueful expression in his eyes, I could tell he did. Suddenly, I didn't feel so miserable any more. I smiled at the little tailor and managed to say, 'Thank you so much, sir, she always spoke most highly of you.'

Zain threw me a reproving glance that spoke volumes as I uttered this total whopper of a lie. Master Kamruddin shook his head sadly, said 'Great lady, great loss' again and was wheeled away.

Not knowing whether to laugh or cry, I turned to face Zain, but just then Munni, Tawny and TB took an almost synchronized step forward which brought then right in line with both of us. Zain's face shuttered over instantly.

'Hello, dear,' Tawny acknowledged him. His jovial voice had a rather cool edge to it.

'Adaab,' Zain replied politely, handing him the marigolds.

All of us just stood there, in a tense semicircle in the middle of the temple square. Behind us, the mourners were keeping up their chant of *Till the sun and moon remain,* louder and more vigorous now, probably for the benefit of TB. The press, thrilled at the possibility of getting a shot of the *Neck to Neck or Necking* opponents together, had gathered behind us, the lenses of their cameras glinting in the hot sunshine.

Zain's jaw tightened. He looked more grown-up than I'd ever seen him. He looked around at my crack team, the press, the crowd, the Top Brass, then he shrugged and turned determined dark eyes on me.

'Sarojiniji,' he said formally, a tiny pulse jumping at the base of his throat. 'I just wanted to offer my condo—'

But I didn't let him finish.

With an exquisite sense of relief, of laying down a burden,

of bursting out of a cold, dark well into hot, bright sunshine, I threw myself into his surprised but incredibly steady arms, laid my head against his superbly muscled chest, and sobbed like my heart would break.

There was a gasp, a loud, clearly audible mass gasp, as if all the people in the temple square had had a glass of ice-cold water flung at them at the same time and sucked in their breath together.

But Zain was totally cool. He held me gently, so gently, patting my half-mad-full-crack hair. I never knew Zain could be so gentle. And when I was done dribbling snot all over his nice white kurta, behaving like a hysterically overwrought, disoriented moron, he kind of handed me back to TB, who told him, in a cool level voice, as he patted me awkwardly, 'I think you had better leave now, young man.'

Zain nodded but continued to stand a few minutes more, looking down at me as I hiccupped in a pathetic, watery kind of way.

'Bye bye, Moti Nagar,' he said gently. 'Chin up, okay? I'll see you soon. Take care.'

And he turned on his heel and strode out, curtly telling the press people to *move out of the way, please. This is not some bloody new year party.*

I would've raced after him, I was so disoriented and demented, but the TB held me firm, murmuring into my ear, 'Pull yourself together, child. We've finally spoken to your mother. Her phone was switched off because she was on a flight to Delhi. She'll be here shortly. Now, sit down and try to compose yourself.'

Which, I must confess, made me feel much, much better.

I allowed myself be to be led back to the whirling dhurrie and didn't budge till Ma came to get me.

It was late afternoon, the funeral was over, and I was sitting in front of the TV in Saket Bhavan, mindlessly surfing channels. It didn't matter which one I switched to, they were all showing the same thing: *Sorrow, shock and scandal mock freedom fighter Pushpa Pande's funeral!* All the under-employed TV channels who do 'breaking news' stories every time the first cousin of a minor celebrity breaks into a prickly heat rash, were having a blast with the little footage they had managed to shoot of the 'embrace'. *Love and War!* screamed their headlines. *Freedom fighter's memory desecrated! Granddaughter cuts off nani's nose at funeral! Indian politics reduced to a mockery!*

It was breaking news on every single channel.

NDTV featured red-faced Pragati Party spokespersons bleating weakly about childhood friendships and a new, civilized way of fighting elections that didn't necessarily involve vilifying the competition. This didn't go down too well because they were instantly asked about all the mudslinging, allegations and counter-allegations that had gone on in Bittora for the past two weeks.

Aaj Tak's panel was talking about whether the influx of so many young people was destroying Indian politics. It featured half a dozen geriatric MPs, all agreeing with each other, saying the same thing again and again. Would you want a young, inexperienced doctor to operate on you? No! Would you want a young, inexperienced lawyer to fight your case? No! So why would you want a young, inexperienced MP, whose hormones were totally out of control, to represent you? Politics was not a sport, argued the oldies, where youth had a natural advantage. Take it from us, they declared, all these young people, who think erection is more important than election, are going to rip apart the moral fabric of the country!

Thumka TV had harassed-looking election commission officials saying there was nothing in their code of conduct that forbade a romance between competing candidates for a Lok Sabha seat.

Star News kept replaying a two-minute piece where Karan Sethie was being chased by their reporter, who was shouting, 'Sir, what do you have to say about the incident at Pushpa Pande's funeral today? What about your brother-sister agenda *now*?' In reply, Karan Sethie promptly accelerated his pace, flung 'No comment, no comment' over his shoulder and hurried towards his car so fast he tripped and practically *fell* into it through the open door. They kept replaying the shot of him falling down.

CNN-IBN had dug up the Hyderabadi Muslim cleric – the one with the 'Conversion through Love' agenda – and he declared that he was proud that Zain was following his (the Muslim cleric's) preachings. 'He's got that girl under his *thumb*,' he gloated, waggling his own thumb at the camera. 'See how she threw herself at him!'

'I *told* you you had feelings for him,' Ma said from behind me, as they replayed the footage of me bawling my eyes out in Zain's arms for the nth time. 'If you'd dealt with them earlier, instead of trying to deny them, this wouldn't have happened.'

I zapped off the TV, turned around and glared at her.

'Excuse me, but if *you'd* showed up earlier, I wouldn't have been driven to fall into the arms of the only person there whom I knew from childhood,' I replied.

Her eyes danced. 'Oh, was *that* your criteria?' she asked as she swooped down on me and gave me yet another thorough hug, squeezing the air out of me, rubbing my back and practically *inhaling* my hair. 'You picked Zain because he's the person you'd known the longest? How logical!'

'Yes,' I said, somewhat indistinctly. 'And also because everybody else there was just so *thrilled* about Amma's impeccable timing. I could totally tell they were gloating!'

'Jinni,' Ma sighed. 'That's not fair. A lot of those people loved Amma. I know Jugatram did. And Gudia too. And… if she had to go, this *was* a good time to go, right? Can't you forgive them for looking at the rather fat silver lining?'

I shook my head, my eyes full of tears. 'How can you *say* that? It's so cold.'

'I believe death is just the beginning,' she said gently. 'Amma's in a better place now. I *know* she is.'

I threw up my hands, tears spilling from my eyes. 'Ma, don't! *Please*. Don't go all new-age spiritual now. I'll throw up. I really will.'

'Okay, I won't,' she said as she hugged me again.

'Ma! I can't breathe…'

'So *don't* breathe,' she said unrepentantly, not letting go.

'Ma,' I said again, after a while.

'Okay, okay,' she sighed, releasing me. She pulled back, looking at me, then reached out to stand my hair up in random peaks. 'Love the cut, by the way,' she said, tilting her head to one side. 'You look like a rosebud.'

'If you'd let me cut it short when I was young, I could've looked like a rosebud sooner,' I pointed out grumpily, as I finger-combed my hair back to the way I liked it. 'Instead of spending most of my life looking like the pigtailed warrior Obelix.'

'Most of your life is in *front* of you, Jinni,' Ma said gently. 'Do with it what you will.'

'Ma!' I groaned. 'I *told* you. Please don't go all philosophical on me!'

'Then *you* don't,' she said firmly, giving me a hard little shake by the shoulders. '*You* don't go all sad old woman on me!'

I tried to push her away. 'You should've got here sooner,' I said abruptly. 'Wasn't your daughter's first election more important than grading papers in Ontario?'

She let go of me suddenly, her lower lip quivering.

'Oh, Jinni.' She sighed. 'If I'd showed up, all the fights would've just started again.'

Well, she did have a point there. She would have made Amma and me feel like axe-murderers for every rupee we spent that crossed the EC limit of twenty-five lakhs. She's like Bauji in drag. Only, much prettier, of course.

'And you didn't even get to meet Amma,' I said sadly.

Ma looked a little smug. 'Oh, I wouldn't say that,' she said. 'We had a long chat the night before your rally. I called her on my way to the airport. She knew I was coming, you know. She was all excited about surprising you.'

Really, I thought with a twinge of irritation. It seemed like all Amma had done was keep secrets from me.

'So, did you talk about me?' I asked.

Ma chuckled. 'Alwayj thinking about yourself,' she said, doing a spot-on Amma imitation. 'No, we talked about *me*. And made peace on a lot of different issues.'

'Good for you,' I said, with a sigh.

'Anyway,' said Ma, 'don't beat yourself up about behaving impulsively in the temple, Jinni. You did what you felt compelled to do. And Zain did what *he* felt compelled to do. Otherwise, he'd never have showed up there in the first place. Either way, it's okay – one of you will become MP and the other one can help him.'

'Or her,' I muttered, not even bothering to comment on the impossible sunniness of this future scenario.

'Or her,' she agreed. 'It doesn't really matter, baba. Stop fretting about it. Now, tell me what Amma and you talked about before she died.'

I smiled.

'Thank god,' Ma said, swooping down on me with yet another fervent hug. 'I thought you'd *broken* your smile. There it is, big and wide and as scary as ever.'

'She said not to let Katrina play her in *SKAA*,' I said.

Ma gasped. 'Because she's *Muslim*?'

'No.' I rolled my eyes. 'Because she's *fat*. And she told me to read Bauji's diaries whenever I get confused. She said you had them.'

Ma went very still. 'She said that?'

I nodded.

'In that case,' she said, her voice deceptively casual, 'here's one of his diaries which I happen to have in my bag, and I think you should read it, right now.'

She stood up as she spoke, and rummaged through her boho sack-like handbag. Then she held out a limp, brown leather-covered diary. 'It's one of his last ones,' she said. 'Written in 1991.'

'Oh,' I said as I took it from her carefully. 'Amma did say he left them to you, not to her. It seemed to be a bit of a sore point.'

'Yeah... well.' She shrugged. 'I don't know, Jinni, they had a complicated relationship.'

'What's in it?' I asked as I gingerly turned over the yellowing old pages which were filled with shaky, spidery handwriting.

'Lots of stuff,' she said, still in that carefully casual voice. 'General ramblings – some prayers, his grocery lists, letters from all kinds of people – and, of course,' she rolled her eyes, 'Sarojini Naidu's poetry.'

I laughed. 'Bangle Sellers?'

She nodded. 'And Palaquin Bearers. Lots of them. But there is one right *here*,' she reached for the diary and opened it to a page somewhere in the middle, 'that I particularly want you to see.'

I took the diary from her curiously – there was a strange, unsteady note to her voice – what was this poem that she wanted me to read so badly?

It was a long poem, taking up more than two pages, even in Bauji's tiny, cramped handwriting.

I started reading.

AN INDIAN LOVE SONG
by Sarojini Naidu

HE

Lift up the veils that darken the delicate moon of thy glory and grace,

Withhold not, O love, from the night of my longing the joy of thy luminous face,

Give me a spear of the scented keora guarding thy pinioned curls,

Or a silken thread from the fringes that trouble the dream of thy glimmering pearls;

Faint grows my soul with thy tresses' perfume and the song of thy anklets' caprice,

Revive me, I pray, with the magical nectar that dwells in the flower of thy kiss.

'Wow,' I said. 'It's tinkly, lyrical porn.'

'Jinni, don't be facetious,' Ma said sharply. 'It's Bauji's diary. Just read, okay?'

So I read.

> SHE
>
> *How shall I yield to the voice of thy pleading, how shall I grant thy prayer,*
>
> *Or give thee a rose-red silken tassel, a scented leaf from my hair?*
>
> *Or fling in the flame of thy heart's desire the veils that cover my face,*
>
> *Profane the law of my father's creed for a foe of my father's race?*
>
> *Thy kinsmen have broken our sacred altars and slaughtered our sacred kine,*
>
> *The feud of old faiths and the blood of old battles sever thy people and mine.*

'Ma,' I said, stopping again. 'This is *so* lame.'

'It's *lyrical*,' she replied, her face straight. 'Romantic. My father had a romantic soul...'

'He was *crushing* on old Mrs Naidu,' I said, 'She must've been, what, thirty years older than him? That's *sick*.'

'Uff, Jinni, he appreciated her poetry,' Ma said, prodding me impatiently. 'How much you can *talk*.'

So I shut up and read.

> HE
>
> *What are the sins of my race, Beloved, what are my people to thee?*
>
> *And what are thy shrines, and kine and kindred, what are thy gods to me?*
>
> *Love recks not of feuds and bitter follies, of stranger, comrade or kin,*

Alike in his ear sound the temple bells and the cry of the
muezzin.
For Love shall cancel the ancient wrong and conquer the
ancient rage,
Redeem with his tears the memoried sorrow that sullied a
bygone age.

The poem spilled over onto a third page, so I had to turn a leaf to read the last two lines.

And when I did, I discovered a black-and-white photograph, carefully taped onto the back of the page. Two worm-infested looking children, aged about five or six, scowling into the camera from the branch of a mango tree, their skinny legs dangling, the sun in their eyes.

Under the picture, Bauji had written, in a shaky, painstaking attempt at calligraphy:

An Indian Love Song.

They were Zain and me.

The photograph freaked me out completely. Don't ask me why. I was conscious of a sudden, searing sense of loss for Bauji and Amma, as well as an entirely unreasonable savage anger at them for trying to *manage* my life.

This weird combination manifested itself in a massive weeping jag. I just *couldn't* stop crying. It didn't help that, as the sun set and the buffaloes began their walk home past our house and the slightly acrid scent of woodsmoke drifted into the garden, Amma's absence hit me like a physical blow. It didn't help that Ponky wouldn't stop howling, sitting out on the verandah, his eyes liquid pools of dumb bewilderment.

Or that the dhobi, his face contorted with grief, showed up with a big bundle of Amma's cotton saris, all freshly washed and ironed.

I grabbed the first one in the pile, a soft, faded, ice blue maheshwari with a tiny pink border, buried my face in it, and wept.

Ma, after a muttered 'Oh, *great...*' grabbed the second one in the pile, a leaf green Rajasthani block print, dropped down beside me, and sobbed quietly too.

'Didn't he know,' I demanded finally, after what felt like ages, my voice still shaking a little, 'that child marriage is against the *law?*'

Ma looked up, frowning, her delicate, Amma-like nose very red.

'Don't be so literal, Jinni!' she said. 'It was obviously just his fondest dream.'

'Oh, please,' I told her, 'if he had this great big dream, how come it skipped a generation? Why the hell didn't he make you marry the lecher and wastrel Zaffar Ali Khan, huh?'

'Now you're being stupid,' she said. 'Bauji wasn't hell bent on some politically correct Hindu-Muslim wedding – he was just hell bent on *your* and *Zain's* wedding. He must've felt, even when you were at that age, that you were made for each other.'

'Which proves that he was *senile*,' I said gloomily. 'And anyway, Ma, I wish you'd stop with all the boy talk. Let's talk about Amma.'

'Okay,' she said obligingly. 'Amma thought you should marry Zain too.'

I gasped. 'How could you possibly know *that?*'

'She told me,' she said smugly, 'that night, when I spoke to her on the phone for the last time.'

'You're lying,' I accused her.

She shrugged.

'Maybe,' she said. She got up, draped her snotty green Rajasthani sari on top of my head like a bride's veil and went towards the loo. 'But you'll never know for sure, will you?'

I blew my nose into both the saris gloomily.

I tell you, my entire family, living or dead, is nuts.

'I heard you.'

Not recognizing the furious, trembling voice, I looked up, blinking. It was Munni. The dupatta wound tight around her neck looked like it was choking her. Her eyes were red and bulgy.

'Talking about getting married,' she continued, her voice still shaking. 'That's all that matters to you and your mother! Just your stupid little romance! Do you care that aisey IJP candidate ko gale lagake you have made laughing stocks of all of us? Of me? What am I supposed to tell my workers in Champapul? To start hugging IJP workers? To *marry* them?'

I looked up at her, open-mouthed. 'Uh, listen, Mun—'

She pointed a finger straight into my face.

'No, didi, *you* listen,' she hissed violently. 'You people...' She shook her head. 'Lok Sabha tickets fall into your lap like ripe mangoes – so you think it is all a joke. Arrey, I am also young! And I have done party work for many many years – but did jiji think of recommending *me* for the ticket when TB wanted a young candidate? Of course no – she recommended her darling granddaughter from *Canada*, who knows nothing, who understands nothing – who is set on drowning herself and taking all of us down with her – just because she can't control her feelings for some *boy*!'

She was right, I thought, feeling sick. She was absolutely right.

But Munni wasn't done.

'Do you know what people would have done to me if I embraced the IJP candidate at my grandmother's funeral? Expelled me from the party!' She snapped her fingers. 'Assi minute phata phat! But because it's *you*, we have to be so *understanding* – poor didi, unko itna bad feel ho raha tha na – she couldn't control, they are old friends, na… Now we have to run around cleaning up your mess – and keep our mouth shut tight and say *nothing* to you! But I can't stay quiet! Somebody *has* to tell you! Jiji gave up her life so we could win – but now we won't; and I'll never get the MLA ticket from Champapul – because *you* have dubaoed all of us!'

Reduced to mute misery, I just sat there, letting her words wash over me in waves.

But then Munni suddenly said, 'Super, didi, super,' and, looking spent, sank slowly into a moodha, buried her face in her hands and started to weep. Soundlessly. Steadily.

I took an uncertain step towards her.

The guard called from outside. 'Didi. Visitor.'

Thankful for the diversion, I muttered an awkward 'Um… we'll talk more later' and hurried outside.

And beheld a lanky figure draped over the green gate.

'Nauzer,' I said and motioned to the guard to let him through. 'Hey.'

He loped up, looking… different. He was still wearing the white kurta he'd been wearing at the temple – but that wasn't what was making him different. It was the expression on his face.

'You need to know something,' he said, as he sat down beside me.

'What?' I asked, my head still reeling from Munni's stormy

outburst. What was with his expression, anyway? He didn't look sympathetic, or madly in love or anything. He looked… pissed off. What was he pissed off about?

Abruptly, he said, 'Remember those pamphlets?'

I nodded. I didn't like the way he was looking at me. My stomach started to churn for some reason. I could *hear* it churning.

He looked around, leaned a little closer and said, 'Look, before I tell you, I just want to say that I'm very *very* sure of my sources. And I have *proof.* I'll send it to you tomorrow. So don't lose it and start yelling, okay?'

'Okay,' I said impatiently. 'I *won't* lose it. So who printed the damn pamphlets, already?'

Nauzer looked at me in a critical, assessing sort of way, almost the way in which Munni looks at rickety chairs during campaigning, like she's wondering if they're sturdy enough to take her weight. Then he shrugged and said, very matter-of-factly, 'Anthony Suleiman.'

Huh?

I opened my mouth to speak.

He held up a finger. 'No yelling,' he said. 'You promised.'

I shut it again, abruptly.

He looked relieved.

'But—' I began loudly.

He held up his finger again.

I closed my mouth, thought over it a little, then finally said in a strangled whisper, 'But Tawny uncle is a family *friend*!'

'Family *frenemy*,' said Nulwallah. 'Your word, remember?'

'Rumi's,' I said automatically, then added, 'Are you *sure*?' My head was reeling.

He nodded, his demented eyes gleaming. 'I'm sure. I tracked

down the printer who did the job. The order was clearly placed through somebody in the Suleiman camp.'

I stared at him, my mind racing. The pamphlets had broken out the day after Titu's visit to Begumbagh, that much was true. But... *Tawny uncle?* The AIPC General Secretary? The man who'd talked my family into letting me study animation? The man who had bought me my first cell-phone?

Why?

Nulwallah said, 'D'you want to know why? Coz I have a theory.'

I glared at him, simmering with resentment. Who the hell was he, anyway, pointing fingers at my oldest friends. How long had I even known him? I'd known Tawny uncle all my life!

'What?' I said coldly.

He looked at me intently, not at all perturbed. 'You know the forests of Durguja?'

'FUCT,' I said knowledgeably.

'Excuse me?' he said, startled.

'They're Full of Unemployed Christian Tribals,' I explained.

'Yeah, that's right,' he said, looking at me a little strangely. 'Anyway, apparently, there's shitloads of illegal stuff going on there. Illegal logging of the reserved forests, bauxite mining. It's a multi *multi* crore scam. Everybody's involved in it up to their eyebrows. The local officials, the IJP state government *and* Tawny and Son, our men from Tiloni.'

'If you say so,' I said doubtfully.

'That's why the IJP state government is hell bent on getting the missionaries out of there – because they take up for the tribals. Tell them their rights and help them to fight and stuff.'

Okkayy.

Nulwallah continued. 'Anyway, after the delimitation five

years ago, more than half the forests came into Bittoragarh. So then it suited everybody concerned to have a nice, cooperative MP in Bittora. Which Pushpa Pande was not.'

That much was true. Amma was fiercely protective about the Durguja tribals. Not because she was madly idealistic or anything, of course. But because of her passionate Tarzan-n-Jane honeymoon there eons ago.

'You may recall,' said Nulwallah, his voice slipping slightly into Karan Thapar mode, 'that she created a big shindig about the tribals being persecuted back then. But then the morphed photo scandal came along and she got all… err… distracted.'

'So?' I said defensively.

Nauzer leaned forward, his eyes gleaming. 'So, I think Tawny leaked that morphed photo story just to fix her, so she'd be too busy to go poking about in Durguja.'

'*What?*' I shook my head. 'That's *insane,* Nauzer.'

'He did,' Nauzer maintained doggedly. 'I *know* this. I tracked down the guy in the photo studio in Noida. The one who morphed all the pictures on your grandmother's orders. He said Tawny paid him to rat on Amma.'

Could this be true?

Nulwallah continued, his eyes intent. 'Tawny got Dwivedi in instead, as MP for Bittora, gave him a fat cut of everything, and things went on swimmingly for a while. But then Dwivedi went and blotted his copybook with TB and failed to get the Bittora ticket this time. So Tawny was back to square one.'

I shook my head in protest.

'I don't buy this. I mean, Tawny uncle is a bit scheming, but he's sweet… he has three moustaches… he's a *joker,* not a villain.'

'Re-read your Batman, Pandeji,' said Nulwallah, looking irritatingly superior. 'The joker *is* the villain.'

I wanted to slap him.

'But he *helped* Amma,' I said. 'He got her the Tughlaq Road house for life!'

Nulwaalah leaned forward. 'To keep her *far* away from the constituency and all the hanky panky going on there.'

'He asked me to marry his *son*!' I exclaimed.

'To neutralize you, obviously,' said Nulwallah. 'And, by the way, big *ewwwwww.*'

'But how would printing pornographic pamphlets about me help him?' I asked, ignoring this.

'He wants you to *lose*,' Nulwallah said explosively, now looking like he wanted to shake me. 'Don't you *get* it? He'd rather the IJP win! The logging and mining is basically an IJP scam, so an IJP MP will have no option but to shut up, take a small cut and let the plunder continue.'

'But he's an All India Pragati Committee General Secretary…' I started to say, then trailed off weakly.

Gudia aunty's words had come back to me. *Don't be so sure Mr Suleiman is on our side, Jinni. He'd be superhuman if he didn't resent a Pande family dynasty blooming right here on his home turf.*

I'd ignored her when she said it, thinking she was just being her usual insecure, insinuating, *no-one-shall-get-closer-to-Pushpa-Pande-than-me* self. But now I had a sudden vision of Tawny uncle, his expression a sinister smirk, as he bribed the TB's helicopter pilot to say the chopper had engine trouble. 'Thank you, dear,' he would have said. 'Don't tell anyone, dear.'

I said slowly, 'So you're saying *he* screwed us by somehow sabotaging the TB's visit here, aren't you? That was all part of his plan?'

Nulwallah nodded. 'And here's where I have to ask you not to shriek and shout again…'

I ran a shaking hand through my hair.

'*Now* what?' I asked. 'What could be worse than *this*?'

He got off the moodha, and kneeled in front of me, tucking both my hands into one of his large knobbly ones.

'I wouldn't have told you this today for the world,' he said gently. 'I *know* what's going on – I'm not blind, you know. But after what happened at the temple, it would be injudicious not to tell you.'

'*What*, Nauzer?' I snapped, gripping his hand painfully. '*Tell* me.'

He shrugged, then leaned back, not letting go of my hands, and said, in this very casual, off-hand tone, 'Well, if we just hold on to that thought – that Suleiman is out to screw you – and ride with it for a bit, then it becomes pretty clear that he wouldn't stop at just trying to spoil things for you. He'd go further, surely?'

'Further, like how?' I asked, wishing he'd just get to the point.

'Well...' he said, a little reluctantly. 'Obviously, by actively supporting someone *else* – helping that someone else win, giving that someone funds, and contacts, and information about your plans well in advance – how else do you think the Salmon Khan rally happened on exactly the same day and at the same time as yours?'

Something large and heavy fell right through my stomach.

Nauzer leaned in again, his thumb caressing my white-as-chalk knuckles and said gently, almost pityingly, 'Jinni, it's pretty clear, to an unbiased outsider, that Anthony Suleiman, half-Christian-half-Muslim-and-full-opportunist would have to have been hand in glove *right through* this campaign with—'

'Zain,' I whispered, feeling like a Nave nymho fool who'd just been slapped in the face.

12

Shortcut confirmed it. He'd been out of town and he came scurrying over to commiserate early the next day, fretting and afsosing and tch tching and asking me if I'd managed to get any sleep last night.

Which, of course, I hadn't. Well after midnight, a ragtag bunch of our own party workers, their eyes bloodshot, their faces as black as thunder, had marched in delegation to the garland-wreathed green gate, bearing placards condemning my embrace of Zain, and said that the pamphlets had been right about my moral depravity after all. Ma and I had lain huddled in Amma's big double bed and listened to them chant obnoxious slogans till they were creeped out by Ponky's mournful howling and slunk away after flinging a couple of half-hearted stones at the house.

But even then I couldn't sleep. Lying awake, burrowed next to my sleeping mother, I thought about what Munni had said, I thought about Amma and the happy movie ending she wanted for *SKAA*, passing on the baton from grandmother to granddaughter, and how it had been within arm's reach till I screwed it all up with my stupidity. Bloody haarmoans, I thought bitterly, they'd led me up shit creek good and proper. I was going to be the only person in the history of Indian politics to lose an election *in spite* of a sympathy wave caused by the death of a major political leader.

I finally fell into a fitful sleep around five, the picketers' sarcastic chanting still ringing in my ears.

> *Sarojni Pande thu-thu-thu*
> *Pragati workers spit on you!*

Anyway, when Shortcut arrived, I glared at him with my bleary red eyes and asked him point blank if he'd been sending money to Zain from Tawny – and he admitted to it! Large sums of money had indeed been given to his people in Delhi by Tawny in exchange for large sums of money which had been released to Zain by Shortcut's people here in Bittoragarh. It had been going on right from the start. The first installment had arrived the day after Zain filed his nomination papers. Which meant that Tawny, Tits and Zain must have discussed it at the wedding reception itself. And I'd pulled him down and kissed him that very night! God, I was cheaper than mangoes in June.

Shortcut claimed he was telling me because he was 'on my side', so to speak, but I wasn't Nave enough to fall for that. He was a businessman, and it made sense for him to keep all sides happy. The *real* reason he had come out and told me, I knew, was because Amma's demise had suddenly turned the tables in my favour. I was pretty much set to win – or at least I had been, but now god only knew how my stupid public embrace would play out. Shortcut didn't watch much TV, obviously; he seemed to have no clue about my political harakiri.

What a shock he would get when he saw the papers, I thought grimly.

Either way, any hopes I had had that Nauzer was cooking

up a crazy cock-and-bull story because he was madly jealous of Zain and fully enamoured of me, had to go straight out the window now. It was proven, beyond doubt, that Zain was a cunning, scheming bastard. Whatever early promise he might have showed when we were kids had obviously withered away as he grew up. He was nothing but a snake, a devastatingly hot, rough velvet-voiced snake with vulnerable dark eyes, a wicked sense of humour, and gentle, gentle hands and I was going to have to rip him out of my bosom (*Can we please not talk about your bosom?*) and fling him out into the political wilderness where he belonged.

But when the papers arrived, a few hours later, it looked like I was the one who was going to be flung out into the political wilderness. All the papers, and I *do* mean all, had the same damn cover picture. Me sobbing against Zain's chest, his arms cradling me, his chin resting gently on top of my head. His face was clearly visible while mine wasn't, and his expression, under the white bandana, was utterly compelling. He looked sombre and strong and young and tender and sympathetic and superheroic and like he totally deserved your vote. If a man could care so much for his closest opponent, any intelligent voter would reason, surely he would care for his *electorate*?

I, of course, looked like the loser, clinging vine that I was.

It was a fitting culmination to a campaign marked by fabulous pictures – me with a rubber penis, me with a naked wrestler, and now, me sobbing in the arms of my arch rival. At my grandmother's *funeral*. And oh, did I mention that my party Top Brass was in the picture too, watching from a distance, an expression of utter consternation on his face?

Even *I* didn't feel like voting for myself after seeing the picture – why should anyone else?

After I got dressed, Ma and I drove to Normal Public School to cast our vote. Or rather, *my* vote, since Ma was a Canadian citizen. After that, we were going to patrol as many polling booths across as many areas as we could, checking to see that the voting was proceeding smoothly.

We reached the booth to find a whole bunch of news vans, all eager to get a sound byte from me. I thanked god that Zain would vote in the Purana Bittora area, so there was no chance of banging into him here and tearing out his eyes and making headlines all over again tomorrow.

I ignored the gaggle of desperate hungry mikes magnificently, and had a chat with the party workers at the Pragati table. The envelope money had obviously reached them safely – they were all kitted out with scarves and caps, and had massive posters of Amma festooned in their stall. They began to chant

> *Till the moon and sky remain,*
> *Pushpa we will say your name*

as soon as they saw me and I had to blink back sudden, stupid tears as I went into the booth to cast my first ever vote as an Indian citizen. In spite of everything, the way I'd been dragooned into standing, Amma's death, and the whole messy PR disaster I'd created, it was a proud moment. I swear I felt Amma smiling her gap-toothed grin beside me, with Bauji just a little behind her, as I pressed the button next to the pointing finger symbol where it read, in indigo blue ink, in not-very-big letters: Sarojini Devi Pande, Indian National Pragati Party.

I got my finger inked – a messy business – and the ink turned out to be deep blue, not black, like I'd always thought it to be. 'It turns black later,' the inker told me, smiling, not at all like he thought I was a clingy loser looking for a manly torso to cry on, and I exited the booth, feeling slightly better about the whole thing.

I posed for the press with my pointing inked finger, and then we drove back home, stopping at various booths along the way. 'Not bad,' said Ma, as we sat down to a cup of tea around eleven a.m., 'things seem to be going fairly peacefully.'

But then trouble broke out in Purana Bittora.

The area was unfamiliar to me; we hadn't campaigned there at all, and all my memories of the place were from when Zain and I were kids. I remembered it as a gracious old quarter, full of Krystal ice-cream carts and massive, gnarled neem trees. The Taj Bittora was there, and the Bittora Fort, a couple of cloth markets and the old financial district. It was the area Our Pappu had categorized as ROMP – Rich, Oversmart, Muslim People – and it seemed they hadn't taken too well to Zain's 'mixed' dalliance with the opposition. A table of his party workers, very cocky because this was their home turf, had shouted something lascivious about me to a table of our party workers, who'd shouted back something equally complimentary about Zain and Bunty and then a major scuffle had broken out. The police – who were on full alert, the district magistrate and police chief having anticipated something like this after the funeral – had moved in and thrown pretty much everybody into the lock-up to cool their heels for a bit.

We got this news through Our Pappu, who was quite sanguine about the whole thing. 'Didi, if there is low turnout because of rioting and violence in Purana Bittora, it will help us a lot!' he said. 'Because Zain bhai is expecting a lead of eighty thousand from there! Just as long as it doesn't get bad enough for the EC to cancel the election!' Which wouldn't happen, he explained, because the people of Jummabagh and Champapul were too sensible to join in the rioting. 'Actually, they were *happy* when they saw your… heh heh… photu – they said we will get the best of both worlds – and they *know* you both are anyways friends because you sat together at the milad-un-nabi function.'

'He's right,' Ma agreed as I gawped at Our Pappu, amazed at this total volte-face in Zain's favour. 'Poor people are always much more broad-minded than the richer classes – they don't have time for all that hypocritical crap.'

Okay, whatever. So maybe I wasn't going to be such a washout after all. And in the rural areas, mercifully, there had been power cuts yesterday, almost all day long, so none of them had seen the damaging footage of me at the funeral. Besides, the papers got there a day late. I finally had something to thank the extremely inefficient IJP state gourmint for!

'Also, we have instructed our workers to pick them up in tempos to take them for voting early morning,' Rocket Singh told me comfortingly. 'Very early morning – too early for them to get the news from here and there. And at the booths, we have put big-big portraits of jiji, smiling, laughing, with big marigold garlands around the frames, and we have lit agarbattis also. Doodhiya-Durguja will see you through, didi – pukka.'

Hasina Behenji phoned halfway through the day to say that the polling in Tanki Bazaar had been 'funtaastic'. 'And didi, there will be hundred per cent turnout here,' she shouted down the line, 'because all of Tanki Bazaar is doing an Offer! If a man comes to the house tonight with an inked finger, he gets a free ride from the ladies – a free ride on the house! *All* the houses are offering a free ride, so don't worry, you will definitely get Tanki!'

We had no news from Sujanpur but Rocket Singh was optimistic. 'All these years, Sujanpur has voted Pragati,' he said. 'There's no reason why they won't do it again…'

Another bit of news that totally gladdened my heart was that apparently the Hijra in the next constituency had supplied huge amounts of alcohol to the Rapist's workers. They'd been so excited about the success of their TB rally that they'd drunk till dawn and woken up too late to shepherd voters to the booths. Of course, it was too soon to say, but hopefully, god willing, Tits was screwed.

The day passed by in a total blur, the news channels showed the mandatory shots of movie stars, cricketers and top-notch industrialists sporting flashy sunglasses and standing condescendingly in queues with regular people to cast their votes, giving the we-are-like-everybody-else-only ones, and before we knew it, the sun was setting, the buffaloes were walking home and the EVMs had been packed up.

It was over.

I went into my petal room, sat down heavily on my bed, peeled off my tight cotton blouse and sweaty sari wearily. It had been a horribly sticky, stressful day and I was longing for a bath.

Fifteen minutes later, as I was standing under the scanty shower, soaping myself, my mind a thankful blank, Ma's voice came floating through the door to me.

'Oh, Jinni!' she called out gaily. *Too* gaily. There was definitely somebody with her. 'Zain's here! He wants to meet you! Come on out!'

Of course, I got the hell out of there. I yanked on my tracks and a ratty old tee and sneaked out the back door. I was in no mood to meet saakshaat saanp Zain Altaf Khan – especially not in front of my romance-obsessed, Sarojini-Naidu-love-poem-reading mother, who, like all visiting NRIs, was obviously hoping to squeeze both a funeral *and* a wedding into one India trip.

I started walking really fast, almost running, actually, and didn't stop till a stitch in my side *made* me. Doubled up and gasping, I found myself standing right beside the Lion Bridge, looking blindly down at the Bitwa. The water passing below the bridge was a soothing grape green under the gathering clouds. The smell was tolerable, almost pleasant, in a dank sort of way. Still panting, I put my palms down flat against the cool concrete top of the low boundary wall and took several deep breaths. Then I hoicked myself up to sit on the wall.

I gazed at the water for what seemed like a very long time. The wind tugged at my clothes. Birds wheeled around me, the clouds rumbled, the scent of wet earth filled the air. The rain should have cheered me up, like the first rain is supposed to, but it didn't.

'First bhutta of the season, you want?'

He didn't wait for me to answer, just put the cob down on the wall and leapt up lightly to sit beside me, dangling his long legs over the wall.

I had a sudden mad urge to just push him in. *Baazigar,* I'd hiss with a demented grin, and give him one strong shove into the churning water. But then I remembered, with some chagrin, that he was a really good swimmer.

He held out the bhutta placatingly and looked at me, the familiar dark eyes full of phoney concern. Behind him, the sky suddenly darkened to pitch black. Thunder rumbled menacingly. A long crack of forked lightning rent the sky in two.

Well, why wouldn't it? After all, the super villain had just made his entry.

He said lightly, 'You know, Master Kamruddin was right.'

I didn't say anything, just snatched the bhutta and started on it. I didn't trust myself to speak just yet.

'When I was about five, she used to tell me I looked like Dilip Kumar. She told me he was this big movie star. I was really kicked about it until I saw a picture of him in the Sunday papers – the guy was a raddled wreck, all dyed black hair and shiny shoes! Every time she saw me, she'd put one bony finger under my chin, lift it, and proclaim my Dilip Kumarness to the world. It used to embarrass the hell out of me.'

I chewed on my bhutta and continued to say nothing. It was really good, not too soft, crisp, and with just the right amount of nimbu masala.

'She gave me all these fat lifafas full of cash on every birthday,' he continued. 'And Jinni, I'm not sure I remember this right, but I have a distinct memory of sitting in her lap and being fed puri and halwa by hand. By *hand*. D'you have any idea when that could've been?'

I shook my head.

He looked out at the river and said, with wonderfully simulated sincerity, his voice pitched just right, 'I'm really sorry she passed on. She was a great lady.'

In reply, I tossed my meticulously-picked-clean bhutta core into the river.

He leaned forward, laying a large warm hand over mine. Wow, that one hug at the funeral sure had made him cocky.

'Jinni?' he said gently. 'Your mum told me you may have nicked out the back door. So I followed you. I hope you don't mind, did you want to be alone?'

I turned to look at him at last.

'Bet she didn't tell you,' I said, my voice trembling, 'that I'm *on*to you.'

He went very still.

'Sorry, what?'

'I *know*,' I said slowly, so he would get it, 'that Tawny and you are hand in glove. How could you keep accepting money from him for your campaign fund? Shortcut himself told me, so don't bother to deny it!'

He frowned. 'Shortcut?'

'Shafquat ul Haq,' I said tightly.

He didn't look particularly guilty at this accusation, just mildly exasperated.

'So?' he asked.

'You *knew* he was betraying Amma,' I said heatedly.

'So?' he said again, his fine nostrils flaring.

'Didn't it bother you that Tawny is from the Pragati Party?' I demanded. 'That he was doing something ethically wrong by backing another candidate against his *own* party's official candidate?'

Zain shrugged.

'Well, if it didn't bother *him*, I really didn't see why it should bother *me*,' he said matter-of-factly. 'He was giving me funds – no strings attached – and all he wanted in return was that I should defeat you. Which I wanted to do, anyway. There was nothing underhand about that!'

'That's what you *think*,' I said hotly. 'He'll make you sit quietly while he screws the tribals in Durguja!'

'Jinni, I have a plan for that, believe me.'

'You could've warned me,' I said and instantly wished I hadn't. It sounded pathetically Nave.

He shot me this very dirty look. 'Yeah, just like you warned me that you *weren't* going to withdraw.'

I flushed.

'But you betrayed the IJP's trust!' I said.

He did the lazy eyebrow raise.

'How?' he asked, reasonably enough.

I made a small, frustrated noise in my throat. 'Tits got those pamphlets printed!'

'Says who?' Zain demanded.

'Nulwa—' I started to say, then stopped. I didn't want to blow my sources but it was too late.

'Young *Nauzer*,' said Zain icily. 'You've been getting pretty thick with him...'

I ignored this extremely ignorable remark. 'You *knew* Tits and Tawny got them printed, didn't you?'

Zain sighed. 'Well, maybe I suspected.' Then he turned to look at me, his dark eyes earnest. 'But I didn't know they were going to do it.'

I laughed. 'I'm sorry – but *that* I don't believe.'

A long silence.

Except for thunder.

Except for lightning.

Finally, he shrugged, looked at the river tumbling below us, and said, 'Look, I'm tired of these games. You met me so sweetly yesterday. We'd been fighting, I had no idea what kind of reception I'd get, Bunty said I was crazy to go to the funeral... but when you met me like *that*, I thought, wow, she's glad to see me, she values this relationship too! I thought we could put this whole stupid election behind us and move on to something good. I was...' he hesitated, his face twisted, 'well, I was ecstatic.'

'I'm sure you were *ecstatic* when you saw the picture in today's paper,' I muttered resentfully, hugging my knees.

He looked at me in total disbelief.

'Whoa! Don't you *dare* pin that one on me! *I* wasn't the one who fell into your arms in public and cried a river!' His voice softened, as he added musingly, 'It felt really nice, by the way. Made me feel like this strong, silent *rescuer* guy.'

I didn't say anything. Bad mistake. Because his voice promptly grew deeper, more intimate. 'I wanted to scoop you up right there in that stupid temple, and carry you out and make love to you forever. I have no idea how I restrained myself.'

'It's not a stupid temple,' I muttered, looking anywhere but into his disturbingly warm eyes.

'Okay,' he said, looking amused, and tapped the tip of my nose with his finger. '*Clever* temple.'

'And anyway,' I continued, 'what kind of sicko sociopath has thoughts like that at a *funeral*?'

'You're twisting my words,' he said mildly.

Then he added, his voice a husky caress, 'No sweet, clinging hugs for me now that we're all alone in the rain, Jin?'

I sucked in air so fast I almost choked. 'Are you *nuts*?' I hissed, outraged. 'I don't trust you! Not for a moment! You've just admitted that you've been lying to me all along. I hadn't managed to piece it together at the funeral, unfortunately. I was feeling lost and lonely and you showed up, oozing fake concern... and now,' I swallowed convulsively, blinking back sudden tears, 'now, I'll probably lose the election because of that one stupid, *stupid* gesture.'

He flinched. His eyes, so warm a moment ago, became unreadable. The wind had died down a little, and in the whipping stillness that remained, his voice finally rang out, low and steady and furious.

'Fine. If we're getting into *trust*, let's just go over it once from *my* point of view, shall we?' His accent had gotten all clipped, never a good sign. He held up his hands and started ticking off on his fingers. 'You took money from my uncle. You said I'm homosexual and that I'm dating Bunty Sisodia and we have *orgies* at the Taj. You claimed my father was an indiscriminate, incestuous lecher and that my family has robbed the people of Bittoragarh for centuries. You boasted that you were having an affair with me in order to get some guy you – or maybe one of your drivers? – ran over, admitted into my hospital. And oh, I nearly forgot, you tried to get me *disqualified* by planting a whole lot of your illegal campaign money into my vehicle. So please could you tell me why *I* should trust *you*?'

I bit my extra large lower lip. Damn. I'd forgotten all about my foiled attempt to get him disqualified. And all the mean things Amma and I had said about him during the campaigning. So maybe he had a point there. But I hadn't run over anybody! How *dare* he think so?

'Look, Zain,' I said, trying to fight the constricted feeling in my chest. 'I know I said some pretty nasty things -- we *both* said pretty nasty things! But—'

He flung up one imperious hand.

'No, Jinni,' he said, in that same quiet, clipped voice. 'Enough is enough. I know you're devastated about losing your grandmother but frankly, I've had it. Just too many unforgivable things have been insinuated here. Obviously, re-igniting this... this *thing*, whatever this thing is, was a bad idea. I blame myself. I've been an idealistic, nostalgic idiot. It was nine years ago that I saw you last and, frankly, nine years won't be soon enough not to see you again.'

And with that, he leapt off the wall, the same one we used to run along when we were kids, and strode away in the rain.

The next few days passed in a blur. Ma and I endured the four day ceremony somehow, and then took the train back to Delhi like a couple of physically and emotionally wrung-out rats. The driveway of the house on Tughlaq Raod was knee deep in floral tributes to Amma, but when we finally waded through them and managed to enter the house, the phone was ringing – it was the CPWD, telling us very gently but firmly that the house had to be vacated within three months. It was a Grade A Lutyens' bungalow, bang in the heart of Delhi, and many cabinet ministers, Supreme Court judges and party general secretaries had been lusting after it during the thirty years that Amma and Bauji had occupied it. Very often, during that depressing monsoon, as I sat in the verandah, straggly haired, having my very own staring-at-the-jamun-trees crisis, just like Amma, I would see white Ambassadors slowing down on the road outside and random VIPs leaning out to count the number of bedrooms and trying to assess the state of the loos, like burglars casing a joint.

'Vultures, all of them,' said Ma in disgust. 'I tell you, this whole political system sucks. Jinni, promise me, if you win you'll keep your dignity and never stay in these stupid, crumbling, termite-ridden, bandicoot-overrun, anthill-infested houses.'

I tried to tell her that as a first-time MP I would be lucky if I was assigned a tiny flat somewhere, but she wasn't listening. She was too busy losing it because we were having to pack up the whole house.

Amma had been a compulsive hoarder. The furniture in the house was mainly CPWD, thankfully, so that wasn't a big deal – but there was an entire room full of photo albums and every single issue of Bauji's firebrand pre-independence newspaper *Azaadi*. There were three cupboards full of saris and four full of expensive shawls, seventeen cane chairs that Bauji had woven in prison, and an entire garage full of gifts the two of them had received from visiting dignitaries from all over the world.

Gudia aunty, who would've been of great help in sorting through the garage, had mysteriously melted away. Or rather, she'd decided that now that Amma was no longer around, there was no need for her to hang out with horrible, accusation-hurling me. Besides, she couldn't stand Ma. Or maybe she'd just decided that our ship was going to sink and had sensibly deserted it.

Ma spent an entire week going through the stuff. Every now and then I'd find her weeping over some old article of Bauji's or a photo of Amma with Golda Meir or something. But mostly, she just grumbled about how much junk there was.

'There are *eleven* sets of wooden elephants in different sizes,' she would report in a slightly stunned voice. '*Sixteen* sandalwood chariots, with horses attached, of Arjun listening to Krishna's discourse. *Forty-nine* boxes with silver, or more likely white metal, bowls. There are countless nylon blankets, most of them featuring horridly cheerful sunflowers, roses or ducks. There are cuckoo clocks and grandfather clocks and *fourteen* melmoware dinner sets in ghastly colours. There are *nine* Chinese vases, *four* Mah-jong sets, *seventeen* chess sets, two of them probably made of illegal ivory. There are stuffed toy koalas, giraffes and Assamese water buffaloes. *Any* number of ugly garlands made of sandalwood bark shavings. And nine, no *ten* carpets featuring dragons. Jinni, this is insane, my mother had all of Vishal Mega Mart inside her storeroom!'

Meanwhile, the monsoon continued to pour down with a vengeance. The house dripped constantly, and the grass in the garden, deserted by the gourmint gardeners since Amma's death, had grown almost as tall as a paddy field. Too scared to wander into this wilderness which was probably 'seething with bandicoots and monitor lizards', as Ma darkly put it, the two of us had taken to pacing up and down the driveway every evening, earthworms and jamuns squishing below our feet.

I don't know why I didn't just tell her about the Tawny-Zain tie-up. Maybe I was worried she'd go confront Tawny or something. Maybe I was just too vain to level with her that Zain, far from being in love with me, had been playing me for a sucker all along. Maybe, pathetic loser that I was, I kind of liked hearing her air her Sarojini Naidu Indian Love Story theories. Whatever. I didn't tell her.

Instead, I spent a lot of time watching TV, where the news channels were still frantically covering the election. Ours had been in the third phase and there were two phases more to go, mainly in the south, but also in Himachal, Haryana and some parts of Pavit Pradesh. The counting was to be on the twenty-seventh of June, exactly two weeks after our polling. Whenever I thought about it, I felt physically sick. It was worse than waiting for my class ten board results. Really.

Thankfully, the shock and scandal at Pushpa Pande's funeral had died down. Mostly because a renegade nephew of TB, a young, butcher-like, heavily eyebrowed and sideburned IJP dude, had managed to eclipse Zain and me in the popular media. He'd made fun of Muslim names and surnames, saying they sounded scary and barbaric. Then he'd said something blatantly incendiary, like 'if any hand raises itself against the Hindu majority of India, I will cut off that hand'.

The IJP was appalled at such unvarnished, unwarranted frankness. They started scurrying around, spewing political double-speak or claiming *Doctored tapes! Manipulated footage! Pragati Party conspiracy!* But nobody really bought it.

So then, hoping to deflect everybody's attention from the husky young butcher's doings, they promptly went back to gushing about their 'brother-sister' policy for Hindus and Muslims. They even attempted, briefly, to pass off our embrace as an example of such brotherly-sisterly love.

A very senior IJP leader from Gujarat snarled into the news channel mikes that it was all very well to sit in Delhi and Mumbai and *talk*, but the truth of the matter was that practically all of rural India – and most of urban India – was against mixed marriages. 'It is every Hindu mother's nightmare,' he said, 'that her daughter will end up wearing a burqa.' He wound up this shockingly chauvinistic statement by adding that he was confident that, urban flak notwithstanding, the anti-mixed marriage policy would pay rich dividends at the hustings.

So then all the big Bollywood Khans with mixed marriages came out strongly in protest of the policy.

All this excitement seriously rattled the cage of the maverick Muslim cleric from Hyderabad, who started on his 'Conversion through Love' agenda again, exhorting young Muslim boys to seek out, marry and convert Hindu girls. Finally, the district magistrate got the police to crack down on him. They placed him under house arrest and told him to shut the fuck up, which he did, albeit unwillingly. The IJP, thrilled at the unholy mess they'd managed to create, gleefully denounced him in public. They also tried to smarm up to Khiladi Kumar, the only Bollywood superstar with what they called a 'normal' marriage, to push their agenda, but were struck catatonic by the massive fee he quoted.

And so, looking around for some fun and high jinx to end the final phase of their campaigning on a high note, they zoomed in again on the embrace between Zain and me, interpreting it this time as a symbol of non-brotherly, non-sisterly lust.

'*Ho ji!*' they screamed from the rooftops. 'Shameless Pragati Party hussy throws herself at a *paraya mard*, a strange man! A Muslim boy! Her political opponent! At her grandmother's funeral! *Dhikkar!* Shame shame puppy shame! Is this the *sanskar* the Pragati Party wants our children to learn?'

The press kept asking for Zain to come and tell them if he felt violated by my flagrant behaviour but he proved elusive. So they kept replaying the footage of me launching myself into his arms again and again.

The ploy seemed to go down pretty well, especially in Pavit Pradesh and the other northern states, but of course, no one could really tell for sure – not even Mr Urvashi, the man with the name of a woman. Either way, I thought gloomily, all the negative publicity would surely make me unpopular with my would-be colleagues in Parliament *and* with the Top Brass. That is, if I managed to win, which was looking more and more like a total impossibility.

'I wish I could just slip into a coma or something,' I told Nauzer fervently over dinner on one of his visits to Delhi, 'and wake up on counting day and know my fate once and for all.'

'Like Zain, you mean?' he said, taking a sip of white wine.

My heart went bump, like a blind person walking into a stone wall. 'What?' I asked faintly.

Nauzer looked up in surprise. 'Not literally,' he said. 'But he's switched off his phone and hit the Manali-Leh road. It just opened for the summer. Your dude – the one who taught you guys to drive – has gone with him.'

I looked up, my fork halfway to my mouth.

'Jugatramji?' I asked. 'Really? He didn't say a word about it to me!'

Nauzer shrugged. 'Maybe he thought you'd feel,' he made dramatic quote marks in the air, 'betrayed.'

'Oh,' I said, feeling absurdly deflated. 'Whatever.'

I had somehow assumed Zain hadn't spoken to the press about my Hindu wantonness because he was a decent guy with *some* residual feelings for me. Now it seemed he hadn't spoken to them because there was no signal in Ladakh. Bummer.

Nulwallah leaned back in his chair and regarded me with squinting, half-shut eyes.

'Did Zain and you have a falling out?' he inquired.

'Now *why* would you think that?' I replied sarcastically.

'So you did!' he said. 'Did he deny the tie-up with Tawny?'

I shook my head gloomily. 'No,' I said. 'He admitted it. In fact, he seemed rather surprised that I was hassled. He said trying every trick in the book was part of the game.'

'Fair enough,' said Nulwallah, pursing his lips. 'You know what, I *like* that guy. He's straight.'

'Huh?'

He continued. 'It's really your Uncle Tawny who's the snake here.'

Well, I wasn't as ready as Nauzer to absolve Zain of all blame. Because, of course, Zain hadn't looked deep into *Nauzer's* eyes and told him that the relationship they shared was special. Or, to be more exact, that he hadn't known all these years that the relationship they shared was special, but *now* he knew. Or words to that effect, you know what I mean.

'So there's nothing going on between the two of you?' he asked, penetratingly.

'Nothing!' I snapped.

He actually looked a little disappointed.

Hello, I thought he was supposed to be in love with me!

'It would've made a great news story,' he explained regretfully.

I made a small frustrated noise in my throat and reached for my drink.

So Zain was doing something glamorous and adrenalin-pumping in the hiatus period between the polling and the counting. Typical. I, of course, was doing nothing constructive or impressive. Just gnawing on the fingernail on my right index finger, watching the tiny black voting dot on it climb higher towards my fingertip as time passed, waiting compulsively for the twenty-seventh, after which... after which, my life was just one big black hole.

'Can you smell loser stench on me?' I asked Nulwallah worriedly.

A lanky brown hand closed comfortingly over mine.

'Not a whiff, Pandeji,' said Nauzer soothingly. 'Hang in there. Just a week to go.'

13

'Didi,' whispered Our Pappu, 'I smuggled the phone inside in my underwear! I am talking from the bathroom! They have just opened the machines!'

'Well done, Pappu!' I whispered back, then realizing *I* didn't need to whisper, said loudly, 'Now, don't come to the loo too many times to talk or they'll suspect. Go back and watch your table. We are sitting in front of the TV, the updates will start any moment now!'

'Okay, don't worry, didi!' he said. 'I think so that Sisodia has just come into the bathroom. He must be having a phone too. No shame, breaking the rules!'

'Never mind Bunty Sisodia,' I hissed. 'Go outside!'

I put down the phone and flashed a grin at Ma. 'Pappu's in, phone and all.'

A lusty cheer greeted this announcement.

It was finally the day of the counting and we were sitting in front of the TV in the finest suite of the extremely seedy Hotel Gangadeep – traditional dugout for all political parties for all countings in Bittora, because of its proximity to the counting venue at Normal Public School, only a three-minute walk away. Everybody was here, my crack team, *their* crack teams, the grassroots workers, families and friends. It was an unruly, boisterous lot of people, most of whom had been drinking since last evening and parading through the seedy hotel corridors in their underwear. They were also being painfully shy – when they spotted either Ma or me, they would giggle, cross their arms over their chest bashfully, duck back into their rooms and howl with mirth.

The IJP gang was also camping here, holed up exactly one floor below us. Every time we set up a cheer, they set up a louder one, which of course we felt honour bound to outshout, pounding on the floor with gusto. The hotel, very proud of its status as the traditional counting venue, tolerantly turned a deaf ear to the racket everybody was making.

The local press was stationed outside, munching on elaichi cream biscuits and little cups of bright orange tea provided gratis by Hotel Gangadeep, while they frantically checked their phones for updates. Their phones rang so often that there was a constant hum of Hindi movie songs in the air.

We'd checked in the night before and barely got any sleep on the stained, worn sheets, due to a lethal mixture of nerves and mosquitoes. Ma and I had ingested a massive breakfast of greasy puri-aloo and were now plonked on the brown velvet sofa, looking at the TV, fully hypnotized. The table before us was groaning with presents – blessed prasad from about seventeen different temples, coconuts, amulets, tinsel bandanas and baskets of fruits. Rocket Singh was sitting with us, prayer beads clasped in one hammy fist. Munni was still steadily eating puri-aloo. Jugatram, who had returned from Ladakh, slightly shame-faced, tanned deep maroon, and with a dazzling new collection of fake Ed Hardy T-shirts, was sitting near the door, on guard, in case any lowly minions tried to push their way into this sanctum sanctorum.

Ma looked at me curiously. 'What was that about Bunty?' she asked.

I shook my head. 'Nothing, Ma.'

NDTV's election special programme came on just then, with its grand, vaguely patriotic theme music, accompanied by a montage of images, party symbols – the pointing finger, the flower, the elephant, the bicycle, leaders in the middle of speeches, crowds, flags, posters and buntings, two cackling old village women with brightly coloured headscarfs slipping off their wrinkled faces, and ended with a freeze frame of a young rural dude showing his inked finger to the camera. The words INDIA VOTES formed with a dramatic sound effect across his face, and then they cut to the studio and to Pran Bishnoy, looking all bright-eyed and bushy-tailed in a jaunty orange tie, and practically licking his chops in anticipation of the goodies to come.

'Good morning and welcome to *India Votes*!' he announced, blinking rapidly, his beard and his voice both quivering slightly with excitement. 'Today is... D Day! The culmination of the world's largest universal adult franchise, the free, fair and periodic general election in which the votes of an estimated sixty million Indians will be counted! It's the biggest reality show on TV and it will be unfolding live *right* here, throughout the day, with updates straight from five hundred and fifty counting booths across this great country! Kings will be dethroned today, rookies crowned, demigods banished, myths shattered, and history made. Because this is India, this is democracy at its vibrant, pulsating best, this is the place and the day when the public giveth and the public taketh away.'

He paused for breath, looking slightly at a loss for words at the end of this obviously rehearsed piece, goggled at the teleprompter for a moment and then continued, in a much more normal voice, 'And here's our very first update – from Belgaum, Karnataka!'

The update from Karnataka said that a senior Pragati Party leader was trailing by seven thousand votes in Belgaum, but of course, it was early days yet, as about six lakh votes remained to be counted. Bishnoy nodded intelligently and turned to Sameer Marwah, a nervous looking historian dressed in a shabby tweed jacket, who looked like he'd just been dragged through a hedge backwards, and asked him some complicated question about the recent electoral history of Karnataka.

'Oh man, who gives a shit about bloody Karnataka!' Ma muttered, reaching for the remote, which I was holding tightly in my hot, sweaty little fist. 'Switch to one of the local channels, Jinni, the Pavit ones.'

She pried the remote out of my hand and flipped channels until she found the garish graphics of Thumka TV, where a well-endowed lady with lashings of bright red lipstick was sitting behind a sign that proclaimed *Voters ka hai zamana* in neon orange, white and green. 'Ji haan, voters ka hai zamana, it is a voters' world out thyeure!' she was saying archly. 'This is the public, dear, and it will beat you up very badly if you don't it fear! And now, our first update is here! Sarojini Pande, granddaughter of the recently, tragically expired Pushpa Pande trails by thirteen thousand votes in Bittoragarh.'

A huge roar rose from the floor below us, causing the walls of the room to practically shake. Almost at once, our workers in the rooms and corridors outside retaliated, setting up massive chants of

Jab se aayee Sarojini Pande
Chud gayeen IJP ki gaande.

Munni leapt up immediately. '*Not* that one!' she cried out shrilly. 'I have told you *many many* times. Not *that* one!' She wound her dupatta tightly around her neck and rushed out of the room.

Thirteen thousand, I thought, my heart plummeting like a boulder down a bottomless chasm. I was lagging behind by thirteen thousand votes. How did one even begin to recover from a mortal bloody blow like *thirteen thousand votes*?

I clutched convulsively at Ma's shoulder. She pulled me closer and patted me gently. Rocket Singh stopped telling his beads long enough to say, 'Must be Purana Bittora. Khan is strong there.'

Jugatram grunted. 'System has changed since your time, Rocket Singhji,' he called out from his post by the door. 'They count all eight assembly segments together now. It happens in rounds. One EVM from PB, one from Jummabagh, one from Durguja, and so on. This is an *overall* lead, not only from one place.'

Rocket Singh sat up straighter. 'What do you mean by *my* time, Jugatram Sharma?' he demanded combatively. 'Don't talk like you are some young cock, just because you did some chota-mota jeep driving in Ladakh.'

I blinked in surprise at this rather random attack.

Jugatram flushed even marooner. He opened his mouth to say something, but Ma cut in, her voice like thin steel, 'Do you mind? We're trying to watch the counting here. You guys can take this outside, and Jugat, if you're so keen on Zain, go watch the counting from his digs downstairs, okay?'

They looked instantly abashed. Jugatram subsided, muttering that he was in my team only, in Amma's team only, and Rocket Singh repeated staunchly, with a fierce, defiant look at Jugatram, that the thirteen thousand lead must've come from Purana Bittora undoubtedly.

We stayed glued to the TV, hoping for updates as the clock inched slowly towards nine-thirty. It would be finished by noon, Our Pappu had said. Which meant, I thought, doing some rapid math, that about one-sixth of the counting was done. Please god, let the other five-sixth go my way!

Type-written updates from all over Pavit Pradesh now started crawling across the bottom of the Thumka TV screen. The butcher-like guy with the hate agenda was leading in his constituency up north. The Top Brass, both father and daughter, were leading in theirs. The dude who played Ravana in the Ramanand Sagar tele-serial *Ramayana* was leading too. The transvestite in Tiloni was trailing by three thousand. And every seven minutes, crawled the damning words *Sarojini Pande trails by 13000 in Bittoragarh*.

I'm trailing, I whispered to myself. It's official. Amma, how can this happen? We have a sympathy wave, surely? Could that one embrace really have had such a big impact?

'It's stuck,' Ma said in answer to my unspoken question. 'They haven't got any updates from the area so they're flashing an old update. Why isn't Pappu sending us anything?'

At that moment, my phone glowed. I snatched it up and checked the inbox with shaking fingers.

Leading by four, by the blessing of God and jiji, Our Pappu had written.

Ma swore. A very rude Pavit word.

'Ma!' I remonstrated, shocked.

'Four *what,* Jinni?' she demanded. 'What an idiot that Pappu is! Four hundred? Four thousand? Four lakh?'

'Must be *four* only,' I said gloomily, wondering why my headache hadn't eased at this good news. The rusty vice gripping my head was as tight as ever. 'One, two, three, *four*. That's one less than five.'

'Should we message him back?' Ma asked.

'I don't know,' I said dubiously. 'He may not have been smart enough to put it on silent. And if his underwear starts beeping, people may notice.'

'And if it's on vibrate he may get turned on and all,' Ma said, with a sudden giggle. 'Eww. Chalo, let's just wait and watch then.'

I looked at her fretfully. She was acting like this was all one big joke and not the most major crossroad of my life. I bit my lip and restrained myself from saying something rude to her, because then she would start talking about *perspective* and *pitfalls* and the *futility of living in the flesh* versus rooting yourself in *The Forever*.

We watched and listened. We flipped back to NDTV, where Bishnoy, looking flushed and happy, was holding forth to Sameer Marwah about the north east, Sikkim in particular.

'Oh, for heaven's sake, there's only *one* measly Lok Sabha seat in Sikkim!' I said in frustration. 'As opposed to *seventy* in PP! Where are the Pavit Pradesh updates?'

Ma shook her head at me. 'It's because people like you talk in that fashion that north-easterners end up feeling left out of India,' she remonstrated.

'*You* don't talk,' I said rudely. 'You live in Canada.'

'Oh my god,' said Ma. 'You're channelling Amma's spirit. You'll be calling them *chaptas* next.'

'I *miss* her,' I said fervently. 'She would've been hunched up right here, gnawing on Vicks ki golis, periodically messaging little rockets to Our Pappu's underwear. And I would have been sure that everything was going to be all right in the end.'

Ma reached for the huge bunch of litchis on the table. 'I know,' she sighed as she peeled one and popped it into my mouth. 'Anyway, she's probably hovering in spirit over the counting officers right now, hexing the EVMs.'

My phone beeped again. My heart leapt like a nimble athlete, lodged neatly in my throat, and promptly started choking me.

'Look, baby, look!' urged Jugatram, as I stared at the phone in horrid fascination. 'Must be Pappu! What does it say?'

I shook my head. 'I can't look,' I whispered. 'I just can't.'

'Don't look then,' Ma said soothingly, cupping her hand under my chin and patting the back of my head coaxingly.

I scowled at her. 'What are you doing?'

'Spit out the seed,' she said matter-of-factly. 'You're about to swallow it.'

Meanwhile, Rocket Singh grimaced, reached forward and picked up the phone. He peered at the message screen, his lips moving slowly.

'What does it say?' I asked, fearfully.

He looked across at me, then shrugged and read out, somewhat gingerly: 'Jinni baby, worry not, you'll kick him in his lush… cious crotch.'

'There are some Xs and Os after that,' Rocket Singh added conscientiously.

'It's Rumi,' I told a confused looking Ma. 'He's a friend of mine. From Mumbai.'

But then the phone beeped again. Rocket Singh snatched it up. 'Message from Pappu,' he said excitedly. 'Leading by five thousand now, thanks to God and jiji.'

Yessss.

I sank back into the sofa, weak with relief. On Thumka TV, *Pande trails by 13000 in Bittoragarh* crawled by again, and the

IJP gang below set up another earth-shattering roar, but this time, I didn't shrivel up and die. I handed my phone to Munni, who got up and walked out to the corridor where our workers were gathered, and brandished my phone about. 'Don't believe what the TV says!' she shouted. 'Read *this*, it is the absolute latest latest report!'

A short guy with a crew cut and a vest with my face on it, grabbed the phone from her hand and shouted out Our Pappu's message loudly. Everyone whooped and cheered.

Ma made a small satisfied sound in her throat. 'Superb,' she said, 'we're really on the road to victory now! You're going to be the youngest MP ever, Jinni! You know, we should start speaking to the printers about some thank you posters…'

But I held up my hand and pointed to the TV. I'd flipped back to Bishnoy, who *finally* had a Pavit Pradesh map behind him. He was saying, 'And things are getting really exciting in Bittoragarh, setting of the high-profile Khan-versus-Pande face-off. We're told the counting there is about half done. Sarojini, who started off by trailing by over thirteen thousand votes, recovered quickly to take a lead of over seven thousand, but our latest report shows that Altaf Khan is back in the lead – presently, he leads by over two thousand votes…'

I looked wildly at Ma, who reached out and grabbed me for another one of her lung-busting hugs. 'Relax,' she whispered. 'Relax and just breathe, okay?'

I nodded, eyes shut tight, my body shaking uncontrollably. I couldn't lose to Zain. I *couldn't*. Not after I had found out he was in league with Tawny. Not after Amma died. I had to kick him in his luscious crotch. I *had* to!

The cheers from the floor below us were deafening. I stood up.

'Get up, Ma,' I said calmly.

'Jinni, what are you doing…?' she asked, standing up warily.

In reply, I grabbed one arm of the sofa and lifted it off the ground. 'Rocket Singhji?' I said, looking around at him enquiringly.

He walked over and lifted the other end of the sofa.

'One,' I counted softly, as we lifted the sofa higher. 'Two. *Three*.'

We dropped the sofa. It landed with a horrible, guttural *dhadaam* and things went quiet on the floor below, well, at least for three minutes.

'Wow,' said Ma shakily, as she sat down again. 'That's telling them…'

On the news, Bishnoy was now blathering on about totally extraneous issues, like which party would win the general election this time. 'The exit polls conducted by this channel have clearly predicted a simple majority for the Pragati,' he babbled seriously, like he didn't know that exit polls were the only avenue a disgruntled public had to take the piss out of news channels and politicians. 'But nobody knows if they'll be able to find partners to cobble together a coalition and reach the magic 278 figure.'

He turned towards his studio guest. 'Sameer, how significant is the demise of Pushpa Pande to the verdict in central Pavit Pradesh?'

The untidy looking historian-psephologist scratched the back of his head thoughtfully. 'Hmm… uh… Bishnoy, we must remember that these are rural areas. Literacy is low, television reach is erratic because electricity is erratic. Mrs Pande's passing actually occurred very close to polling day – just two days prior, if I'm not mistaken – so the impact will probably not be as huge as it could have been. Also, let's not forget there was that other... err...' he paused and blushed pink, '*incident* at the funeral. *That* would've definitely confused the voters.'

Bishnoy permitted himself a hesitant, wintry smile. 'Ha ha,' he said wittily. 'Well, Bittoragarh certainly seems to be the place to be this election, but in *other* places, leads are quickly converting into victories...'

And then he went on to inform us about all kinds of victories across India. Like we gave a damn. TB had won by ninety thousand votes. Karan Sethie had scraped through by three thousand. An independent with a commode as his symbol had won in Bihar. The renegade TB nephew with the hate agenda was through from eastern PP. An IJP candidate who'd been denied a US visa for his alleged involvement in the Muslim killings in Gujarat had romped home with a margin of over two lakh votes. A Pragati Party man whose son was in prison for mowing down seven people in his BMW had won by three lakh votes. A lady involved in a six thousand crore scam had won in Chennai. The woman who played Sita in the *Ramayana* serial had lost by seventy thousand votes, standing on an IJP ticket. An independent bearded holy man who could haul a tractor by his testicles had won in Punjab. A famous intellectual and Nobel prize winner had lost from the educated, urban constituency of Mumbai West. And in Nagaland, a petite, twenty-six-year-old *Indian Idol* winner had totally *destroyed* a candidate who'd reigned supreme in that constituency for thirty years.

I watched the crawlies frantically as Bishnoy dished out all this good news. Every forty-five seconds, a crawly would whizz by, saying *Sarojini Pande trails by 2000 votes in Bittoragarh, PP*, and the gang below would send up huge, blood-curdling victory whoops.

'Didi?'

There was an urgent hand on my shoulder. I looked around, wondering who had breached Jugatram's fierce guardian-at-the-gates demeanour and entered this hallowed zone, and beheld a beaming Hasina Behenji. She was soaked through from the rain outside and her wet white sari clung lovingly to her hefty, muscular form, making her look like some kind of Bollywood rain song fantasy on steroids. There was a small revolver dangling casually from her right hand.

'Hi, Hasina Behenji,' I said. 'What's with the… err… *gun?*'

She grinned. 'Oh, that's just for shooting off when we win!' she boomed. 'We *will* win, for sure, you know. You'll see! Hasina Behenji always knows!'

'D'you have a licence for that?' enquired my NRI mother, standing strategically behind my shoulder.

I dug her fiercely in the ribs. '*No*,' I whispered, out of the corner of my mouth. 'But she bites off her armpit hair with her *teeth*. You wanna argue with her?'

Ma frowned. 'Don't *poke* me, Jinni,' she said austerely. 'You're not my mother. Hasinaji, won't you put down your gun and have some fruit?'

Hasina Behenji smiled and sank down on the sofa graciously, but not without shooting a triumphant look in Jugatram's direction. 'I would shut the doors now, if I were you,' she advised Ma in a loud, confiding whisper as she picked up a hard, green guava and split it open effortlessly between her palms as if it came fitted with a hinge. 'All kinds of gatecrashers will try to thrust themselves in otherwise.'

On Thumka TV, they had cut to an ad break where all the advertisers had done extremely unfunny 'topical' take-offs on the elections. A chick got dumped at the wedding mandap when her bridegroom-to-be started to put sindoor into her maang and realized she had dandruff. He went all *ewwww* and stormed out, and a social worker type stood up and told the weeping, jilted bride to 'Vote for Clinic All Clear Shampoo. They promise to rid the nation of the Social Evil of Dandruff!' Next, a hot chick licked an ice-cream cone meaningfully, while she stared at a hairy chimpanzee-like man doing push-ups by the pool. 'Vote for Manforce condoms,' cooed the hot chick, as the chimp-like guy clambered into bed with her, waving a packet of condoms about.

'Wow,' said Ma, impressed. 'Indian ads have become really bold! Which company makes Manforce condoms, Jinni?'

'I don't know Ma, okay?' I said crossly, just as Our Pappu messaged us and confirmed what Bishnoy had said ten minutes ago – I was trailing by two thousand votes.

Rocket Singh said comfortingly, 'Baby, don't worry. Sujanpur will save you! Hundred per cent.'

'I keep telling you, old man,' Jugatram said with savage restraint, 'they don't count assembly by assembly!'

Meanwhile, a huge scrum of people had built up near the door of our room. When I got up, simply wanting to go to pee, they reached forward and lunged towards me. In the front line was a venerable gent I recognized vaguely. 'Bitiya, pehchana?' he called out in a wheezy voice. 'I am Printer Vohra, I have printed all your posters and buntings!'

'Namaste, Vohra saab,' I said politely.

From behind him, another gentleman spoke up. 'Myself Mr Rohtaash from Rohtaash Caterers,' he said. 'We provided snack boxes for all your public meetings.'

'Oh, how nice,' I babbled, a little blankly. 'Thank you.'

Munni swooped down on me and hissed, 'Just go to

the bathroom, didi! They are here just to nag about their outstandings…'

'But haven't you paid them yet?' I asked in surprise. 'I mean, it's been almost a month since the polling!'

'All in good time,' Munni murmured. 'Such inflated bills they have presented, you will not believe! Don't get into a *conversation* with them!'

So I sneaked into the loo quickly. As I splashed cold water on my face and looked into the mirror, I saw a flushed face with wide, worried eyes staring back at me. That was your last pee as a regular person, I told myself. The next time you pee, you will be an MP. Or, of course, that pathetic thing – a could-have-been MP, drowning in loser stench. The girl who, with one stupid embrace, destroyed her entire family's political legacy.

Just then, my phone beeped. *Didi, ahead by fifty votes, only one machine left to be counted.*

Oh My God.

This was way too close.

I ran my shaking fingers through my hair and took a deep, unsteady breath. The phone beeped again. But I didn't have the guts to look at it in here, all alone.

And then suddenly, the workers outside started chanting, loud, exultant, *all-out* chanting, the beating of their drums deafening.

> *Sarojineeeee… Sarojini!*
> *Pragateeeeee… Pragati!*

A scent filled the air; a cool, shining, intangible scent, redolent of confetti and champagne, of tapes being breasted and national anthems sung. It carried with it a sweet hint of desi gulab, a sharp tang of chrysanthemum, a jolting electric charge and the crisp taste of money.

I knew what it was.

So when I looked down at the SMS, I already knew what it said.

Didi, we have won. By six hundred votes. Mubarak ho.

I unbolted the door and rushed out, shrieking.

Ma looked at me in incredulous, wordless disbelief and then screamed madly, pumped her arms in the air and swooped upon me, laying smacking kisses on both my cheeks. Then, while Hasina Behenji fired six bullets into the air, Rocket Singh banged the velvet sofa again and again on the tiled floor and the crack team collided into a laughing, sobbing, euphoric huddle with Ma and me at its centre. I thought dazedly, We've done it! We've won the Battle for Bittora! We've upheld the family legacy, we've foiled Tawny's shady plans, we've shut up the sniggerers, we've rubbed Zain's nose in the mud! And I, I am Eau de Victory incarnate. I am the MP from Bauji's old seat, I am the youngest Member of Parliament India's ever had.

The moment was everything I'd ever thought it would be. For that one moment, the world seemed spun out of pure, shimmering gold.

14

It didn't last long. Not even one month later, I was a very depressed person. Maybe it was because it took the TB and his cronies *ages* to cobble together a coalition and we had to just twiddle our thumbs and wait it out till then, feeling fully anti-climaxed. Maybe it was because I kept thinking about how much Amma would've gloated about my victory to everyone in Delhi. Maybe it was just the realization that I was never going to be a full-time animator and make a movie like *Avatar*. Whatever. The bottom line was that I was exuding loser stench from every pore. It rose from me in waves and caused happy, healthy flowers to wilt upon their stems.

'Didi, why are you crying?' piped up Our Pappu as I drove home the entire crack team, which had swung into town to witness my swearing in the day after tomorrow.

'She's crying,' said Ma flatly, 'because the car in front of us is a Maruti Zen.'

Our Pappu looked around the Sumo we were in. 'You'd rather have that cheap car than this nice jeep?' he asked, confused.

'I'm not crying,' I returned shortly, looking straight at the road ahead.

Ma snorted. 'Well, you're about to start any moment,' she retorted. 'It's pathetic.'

God, she was getting on my nerves.

'No, I'm not. And where else do I look?' I demanded, nettled, turning around to glare at her. 'I mean, I'm *driving*, and the damn thing's right in front of me. Perhaps you'd rather I look at my lap and have an accident?'

Ma hunched her shoulders. 'I can't *believe* I'm having to go through this all over again!' she said broodingly. 'It was bad enough when you were sixteen. It took me *age*s to pull you out of it – and now, nine whole years later, you're back in the same mess. It's like a dog returning to its own vomit.'

I glared at her through the rearview mirror. 'Do you mind, mother?' I snapped. 'Can we not please discuss this in a car full of people?'

'Didi, we are family,' Munni piped up from next to Ma. 'Don't mind us.'

'And don't call me mother,' put in my mother. '*Cosmopolitan* magazine says that children who call their mothers mother are trying to dominate them.'

'I know,' I said tiredly, changing gears. 'You've told me that before.'

'Anyone would think you would be happy now,' she continued fretfully. 'You were on *MTV Democrazee* for thirty whole minutes! And on the cover of *India Today*! You're going to *Parliament* soon! You can make all your plans and schemes come true – remember all the stuff you wrote about in Enforcer 49? What's the problem?'

'I didn't write the Enforcer 49s,' I told her shortly. 'I just drew them.'

There was silence. Then she started muttering again.

'God knows what happened that night,' she said. 'He came

home, just walked in, hugged me, and asked where you were. *One* look at him and I knew! He *still* had feelings for you!'

'Ma!' I protested, looking around. Everybody was listening avidly. *'Please!'*

Everybody smoothly assumed impassive expressions and continued to listen avidly.

'So I told him you had just left,' Ma continued gloomily. 'Then I got into bed and *prayed.* But you came back looking like a wet, suicidal rat. Really, Jinni, I don't get you! The two of you are perfect for each other! You have a big mouth – he has big ears – whole day you would've talked and he would have listened! How can you trade him in for that zoo exhibit Nulwallah?'

'I thought you liked Nulwallah,' I shot back at her. 'You said he was friendly and funny.'

'I think Ponky is friendly and funny,' Ma said darkly. 'Why don't you marry him?'

Munni giggled. So did Rocket Singh. So did – they were all giggling, dammit!

I slammed the brakes and glared at them.

'What's with the *marrying,* anyway?' I demanded. 'I'm not marrying *anyone* for a long long time!'

'Bitiya, marrying into a minority community is a good idea,' Rocket Singh volunteered. 'It will increase your vote bank and show ki you are a progressive. But be practical, please choose a large, healthy minority! There's no such thing as a Parsi vote bank – they're practically extinct.'

'But they're rich,' interrupted Our Pappu, with a worldly wise air. 'All the richest Mumbai families are Parsi...'

'Thank you, *everybody* for your invaluable advice,' I said coldly. 'And I'm sure you guys will be kind enough to tell me which minority I ought to cold-bloodedly, strategically pick out?'

Complete silence in the car.

Then Jugatram, who had been quiet until now, cleared his throat and opened his mouth.

'Don't say anything!' I thundered at him. '*Especially* you, Jugatramji. Do *not* speak.'

'Baby, I was just going to say ki I can drive if you are tired now, that's all,' he said in an injured voice.

Which, of course, put me even more firmly in the wrong.

A long, reproachful silence followed.

Broken by Ma, muttering, 'Really, Jinni, winning that election has gone to your head. You've become so unattractively bossy…'

Which infuriated me so much that I stamped down on the accelerator instead of the brake and pranged the Maruti Zen in front of us right in the ass.

That evening, I was wandering moodily under the squishing, dripping jamuns at Tughlaq Road, when a voice called out my name. I turned.

'What?' I snapped

There was no reply.

I peered into the darkness. Now that Amma was gone and her security guards had been withdrawn, people could just wander in and out of the gates at will.

'Who's there?' I called out.

A sari-clad form stepped out hesitantly from behind a jamun trunk.

I squinted into the darkness.

Large watery eyes, a thin tremulous mouth and a vague smell of vodka.

'Gudia aunty!' I exclaimed. 'Hey, where've you been?'

'Jinni,' she said, her voice very slow and dramatic. 'I need to speak to you.'

'Okay,' I said. 'Hey, it's nice to see you! You just vanished! My god, I don't think I've seen you since the day—'

'Jyoti came,' she said with a little sniff. 'Yes. We never got along too well, you know, your mother and I. She was too insecure about how fond madam was of me.'

'Uff, that's all in your head, come *in*,' I started to say, grabbing her by the shoulder, but she shook her head firmly.

'No,' she said. 'Not inside. Here.'

And with that, she sank down onto the grass, amongst the squishy squashy jamuns.

'Gudia aunty?' I asked, a little alarmed, as I sank to my knees too. 'What's up?'

She gripped my arm tightly, too tightly, and said, her voice sending goosebumps down my spine, 'Do you know what day it is?'

'Uh, yeah, I guess,' I said. 'The sixteenth of July?'

She shook her head urgently, her eyes glassy and wide.

'It is the *last* day,' she said, 'for filing complaints against any EC violations committed during campaigning.'

'So?' I asked, perplexed.

'So, even if anyone had *proof*, any concrete, documented, irrefutable proof, bills for instance, signed by the candidate or her election agent, which prove that more than twenty-five lakhs have been spent on campaigning – and if that person were to submit those documents to the election commission *now*, after the last date is past, the election commission can no longer disqualify the erring candidate.'

I looked at her, puzzled. She sounded like she'd swallowed the Election Commission of India Rule Book whole. 'Matlab?'

'Matlab, even if there is any evidence against you, it can't be used against you any more.'

'Okay,' I said, still confused. 'Cool. So... why are you telling me all this? So I can relax?'

She just looked at me.

My eyes widened in horror. 'Is there proof? Was there *proof*? Oh my god, did someone submit it and file a complaint? Will I have to resign now? Will Zain get my seat?'

She shook her head. 'There was proof all right. I gave it to him with my own hands.'

'What?' I squeaked. '*Why*? To *whom*? How *could* you?'

'That day,' she said reminiscently, her voice slipping into its familiar, pain-laced Meena Kumari impersonation, 'that black day, when you accused me of...' she paused and closed her eyes, like it was hard for her to repeat such crude words, then continued resolutely, 'of wearing your undergarments...'

'Aunty, stop,' I interrupted. 'I'm sor—'

But she carried on. 'Simply because I happen to have a lilac slip as well! The very *same* shade! Why,' she gave a tinkling little laugh and tossed her head, 'many's the time I suspected you of wearing *mine*!'

'Of course,' I replied dutifully. 'Now can you tell...?'

'I was very hurt, Jinni.'

I nodded, bewildered, wishing she'd get to the point.

'Gudia aunty...' I said awkwardly, 'I'm sorry. I've been sorry for a while... but what are you *saying*?'

'I was *so* enraged that I went to madam. But she was...' she gave another tiny sniff, '*unsympathetic*. Later, of course, I realized it was because she was so unwell. But at that time, I did not know. So I decided to finish off your whole family for good. I took the bills – not all, but the ones which had your signature on them, totalling to well over three crores – drove over and gave them to Zain.'

I gave a small, choked gasp and sat back on the wet grass with a loud squelch.

'And he waited till today to submit them,' I said flatly. 'God, that's *really* cruel.'

'For one whole month,' she continued dramatically, 'I have been living with a sword dangling over my head. Because I regretted my action almost immediately. And when madam,' she gave a little gulp, 'passed on... oh! I was *crucified* with guilt. I couldn't face you. That's why I went away. Please, please forgive me, Jinni!'

'I forgive you,' I said sadly. I mean, what else could I say? She was so pathetic, with her enormous nose and large watery eyes and her hysterectomy at twenty and her husband who-left-her-and-not-even-for-someone-else. 'I was horrible to you. *You* should forgive *me*.'

Silence.

I popped a squirrel-nibbled purple jamun into my mouth and chewed on it gloomily. A muggy breeze blew. Crickets hummed. Mosquitoes sucked blood. The recycled-sewage water the gardeners flooded the lawn with every evening pooled below us and stank.

So this is how it would end, I thought. Humiliation. Disgrace. Public vilification. No wonder I'd been exuding loser stench.

I fished out the plastic MP badge I'd been issued for the swearing in day after tomorrow and turned it over in my hands a few times. 'Well, I guess I'd better return this then!' I said lightly. 'The photograph's awful, anyway.'

She looked up at that, blinking, shaking her head.

'Jinni,' she said, grasping my hands, urgently. 'You don't

understand. I just came to *tell* you. To confess. *No* complaint has been filed – I've been checking at the Nirvachan Sadan – the election commission office – every single *day*. Sometimes *twice* a day. Zain didn't use those documents. He spoke to absolutely *no one* about them! I thought,' she stopped, blushed and gave me a timorous smile, her large watery eyes glowing almost maternally in the dark, 'I thought you might like to ask him *why...*'

The sun was rising behind the Lion Bridge over the Bitwa when I drove up there the next morning, a cheerful, India-Gate-balloon sun, reflected in a river of sparkling glass, green as a champagne bottle. Birds wheeled in formation over the gleaming water and a veritable army of monkeys – moms, kids, grandparents and bachelor uncles – promenaded along the low boundary wall of the bridge. I peered into the rearview mirror, rubbing my gummy eyes, and winced at my reflection – skin grubby, eyes manic, mouth huge under a half-mad-full-crack mop of hair. I looked like an underfed dolphin with a bad quiff. A quick halt at Saket Bhavan was clearly indicated.

An hour later, I drove into Purana Bittora, looking and feeling much revived. If the welcome Zain gave me was even one-*hundredth* of what Ponky had just come up with, I would be extremely satisfied.

I drove slowly, looking around, as I hadn't been in this part of the city since I was a child. The roads were wide – and quiet at this time of the morning; crows cawed lazily on the blossom laden gulmohar branches above. The sunshine that touched everything had the slightly unnatural sparkle it gets when it bursts out after several days of rain and thunder. Herds of buffaloes ambled past, staring at me with soft dark eyes. A particularly large one eyed me compellingly, then shot out a long pinkish-grey tongue, flicked it upwards, and stuck it into his nostrils one by one, giving them a thorough, fastidious cleaning.

Ewww! I groaned.

And then, abruptly, I saw the palace.

I wasn't prepared for it. I mean, I knew it had been done up, of course – I'd seen pictures and stuff – but I still wasn't prepared. There were these towering cast-iron gates that I had no memory of. After that, there was a long, sweeping drive, almost a kilometre long, flanked by glowing, ruby red bougainvillea. And finally, there was the palace itself – sprawling, low rise, yellow-stoned, exquisitely restored. In front of it were sleek vintage cars, fountains, lotuses and liveried men.

I swallowed convulsively. Suddenly, my crisp blue-n-purple sari and ruby red blouse didn't seem so crisp any more.

One of the liveried gents bowed low as I emerged from the dusty Sumo, feeling small-time and rumpled and nowhere in the league of all this understated opulence.

'Madam has a reservation?' he asked smoothly.

'Uh... no,' I said. 'I'm just here for... umm... breakfast.'

He bowed again, the top of his turban at level with my chest. He extracted the Sumo keys from my nerveless grasp (there was dirt under my fingernails and I quickly curled them under my palms) and indicated that the coffee shop was in through the lobby and to the right.

'Thanks,' I told him. 'But what I want know first is, where's the loo?'

He indicated discreetly in the opposite direction and I put my head down and scurried off. I zipped through the lobby like a speeding blue, red and purple bullet and dived into the ladies'.

The restroom was sumptuous, as large as a banquet hall, with full-length mirrors, plump sofas, subtle lighting and massive bowls of white roses everywhere. An extremely snooty looking cloakroom attendant was presiding over the whole setup. She didn't even glance at me when I burst in.

Rushing over to the dressing area, I peered into the mirror, combed out my hair, adjusted my sari pallu, and executed a few three-sixty-degree turns to see if I looked presentable from every angle.

You've just come to say thank you, I told myself firmly as I checked for boogers up my nose. Thank you and sorry. Thank you for being such a gentleman and sorry for being such a bitch. There was nothing else to say, really.

Because to say or expect anything else would be, to use Gudia aunty's words, *Ridiculous. Bizarre.* And *unbelievable.*

Wow, I totally forgave her that remark now. If I had seen Zain's home earlier and realized it was no longer the mouldering ruin I remembered, I would never have fallen sobbing against his chest. I would've been all, oh no, if I touch him the Aukaat police of Ahri will stone me to death for getting-ideas-above-my-station.

Then, just as I was finally turning to leave, reconciled, if not satisfied with how I was looking, I felt a tap on my shoulder.

I whirled around.

It was the snooty cloakroom attendant. She'd slunk up behind me silently. As I looked at her, my mouth half open, wondering if she expected a tip or something, she gurgled, 'Didi!' and dived for my feet.

'Heyyy!' I exclaimed. 'What are you doing?'

She straightened up – she was really quite a beautiful girl – and informed me fervently, in the chastest Pavit Pradeshi, that she owed me her life.

'No, no,' I said weakly. 'How could I… I mean, how could you possibly?'

'Didi, don't try and deny,' she returned mistily. 'I am Rita Mishra. You saved my Him from the Brahmins of Ahri. I would have suicided if He had died!'

Huh?

Then something clicked.

'Oh my god, you're Babu Ram's chick!' I cried out, delighted.

She nodded, giggling a little, her snootiness a thing of the past. 'That is not His real name,' she said, 'but yes, *now* you have understood!'

But I hadn't understood. What was she doing as a cloakroom attendant at the Taj Bittora? Was she all right? Had her family been hard on her? Had she been married off to some weirdo pandit? Suddenly, I felt horribly guilty that I'd managed to forget about her completely.

She didn't seem to bear any grudges though. Pressing me into one of the sumptuous winged armchairs, she quickly filled me in.

Basically, after Rumi and I had spirited Babu Ram away that night, her family had realized they were stuck with an unmarriageable daughter. Nobody would marry Rita if her 'lover' was still at large. Being too delicate-minded to murder her outright, they settled for locking her up in a small room and leaving her to starve to death. She became sick and skeletal there, with no food or loo or water, until some gutsy ladies in the area alerted the local NGO of her plight. Then Zain's cousin Pinky, who headed the NGO, arrived at her home. Ugly scenes ensued, but eventually the family surrendered her to Pinky didi, who introduced her to Zain bhai, who got her this job. Then he produced her lover boy from somewhere and organized a quiet court marriage. The family tried to make a fuss, but once Zain bhai gently hinted that the footage on Rumi's camera could get the whole Brahmin community of Ahri into big trouble, they piped down and shut up.

Next week, she wound up breathlessly, she and her Him were going to Goa. Zain bhai – who obviously thought of *everything,* I thought sourly, unlike me who only thought of Zain bhai – had arranged for jobs for both of them at a Taj property there.

I smiled and hugged her and wished her all the best, but I couldn't help feeling rather deflated. The way the words *Zain bhai* and *Pinky didi* had tripped together so easily from her tongue had suddenly given me a headache. They both had so much in common, it made sense for them to end up together. Was I about to make a complete idiot of myself here?

Still, I had to say my thank you and sorry; that was only polite. So after hugging her again, I squared my shoulders, raised my chin and stepped into the lobby. My heart was beating fit to burst and I could hear nothing but its demented, impossibly high-decibel thumping. It drowned out every other sound. I was suddenly, miraculously, a unique medical case, a Guinness Book entry, a person who had shattered her eardrum with the sound of her own heartbeat.

In this numb, deaf, heart-banging condition, I wandered around the lobby, looking for Zain. Of course, I hadn't been smart enough to check if he was even here. For all I knew, he was back in Ladakh.

I must have been giving out mad-woman-loose-in-the-lobby vibes because a liveried dude slithered up to me right away and asked me what I was looking for.

I told him.

He looked a little taken aback, but then he pointed to a set of crystal double doors in the distance. 'Sir is there,' he said, 'You are here for the septic tank conference, I suppose.'

It was a statement, not a question. Which was very depressing because it seemed to suggest that in spite of all my frantic primping, I was somehow managing to radiate an aura redolent of septic tank. So be it.

I walked towards the crystal double doors and past the sign that said *Fifth International Engineering Conference on Waste Water Management*, took a deep breath, and flung the doors open. Here goes nothing, I thought.

The hall was dark. And huge. About two hundred people, all seated in groups around circular tables, were looking ahead at some kind of presentation. Except Zain. He was standing in front of a podium, spot lit, dressed in scruffy jeans and a cheesy red Ed Hardy T-shirt, holding a section of what looked like a PVC pipe in his hand. He had on a lapel mike and behind him, on a slide, there was a projected image of what looked like a mountain of dirty brown sludge.

I sank down in the darkness at the table closest to me and proceeded to listen to a long lecture on waste water management like my life depended on it.

He talked about solid waste and liquid waste. Kitchen waste and bathroom waste. About how the pipes they'd used in the renovation of the property were made of some corrugated, non-corrosive polymer to withstand the extreme toxicity of the freight they carried. How the waste water was cleaned thoroughly inside the septic tanks and only then released harmlessly into the Bitwa. How the tanks were equipped to handle two hundred and fifty metric tonnes of human waste. How (this with a grin and a modest duck of the dark head) his team must've done something right as the waste water model of Taj Bittora had been awarded seven awards for excellence in waste water management by the world environment council.

Basically, I just watched him. Bouncing a little on the balls of his feet, his voice rising and falling, his hair all tousled, his enthusiasm for the subject electrifying the room. He was always so *enthusiastic*, I thought besottedly, whether he was writing comics or making kebabs or rally driving or running for parliament. He had so much energy. He talked for forty-five minutes about susu-potty disposal and managed to reduce me to a state of pathetic, worshipful lust. Finally, he stopped, asked for the lights to be switched on, and asked if there were any questions.

I ducked my head, held my breath, and prayed there were none. But of course, a thin, bug-eyed blonde guy behind me raised his hand and asked some interminably long and appallingly ill-informed question about how this system was taking away the livelihood of the erstwhile untouchable caste of night soil workers and what had Zain done for their emancipation, if anything. I groaned silently as I slid lower into my chair and sank my chin into my chest. This was going to take *ages*.

And it did. The questions came thick and fast, most of them totally incomprehensible – at least to me. Finally, just when I thought I couldn't take it any more, Zain said, 'Well, that's it then. The lady there has a question too, I know, but we mustn't trespass onto the time set aside for the next session. Ma'am?' His voice was low and pleasant over the mike. 'I could answer your question now during coffee break, if you like?'

I looked up with a start and realized he was looking straight at me.

'Yeah... sure,' I fumbled out, stupidly. 'Coffee would be nice. Thank you.'

Then I stood up and, hit by a massive nerve attack, walked briskly, not in the direction he was indicating but out through the crystal double doors, heading blindly for the safety of the lobby. There must've been more than just one set of crystal doors, though, because I suddenly found myself outdoors. A low rocky wall and a chain link fence faced me, and I could see tennis courts beyond. I was still trying to figure out where the hell I was, blinking in the warm sunshine, when running footsteps sounded behind me, and then, suddenly, there he was, his dark eyes glowing, his breath coming fast, as though he'd covered a much longer distance than the length of the conference hall.

'Hey,' he said, coming to a sudden halt.

'Hi,' I replied.

There was a weird little silence. I raised my chin and forced myself to look him in the eye.

And still he said nothing. Just looked at me, like there was nothing else to look at in all of Bittoragarh.

Finally, I said, like a very polite moron, 'That was a very informative session.'

His face changed. Closed down, somehow.

'Why, thank you,' he returned a little sarcastically. 'I'm glad my local MP approves of my small environment initiatives.'

I flushed.

'I wasn't being patronizing,' I said awkwardly.

'No?' he asked, a queer little smile twisting his mouth. 'So what's up? How come you're here? No magazine covers to shoot? And isn't the swearing in today?

'It happens alphabetically,' I told him. 'Andhra, Andaman, Arunachal, Bihar... PP is wayyy down the list.' Then I squared my shoulders and added quickly, 'Anyway, I just came to say please and thank you.'

'*Please?*' One eyebrow rose interrogatively. 'What's the please for?'

Uff! I'd said the wrong thing as usual.

'I mean sorry,' I amended quickly. 'For being rude. That day, on the bridge. Not please.'

He stood lounging against the chain link fence, a small smile still playing at the corner of his mouth, the dark eyes glowing strangely. 'Are you sure?' he asked.

Flushing bright red, I pushed past him, shaking my head vigorously. 'I'm sure,' I said airily, as I hurried away. 'In fact, I should be going now. Bye, then.'

'Whoa, hey, hang on!' he said, jack-knifing up from his lounging stance against the fence so fast he made my head spin. But I didn't look back. I was almost running.

I mean, what was I *thinking*? That I'd find him all broken and brooding and I'd *save* him somehow?

Sneakered footsteps sounded lightly behind me, an insistent hand closed around my wrist and the next thing I knew, my back was up against the chain link fence and he had me pinned, a sinewy arm on either side.

'Sure you didn't mean please?' he asked teasingly.

'Yes!' I snapped. 'Why would I be saying please to *you*, anyway?'

'Oh, I could think of a few reasons...' he drawled, running a finger down my cheek in this very cocky, suggestive way that made me want to hit him.

'Are you trying to be all *suave*?' I said witheringly. 'Because it isn't working.'

'No?' he enquired, not looking too worried about this

feedback. 'You've gone the exact colour of a pink guava, by the way. Did you know?'

'*No*,' I said irritably. 'Your T-shirt's really cheesy. Did you know?'

He looked taken aback. 'It's a present from Jugatramji,' he explained.

Intensely irritated that Jugatram hadn't got *me* a T-shirt, I glared at him.

'Anyway, why are you following me? I thought nine years wouldn't be long enough for you not to see me again?'

He grinned.

'That obviously rankles,' he said, with great satisfaction. 'Good.'

I glared straight into his chest, avoiding his eyes. His stupid T-shirt left the golden skin at the base of his throat bare. That golden skin had started a whole separate conversation with me.

Giggles sounded behind us. Two small blonde boys were walking towards the courts, racquets in hand. They were pointing at us and whispering.

'Hey, Zak!' One of them waved.

He raised one arm to wave back and quick as a flash, I ducked out and away, restarting my mad, thoughtless dash to god-alone-knows-where.

He didn't say anything, just fell in step beside me and somehow, I don't quite know how, managed to manoeuvre me back into the lobby. Here, he pointed out the numerous restorations that had been made – the chandeliers, the floor, the vaulted ceilings – in a most natural manner, politely ignoring the fact that I was acting like some kind of skittish, headless psycho. He even told me that all the dead mounted animal heads had been moved to a bar lounge on the third level. 'It's got a sort of Jungle Hunt theme,' he said. 'I'll show you later. Come this way.'

So, of course, I came that way. I was walking like somebody hypnotized.

He guided me into a large elevator with mirrors on the walls, punched a button marked Zain Mahal, and a couple of seconds later, we entered a deep blue and gold floor. It was beautiful but untidy, mostly because there were dusty stacks of campaign posters everywhere, including a massive framed one on the wall. 'Vote for Youth! Vote for Change! Vote for IJP candidate Zain Altaf Khan!' it said below a smiling picture of Zain.

I stopped.

'Zain,' I said uneasily.

He turned around and looked at me, smiling a little.

'I keep meaning to get rid of all this stuff,' he said lightly. 'But then I keep forgetting.'

'Zain, I'm sorry,' I said, even as a huge lump formed in my throat.

He just looked at me. 'Oh, I'm sorry too,' he said ruefully. 'You have no idea.' Then he added, 'Come on through. The décor's a bit oppressive, but I'm sure you'll like the view.'

I walked slowly into the sumptuous suite. It was a really male space – done up in deep reds and emerald greens and Persian blues. Humongous floor-to-ceiling windows looked onto rolling golden fields outside. A deep pool of brilliant sunshine lay shimmering across the plump, inviting, white linen covered bed.

'C'mon here,' he called as he threw open a few of the bay windows. 'I bet you remember this!'

I walked slowly towards the window and looked out. Of course I remembered the view. The rolling fields on one side, the single-storied, yellow brick houses of Purana Bittora stretching out for miles on the other, the glinting water of the curving river, the Lion Bridge, and far away, the hazy golden domes and ramparts of the old Bittora Fort.

I stood there for a long time, inhaling the wood smoke, then turned my back on the view, crossed my arms across my chest, and came to the point.

'So whyn't you use the stuff Gudia aunty gave you?'

He'd been tidying some papers at an ornate wooden desk but he went very still at this.

'What stuff?' he asked casually.

I rolled my eyes.

'*The* stuff,' I said. 'My *bills*. For well over three crores.'

He shrugged. 'Oh, *that* stuff,' he said. 'Who told you about that?'

'Gudia aunty told me,' I said, trying hard to get him to look me in the eye. 'She waited and waited for you to submit them – consuming a few gallons of vodka in the process, I'm sure – and then, when the last date was past, she came and told me. So I would *know*.'

'Know what?' he asked.

'How *nobble* you are.'

He frowned.

'I'm not *nobble*,' he said, shaking his head. 'I *wanted* to use the bills. I couldn't believe it when she just walked in and gave them to me. And for free. I decided it was divine intervention – that *god* wanted me win this thing. It was my *duty* to expose Pushpa Pande's hypocrisy. Her pseudo-secularism and so-called Gandhian values. Even your poor aunty was a victim! She told me, crying bitterly, that your grandmother had repaid all her years of service by accusing her of being a thief!'

Err, that was me, I thought but didn't say. And she *is* a thief.

'I quite liked her,' he continued. 'She's a bit weird, of course, but in a *nice* way. She reminded me a little of you, actually – she had the same kind of wild rose smell.'

That would be my Body Shop Moroccan Rose perfume, of course, I thought sourly.

'So then?' I asked in an even voice. 'Why didn't you go ahead and *expose* Amma?'

He pushed his dark hair off his forehead.

'She *died*, Jinni,' he said. 'And you cried. And your Gudia aunty looked at me from behind you as you cried, with huge, mute, pleading, golf-ball eyes. And then that Saheli Boutique Masterji swung in from nowhere, gushing. How could I do it after that? It would've been… indecent. Besides, once Babu Ram recovered consciousness and talked to me…'

'You figured I wasn't really a hit-and-run-to-hospital driver after all,' I finished. 'Really, how could you even think I'd run over somebody? You *know* I'm a good driver!'

'He told me what you did that night,' said Zain, ignoring me, his eyes glowing. 'You pulled off that gag from the old Enforcer 49 comic! That was *awesome!*'

'It was *your* gag,' I reminded him. 'And let me tell you, it was a very stupid, *impractical* gag. It—'

'Jinni, it was *fiction*,' he said, shaking his head like he couldn't believe I was for real. 'A fourteen-year-old boy's fiction. You weren't supposed to actually *do* it!'

I shrugged awkwardly. 'Yeah… well, whatever. Anyway, I think what *you* did was awesome. Saving Rita. Getting those two together. Organizing their getaway.'

'That was just good follow-through,' he said dismissively. '*You* did all the heroic stuff. And it confirmed what I'd been suspecting for a while.'

'What?' I asked fearfully. He thought I was mentally unhinged and that escapade had confirmed it?

'That you weren't just this little puppet dancing on your Amma's strings. You were smart and spunky and so Enforcer 49ish…' he paused, looked up at me and said simply, 'that you totally deserved to win.'

I looked at him in stunned disbelief.

'Just like that?' I whispered, awed.

He flung up his head.

'Of course *not* just like that!' he said, his sudden vehemence making me jump a little.

'Then?' I asked, confused.

He gave a short, mirthless laugh. 'I agonized over it *every* day. Especially because the margin we lost by was so small. Only six hundred votes! And, by the way, we *rocked* Sujanpur, the traditional, loyal Pragati bastion! You know what that means, right? If she hadn't died we would've won for sure! She *out-manoeuvred* me. I kept brooding over it. Wallowing in loser stench, as your buddy Rumi would say. I kept trying to justify ratting on you, telling myself *you* had been less than fair – you'd tried to get me disqualified, you'd insulted my family. Every night, I'd decide to go to the EC *tomorrow* and have you disqualified. Thrown out. Humiliated. Or I'd think about phoning you and telling you I had the goods on you, and making you *beg*.'

He stopped, panting slightly, his eyes looking beyond me.

'Then every morning I'd think that I was no one to take a high moral stand. God knows I spent more than three crores on *my* campaign! Besides, what about your stupid aunty – she'd get into trouble for sure – and your mother, who sent me a friend request on Facebook a fortnight ago! I couldn't bring myself to just burn those wretched bills and end the uncertainty once and for all, either. I took them out every day and looked at them and told myself I wasn't such a loser after all... Luckily, Bunty wasn't there when your aunty came – if he knew I had the goods on you, he would have persuaded me to go to the EC for sure. And the day you gave that crowing interview to Nulwallah on Democrazee – that was a really black day.'

I still didn't say anything.

I couldn't think of anything to say.

'I think, finally, it was the fear that your grandmother would *haunt* me that stayed my hand. Can't you just imagine her, floating in through this window here and pitching into me like I was Master Kamruddin?'

'No,' I finally managed to say. 'But I can totally picture her floating in tonight, cooing, *You good little boy! Sit in my lap and let me feed you, little Dilip Kumar!*'

'Nooo!' He groaned and flopped back in his chair, throwing up his arms. I carefully averted my eyes from his lap and the denim stretched taut across his thighs – it was sending out its usual hello-this-seat's-not-taken signals.

'So!' I said resolutely, getting to my feet. 'Like I said, I came to say sorry and thank you. So, sorry and thank you, Zain. You're a good friend.'

He looked up abruptly, his dark eyes glittering below his messy hair. 'You're welcome,' he said. 'Next friendship day, I'll give you a friendship *band.*'

I ignored this stupid remark.

He continued, still sprawling back in his chair, in a very neutral voice, 'Babu Ram *also* told me that you were aided in your desperate rescue expedition that night by Nauzer Nulwallah, and that the two of you appeared to be an item.'

I sat down again.

'And *Mrs* Babu Ram told me you seemed very cosy with your lovely cousin Pinky,' I said steadily.

'*What*?' He laughed, like this was a really good joke. 'That's just plain weird.'

'*Any*way,' I said, tossing my head, secretly relieved but refusing to show it, 'why shouldn't I be an item with Nulwallah, huh? He thinks I'm nice, *and* he votes Pragati, *and* we don't squabble every three minutes like we're both three years old!'

Zain looked up, his dark eyes glowing.

'*I* think you're nice,' he said quietly.

I stared at him.

He was doing it again. That just-kidding grin with the disturbingly serious look in his eyes. My heart began its deafening drum roll again.

But then, abruptly, he flung up one hand and shook his head. 'Forget that,' he said. 'You're starting a whole new phase of your life now, you'll get to meet all kinds of interesting people... You should begin on a clean slate.'

'Oh yeah,' I said shakily. 'Because there are all these cool seventy-year-old dudes *dying* to date me in Parliament.'

'There's Tits,' he reminded me, his voice none-too-steady either. 'And lots of other young guns too.'

'Shut up,' I said.

'Jinni, it won't work,' he said slowly, his voice almost pleading. 'This whole situation is a disaster zone.'

But I wasn't listening to his words, which, of course, were absolutely wrong. I was listening to his voice, which was absolutely right. In fact, it was a voice I hadn't heard in nine years, but remembered very well indeed.

I want to kiss you, Jinni. I want to kiss you very much.

It was all the opening I needed and I grabbed it with both hands. And why not? Life is *sort*.

'Of *course* it'll work,' I murmured persuasively, as I sank into his lap and slipped my arms luxuriantly around his neck. 'Unless, of course, you're not man enough to take on a woman who has bested you so comprehensively, hmmm?'

It worked. He grabbed the back of my neck instantly.

'Listen, Kidwai Nagar,' he said, shaking me not very gently. 'You only won because I *let* you.'

I yanked at his hair, hard.

'That,' I shot back cockily, 'is an entirely *debatable* point. I mean, I could've answered all the questions to the EC's satisfaction and been cleared of all charges.'

One dark eyebrow rose at this, not impressing me a bit.

'Like how you spent twenty-three lakhs on alcohol?' he asked. 'And *twelve* on twenty-four carat gold nose rings?'

'I would've worked out *something,'* I blustered.

'You know what, you're right,' he replied wryly, letting my neck go. 'You probably would've.'

We were both quiet for a while.

'D'you think I'm going to slowly turn into a mindless TB sycophant or a cynical line-toer, or siphon off millions from famine relief funds into my personal Swiss bank account, doing this job?' I asked doubtfully.

'No,' he said steadily. 'Not if you don't *choose* to. Unless you believe I'm going to turn into a rabid soldier of Hindutva doing *this* job?'

I groaned and stood up. He let me. 'Don't tell me you're going to keep up this sicko flirtation with the IJP?'

'They're going to rename it,' he said doggedly, getting up

too. 'I'm pretty confident it's going to mutate into another kind of party altogether. And soon. It *has* to. The country's waking up to the need for an alternative to your fat-cat, screwed up Pragati.'

'Speaking of which,' I said thoughtfully, 'should I tell TB that Tawny was slipping crores of official Pragati Party funds to you right through the campaigning?'

He looked thoughtful.

'It might be smarter to hold that knowledge over Tawny and pressurize him to wind up all that crap he's been pulling in Durguja, instead,' Zain said. 'But *gently*. Don't antagonize him. He's powerful. Besides, he's genuinely fond of you.'

'That's good advice,' I allowed grudgingly. Then I snapped my fingers. 'Hey, the first thing I'll make him do is give Munni the assembly ticket from Champapul in the state election! Hah!'

'Good for Munni,' Zain remarked. 'Whoever she is.'

I looked at him a little suspiciously.

'Are you going to tell me what I should be doing all the time now? I won't let you.'

'Okay, okay,' he said peaceably enough, though I didn't like the way his eyes were dancing. Then he grabbed the end of my sari and pulled me closer. 'But will you let me pull this off? Slowly? Pleat by pleat? It's become a bit of an obsession with me.'

Oh, with me too, I thought fervently. You have no *idea*.

'Jinni?' he asked, his voice uncertain.

In response, I slid my hands up under his cheesy red T-shirt, my palms tingling as they encountered the muscled warmth beneath. And then I was struck by an awful new possibility.

I looked up at him, panic gripping my belly.

'Oh my god, Zain, what if we've both been building up this

whole thing in our heads for years and years, and that's why our sexual encounters with other people never felt *really* awesome, but now that we're finally about to consume this relationship, what if it turns out to be a total anti-climax?'

He blinked.

But only for a moment. 'Excuse me, please speak for yourself,' he objected even as his hands slid smoothly down past my waist to the swell of my butt and pushed me firmly up against him. '*My* previous sexual encounters totally rocked.'

'So did *mine,* you bastard,' I replied, stung.

'In which case,' he murmured into my ear, sounding suspiciously like he was trying not to laugh, 'I don't see any problem, do you?'

'Umm... none,' I agreed rather dazedly as he pushed me against the pillows.

I fell back, but then sat up and said worriedly, 'Suppose this is just unfinished business? Suppose once this is done, we get totally *over* each other?'

'Then you can go off with Nulwallah,' he said soothingly, as he lifted my pallu off my front, threw it aside and slid his large warm hands down to the knot of pleats at my waist. And I...' he was definitely laughing now, 'I can go off with Gudia aunty.'

'With Bunty,' I corrected him.

'With Bunty,' he agreed, somewhat huskily.

A while later, my sari lay unspooled at the bottom of the bed.

'Jin?'

'Hmm?'

'It's not consume, by the way, it's consummate.'

'I *know* that,' I retorted fiercely, rearing up at once. 'I'm not *stu—*'

But he didn't let me finish. Shoulders shaking with suppressed laughter, he pushed me back down on the big sunshine-filled bed, lowered his tousled dark head, and kissed me.

Epilogue

I almost missed the swearing in.

Zain drove us back to Delhi, tearing down the bumpy highway in the dark pelting rain like a maniac, swearing at the trucks on the road and yelling at me for being dumb enough to drive to Bittora a day before what he kept calling 'the biggest day of your life'.

I smiled at him, too replete and happy to argue, even when he cursed the condition of my Sumo (which he had no option but to take because of the brand new Parliament House parking sticker pasted on its windshield).

'Don't put the glass down,' he yelled when, still in a fuzzy romantic daze, I slid my window down just a couple of inches to inhale the falling raindrops. 'You'll mess up your hair!'

'Okay…' I muttered, then brightened at the sight of a passing tea-stall. 'Hey, d'you wanna get some chai?'

'No,' he snapped, his eyes on the road. 'I'm trying to get you to Parliament in time. Would you please try to get with the programme?'

'Oh, please.' I stretched back in my seat languorously. 'What's the big deal about going to Parliament? I've been there tons of times, to withdraw money from Amma's SBI account.'

'There's a difference between running errands and being sworn in as a member,' Zain told me grimly. 'You'll see.'

'And afterwards, she'd sometimes buy me this awesome tomato soup from the railway canteen upstairs,' I continued, my mind still on the tea he hadn't let me buy. 'It used to be fully subsidized. Just two bucks a bowl, at least that's what it *used* to be back in the nineties…'

He ignored these reminiscences completely, so I shrugged, lay back in my seat and closed my eyes. God knows why he was hyperventilating so much. We had *ages* to make it to Parliament. And the swearing in was no big deal, really. I'd seen it happen loads of times.

'See?' I told him smugly, three hours later, as we sped down Ashoka Road and turned onto Sansad Marg with over fifteen minutes to spare. 'There was no need to lose the plot.'

He shot me an exasperated look even as the sentries at Gate No. 1 looked at the brand new 'MP Fifteenth Lok Sabha' sticker and waved us through. Then he turned into the lane that leads to the main porch of Parliament House.

And there, the sight of a thousand news channel vans, the hypnotic *khit khit khit* of flashing cameras, the revolving blue and red lights on the white cars clogging the drive, disgorging the triumphant looking Ugly People Mafia onto the porch, suddenly turned all my muscles to water.

I can't go in there, I thought. I can't. I just *can't*.

Honestly. The nervousness I felt lurking outside the Taj Bittora yesterday was nothing compared to the panic I was feeling now.

I wanted to run back to Pixel animation and design kitaanus for the rest of my life.

Zain, the bastard, fully aware of the consternation inside

my primly-encased-in-grey-and-pink-khadi breast, killed the engine, turned to me and smiled.

'All the best,' he said with a wicked grin. 'Get in there. Kick some ass.'

Was he *insane*?

The press had seen me now. Worse, they'd seen who was driving my vehicle. The windows of the Sumo, designed for campaigning, gave them a clear view of both of us. As they surged towards us, waving their microphones and shouting questions, I resisted the urge to duck.

'Sarojiniji!'

'Youngest MP! How does it feel?'

'What's the biggest challenge your state is facing?'

'What's your view on the growing Naxal presence in the province of Durguja?'

'Will you convert to Islam when you get married?'

Cars behind us were starting to honk so I took a deep breath, opened the door of the Sumo, and narrowly missed knocking somebody down.

'*Pande* junior.'

It was TB. Flanking him was that prince of snakes, my late grandmother's best friend, Tawny Suleiman. They'd obviously showed up to see their respective progeny being sworn in as PP MPs. How sweet.

'We were so happy to hear you scraped through! Weren't we, Anthony?'

Tawny nodded enthusiastically. 'Thrilled. Thrilled,' he said, smiling at me with what looked like real affection, his shame-lessness quite sucking my breath away. 'I *told* you she would win, sir! Though it was close. Two hundred votes, wasn't it, dear?'

'*Six* hundred actually,' Zain's lips smiled politely enough, though his nostrils flared warningly.

TB looked around, astounded at my outspoken 'driver', did an infinitesimal double take, and then said smoothly, 'Ah, young... err... Zuber. How nice.'

'Congratulations on your victory, sir,' Zain said.

'Yes, yes, such as it is,' responded TB a little grumpily. The wrangling preceding the formation of his coalition government had been the only thing in the news all month.

Meanwhile, the press hounds, who'd been clicking away gleefully, now started emitting hoarse, uncouth shouts. 'Hug her, Zain!' they heckled from behind their cameras. 'Kiss him, Jinni!'

TB cast a jaundiced eye around the porch. 'Politics in this country is just not what it used to be,' he murmured dryly.

Tawny hastily stuck his head into the Sumo and tackled Zain. 'So!' he said jovially. 'Come to see Jinni's swearing in?'

Zain looked taken aback, and cast an involuntary look at his scruffy jeans and Champapuli chappals. 'Err... I'm not properly dressed. Besides I don't have a pass.'

'Arrey, pass humare paas hai!' said Tawny, all bluff good humour. 'You come up and sit with me in the Rajya Sabha gallery!'

I looked ahead, noncommittal, and fiddled with the end of my pallu. It would be awesome if Zain watched my swearing in, of course. But I hadn't asked him to, partly because I'd already given all my passes away to the crack team, but mostly because I was trying to be sensitive. Watching me being sworn in when he had hoped to be sworn in himself? That would be too painful, surely.

So now, I steeled myself and waited for him to make some excuse.

Instead, he said, his dark eyes totally lighting up, 'Thanks so much, sir. I'd love to see Jinni being sworn in.'

Huh?

I know, I know. I don't deserve him one bit.

I almost hugged him in public again, but managed to stop myself just in the nick of time. (Well, to tell you the truth, I kind of half-lunged into the Sumo but then TB's hand closed warningly over my arm.)

'Yes, yes,' said TB, as he patted my arm austerely. Then he leaned into the vehicle and addressed Zain. 'Come and see me sometime, when you're properly dressed. Young men like you have no business being in the IJP.'

'It's like you said, sir,' Zain replied pleasantly. 'Politics in this country is just not what it used to be.'

Saying which, he grinned, restarted the engine, tossed a casual, 'Meet you at the public gallery entrance in ten, Mr S' in Tawny's direction, and drove the rattling mud-spattered Sumo out of there with the air of a world-saving superhero cruising off behind the wheel of the Batmobile.

As for me, I wiped the stupid, adoring smile off my face, took a deep breath, and followed the luminaries of the fifteenth Lok Sabha into the House.

And it was exactly like Zain had said.

Being sworn in *is* completely different from visiting to drink tomato soup.

I walked like someone in a dream, through the security area and into the stately pillared corridor, dotted every now and again with dark, wooden benches. The grassed courtyard within and the three life-sized stone statues of the founding fathers, were wet with morning dew. I sent up a fervent application for their blessings, and then, lifting my sari pleats a little, followed the other new MPs past the Library Hall, the Central Hall and the Rajya Sabha, into the House of the People.

The Lok Sabha was pretty much as I remembered it. Semicircular, reminiscent of the interiors of a large, slightly tatty, multiplex movie theatre, and done up in pool-table green. The white bearded portrait of Vithhalbhai Patel, the first elected President of the Central Legislative Assembly, glowered down fiercely at everyone.

I walked sedately to the humble backbencher seats at the right hand side of the Speaker's chair and looked up at the galleries, hoping to spot Zain, Ma and my crack team, and did so almost immediately, probably because of the incandescent glow on Ma's face. Smiling the world's biggest smile, she pointed at Zain and did a double thumbs up. I beamed back at both of them. Zain immediately staggered back in mock alarm, his hand going to his heart.

Whoa, smile impact.

Blushing bright red, I stumbled and almost fell, but managed to make it look like I was just sitting down. As I adjusted my sari and looked down at the buttons and gizmos of the automatic voting system on my desk, a dulcet voice spoke in my ear.

'Hello, so nice to meet…'

Both of you, I thought with a sigh. And smiled. 'Hi, Titu.'

'Hello, Sarojiniji,' he said politely, like he was this really khandaani person who hadn't been trying to sabotage my campaign all summer. 'Meet Saurav and Manish and Madhu.'

I folded my hands in a namaste to the other nervous-looking first-timers in our row and sat back, head bowed, waiting for my name to be announced.

Which is when a strange thing happened.

As I listened to MP after MP taking the oath, all the foolish skittering notions of impressing the Pragati Party Top Brass, the other big shots in the party and the cynical press with my perfect enunciation, my pretty sari or the simple sincerity of my oath-delivery faded from my mind. Amma and Bauji, who seemed to be hovering by my side since I entered Parliament House, all misty-eyed and full of unsolicited advice, withdrew too. Ma retreated. Even Zain grew a little dim.

They were all unceremoniously pushed aside by an aggressive horde which shouldered its way into my mind, without a VVIP pass of any sort, refusing to be disallowed. Dour faced and unblinking, the eleven lakh plus people of the eight legislative assembly segments of Bittoragarh took centre space in my head. Not so subtly reminding me that *they* were the ones who'd sent me here. For whatever reason. Out of love, or hope, or a gold nose-pin, or lack of choice, or force of habit, or by simply not showing up to cast their vote. I could see them clearly, I could read their minds. Frowning down at me, brows furrowed, lips pursed and fingers crossed, they were thinking darkly, *Okay, let's hope we haven't screwed up here, choosing this cartoon-college graduate to represent us...*

The thought humbled me and made me incredibly proud, both at the same time.

Which is why, when my turn finally came, I was able to swallow the lump in my throat, raise my chin and speak clearly, the words coming with fierce, painful intensity, straight from the bottom of my heart.

I,
Sarojini Devi Pande,
having been elected as a Member,
in the House of the People,

do solemnly swear,

with God as my witness

that I will bear true faith and allegiance to the Constitution of India,

as by Law established,

That I will uphold the Sovereignty and Integrity of India,

That I will faithfully discharge the duties

to which I am about to enter.

So help me God.

Acknowledgements

My mother-in-law, Margaret Alva, whose many hilarious stories about her 'office' made me want to write this book in the first place. Thank you, Mamma.

My mother, Pushpa Raman, who let me borrow her name, and her memories. Thank you, Mummy.

My ammaji, Leelavati Thakur, who taught me that a maternal grandmother's home is indeed Home. For my sisters and me, it will always be 898 Saket Bhavan, Pyaare Lal Sharma Road, Meerut Cantt.

Niharika, for her effusive praise *and* brutal criticism.

Nayantara, whose sudden, wide, sweet smile I stole for Jinni.

Daivik John, who continues to inspire. (No, Daivik John, you may *not* have Grand Theft Auto, not even if you buy it with your own money. Not even Grand Theft Auto Chinatown even if it has 'no sex – only violence and bad words'. Not even if you 'play it on mute and don't even *hear* the bad words'.)

My sister-in-law, Manira, who, when plied with cups of midnight chai, supplied anecdotes and insight and major plot points.

My Mini didi, who found the manuscript 'unputdownable' and read it in four hours flat on a hectic working day. (But who's a member of a Facebook group called 'I'll Read Anything' so let's not get too excited here…)

My sister, Nandini, for her totally excellent, vital early advice on my hero.

Early readers, Shalini Beri and Alok Lall.

Neelini Sarkar – nit-picky Virgo editor whose eagle eye missed nothing. *(Neelini's log, 7:20 am: Technically, if she's five- feet-two and he's six-ish, their navels can't be kissing. Think about it…)*

VK Karthika, for being both giggly girl and savvy chief editor.

The poetry selection *Panorama* which exposed entire generations of class ten students to Sarojini Naidu's poetry.

P Sainath's *Everybody Loves a Good Drought*, for its 'legend of the water-thieves'.

Anupama Ramaswamy, Cannes Gold Lion winning art-director, who designed at least seven hundred and ninety-three cover options – including this one.

Sidhaarth Dyalchand, whose store of 'desi English' gems I help myself to liberally.

My entire family – Alva and Chauhan both – who had to put up with me rabbitting on and on about this book all year.

Ditto, my entire office.

All the staff at 23 Ashoka Road and 12 Safdurjung Lane – especially the Late Ishwar Dasji. I think the odds on Sean Connery possessing an I LOOK LIKE ISHWAR DASJI T-shirt are extremely high.

Goldy, the resident Ponky at the Raj Bhavan, Dehradun.

And finally, the big three.

Our Lord Jesus Christ, in whose peace we dwell.

Choku, my first reader – for his patience, his clarity and his childhood memories. And for his testy *no-no, it's okay, keep going, I've gotten used to falling asleep to the sound of the laptop keys tapping away, anyway...*

And my grandparents-in-law, the late Joachim and Violet Alva, the first couple in India's Parliament, whose romance and idealism inspired this book.